Praise for

"Robert Antoni doesn't make giant steps. He makes quantum—and sometimes hilarious—leaps past whatever we call metafiction to the same territory as Richard Powers and David Foster Wallace. But like those men and unlike nearly everybody else, he never forgets that at the core of it all you've still got to tell a rip-roaring story."
MARLON JAMES, author of *A Brief History of Seven Killings*

"*As Flies to Whatless Boys* is a brilliant novel that is rivetingly localized in a distant time and an untouched place, and yet somehow speaks vibrantly to this present age and to the universal human condition.
Robert Antoni is a treasure of our literary culture."
ROBERT OLEN BUTLER, author of *A Good Scent from a Strange Mountain*

"Antoni is an audacious storyteller, mining his very own language and ways of telling from the linguistic cornucopia of Trinidad. His novel is moving and is also hilarious."
LAWRENCE SCOTT, author of *Leaving By Plane, Swimming back Underwater*

"A marvel of a novel, layered in histories, Robert Antoni's unique and engaging *As Flies to Whatless Boys* is an unforgettable and matchless work of fiction. A crowning achievement in an exceptional body of work by this amazingly talented writer."
EDWIDGE DANTICAT, author of *Breath, Eyes, Memory*

AS
FLIES
TO
WHATLESS
BOYS

ROBERT ANTONI

PEEPAL TREE

Published in Great Britain in 2015 by
Peepal Tree Press Ltd
17 King's Avenue
Leeds LS6 1QS
England

ISBN13: 978 1 84523 121 7

This is a work of fiction. All names, characters, places, and
incidents are the product of the author's imagination.
Any resemblance to real events or persons, living or dead, is
entirely coincidental.

Supported using public funding by
ARTS COUNCIL
ENGLAND

Also by Robert Antoni

Divina Trace

Blessed Is the Fruit

My Grandmother's Erotic Folktales

Carnival

for Ali

As flies to wanton boys are we to the gods
They kill us for their sport
                    —William Shakespeare, *King Lear*

I met History once, but he ain't recognize me
                    —Derek Walcott, "The Schooner *Flight*"

Contents

Appendix*
Where an icon appears followed by a large asterisk, enter the internet link found in the Appendix to view the document on the novel's companion website, whatlessboys.com.

First Message

3/7/10

Dear Mr Robert W Antoni:

Thank you for your generous offer to donate the letters and
maps and personal writings—a notebook from 1845 you
say?!—of your great-great-grandfather on your mother's side,
WILLIAM SANGER TUCKER, to the Permanent Collection
of the Trinidad & Tobago National Archives. Please excuse the
informality of this email, but as your own message came to us via
electronic format without postal address, I can only respond in
like manner.

I am of course familiar with the surname Tucker in relation
to the shipping industry here in Trinidad since longtime.
In answer to your various other queries, however, I must
inform you that I have never before heard of any man named
ETZLER in connection to the history of THIS island, nor am
I acquainted with any such organisation called the TROPICAL
EMIGRATION SOCIETY, so I don't know anything more
about this business than you do, which is to say nothing much
at all (though I think it was Barbarossa who brought out a
Carnival band last year called TROPICAL INEBRIATION
ASSOCIATION or something so). Furthermore, I have
looked good on the map and there is NO place called
CHAGUABARRIGA nowhere near the south coast of THIS
island, not that I could see, Mr Robert, so I suggest you check
your references again and make sure you got all your spellings
down correct. Of course, everybody living here in T'dad knows
the STOLLMEYER surname good enough, he being the man
who built that big fancy fallingdown house beside the Queens
Park Savannah known as KILLARNEY CASTLE, a documented
historical relic erected sometime around 1904-or-5 I think it is.
And you will be pleased to hear that all of HIS own personal

papers and writings were donated by the family to the Archives a good while ago, and you will find them when you visit us right here in the C F Stollmeyer Esq Collection just beside my office at the back with the photocopy machine.

So maybe STOLLMEYER is the famous German inventor who bring your family here to T'dad from London in 1845 as you say? In any case, my suggestion to you Mr Robert is that you get all your pekings in line and doublecheck your spellings before you embark on any such project as this book you say you looking to write. And please be assured that my assistant Miss Samlalsingh and me will be happy to offer you any kind of assistance we could in this regard, and we look forward to making your acquaintance and showing you little something of the hotspots in Port of Spain as you suggest.

Cordial,
Miss Ramsol
Director, T&T National Archives

PS in answer to your final query I recommend the Hilton Hotel up on the hill above the Savannah with a nice view of p-o-s right down to the La Basse beyond Beetham Highway, very romantic with the lights at night, & you might even see Stollmeyer's own house from the terrace 2 in case you decide to write out your book on HIM instead, because that seems to me a much better idea since I could assure you sure-as-Shiva he DID exist, which is more than I can say 4 this man Etzler, & I have 2 tell u my OWN personal preference in dining is curry crabbacks at Ganeshhouse & fresh seamoss drink, with my #1 choice 4 bars down the hill from the Hilton very convenient by the name of Pelican, but please please Mr Robot dont let nobody hear u calling it that as they would all know straightway u is nothing but a yankee tourist just-pass-through-Piarco as we does call it PELO

3 Letters

19 July 1881

Dear Mr. William Tucker,

You may be surprised to hear that your fame as a taxidermist, and illustrator of hummingbirds native to your island of Trinidad, has reached our shores. But this is so. Indeed, for some time now I have heard of your achievements from acquaintances that have travelled to the West Indies, and recently I was privileged to examine one of your exhibits myself. It was shown to me by a colleague, Dr. Lance Parks, who purchased at your workshop 'Male purple-throated Carib hummingbird on heliconia in flower.' I was fascinated. I daresay enchanted. I have since had the opportunity to study this handsome little gentleman at length. And I have demonstrated him to several members of our scientific community.

Dr. Parks has encouraged me to contact you, and he has provided your postal address in Port-Spain. Hence this letter. It is my pleasure, therefore, under the auspices of Director of the Natural History Museum, as Professor of Biology at Christ Church College, and as Chairman of the Ornithological Society of London, to invite you to visit us and offer a cycle of lectures on your techniques for preserving and displaying hummingbirds. It would be expedient if you could bring along some of your exhibits for illustration purposes. I am further informed that you are the first to capture images of living hummingbirds in talbotypes. It would be an added treat if you could bring some of these plates to show us as well. Whilst here you would be welcomed to share my laboratory at the Museum. In addition my wife and I would be happy to offer you modest accommodation in our home, located adjacent to the Museum grounds. Unfortunately the Museum is not in a position to fund your passage out from Trinidad. But Dr. Parks tells me that aside from being an accomplished taxidermist, you are the owner of an expansive shipping line in the West Indies. So I imagine the possibility exists of coming out to visit us on one of your own vessels.

I do hope so! And I anxiously await your reply.

Sincerely,
Dr. Francis M. Evans
Director, Natural History Museum

PS It occurs to me that you may have heard mention of a certain A.J. Etzler, a German inventor and scientist who some years ago established the Tropical Emigration Society here in London. He led his first group of 'pioneers' to Trinidad with the intention of forming an experimental community there, his followers meeting only disaster, Etzler himself fleeing to America with the remains of his investors' money. As it turned out my father lost the entirety of our modest family fortune in Etzler's scheme, and he and my mother and myself narrowly escaped the fate of those unfortunate emigrants in Trinidad. I would be interested to hear anything you may know on this subject.

DRAFT

27 August 1881

Dear Professor Evans,

Thank you for your invitation to visit the Museum & 'lecture'
as you say on my techniques for preserving and exibiting
hummingbirds. I am certainly surprised to hear that my modest
hobby should attract the interest of a scientific mind such as
youself, & I must inform you with some embarrassement straight-
off-the-bat that my own education ended abrupt at age 15—in
truth I will have to ask my eldest son to writeover this draft
before the letter can be sent! None-the-less if you are willing to
hear a 'lecture' from a man with little or no formal education,
but greatly enthusiastic about wildlife & nature & my little birds,
then I am happy to come & bring along some of my exibits &
the talbotypes. All of my own ships are of the lighterage capacity
only & opperate local exclusive amongst the islands. But on
receipt of your invitation I made enquiries with a close friend just
in port who is Captain of the Condor, & he has kindly offered me
passage as well as transport of my exibits.

Due to the demands of my business activities here in Trinidad
& especially considering the length of the passage (4 weeks out
approx. & same back) I will not be able to stay long in London. I
would guess the Condor will remain at port a fortnight or so before
she must turn round to make her return voyage, but that should be
adequate for a few 'lectures' at least. In addition I would not want
to take overadvantage of your generous offer of accommodation
in your home. Please expect me then to arrive with the Condor &
upon landing I will make my way direct to the Museum.

I look forward to meeting you & your wife & thank you again for
your invitation.

Sincerely,
William Sanger Tucker
Director, Trinidad Transport Co Ltd

PS It is interesting you ask about Etzler & the Tropical
Emigration Society as my family came out from London in 1845
as part of that very venture. My father & I being two of the
pioneers you speak of who went off to Etzlers settlement on our
north coast. Equally coincidental is that only the other day my
son asked me to give him this tale of how the Tuckers came here
to Trinidad. But I put him off as I wanted to search the attic first
for a old cigar box containing my fathers notebook from that trip,
plus a handful of maps & letters & other artifacts to coincide with
the storytelling. In any case I have now retrieved the box, & I will
be sure to bring it along & eager to tell you of my & my fathers
experiences with Etzlers TES.

PPS I wonder if I could trouble you with another matter in some
ways related to this subject. Counted amongst our group was a
Miss Marguerite Whitechurch who came to Trinidad with her
aunt & uncle a prominent gentleman in the business circles of
London of those times. One of Etzlers principle supporters. Miss
Whitechurch may well have given up her sirname by now. None-
the-less I wonder if you could make some inquiares & perhaps
locate her postal address & forward the attached letter to her?
Her uncle was amongst the first to succumb to the misfortune of
Etzlers plan, after which Miss W. returned with her aunt direct to
London. I have not heard of her since.

DRAFT

c/o Dr. Francis M. Evans
27 August 1881

Dear Marguerite,

You will no doubt be surprised to hear from the boy you once knew many years ago as 'Willy.' I have requested Professor Evans of the Natural History Museum to enquire into your postal address, & he will hopefully forward this letter. I am sure you'll recall my giving to you as a keepsake my first bumbling attempt at what has since become a modest but enthusiastic hobby—that female blue-chinned sapphire in her little wooden box labeled 'buttons.' As it turns out Dr. Evans has invited me to visit the Museum & offer a few 'lectures' as he calls them & demonstrations of my techniques for preserving hummingbirds. The point then of this communication is to inform you of my empending trip, & to request a reunion while I am visiting in London.

I have on my desk before me the letter you wrote on the eve of your departure from Trinidad. Only fate kept me from reading it before you were already aboard ship, otherwise I would no doubt have returned to England with you. Indeed I tried my hardest to get to the Caroline before she sailed, & very nearly managed. Fate as I say had other plans for us. That was 36 years ago. I imagine you are now married youself, & I am happy to say that in addition to being married we have six children of our own, one son already three years older then I was at the time of our story together! I understand perfectly well if you choose not to meet again. For as you wrote to me in your letter— 'who is to say we are not better off left with our memories? if those memories are not better off left intact? untouched by further sadness? another farewell & another departure?'

Whichever way you choose I am prepared to accept. Know then that you can find me in the home of Dr. Evans & his wife who have kindly offered me accommodation while I remain in London. They home as I understand it is adjacent to the Museum grounds. No doubt you can also contact me through Dr. Evans heself. And now I must return your letter to the safety of its pasteboard box.

Sincerely,
William Tucker

Preamble
7 September 1881

Awaiting the Tide

I couldn't tell you, my father said, and I knew I was in trouble. I had a long night of listening ahead of me.

I couldn't tell you how this Etzler managed to mongoose everybody. He wasn't nothing to look at. A funny little man with a big beard & piercing eyes & a face consisting of 50% brooding forehead. Shaped like a sucked mango seed. A squeaky voice that whistled when he got excited—which was most of the time—and the more excited the harder he was to decipher with the German accent. But he had the gift: boldface bamboozlement. Shameless mongooseeocity. Some would say 'amongst others'—that he was a genius & prophet & saviour & all the rest—but son, I couldn't tell you about none of that bubball neither. It wasn't the Etzler I saw. Despite that in his own way he had me mongoosed good as everybody else. Mind you, that was thirty-six years ago. I was only a boy of fifteen. Three years younger than you are youself—not so, R-W?

There weren't any furnishings on this back deck. Not even a railing round the side. Only some enormous coils of weathered rope my father and I reclined against while he smoked his cigar. It was the highest part of the ship, and so isolated we could have been the only two people aboard. We couldn't even hear the noise below of the other passengers getting settled for the night, sailors still preparing to go to sea in the morning. Everything quiet. The sea quiet too without scarcely a ripple, the ship having swung round with her stern facing the shore. The two lights at the end of Kings Wharf had come on in the distance, reflecting at us in wavering lines across the flat water. With a few other lights already tinkling round the curve of the bay, a handful more in town and higher up in the hills. The mountains behind them had turned to such a dark green they were almost black, sky smoky gray without a cloud or a star yet. Flat and still as the sea. Whatever lights there were below on the ship you couldn't see them. Here on deck there was only the glow of my father's cigar.

First one he mongoosed was another German inventor named Roebling. His friend longsince childhood. As young men, these two left on the same ship bound for New York. But that was still a good while before the start of this story. Etzler was on the run because the authorities were taking a lag on he tail over something-or-the-other—they'd jailed him once already—and he was running from his creditors too. Etzler never went nowhere that he wasn't running from creditors. But he had he friend Roebling bamboozled, as I was telling you, and together they led a group of working-class emigrants on this ship. Yet by the time the ship disembarked the two leaders had fought. Half the group went with Etzler, other half with Roebling. They went they separate ways, despite remaining friends. Roebling to start a cultivation in Pennsylvania, Etzler to begin a expedition exploring the western frontier, looking for the suitable place to establish he own experimental community. But as it turned out Roebling would be the one to leave he mark in the history book. Not Etzler. Understand, Etzler's public life occupies only a few years, before and after which everything looks hazy like you seeing it through a gauze. Roebling, on the other hand, wasted little time deciding he wasn't no kinda weed-puller a-tall. He converted his farm to a factory to mass produce his newest invention: steel rope. He became obsessed with this thing. And he remained obsessed with it the rest of his life. Same steel rope that eventually enabled him to design and erect the grandest, most magnificent madman-monstrosity ever imagined to we present day: the Brooklyn Bridge.

Son, I couldn't tell you because I never been there. Since I arrived here in Trinidad at the age of fifteen I've never set foot from it, except to travel to a fistful of other islands. I never seen this bridge. All I can tell you is that

even Roebling kowtowed heself before Etzler's genius. Yet even Roebling
couldn't sit in the same room with he childhood friend five-minutes-together
without busting-out in a row with him neither.

My father had asked me to help him load his things aboard the
Condor, a newly built steamer under charge of his friend, Captain Vincent. He'd had one of his own TTC lighters ferry us
out to the ship at anchor in the harbour. His luggage a half-
dozen crates containing his hummingbird exhibits, a small grip
with clothes, and three clumsy thatched baskets filled with every
kind of still-green fruits and vegetables. Because my father's the
only West Indian non-flesh-eater I've ever heard of aside from
the Hindus. We got his crates onto the deck and down into the
hold, his other things up into his cabin, there beside Captain
Vincent's quarters just behind the wheelhouse. By now it was
dusk. We were just about to go down again for me to catch the
ferry ashore, my father taking up a cigar to smoke while we waited. Then we discovered the door at the back of his bathroom,
opening onto the ship's aft deck.

   My father had brought a pitch-oil lamp but he hadn't lit it yet.
For now there was only the glow of his cigar. He'd also brought
out his leather briefcase, the same one he took every day to work.
Which didn't make any sense to me—what could he want with this
briefcase in the dark on the back deck of a ship? And it wouldn't
be until a good while after he'd launched into his story—after he
lit the lantern—that he'd open up his briefcase to take out a slightly battered pasteboard cigar box. With a single word handprinted
in hard capitals cross the cover: *CHAGUABARRIGA*. I'd never
seen the word before. Didn't know what language it came from.
Or languages. Even the box was a mystery—when my father first
took it out I'd thought he wanted to smoke another cigar.

Inside was a collection of old papers, smudged and ragged-looking round the edges, that he would ruffle through occasionally and select one to illustrate something from his story: maps, letters, clippings from some ancient newspaper I'd never heard of called *The Morning Star*. He'd take one out and we'd squint together to decipher it beneath the glow of the pitch-oil lamp. But the main thing he wanted to show me—the principal 'artifact' as he called them from out of his box—was the little notebook that had once belonged to his own father. It told of the twenty-three days they'd spent together on some estate up on the north coast. A commune where all the labour would be done by machines of Etzler's own invention. Machines powered by Mother Nature: by wind & water & waves.

The notebook measured four-by-six inches square. On the tattered cover, printed out by the hand of a grandfather I'd hardly heard of or knew anything about, was the same mysterious word: *CHAGUABARRIGA*.

Whatever-the-arse Etzler was doing leading his band of emigrants stumbling round the American West, like Moses leading the lost Israelites, nobody knows. Presumably he was evangelising his machines and ideas. But he couldn't convince those frontier yankees not-for-nothing, and before long he'd lost he handful of German followers too. They were simple people looking to improve they lives with a few simple creature comforts. They didn't give a pum about changing the world and turning it into a earthly paradise. But Etzler's biggest problem beginning-to-end was his inability to accept contrary opinions. Especially when those opinions were coming from people he considered both backwards and boobooloops. He abandoned the West, turning now to explore the South. But there he bounced up face-first with American slavery—which of course his conscience could never condone—and he'd run out of money again.

He went to Pittsburgh, maybe back to his friend Roebling, to start the first German newspaper in that town. But Etzler's ego had taken a serious blow, and before long he left America altogether, disappearing again. Now he turned to the Caribbean. He went to Haiti. Possibly during this time he travelled the other islands as far down as Trinidad. Most likely. But whatever he did during that time, Etzler managed to recover heself. At least good enough to write out what would become his first publication, printed upon he return to Pittsburgh.

And here is where history begins to play she hand. Because that same day that he published Paradise, *he travelled to New York for the birthday celebration of a famous Frenchman-socialist by the name of Fourier. And it was at this birthday fête that Etzler met the man who'd become he biggest acolyte ever—C.F. Stollmeyer. (Yes it is, son. The same Stollmeyer who built that big, crazy-arse house round the Savannah, known to us as Killarney Castle. Complete with turrets & towers & Italian stained-glass windows & balustrades of purpleheart-wood lugged out the jungles of Guyana. Same man they used to call 'Shit-Slinging-Stollmeyer' because he went round the place collecting up cowshit & horseshit & goatshit & any other kinda caca he could get he hands on, only to compress it into fuel and sell for 5¢-a-brick. But what he eventually made he fortune from was refining pitch he got gratis out the lake at La Brea (that same pitchlake where Columbus heself went to fetch tar to cork the hulls of his ships), and Stollmeyer dug it out & refined it & sold it off as kerosene—what we call pitch-oil. Because that's the kinda men we talking about here, R-W. That's the kinda characters peopling this story. Because as it turned out Stollmeyer never followed Etzler back to America, when he went running from Trinidad with he stones shriveled up between he legs. After the TES had gone to hell and the whole bloody thing was dead and done with. Even Stollmeyer had he fill of Etzler by then.)*

My father paused here a minute. And as if he'd orchestrated it himself, at the end of that minute we were shaken from out

our solitude by the clanging of the captain's bell down below—
ca-clang ca-clang ca-clang ca-clang. Now we heard Captain Vincent
call out—

Last ferry ashore till mornin!

Yet even as I heard the captain's hoarse voice I knew I was
in trouble. I didn't have a chance to escape. Not a chance. I was
here for the night. Thing is, only the other day I'd asked my
father to tell me this story of how the Tuckers ended up here in
Trinidad. My family. It was the first time I'd made the request.
Oddly enough, before I turned eighteen, I'd never even thought
to ask. Suddenly I had this itch that wanted to be scratched.
But my father put me off, giving me some excuse, like he didn't
feel I was ready. Then, a few nights ago, he asked me to help
him writeover a couple letters concerning his impending trip to
London—not exactly *business* letters, either—and those letters
made my itch scratch me even worse.

Now, despite my curiosity, *I* was the one who wasn't sure.
Suddenly my itch was gone. Washed away clean. Suddenly I
wanted to be someplace else—out liming with my friends, busting bamboo round the Savannah, or down in the pit at Roxy
Theatre. I did not want to be sitting here listening to this. But I'd
asked him for it, and now I was hearing it. My story. In the most
unexpected of places—on the back deck of this ship, reclining
against some big coils of weathered rope. Because my father
hadn't even begun yet.

*Stollmeyer was a fellow German who'd emigrated to Philadelphia a few
years before. He was a publisher and he edited a German newspaper too—
which only leads you to wonder how he hadn't run into Etzler already. But
that was history taking in a deep breath. Getting sheself ready. Because
now at this birthday fête in New York he not only met him, he read Etzler's*
Paradise. *Stollmeyer became a instant convert. More important, he became*

Etzler's business-partner. Stollmeyer brought him back to Philadelphia, and there the two began to scheme. The place, they decided, for Etzler to propagate his ideas, was England. Not America amongst a bunch of backwards country-bookies and racist slave-owners. England was the place. But that was only the first step. And here Etzler added the twist: he'd get his British followers to emigrate to the Caribbean. To they own West Indies. A place where land was available, free for the asking, closer to the equator where the powers of Mother Nature were a hundred times more potent. Only waiting to be harnessed by Etzler's machines. And now it was as if he reached into he hat or a sack-of-pommeracs and pulled one out—Trinidad, he decided. With its unlimited natural resources and expanses of available fertile land. Perfect for cultivation with he own Satellite.

That's what snagged Stollmeyer. And eventually it would snag the whole of England too. That's the difference between Fourier's airy philosophizing and Etzler's practical plan—machines. Understand, like all these men we talking about here, this Stollmeyer fancied heself a scientist and mathematician too. And although he didn't have no formal university training in engineering like Etzler did, he saw the potential for he new friend's machines. Whether or not it was potential to make them a bloody fortune, or save the labouring-masses from toil and starvation, or both, I go leave up to you to decide. Thing is, here was Etzler with he machines already proven. Not practically, mind you—not in real life—but mathematically. And that's all that mattered: numbers speak the truth. They could not lie. And let me tell you, Etzler had plenty plenty numbers propping him up.

Within days of arriving in London they formed a joint-stock company called the Tropical Emigration Society. Now not only the British aristocracy and wealthy capitalists could pour they pounds into Etzler's open purse, but the destitute labourers could dump they handful of sticky pennies in as well. At last Etzler had the two things he'd always needed. Two things he always dreamt about: a disenchanted populace ready to embrace his ideas for change and emigration, a people anxious to line he pockets too. Everybody-and-he-

brother only buying up shares of the TES like tanyafritters, one-penny-at-a-time, with hopes of immediate emigration to Trinidad.

 Here, son, in a relatively minor way, is where the Tuckers enter into the picture. But via a circuitous and rather unprecipitated route. Understand, my father, together with his closest friend—a Scotsman-ironmonger named Thomas Powell—Papee and he friend were former members of a underground group based in London known as the Chartists. They'd been radical & militant & until the end, secret. Fighting down the Crown for all these charters to improve working conditions for the labouring poor, in addition to voting rights. But the movement had been crushed by the government. And Powell heself—their spiritual and elected leader—Powell turned informer in the middle of the scrimmage to save the skins of he comrades. The authorities turning round soon as the deal was brokered & busting him & tossing him in jail. Papee only narrowly escaping Newgate by the skin-of-he-tail heself.

 So as you can well imagine, this group of just-defeated and still hotted-up Chartists fell straight into Etzler's hands. All-in-a-sudden Papee and he friend began talking about nothing more than the TES and emigration to Trinidad. In they minds they'd left England already. But son, Papee would be the fortunate one—if you want to call it that. Because whilst he was picked by Etzler to help construct the Satellite, Powell was chosen to edit the journal that would become the voice of the TES in England, The Morning Star. *So time as Etzler was ready to depart for Trinidad with he first group of thirty-seven pioneers, he had no choice but to leave the thoroughly disappointed Powell behind to edit the* Star. *On the other hand, Papee and the rest of us—Mum & me & my three sisters; the Tucker clan; you family—we got to go.*

My father had reached the end of his cigar. He took three last pulls to send the tip glowing red. Then he touched it to the wick of the pitch-oil lamp, closed the glass, tossed the zoot over the stern. It was so quiet we heard it hiss as it plopped down into the water. And as the pitch-oil lamp flared to a dim glow, he took out his old-fashioned pocketwatch, fastened to his vestcoat buttonhole by a long goldchain. He clicked it open—

Almost eight o'clock already.

He nodded his chin at the watch—

I might have mentioned to you, son, that this pocketwatch once belonged to a gentleman named Mr. Whitechurch. A close friend of Papee's. He came over with his wife & niece & the rest of us on this same ship with Etzler.

My father paused a beat—

That niece became my first love. Marguerite. Only woman besides you mum I've ever been bazodee over my whole life.

He paused again—

You never imagine telling you own son such intimate details that took place even before he was born. But I couldn't give you this story without telling you about Marguerite. I couldn't make a start. Couldn't finish neither.

My father clicked the cover shut and slipped the watch back into his pocket, reclining quiet a moment. By now more lights had come on, tinkling round the curve of the bay. More lights in town and the hills and up in the mountains too. Plenty stars in the sky. But the moon wouldn't rise from behind those mountains for another hour. Cut with a knife down the middle into a perfect half. So somehow you saw the reflection of the moon's other side, even though that half was caught in the earth's shadow and blanked out completely. You saw it. Even though it wasn't there. But that wouldn't happen for another hour. Now there was only the pitch-oil lamp glowing faintly at my father's feet, there beside his briefcase containing the still-unopened cigar box, the lights onshore reflecting across the flat water and the stars. As the *Condor* hung on her anchor ready to go to sea, nothing left to do but wait for morning and the tide. And I had nothing to do but listen.

We are on the eve of the most eventful moment of humankind.
—J.A. Etzler

I
At Sea
13 October 1845

1
Aboard the *Rosalind*

We'd been at sea five days already, and I'd yet to catch a glimpse of Marguerite. Not even a glimpse. Despite my untiring, solitary wanderings of the deck allotted to the third-class passengers. In all weather and at all hours of the day and night. Despite my continually bouffed attempts to gain access to other parts of the ship. Son, no sooner was this voyage underway than it was made clear that each class would be restricted to those areas of the ship that coincided with we rank and privilege. Not only deck space and sleeping quarters. But also the designated dining halls, saloons and parlours for recreation and relaxation, in addition to washrooms and privy facilities. The third- and first-class passengers not only did not intermingle—socially nor for any other reason a-tall—we were, for the most part, oblivious to each other's existence. There was even a steerage class that I'd remain ignorant of till Papee exposed them to me towards the end of the journey.

I soon came to realise this ship wasn't nothing more than a miniature floating replica of the city we left behind: everybody had they place. With the wealthy passengers congregating forward and nearer the main deck in they elegant cabins, reclining beneath butler-held parasols on the cushioned lounges of they sundecks. And the farther astern and deeper into the ship's bowels you descended—like the basements and sewers of London—the more decrepit the environs *and* they inhabitants.

Papee seemed the sole passenger able to sidestep all this

vigilant segregation. After taking his breakfast with us of porridge tasting like shredded pasteboard, tea concocted from used leaves stirred into lukewarm water—a dollop of coagulated milk plopped in if we were lucky—he'd return to the cabin he shared with Mum to change his outfit. Now Papee put on he new white linen shirt. Suspenders, embroidered vest, pinstripe pants. Silk cravat & frock coat & gloves & tall top hat. Son, I had my own set of fancified clothes too—newly tailored for the selfsame reason as Papee's—but on Mum's orders those garments lay packed up in the trunk with the rest of the Tuckers' luggage, who-the-arse-knew-where down in the hold. Papee then made his way forward, past the deck-steward posted behind the galley, to the first-class saloon. Where he spent the rest of the morning and a good part of the afternoon too, conversing with Mr. Whitechurch and a handful of other gentlemen. I also knew Papee visited the Whitechurches in they first-class cabin, located below the forecastle deck. Adjacent to the cabins of the Etzlers and the Stollmeyers. Those accommodations, Papee assured us—with they private sitting rooms, four-poster beds, and bathrooms with full-length porcelain tubs—were superiour even to Captain Damphier's own.

For me those parts of the *Rosalind* seemed as far away as Marguerite's Knightsbridge had from my old East End borough. And just as out of reach.

Son, you got to realise that the sole reason I'd looked forward to this voyage with such excitement was so Marguerite and me could be together. Much as we could want. And nobody could stop us neither. Yet now the passage was underway, after all the setbacks, I didn't even know for sure if she was aboard ship. Even if she *was* the fact that she'd be travelling in upper class made her perfectly inaccessible.

But after five days I'd had it up to my nostril-holes. And that same afternoon I spied for two long hours on the deck-steward stationed behind the galley. Till I watched him step-way from he post a few seconds to weewee over the leeward rail. Now I hurried past he turned back, leaping a low railing, descending a short flight of steps. Bouncing up face-first with a set of elegant passengers, all dressed to the nines in full feather. Stylish couples promenading the deck arm-in-arm, one-behind-the-next in circular fashion—like the entire operation was orchestrated only so the ladies didn't decapitate each other with the brims of they bloody hats—hot toddies holding in they whitegloved hands. An elderly couple even accompanied by they primped-up poodle, the dog wearing a red velvet vest just like Etzler.

A few minutes later I happened to glance through a window into one of plush parlours, my heart beating out a warm hole inside my chest the same instant: there sat Mrs. Whitechurch, together with a half-dozen other fancy ladies and young maidens. At one end of the room stood an upright piano, with a pair of portly little women sitting on the bench, playing a duet and giggling. A large silver bowl of strawberries-and-cream on the table behind Mrs. Whitechurch, together with an ample tray of biscuits & pastries & finger-sandwiches. Livery-clad steward to pour out they tea or coffee from shining silver pots, holding in each of he whitegloved hands. Needless-to-say, my own lunch a couple hours earlier had included a single boiled potato and a piece of stewed bullbeef so impregnated with salt, I'd spit it back in my tin plate in one. And there wouldn't be no blasted afternoon tea for the likes of none of us.

Yet it wasn't all these lavish victuals adorning the lace-covered table behind Mrs. Whitechurch that had me so defeated. It wasn't even that Mum and my sisters were barred all entrance to this particular parlour. It was the fact that Marguerite wasn't sitting on the Chesterfield couch beside she aunt.

I turned round and walked straight back to my own deck, in my own third-class portion of the ship—hopping the railing and striding boldface past the deck-steward—like I was daring he arse to give me some kinda backbite.

The following morning, as I stood at the rail staring-way at a dirty-looking, whitecap-littered sea, I got an idea. Caper. The beginnings of a plan. Son, by this point I was so desperate to see Marguerite, I never even stopped to contemplate just how vie-kee-vie this caper could be. Nor how dangerous. *That's* how ba-zodee I was—too-tool-bay, assassataps, third degree of tabanca. And you got to remember that I was a restless fifteen years of age too. Reckless.

I turned round and left the deck and the handful of passengers wrapped up in they tattered blankets, descending the narrow stairs. Three levels below to the cabin I shared with my sisters. I knew we cabins would be empty at this hour of the morning, especially now we'd gotten over our initial bouts of seasickness. And in any case we'd all learnt quick enough that the best place to be when we felt queasy was up on deck in the fresh air. Mum would be in the third-class parlour with a circle of other women, sitting on blankets on the plank flooring—Georgina and Mary as well—all with balls of yarn in they laps and a pair of needles in they hands knitting-way. Son, whatever-the-arse kinda garments they could possibly be making I couldn't tell you—sweaters for the tropics? Sometimes they played draughts, gossiped about Lady So-and-So or the French comte travelling in upper class, or they sang songs with the children. Amelia playing with a handful of girls nearby.

Papee would be up on deck with the other men. Deep in discussion over some topic relevant to life in Trinidad or the TES. Unless they were hearing to a lecture from Mr. Etzler heself, or the comte—only two gentlemen aboard who made a point of venturing daily into the commoners' part of the ship—or he'd be forward in the saloon with Mr. Whitechurch.

The cabin I shared with my sisters measured 5½ ft x 5½ ft x 5½ ft. With the four bunks built perpendicular to the bulkheads, two on either side, a narrow passageway between into which the door opened. Meaning, of course, that I had to stoop down boseé-backed to enter into the cabin. And I could only sleep in my bunk with my legs folded up tight like a crab. Beneath the lower births were spaces for clothing and other articles. In addition to the tin poe in case one of us needed to use the toilet (or vomit, as Amelia and Mary had done those first couple nights—when we were all still adjusting to the constant roll and jar of the ship). A pitch-oil lamp hanging from its hook on the forward bulkhead.

Mum and Papee had the equivalent, adjacent cabin. The difference being that on the hull-side, midway between the upper bunk and ceiling, they had a porthole six inches in diameter that opened on a bevel. So when we left our two doors latched back—and we were fortunate enough to be on the windward side of the ship—a cool breeze swept through both cabins.

So far our nights had been tolerable enough.

Mum and Papee used they lower bunks to stow additional clothes, blankets, and other necessities for the voyage. Including the pasteboard box with a dozen apples packed in straw—purchased by Papee at the last minute before we boarded the ferry in London—which we'd all vowed solemn *not* to touch before our sixth week at sea. Son, the truth is we considered weself fortunate. All thanks to the government of Great Britain. Though nobody aboard knew nothing about none of that bubball but us.

I shut the door, locking myself into the cabin I shared with my sisters. Getting down on my knees to rummage beneath Georgina's berth, through her bundle of clothes. Till I found she white lace brassiere. Pair of square-toed shoes. Mary's bloomers with the little pink bows at the hips in the bundle beside it. I took up they little purse—I knew without having to look inside—containing the small cake of Cashmere powder and tiny pot of rouge.

I crossed over to my parents' cabin, which Papee'd left open to air out too. There wasn't nothing much of value to thief anyway, except maybe the apples. I latched the door shut behind me, stripping off my clothes, dressing myself in my sisters' undergarments. But as I went to pull on Mary's bloomers I realised my own drawers would suffice: I stuffed the bloomers into one cup of Georgina's brassiere. Then I turned round to ransack my father's stack of clothes, balling up two of his handkerchiefs and shoving them into the other cup. Now I sat on the edge of the lower birth rolling Mum's silk stockings over my pointed toes. Up over my stringy calves. Clipping them into the snaps of she French garters. From a package wrapped careful in tissue paper I removed Mum's crimson-coloured silk gown—shoulderless, with mutton-sleeves and a heavy quilted border round the hem of the skirt. In a flurry of excitement she'd sewn the gown out for she-self in the final days before the voyage—Mum planned to wear it to the Captain's Ball when we reached the Azores. I shook the frock out and stepped awkward inside. Struggling for the longest time—my spindly arms twisted up and contorted behind my back, navelhole sucked in tight—before I managed to fasten the seven tiny hooks running the length of my spinebones. Exhaling a slow breath.

Using Mum's handmirror and a wad of cotton wool, I brushed the rouge onto my cheeks. Dusted Cashmere powder round the periphery of my face. My neck & shoulders & chest. I pulled out Mum's black lace scarf and spread it overtop my head, tying a floppy bow beneath my chin. Her black Spanish shawl with the little embroidered bullfighters and its stringy fringe spread over my shoulders. I pulled on her black lace gloves, reaching to mid-forearm. Last, I squeezed my duckfeet inside Georgina's square-toed shoes—which I can assure you wasn't no kinda easy enterprise a-tall—buckling the straps behind.

I sat on the bunk, waiting and listening.

Before long I heard the clanging of the steward's bell. Calling the third-class passengers for lunch in they dining hall, two levels above my head. I listened to the thumps and scuffs of they boots as passengers filed into the hall, clatter of tin bowls laid down on the rough plank tables. Even the scrapings of the steward's ladle against the sides of he stewpot.

Son, despite my hunger, I was happy enough to avoid this lunch.

I waited a few more minutes. Till I felt sure all the passengers had assembled theyself in the dining room. Then I unlatched the door.

But at the same moment Amelia came busting through, shoving me back—

Sweet Jesus! she says, staring up into my face.

Son, I couldn't tell you if I felt more embarrassed, panicked, or geegeeree out my bloody skin. But after a few seconds her expression changed. Now Amelia looked up at me with a playful, mischievous amusement—

Good to see you're in a better mood, she says. You were looking so bored and sulky!

Amelia reached past me, searching through the things under Mum's bunk—

Seen Moffie? she asks. Mum told me she packed her under here.

Amelia grabbed up her rag doll and started out. But she stopped short, turning round again—

Better hurry, she says. There's cocoa left over from upper class.

Amelia paused, smiling—

Mind you don't smudge your powder drinking it!

She pulled the door shut behind her.

I flipped the latch and sat on the bunk again, catching my breath. Waiting a few more minutes. Till I'd mustered enough courage to slip out the cabin. I hurried up the narrow stairs, past the noisy dining room, stepping lightfoot as I could manage in Georgina's shoes on the uneven flooring. Though wide at the bottom with its thickly quilted hem, Mum's frock hung a foot-and-a-half short, exposing my bony ankles. Stockings stretched tight over them. Now I had to hide myself for the next hour, maybe two—someplace that gave me easy access to the upper-class deck—till it came time for the ladies to take they tea. I crossed the open deck, vacant with all the passengers down at lunch. A stiff breeze blowing Mum's heavy skirt between my legs, adding to my difficulties of crossing the shifting boards in Georgina's shoes.

I locked myself into the men's privy—the one assigned to the third-class passengers—immediately realising my mistake. The place stenching, with a putrid black puddle in the middle of the floor, sloshing side-to-side with the slow roll of the ship. The bench, walls, even the compartment's ceiling so soiled with nastiness, I feared I'd ruin Mum's fancy gown in one.

I let myself out, exhaling a long breath, crossing over the boards again. Sequestering myself this time in the women's toilet. Which I can assure you was plenty more agreeable, odours tolerable, sitting safe enough to one side of the bench. With the open hole just beside me, blue-gray sea slipping past far below. I untied the scarf beneath my chin, leant my head into a back corner of the stall, shutting my eyes. A salty breeze wafting up through the hole. Rhythmic slap of waves washing past the hull, distant squawk from a handful of gulls perpetually trailing the ship. And after a few minutes I entered into a familiar dreamplace. Memoryspace. Like a daydream, only a notch or two deeper. Floating alongside the slap-wash slap-wash of the waves, soft salt-breeze billowing up against my cheeks.

❁

Victoria Station: piercing screech of metal wheels. The Tucker clan following Papee's lead—five of us in a long line squeezing each other's hands and Amelia's rag doll's hands too—so as not to lose weself on the crowded platform. Weaving we way along like a string of squids. Back-and-forth amongst the excited, shouting passengers, everybody shoving toute-baghi in direction of the Bicester train.

Meanwhile, Papee searched for Mr. Powell and the Whitechurches.

A handful of TES members who'd once belonged to the military had dressed theyself in full regalia for the big event. They'd brought they rusty muskets so a volley of shots could be fired to announce the takeoff of the Satellite. Another group, dressed also in unrelated military garb, formed an orchestra that included a big bass drum, tuba, several bugles, and a triangle played with great delicacy by a chuffchuff former member of the Royal Guard. According to rumor the orchestra had met at Crossed Sabers Tavern early the previous evening. They'd only just exited this facility, after spending the entire night *synchronizing*. Needless-to-say the majority of them were having trouble not only blowing into they instruments, or beating them, but standing atop they feet. The Satellite Ensemble—as they dubbed theyself—rode in an open car adjacent to one the Tucker clan travelled in for we journey to Bicester.

My three sisters put down they hampers and went forward to listen. Whilst back in the compartment where the rest of my family settled weself, Mum napped, despite the jostling train and obnoxious music. Papee studying his mechanical drawings spread out cross his lap, oversized and dog-eared, scribbling last-minute notes.

After a short while Mr. Powell arrived, already red-faced and smiling. He greeted my father, squeezing onto the bench beside him, laying his jacket over the sidearm. The two men entering into a whispered discussion of some glitch in the Connective Apparatus. Papee pointing to something on his drawing, running his finger cross to where the ropes connected with the Prime Mover. Now they sat in silence a minute. Me listening to the chugging train and various va-va-vooms of the Ensemble. Then—as if in answer to they quandary—Mr. Powell reached into the pocket of his folded jacket, fumbling round, producing a pint-bottle of whiskey. He uncorked it with his teeth, offering my father some. But Papee waved him off, Mr. Powell tipping he bottle back for a generous swig.

Then, with a wink, he reached his bottle cross to *me*. First time in my life, I can assure you, I'd been offered any alcohol more than the priest's wine at Easter Sunday Mass—Mum's people came from Alsace, she was Roman Catholic, in which concern Papee cared not a pum.

I glanced over at him: he had his eyes fixed on the drawing. Like he hadn't even noticed.

What the arse? I took a quick swallow. The whiskey somehow splashing up my nose—two little rings of fire burning round my nostrils. I coughed, grimaced, passed the bottle back.

Mum stirred on the bench beside me, but she didn't open she eyes. In any case, Papee and Mr. Powell had already decided to remove theyself to some other part of the train, where they could discuss Papee's drawings more freely. He tied them up in a big roll with a piece of twine, the two men squeezing out.

The Ensemble broke into a waltz so speeded up it sounded like a polka. Waking Mum. On she lap she held one of the picnic baskets with sandwiches she and my sisters had made for lunch, since the victuals offered at the food venues were sure to be priced out we range.

Suddenly I suspected she smelt the whiskey on my breath. Despite that I'd taken only a sip.

My mother looked at me, like if she'd been reading my mind—

I'm expecting decent manners from you today, Willy, she says. Practically shouting over the band. And after a breath—

You're advised *not* to model your behaviour after these gentlemen, understand?

The Ensemble ended with a great bash of cymbals, Mum shifting she basket to the flooring beside her feet—

Finalment! she mumbled. And she went forward to check on my sisters.

Now, despite the overcrowded train, I found myself alone inside the compartment. Just beginning to move aside my family's belongings and stretch out on the seat—maybe I'd catch a few winks before we arrived?—when Mr. Powell's bottle tumbled out the pocket of his jacket, still folded over the armrest.

I sat a minute, contemplating the sloshing amber liquid. Then I uncorked it and took a sniff—like crusty leather doused down with turpentine. Enticing and revolting at the same time. And I took my second cautious, grimacing swig. Then, over a period of a couple minutes, I took three or four more, recorked the bottle, and slipped it into the breast pocket of my own jacket—Mr. Powell would hardly miss it, I decided. Plenty more bottles where that came from.

The Ensemble started into some species of military march—*um-pa-pa um-pa-pa*—and all-in-a-sudden I began to feel queasy. I shoved my family's things aside, stretching out on the seat, which had begun shifting about somewhat awkward beneath me. And not due to any jostlings of the train neither. I planted my unpolished brogue on the floor, attempting to steady the swimming seat, shutting my eyes. Trying my best to relax. And I must've managed, because after a time I dropped off dead asleep. Deep down into the depths.

Son, whether or not it was an effect of the whiskey, I couldn't tell you. It was my first experience with it. But the image that surfaced now in my imagination was disturbing enough. It was, in fact, derived from an illustration of the Satellite printed that same week in *The Morning Star*. Yet in my dream the machine was *alive*. Smoking-way and eating up the dirt. Now I watched it coming in my direction—roaring its way towards me—about to grind *me* up to a pulp too.

I sat up with a jolt, blinking. A clammy sweat crawling cross my forehead. I grabbed up the silly golfer's cap to swab it dry, deciding I wasn't drinking no more whiskey: I'd had enough for one day. I took the bottle out of my pocket again, with the intention of returning it straightway to Mr. Powell's jacket.

Just then the compartment door banged open against my leg. And a little woman I'd never seen in my life entered, standing there before me—

Here's a healthy lad! she says. I can see we're occupied with the same amusements as the other gentlemen on this train!

She swallowed a breath, huffing—

You must be Willy. Your father's told us a good deal about you n' your sisters—I'm Mrs. Whitechurch.

She reached her whitegloved hand towards me. A tiny woman, wearing a bright-coloured cloak and bonnet, despite the warm weather. Like Little Red Riding Hood. Only this woman could've been the granny. Clearly upper class—maybe even gentry—which had me wondering how she and she husband had taken so swift and easy to Papee. Because he'd never mentioned how wealthy they were.

I had to shift the bottle to my other hand in order to take hers, nudging my nose at it—

My birthday, I say, by way of explanation. First thing to jump inside my head.

Splendid, she says. N' how old are we today, young man?

Nineteen, I say, not batting an eye.

Well, she says, in that case I shall have to introduce you to my niece. Let me go and fetch her—train's so crowded we weren't able to find a seat!

With that she hurried out, banging the door behind her.

I'd overheard Papee telling Mum about these Whitechurches. About the same niece—who was eighteen years of age—and how she'd been born *cordless*. Whatever-the-arse that meant. Any other abnormalities, mental or physical, father didn't mention.

Only that she lived with she aunt and uncle under they care, how distressed they were to leave her behind when they emigrated to Trinidad.

Needless-to-say I was already busy conjuring up this girl born without a spinecord. Her head constantly flopping down atop her chest. No doubt she needed to wear some kinda whale-bone-ribbed corset. Two canes to walk with, if she could walk a-tall. Because probably she had to be *heaved* from place to place, like some kinda human-jellyfish. Or a pair of stockings stuffed with walnuts, constantly tumbling from the chair and needing to hauled up off the floor.

In any case, *whatever* this Marguerite was like, I assure you I wasn't much looking forward to meeting her a-tall.

Son, nothing I could've dreamt up would have prepared me for this young woman who entered behind she aunt. And not due to no deformities neither. Both women taking they seats on the bench before me.

To my embarrassment I was still holding the bottle of whis-key. I disappeared it quick inside the pocket of my jacket again.

Mrs. Whitechurch looked up, out of breath—

Willy, she says. Please make the acquaintance of my niece, Marguerite!

And with that the niece reached she own whitegloved hand towards me—I could see it vague and blurry out my eye-corners, because I couldn't raise them up to look at her not-for-nothing. Only staring down timid at the hideous golfer's cap, grateful I wasn't wearing it atop my head. Eventually I managed to lift my arm, aware of little more than the jostling train, of my own skinny bamsee sinking down into the seat.

But son, even the first touch of warm skin through the soft cotton glove sent a set of shivers tingling along my spinebones.

Like a line of batchacks crawling up. My head giddy again, light as air. A floating sensation inside my chest, my whole body. Like all-in-a-sudden I was rising up off the bench.

Now the oddest thing: my hand stuck up inside the cotton glove like it was plastered down with laglee. I just couldn't pull it loose. Take it away. Like if now I *needed* to be holding onto this woman, because if not I'd float up to bounce my head *braps* against the ceiling.

In the midst of all this awkward, laglee-sticking-floating business, my eyes slid cross the flooring. Over towards Marguerite. Beside her feet sat a smallish canvas rucksack, bearing the outlines of two-three books. Below the hem of her lacy white frock, brown leather hiking boots, ankle-high, multiple laces crisscrossing the tongues. Like a scoutboy's boots. Now my eyes began climbing up the lacy frock-folds. Up to her other white-gloved hand poised in her lap, with a row of six bead-shaped, lace-covered buttons along the joint of the cuff. Another line of these same buttons stretching the length of her sternum. Now my eyes began climbing up them, like a little ladder, button by button, up to the nape of her neck. Halting at the soft triangular indentation there at the base of her throat. Draping round her shoulders was a lilac-coloured scarf, tied loose. The brim of her white hat angling almost to eye level, a few strands of hazelnut hair spilling from underneath.

I could make out her strong jaw, lips thin and purple-pink, her nose long & straight & strong too. But son, what struck me most was the burnt-sienna colouring of her cheeks: deep, rich, *not* an Englishgirl's kinda skin—it came from she aunt's Portugee side of the family, but of course I wouldn't learn that for some time to come. And however pit-tim-pam was this Mrs. Whitechurch, she niece is tall like tall—that much I could tell you already—only a few inches under my own spindly, awkward, chickenbone self.

Now, with a warmish electric jolt, my eyes met up with hers. Staring straight back at me: bright, clear, hazel-coloured eyes. Unflinching. Like they'd go on looking forever, those eyes. Like after the last eyes had dimmed & silenced theyself & flickered out, those eyes would keep on looking.

Son, next thing I knew my *own* eyes stuck-up on hers with the same embarrassing laglee business as the glove. Just so. Because I couldn't shift them way, pry them loose—I couldn't take my blasted hand back neither! With that same awkward floating sensation inside my chest, my whole body. Only waiting to feel my head bounce against the ceiling, because maybe *then* I could take my eyes and my hand back.

How long it lasted I couldn't tell you. A minute, maybe two. Till I found myself sitting there with both sweated-up palms inside my lap, staring down at my clunky brogues.

It was the aunt's voice that broke the silence—

Willy, she says, I'm leaving Marguerite in your care a moment. Whilst I go n' extract Mr. Whitechurch from the company of your father n' Mr. Powell. They're making a pretence of studying their drawings!

With that she pushed out of the compartment.

Leaving Marguerite and me alone—distressingly alone.

With me still staring at my scuffed-up brogues, wondering why-the-arse I didn't at least polish them. Mum had sewn egg-shaped patches of the same gaudy gold-plaid material as the cap over the knees of my trousers—hand-me-downs from Papee, same as the brogues—and since I'd already outgrown my father's six-foot stature by an inch, they fit me round my ankles like buccoo-reef trousers. As Papee'd ripped a hole in the left elbow of his jacket, Mum had sewn matching egg-shaped patches over my elbows.

Son, as I sat there I couldn't decide if I looked more like a scarecrow, clown, or organ-grinder's chimp.

Again out my eye-corners, I watched Marguerite opening the buckle of her rucksack. Extracting a smallish book covered over in mother-of-pearl. Thinking at first that it must be a Bible—because Mum had made me a present of a little Bible just so a few years previous for my Confirmation—son, my first thought was that this Marguerite must be some kinda bloody evangelist!

She raised the little book up to her lap—in her cool, calm, whitegloved hands—sliding out a little white pencil from a special pocket along the spine. Now she daubed the lead against her tongue. Slow, three separate times. She opened up the book, lifting out the red ribbon, flipping the page. Scribbling out something. Now she turned the book round, reaching it forward for me to read—

you're not nineteen, are you?

❖

Just then, as I sat sequestered in the women's third-class lavatory, another of the steward's bells startled me—*ca-clang ca-clang ca-clang ca-clang*. Ringing, this time, at some forward location a good distance away. Announcing teatime for the upper-class passengers. But son, now I didn't want to leave the stall, depart from out my daydream. My memoryspace. Not as yet. Not so quick.

I shut my eyes again. Willing myself back onto that train hurrying us to Bicester. Back into the compartment with Marguerite.

◇

She flipped a page of her book, scribbling out something else. Reaching it forward—

I was born without vocal cords

Son, only then did it dawn upon me—like a swift zobell cross the back of my head—what Papee'd meant by that *cordless*. Thinking: but how-the-arse could somebody survive without saying anything a-tall? It seemed impossible—almost more difficult than living without a spinecord. How do you ask for a simple glass of water? Advise somebody where to scratch you back? How do you tell them you got a bloody itch in the first place? How do describe the way leaves in eucalyptus trees glitter at sunset?

Marguerite retrieved her book. She flipped the page, scribbling again. Reaching it forward—

since it's all I've ever known
it's never seemed much of an impediment

I sat contemplating this last remark. Turning it over in my head. And son, it wasn't half a minute before I turned my mind round arse-backwards too. In the opposite direction. Thinking: who needs to talk anyway? since you could write down everything you had to say quick-and-easy enough? clear & simple &

fixed there solid on the page without a chance of *mis*communication neither? Because what-the-arse-good has *talk* ever done
anybody? so many people always flapping they traps? so much
wasted breath? brainless babble?

Son, I hadn't hardly contemplated this profound insight a
moment when the conductor began clanging his bell—*ca-clang
ca-clang ca-clang*—signaling our arrival into Bicester. As the train
came to a screeching halt, Marguerite turned the page. Daubing
her pencil again, scribbling out something else.

She turned the book round—

*I'd be pleased Willy if you'd
escort me to Satellite Field*

◈

Now I heard loud knocking on the toilet-stall door. Pounding.
Like each hard blow was a stiff thump down on the crown of
my head. I sat up, rattled. Spread the scarf quickly overtop my
head, retying the floppy bow. Straightening Mum's frock and
letting myself out.

A handful of women stood queued up before the door—
how they hadn't commenced to hammering on it till now I
couldn't tell you—they tattered wools wrapped round them
against the wind. I swallowed a breath and held my head up,
clutching Mum's stringy-fringed bullfighter-shawl round my
shoulders. Walking straight past them. Clacking cross the boards
in my sister's shoes. And I continued clacking, straight past the
deck-steward at his post behind the galley.

But son, soon as I arrived at the low railing I'd hopped so
easy the previous afternoon, I stopped short: there wasn't no

way I could negotiate this leap in Mum's frock and Georgina's shoes. No way a-tall.

A second later the steward was at my side, grinning peculiar. Bending over to unhinge a part of the rail—I hadn't seen it up till now—doubling it back on itself—

Please, he says. And he winked at me in a manner I recognised straightway was laden with meaning—though what, precisely, the meaning *was* I hadn't a clue—presenting me his arm.

I took hold of it in my lace-clad hand. And I held my head up, stepping through the gap in the rail. Raising up the thickly quilted hem of Mum's frock with my other hand as I proceeded, graceful and dainty as I could manage, down the short flight of steps. Clacking cross the boards.

I made a bolt for that ladies' tea parlour. The one reserved for upper class where I'd spied Mrs. Whitechurch the previous afternoon. But soon as I entered the steward in charge—dressed again in white-tie-and-tails—took notice and put down his silver pots. He approached from the other side of the room, much to my dismay. Yet the steward only offered his arm, same as his companion outside. Escorting me over to a seat near a group of women chattering round the Chesterfield couch, cups of tea and little plates of pastries holding delicate in they hands. With the same pair of portly little ladies sitting before the upright piano, tinkling on the keys and giggling-way.

I settled myself into the chair and took a look round—Mrs. Whitechurch hadn't arrived yet.

This was, in truth, as far as I'd proceeded with my plan: to get myself past those two stewards and into this tea parlour. I hadn't thought it out further than that. Presently I decided that when Mrs. Whitechurch did appear I'd communicate with her—in some secret manner I hadn't yet devised—confirming, first, that Marguerite was aboard ship. Then I'd arrange some secret way for the two of us to meet.

But as I sat back in the plush cushions of my chair—listening to the women chattering on the Chesterfield couch, two ladies at the piano tinkling and giggling—I began to grow bored with myself. I also began to feel *hungry*. Now I realised that I was famished. Hadn't hardly eaten nothing a-tall since we'd boarded the ship six days before. I mustered my courage, stood on my shaky ankles in Georgina's shoes, and I approached the table spread lavish with food. Taking up the pair of silver tongs—a little awkward in my lace gloves—and helping myself to a ham sandwich and another of sliced cucumber, placed careful side-by-side on my little porcelain plate.

But even before I could return to my seat I'd consumed the two sandwiches, inhaling them one-after-the-next in a couple breaths. I went back to the food at the table. Disregarding the tongs this time, I piled myself up a precariously tall stack of five more finger-sandwiches—two cucumber and three of Spanish ham—in addition to pouring out a tall glass of iced lemon-bitters from the pitcher.

As I turned round, one of the portly ladies who'd been playing on the piano approached from behind. She looked up into my face, smiling sweet.

I smiled back. Good as I could manage.

Then, a second later, she realised I wasn't no kinda young maiden a-tall. Letting loose a squeal like a puss-cat with its tail caught beneath a wagon wheel. Causing me, in my state of shock, to toss my little plate and glass into the air—cucumber slices & ham slices & little squares of bread, in addition to chipped ice and lemon-bitters—raining down atop this little lady's head.

I couldn't think of nothing more than to try to clean up my

mess. Reaching down to the floor for my little plate—attempting, at the same time, with my lace-clad fingers, to scoop up several squares of soggy bread. Managing only to slip on a thin slice of ham in Georgina's shoes, cockspraddle cross the floor, slick with lemon-bitters & ice chips & disassembled finger-sandwiches.

By this time several other women had joined in for a chorus of squealing puss-cats. The whole of that tea parlour dissolved to chaos. I struggled, with considerable effort, to regain my feet in my square-toed shoes on the slippery floor, aided by a small woman—her arm wrapped round my waist to help me up—who I believed, in my state of confusion, was the same portly one from the piano I'd just flung my food over.

She turned out to be Mrs. Whitechurch—

Willy my boy! she says. What in heavens?

She peered up into my face. Giving me a curious grin—

Marguerite's been asking for you. Poor girl, she's been seasick since we set sail—*heart*struck more likely!

Son, for a split second I felt my own heart beating happy as soursop ice cream inside my powdered chest. But it only lasted a second. Because now I felt a hand grasping hold of each of my elbows. Firm as vice-grips. I looked round to see that at one side stood the steward in charge of the tea parlour. At my other elbow—I realised with sudden alarm—the deck-steward stationed behind the galley. With the same indecipherable, queasy smirk on his face—

We'll give this he-she some *real* tea-n'-pastries! he says.

Most tasty! states his companion.

They hurried me out the tea parlour via a service door at the back. Lugging me along a hallway, past the first-class dining hall, down a series of narrow stairs lit only by a hatch at deck level.

With me stumbling awkward between them in my cramped shoes, my abductors hauling me brutish down the stairs—

In here! the deck-steward says, running his tongue over his lips.

He indicated a rough plank door with a hole for the handle, latched shut with a short piece of wood nailed cross the middle. He turned it, flinging the door open. Now they shoved me into a dark hallway lined on both sides with other rough plank doors. In the dim light I made out the handle-holes, worn flat with use. But these doors were locked shut with gleaming brass padlocks—

Where's 'em clatty keys? the deck-steward demands. I'm risin up fer the jab awready!

Now the parlour-steward reached deep inside his pocket. Feeling round—

Hold on to yer hoses, he says.

With that the deck-steward slammed the first door shut— *bram*—enclosing three of us in pitch-darkness.

Bloody hell, one of them says.

The other—

Let's give it the jab right here!

Better hope Cook don't come in search of bacon.

We'll give him his fair share of tasty bacon!

I sat on the plank flooring where the stewards had thrown me. Breathing hard, sweating in Mum's heavy gown. Surrounded by darkness and geegeeree out my bloody wits. I pressed backwards, instinctive, to the far end of the passageway. Till I felt the hard wood wall butting me up against my bony bamsee. I heard the stewards pursuing. Feeling they way in the dark. All-in-a-sudden, with a burst, I shoved under and past them—regaining my feet in the awkward shoes—and somehow aware, at the same time, of those seven hooks along the length of my spine snapping open one-by-one.

I moved in a rush towards the single spot of light in the darkened hallway—the small handle-hole in the door at the end. Busting out and slamming it shut behind me.

I turned the latch. Locking the stewards inside.

Now I paused a second, leaning against the latched door, catching my breath. How-the-arse I'd managed to escape, un-scathed, in a matter of seconds, I couldn't say myself. I turned and hurried off, the stewards pounding against the inside of the door, cursing behind me. And I made my way up the narrow stairs, wiping the back of my gloved hand cross my sweated-over brow. At that instant I noticed something—a faint flash—com-ing from the corner of one of the steps. Son, my first thought was to ignore it. Wanting nothing more than to get my bony little bamsee to-hell-away-and-gone from those stewards. Fast as I could manage. Then, with a vaps, I turned round. I reached down my lace-gloved hand to pass it over the floorboard. Tak-ing up, what I realised a second later, was a ring containing eight heavy iron keys.

2

Night Prowling

I slept in my cabin during the day. Now I became a nocturnal animal. Not long after the nine o'clock curfew, when the third-class passengers were required to be in we beds, and my three sisters had dropped off asleep, I'd slip from out my bunk. I'd take down the pitch-oil lamp from its hook on the bulkhead, but I wouldn't light it yet. Still wearing my nightshirt, in the complete dark, I'd tiptoe out the cabin, up the narrow stairs. Already I'd discovered that during the late evening hours the deck-steward was seldom posted at his station. And if he happened to be there a-tall he generally lay in the midst of a big coil of rope, flask of rum holding in he hand, snoring-way. Unless there was some special event for the upper-class passengers—a dance, lecture, or a theatrical performance put on by the passengers theyself—they'd be dead-asleep inside they own fancy cabins by this time too. Only the first mate and his watchman at the helm, or the cook preparing meals for the following day, might be awake at that hour.

Still in my nightdress, on my bare feet, I moved swift and silent as a ghost over the boards. I ducked past the elevated station at midship that housed the helm, enclosing the first mate and he watchman. And I proceeded forward: cross the third-class deck, past the open door of the galley where the cook tended he pots in a pungent cloud of smoke and steam. Cross the empty forecastle deck and down a flight of carpeted steps. Past the deserted dining hall, saloon, vacant ladies' tea parlour. Down the three flights of narrow stairs to the hold. In jelly-thick darkness I felt for my ring of keys, tied with a loop of twine round my neck. Already I'd learnt by touch which of the eight iron keys fit each of the brass padlocks, four doors on either side of the passageway.

My first objective was to recover my frock coat, and all the rest of my newly tailored attire, from my family's trunk hidden somewhere in the hold. So that I could move with impunity between the third- and first-class sections of the ship. Same as Papee. Always careful to lock whichever of the plank doors I'd opened up behind me again. Squeezing the padlocks closed with my dexterous fingers—shoved, convenient enough, out through the selfsame holes that served as door handles.

Yet despite my precautions there'd been a couple of close calls: the cook descending to the pantry for some ingredient for his pot, a steward sent to retrieve a bottle of liquor from another storeroom—there seemed to be at least one other copy of my set of keys. But on both of those perilous occasions I'd managed to out my lantern just in time. Escaping without a scrape. Nonetheless I grew accustomed—even in the midst of my wildest rummagings through this veritable treasure trove of luggage and goods—to keep a cautious ear cocked.

Son, I *should* have been reunited with Marguerite already. I'd been rummaging through the storagerooms for four nights. By this time I knew the ship's layout (at least that part forward of the cabin I shared with my sisters) well enough to diagram and label each level. And according to my calculations the Whitechurches' cabin, as well as the other first-class quarters situated below the forecastle deck—and the very bed in which Marguerite, at that moment, lay peacefully asleep—was two levels up and only a short distance forward of the same storeroom into which I had, on this particular night, sequestered myself. Same storeroom where I discovered, finally, after my exhaustive search of four nights, the whereabouts of the large tin trunk labeled—

TUCKER
TRINIDAD, B.W.I.

By the light of my pitch-oil lamp I shed my nightshirt. Hands trembling with excitement, I dressed myself in my linen shirt with French cuffs. Pinstripe pants & embroidered vest & boots & single-vented frock coat. But son, on this same night that I located the Tuckers' trunk, sure-as-goatmouth, I *also* happened to find—at the other end of the passageway of locked plank doors, in another storeroom altogether, the only one I hadn't yet inspected—I also discovered the compartment where the most valuable and luxurious articles aboard ship were stowed. All those extravagances served to upper class. Together with all the lavish goods destined to be sold off by merchants when the *Rosalind* arrived in Trinidad.

Instead of proceeding direct to Marguerite's cabin the following morning—or even that same night, now with the licence of my fashionable attire—I took off my fancified clothes again. Stripped myself down. Hanging my frock coat from a nail in one of the rafters, top hat safe on a shelf, and I folded up my linen shirt and pinstripe pants. I dressed myself back in my tatty nightshirt. Purposely postponing my reunion with Marguerite another four nights. Continuing my prowling. Returning for four more nights to this particular storeroom at the end of the passageway.

There were bottles of French champagne I taught myself careful to uncork. To enjoy the pop and fizz of the foam surging forth from the bottles' narrow necks. Tingling cross the back of my parched throat. Bottles of twelve-year-old Irish whiskey I learnt to sip slow and patient, savouring the smoky taste. After my second night prowling I'd borrowed Papee's pocketknife from the space beneath his bunk. Now I took down one of the hams swinging beside my head, and using the blunt back edge of the blade, I scraped-way a few remaining salt crystals. The sharp edge to hack off wedges of hard desiccated skin, with a few wayward tufts of hair. And I carved off paper-thin, semitransparent slivers of the finest acorn-fed Catalonian ham, stamped *PATA NEGRA*.

They melted on my tongue like curls of butter.

There were globe-shaped cheeses the size of ships' buoys, encased in they skins of red wax. Labeled *HOLLAND EDAM*. Swiss cheeses. Rounds of Italian *PARMASANO* big as wagon wheels. Smaller cheeses in flat, mould-splattered boxes of light wood labeled *ENGLAND STILTON, FRANCE CAMEM-BERT, ESPAÑA MANCHEGO*.

There were big dusty tins of bonito marinating in oil; smaller tins of cockles & muscles & cherrystone clams; little square tins of herring, sardines, anchovies; tiny tins the size of demitasse saucers containing Russian caviar.

In the shadowy light of my pitch-oil lamp, locked into the hold of the gently rolling ship, I taught myself to eat patient. I taught myself to eat purposeful. Then I paused from my eating for another short sup of whiskey. A cool draught of foamy champagne.

Son, I ate till I couldn't eat again. Till I was satiated, gorged, bloated-out. I drank till I couldn't drink no more. Till I'd filled five champagne bottles with my own weewee, and carefully corked them back. My stools ritually wrapped in ladies' negligees of the finest silk, the packets tucked careful into a large spherical bottle with a clampdown lid—its contents long ago consumed—labeled *ΕΛΛΗΝΙΚΗ ΦΕΤΑ ΣΤΟ ΕΛΑΙΟΛΑΔΟ*.

I outed my kerosene lamp and tumbled with a groan and a thud onto my back. Onto the rough plank flooring at the bottom of the ship with the pleasant sounds of bilgewater sloshing back-and-forth beneath the boards. The unceasing creak and jar of the ship all round me. Those faintly nauseating yet delightful smells of mould on the cheeses and cross the desiccated skins of the hanging hams, swaying to and fro in perfect unison, like a second ocean floating in the air above my head.

I slept and dreamt of eating and drinking. And I awoke again and lit my lantern and ate and drank with such studied, sustained, precise and celebratory enjoyment—such patient purposeful pleasure—that I felt I must be asleep, dreaming that I was awake drinking and eating. Unless I'd died in my sleep and woken up in heaven. Drinking & eating & dreaming.

Lying on my back at the bottom of the *Rosalind*'s hold, my arms folded comfortable behind my head, I gazed up into the hams swaying amongst they shadow-reflections from my pitch-oil lamp. Drifting again in that familiar memoryspace—what do you call a daydream that happens at night?

❖

Marguerite and me happy enough to let the eager crowd surge on ahead. For one thing, I had no idea where we'd go once we reached Satellite Field. I assumed we'd join Mum and Mrs. Whitechurch in the stands. But I wasn't so keen about sitting there with Marguerite, under the maco-eyes of my three sisters. I'd seen Papee exit the station with his oversized roll of drawings tucked under his arm—other hooked round the elbow of an odd-looking little gentleman carrying a cane with a gleaming silver panther at the handle—who I assumed was Mr. Whitechurch. No doubt those two would make a beeline for the Satellite with the rest of the men. But I couldn't see joining them neither—Marguerite would be the only woman out on the field. Son, the truth is I didn't have no idea where we were going. And it wasn't till I spied a place secluded from the boisterous crowd—hidden beneath the smaller of the grandstands and backed by a line of shaggy sycamores—that I caught a vaps.

I veered Marguerite off in that direction.

Suddenly all the shouting and ruckus behaviour seemed far away. Despite that the spectators were perched just above we heads. Marguerite untied her large silk scarf from round her shoulders. Spreading it out on the yellowed grass for us to sit on. I wanted to take off my jacket—not only to spread it on the ground as well, but all-in-a-sudden I'd found myself in a serious sweat. And not due to the warm weather neither. But I kept it on, too nervous to act one way or another: my mind felt scrambled as the guts of a calabash.

Marguerite removed her little mother-of-pearl book from her rucksack again. She slipped out the pencil and daubed it three times against her tongue, scribbling, turning it round for me to read—

I'm sure this isn't the trial you were expecting

After a time Marguerite removed her white gloves, setting them into the bowl of her overturned hat. She unpinned her hazel hair, letting it fall like a sprinkling of water down over her shoulders. Meanwhile, as I stretched my legs out before me, I heard Mr. Powell's bottle give a summoning kinda slosh inside my breast pocket. Somehow I'd forgotten all about it. Now, for some reason I couldn't fully explain, I took it out, offering Marguerite some. She shook her head. But I pulled the cork nonetheless, and after another pause I took a swig, trying my best to hide the grimace. And truth is it eased my anxieties further. Bolstered my self-confidence. And although I never did manage to take my jacket off that afternoon, eventually I became comfortable enough to unbutton it. I loosened my cravat and collar, took off the hideous cap.

I had, of course, learnt a good deal about this Satellite from Papee. I'd studied his mechanical drawings, in addition to the plates and descriptions printed in the *Star*—it occurred to me that Marguerite might've glanced at them sheself. In any case, the Satellite provided an easy and convenient subject to talk about. A subject on which I could even be something of an expert.

I took a next grimacing swig, and I found myself chatting on enthusiastic about Mr. Etzler's machine. Surprising even me— till now I'd taken only a passing interest in it. Marguerite nodded her head. We ate a couple more cheese-and-tomato sandwiches.

As I talked Marguerite reached to her ankles to untie the leather laces of her scoutboy-boots. She slipped them off, setting them aside. Then she rolled her cream-coloured wool stockings down along her brown legs, off the points of her toes, balling them into the cups of her boots. And as I continued chatting-way, out my eye-corners, I watched her rake her long toes through the yellowed grass. One slender foot and then the next. I watched her luxuriate in it, like a puss-cat.

We sat in comfortable silence a minute.

Eventually, Marguerite reached over for her little book, poised atop her rucksack. She flipped it open, scribbling out a line—

> *he's always struck me as something of a buffoon*

I read it twice. Then I put the book down, rubbed my eyes. And I read it a third time—

Who? I say, already a little bit geegeeree to hear her answer.

She scribbled again—

> *Mr. Etzler—though I fear he's nearly as dangerous as he is foolish*

I was stunned. Nobody'd never uttered a condescending word against him before. Not in my hearing. It seemed blasphemous, a sacrilege. It seemed to me outrageous, utterly unthinkable, unsayable—certainly unwritedownable.

I looked up—

What can you possibly mean? I ask.

Marguerite smiled. She took her book back, scribbling—

> *all these unfortunate labourers*
> *he's robbing them blind*

She scribbled again—

> *I shan't lend him my support*
> *nor shall I follow him cross the sea to Trinidad*

I fought a few seconds to gather myself, to assemble my jumbled thoughts. My calabash guts. What she'd said made me vex, plain and simple—like if it was *me* she'd insulted. Though I doubt I could even isolate that emotion clearly inside me. More than anything I felt confused, unmoored, floating again. But not in any welcomed, agreeable, *delicious* kinda way.

I took a deep breath—

That's the significance of all this, I say, slow, careful. That's why we're here. So Mr. Etzler's Satellite can save us.

I paused—

My impoverished working class!

Marguerite smiled at me again. Though not in an unkind way, nor patronizing neither. She wrote in her little book—

he's an unpardonable charlatan

Then she took her book back, and I watched her writing—

*in addition to which his mathematics are unsound:
there's no infinity when it comes to mechanical function for the
simple fact of <u>friction</u>—all things must, inevitably, draw to a halt*

I looked up from the page at her.

◉

Counted amongst the passengers travelling aboard the *Rosalind* were a handful of wealthy English and French estate owners. We never saw them. Excepting the French comte—who made a point of visiting the third-class deck almost every afternoon, same as Mr. Etzler. This Comte César de Beauvoisin as loud as he was large, with the rather disagreeable habit of animating his speech with one or the other of the half-eaten mutton legs held in his whitegloved hands. Having visited his cultivations in the Pyrenees during the pleasant autumn months, he was returning to his properties in the warmer climes. The comte's discourses, almost without exception, dealt with the great hardships suffered by West Indian planters in recent years. Of they enormous monetary losses since the emancipation of the Africans.

Yet despite his litany of complaints the comte's sermons were lively. The estate owners had taken matters into they own hands. They'd sought to solve they *own* problem—this problem created for them by self-righteous, stiffnosed, bill-mongering MPs in London—and in a manner that seemed perfectly West Indian. Hope was, indeed, on its way. It travelled on the selfsame sea that we did. Bound for the same West Indies. For the very same island of Trinidad. This hope, however, came from a different place. And although it was the same general direction in which Africa lay, it originated in another continent altogether. Because at that very moment, on another ship called the *Fatal Rozack*, a cargo of 217 indentured East Indians were making they way from the city of Calcutta. Bound also for the estates in Trinidad.

The comte claimed to have already purchased some forty-five of these same coolies due to arrive on the *Rozack* heself. If the new labour scheme proved successful—and who could say why it wouldn't?—he'd set aside funds to purchase hundreds more. The comte estimated conservative that his cane, cocoa, and copra cultivations in Trinidad could easily employ a thousand coolies.

As you can well imagine this comte was also the particular object of all Mr. Etzler's seething, pent-up wrath. And not simply as a flesh-eater. It was rumored that the comte's only luggage consisted of a hundred cured Catalonian hams, plus a flock of sheep from off his farm in the Pyrenees—one to be slaughtered every other day of the voyage for his individual consumption—kept in a special pen beneath the aft deck. As if the *Rosalind* was he own personal Noah's ark.

For the first couple weeks at sea Mr. Etzler and the comte did not exchange a word together. Though the comte was present for all Mr. Etzler's lectures, improvised and advertised. At each of these discourses he made a deliberate show of dedicating more attention to his pair of half-eaten mutton legs—reclining on a chaise lounge toted by the stewards from deck to parlour to saloon—large white napkin spread diamond-wise over he bigsome belly. Shifting, quite audible and voracious, from one greasy whitegloved fist to the next. Likewise, each time the comte fell into a discourse on he indentured coolies, Mr. Etzler stood at a distance listening. Without so much as opening up he mouth. Till the experience became so painful for Mr. Etzler that he stormed off in a huff.

Not till the afternoon of we fourteenth day at sea was there any direct communication between the two men. I happened to be there, having just awoken in my cabin and ascending to the deck to make a serious weewee. And son, even after hearing Mr. Etzler's animated voice, I wondered if my own necessities didn't take precedence. As usual he was standing atop a sailor's stool to facilitate he delivery, addressing the group of men crowded round him—

West Indian plantation owners, he says, stuck in zee blind prejudices huv zair age-old practises unt customs, are dumb as donkeys. Belligerent unt boorish as billy goats!

He cited, by way of example, the dangerous and labour-intensive method used by the planters for crystallising sugar from cane juice. This procedure could, he maintained, be accomplished virtually cost-free (since there wouldn't be no such labour involved) and danger-free (since neither heat nor fuel would be needed to boil the juice) by employing a procedure of he own invention. This process for crystallising sugar—like all his inventions and discoveries—utilised only the most rudimentary of scientific, chemical, and engineering principles.

Mr. Etzler continued—

Zee problem wiss men since antiquity is zat zey do not reason. Zey do not *sink!* Stuck in zair state huv mental sloth unt barbaric ignorance, zee generality of men do not even open up zair eyes to see what sits in front huv zair noses!

In fact, Mr. Etzler added, his little chest expanding within the confines of he crimson vest, this invention for crystallising sugar could earn him *thousands* of pounds if he offered it for purchase on the international market. And not the advancement of scientific knowledge for all humanity. Nonetheless, this invention utilised the simplest chemical principle—

Known to every knucklehead schoolboy older zen zee age huv seffen!

In the silence that followed Mr. Etzler's speech—a moment that felt, in truth, like he'd sucked the air out the entire deck—the comte got up slow from out he lounge chair—

Écoutez ici, Monsieur Etzler, he says, holding up a slightly soiled canvas sack in he whitegloved hands.

Now we all turned to look at the comte—

You crystallise sugar, he says, without the use of fuel—*ou le feu, oui?*—for everybody here to witness, and I pay you the equivalent of one thousand pounds in gold doubloons!

With that he dropped he bag to the deckboards at his feet, giving out a *shilllink* and an exhalation of ancient dust.

The comte continued—

Fail, he says. Et avant le Christ avec sa Sainte Vierge, Captain Damphier will set you in a rowboat, adrift, *au milieu de la grande mer!*

Another silence followed the comte's pronouncement, with every man-jack on that deck only watching at him recline again in his chaise lounge. He reached to his vest pocket to take out a cigar, livery-clad butler stepping forward to light it. With Mr. Etzler still standing on he stool at the other end of the deck, jawbone hanging open like a zandolee catching flies.[*]

On the afternoon advertised in Mr. Stollmeyer's handprinted announcement the sea was flat as a dishplate. As if to signal the approaching tropics, it was coloured a glittering sapphire. Indeed, the sun shone brighter and hotter that afternoon than it had since the start of we journey sixteen days before. Such fine weather worked well in Mr. Etzler's favour. Adding to the festivities Captain Damphier ordered iced lemonade for the children, a special punch of he own recipe—spiked generous with dark West Indian rum—to be served to all the adults. And good quantity of this punch had already been consumed when, as advertised, Mr. Stollmeyer circulated round the men collecting the admission charge (women and children free, a group amongst which I was happy to hide myself).

---

[*] *The Sugar Question Made Easy,* by C.F. Stollmeyer (London 1844): 'Everyone who is acquainted with the cultivation of sugar knows that the labours of the sugar-house are the most dreaded by the slaves, or free-workmen; also what waste and other casualties are attendant upon the process of boiling sugar. It is therefore with pleasure I can announce that this very difficult point has at last been overcome by a gentleman of great talents, extensive learning, and extraordinary inventive powers—Mr. J.A. Etzler, who has succeeded in crystallising sugar without heat or boiling, at 1/5 the cost of making sugar in the conventional way. Experiments have proved the fact without a doubt.'

Ever since we'd first come aboard the third-class passengers had noticed an enormous and rather sinister-looking, cubelike structure—mysteriously covered over in thick canvas—standing in the aft-most part of our deck. Though by now we'd all learnt easy enough to ignore it. But that afternoon, with a bit of improvised ceremony, Mr. Stollmeyer untied the canvas cover. Revealing to us an obzockee crate lashed down to the boards— no possible hope of getting it into the hold—stenciled with the following lettering:

SATELLITE
exclusive property of
J.A. Etzler
on loan to TES
(all net profits 10%)

Mr. Stollmeyer instructed the sailors to lean a ladder up against the crate. He had them climb it and set a table on top, a small and innocuous enough black box sitting on it. The box painted that colour, somebody hypothesised, to most effectively attract the sun's rays and heat. No one could say what might be its contents. Though it was the general supposition that if the box did not contain Mr. Etzler's invention, it must hold some secret ingredient or chemical substance necessary for he demonstration.

Like a seasoned performer knowing how to best escalate the emotions of his audience, Mr. Etzler arrived a good hour after the time specified on the announcement. He carried a small suitcase, putting it down to tuck his long beard inside his crimson vest. Mr. Etzler took it up again, ascending the ladder, laying the case down on the table and unbuckling the two straps. Now he removed the model of his Satellite, in addition to a miniature version of one of its attachments.

As was his general custom Mr. Etzler buckled his suitcase closed again, placing it on the boards of the crate beneath his feet. He stepped up on top.

Taking proper advantage of the crowd gathered before him—in an English that became increasingly infected with German, and harder to interpret, the more his excitement grew—Mr. Etzler launched into a lecture on his agrarian mechanism. The fact that he happened to be standing atop the crate containing the very machine he now elucidated for his audience only added a further poignancy to his delivery. Of course, a good number of us present—members of the TES and others too—had heard all this palaver, verbatim, on a number of occasions already. The other spectators, including a handful who knew almost nothing about Mr. Etzler nor his machines, were similarly disinterested. We'd offered up we shillings to see a *Scientific Demonstration*—which, to us, meant some compelling show of chemical magic. Some kinda spectacle. We hadn't paid to hear a speech on some chupidee model looking like the plaything of a badjohn-schoolboy—a rabbit-size rack of medieval torture. And if we *didn't* get the spectacle, in the very least we'd surrendered up we hard-earned coins for the somewhat perverse pleasure and privilege of seeing—as advertised in Mr. Stollmeyer's announcement—this peculiar little man puffed up like a porcupine-fish set adrift in a rowboat in the middle of the sea.

One way or another we were going to get our money's worth.

In response to a handful of rather indignant shouts to *Get on with the bloody experiment!* or some such, Mr. Etzler put down the model of he Satellite. Now he took up the miniaturised attachment.

The purpose of this attachment, he explained, was to instantly crush sugar canes of the greatest quantity, with the highest yield of pure juice, by the power of Mother Nature and his Satellite alone. Without the use of any manual labour whatsoever. That is to say, *human* muscle & blood & bone & sinew. Including—Mr. Etzler spoke out bold, his chest inflated, crimson vest bright beneath the sun—EAST INDIAN INDENTURED LABOURERS who were, in point of fact, no different from the African slaves preceding them. Human beings procured by a trade that was now a capital crime in all civilised countries of the world, with the exception of the United States. That abominable practise of so-called CHRISTIANS!

Disregarding the malicious jeers of the spectators before him—the majority of whom could care a jot about these Hindus who were so exotic to us they couldn't hardly be imagined anyway—Mr. Etzler continued shouting. Seemingly oblivious to the growing danger of he own predicament.

Finally, when he couldn't be heard any longer over the protests of his audience, he took up the mysterious black box sitting on the table before him. With his free hand he pulled out a kerchief, swabbing-way the beads of sweat dripping off his brow.

Mr. Etzler waited patient for the boisterous crowd to quiet weself—

Unt now, he says, zee reason for today's gathering. A demonstration huv zee prowcess for crystallisation wissout zee use huv fire or fuel. A chemical principle utilised by my patented invention—soon to revolutionise sugar production in zee West Indies, unt throughout zee worlt!

Here, with the exaggerated flourish of a master magician,

Mr. Etzler lifted his bottomless black box. Revealing to us a dishplate with a glass beaker containing a viscous-looking clear liquid. A pencil lying crosswise over the beaker's open mouth, from which dangled a piece of twine with a rusty nail tied to the end. Encrusted in white crystals—

Ladies unt gentlemen, he says, I give you zee ROCK CANDY!

Like a pirate Captain Damphier swung down on a rope of the rigging, over the heads of the enraged passengers. We were all shouting. Climbing atop each other's shoulders in our vain attempts to reach the top of the crate—where Mr. Etzler stood shaken down to he stones—eager to tear the little man limb from limb. So many had tried to climb the ladder at the same time that it tumbled backwards, sending a dozen men sprawling cross the deck and almost into the sea. Now Captain Damphier landed atop the crate beside Mr. Etzler. Swiftly tying a loop at the end of the same rope he'd swung down on, slipknotting it and pulling it tight round Mr. Etzler's waist. With the same smooth movement he reached behind to the thick post of the mainmast, uncleating a halyard securing one of the enormous mainsails high overhead.

With an efficiency of motion and countermotion that even Mr. Etzler must have admired, the huge mainsail with its thick heavy boom dropped down along the mast—*verrrappps*—canvas sail flapping loose in the breeze. Hoisting Mr. Etzler into the air, simultaneous and smooth, up to the top of the mainmast of the *Rosalind*. Like if he was flying.

He hung there, high above our heads, swinging slowly side-to-side. Safe from out the grasp of the infuriated passengers. His little arms and legs flailing helpless, swimming through the air, a snared black beetle wearing a crimson vest.

After my fourth night locked into the storeroom at the end of the passageway—after the inevitable, inescapable, uninterrupted sleep of seven straight hours right there inside the same compartment—I awoke clear-headed. Despite a persistent throbbing at both my temples. I felt mildly hungry. Most definitely I felt thirsty for a sup of whiskey, a deep draught of cool foamy champagne. But I didn't eat. I didn't drink. Instead, I lit my pitch-oil lamp and located my frock coat. My embroidered vest and silk cravat where I'd hung them from nails alongside the swaying hams. I found my other neatly folded garments, top hat safe on a shelf beside the Stilton cheeses. And I put them all on. Dressing myself in my fashionable attire. Then I made my way towards the plank door. I outed the pitch-oil lamp, reaching deep inside my pocket for my ring of keys.

Mr. Etzler was still hanging from the top of the mainmast as I made my way up the stairs from the hold. But as I crossed the vacant forecastle deck I didn't even pause to glance up at him. When I passed the window at the side of the dining hall for the first-class passengers I did, however, stop a moment. Long enough to identify Mr. and Mrs. Whitechurch, just beginning they breakfast. I continued down another short flight of carpeted steps to the upper-class cabins. Where I recognised Mr. Whitechurch's walking stick, silver panther shining at the handle, leaning against a doorframe.

I entered without knocking. Proceeding past the enormous, empty, four-poster bed—big as the entire cabin I shared with my sisters—walking slow and calm and as if by instinct towards a smaller room off the side. Where I opened the door and found Marguerite, still peacefully asleep.

I went and sat beside her. Sleeping quiet with her hazel hair spread out cross the pillow, a faint flower of the sheet's creases marking her cheek. The tiny horizontal line from a childhood scar below her chin. The ribbon at the nape of her nightdress had loosened to reveal the skin covering her clavicles, soft triangular spot at the base of her throat. For several minutes I sat there, watching her sleep. Feeling her warm moist breath rising up from the pillow.

A book lay facedown on the sheet beside her, reading glasses framed in gold wire poised on the cover. With a stack of three or four more books atop the bedstand, canvas rucksack on the floor beside it.

Eventually Marguerite opened her eyes, still half-asleep. Staring up dreamy into my face. She sat up against the pillow, yawning, reaching for the bedstand to retrieve her little white book and pencil.

Marguerite daubed the lead against her tongue, scribbling—

I've been waiting here patiently
feigning illness so as not to leave my cabin
whatever took you so long to find me?

She took her book back, scribbling again—

eventually I took up the search myself
but you were nowhere to be found

I cleared my throat—
You've no idea what I've been through to get here.
Marguerite took her book, smiling—

& such a silly outfit
wherever did you get it from?

I shrugged my shoulders, embarrassed.

Marguerite turned the page, writing more—

you look like the boy who brings my breakfast!

I took her book and put it aside, reaching to take hold of her hand, looking into her face. Her bright, sleepy, hazel-coloured eyes—

Never you mind, I say, smiling too. I've a place for us finer than these clothes, n' this cabin, n' any breakfast the steward could bring you. Finer than the Royal Chambers of Buckingham Palace!

15/8/10

dear mr robot:

now as i have lil chance 2 catch me breath & cool down some
after all dem boisterous carryings-ons of last night, of which i
can only admit 2 have play my own part in dem 2, my womanly
desires catching de best of me unawares much as i fight to hold
dem down, cause krishna-only-know dis tuti aint get a good
airing-out like dat in many a long day, & now it finish at last wid
all dat amount of pulsating & trobbing & twitching-up so sweet
& i could collec meself lil bit & sit down cool & calm & quiet
enough dis morning 2 write u out dis email & put everyting down
clear in b&w 4 u 2 hear, so LISTEN GOOD what i telling u,
eh: if u tink u could get u hands pon dis copymachine easy as
dat, u mad like effin toro!!! i aint oversee dese national archives
all dis time only 2 be ram-jam-tank-u-mam quick & easy so, u
unnastan? & i dont give a FRANCE if u is wealty whiteman,
or famous bookswriter from amerika, or whateverdeassitis, aint
NOBODY does touch dis xerox machine but me, u unnastan,
& miss samlalsingh under my own supervision, & u could jook
me & miss samlalsingh 2 till BOTH WE TUTIS SMOKING
LIKE BUSHFIRE, but wouldn't get u no closer 2 dis machine,
unnastan?

good

now u unnastan

so mr robot i done check through de cardcatalogue & fortunate 4
u in de c f stollmeyer esq collection is most of de numbers of dat

journal u looking 4, de MORNIN STAR, dating from 5 feb 1845 through de following year approx, & i give dem lil looksee meself & most is still in pretty good shape & not 2 smudge & tear so u could read dem good enough, & i check 4 dem papers of dis man u name, J J ETZLER, & in de stollmeyer collection u got dem 2, PARADISE & all de rest, everyting, & of course u got copies of all de local news from dat era, p-o-s gazette & standard & even london guardian microfish-self

anyways u got dem all, mr robot, & me or miss samlalsingh would be happy to hold dem 4 u at de reserve frontdesk, but bear in mind mr robot what i telling u, eh: rules is rules & laws is laws & u cannot remove NO documents from de place a-tall a-tall, & just as de sign post pon de wall behind we own selfsame frontdesk read out clear enough 4 u & all de world to see in de queens own proper english & let me quote: UNDER NO CIRCUMSTANCES ARE PHOTOCOPIES OF ARCHIVAL DOCUMENTS PERMITTED, AND ALL LAPTOPS, SCANNERS, CELL PHONES OR OTHER ELECTRONIC DEVICES ARE STRICTLY FORBIDDEN ON THE PREMISES, only PENCIL & PAPER mr robot 2 write down what u want & take enough notes 4 u research

cordial,
miss ramsol,
director, t&tna

ps mr robot if u want 2 see me again 2night u could meet me at pelo round 9

pss & mr robot u would find waiting 4 u at de reserve front-desk photocopy of story i find out de london guardian microfish TRIAL OF MR ETZLERS SATELLITE i hope it please u

TRIAL OF MR. ETZLER'S SATELLITE

London Guardian, 9 July 1845

Yesterday morning in the outskirts of Bicester several hundred spectators gathered for the trial of an agrarian mechanism, designed by Mr. J. Adolphus Etzler to be powered by the forces of Mother Nature, called the Satellite. Mr. Etzler is also founder of the Tropical Emigration Society, and he hopes to soon lead its members to the island of Trinidad, whence his Satellite, with its multiple attachments, shall be given the duty of performing for them all manual labours. According to the inventor the significance of his machine is not its extraordinary feats, but the revolutionary mechanical principle it demonstrates: i.e., 'transferring energy from a fixed to a moving place via a series of ropes and bamboo poles,' hitherto believed to be impossible in scientific circles. In addition to all rudimentary agricultural tasks, the Satellite is capable of 1. yanking entire trees out by their trunks, 2. instantly severing steel beams with a saw, 3. pulverizing large boulders with a single blow from a hammer. According to Mr. Etzler the importance of his machine to the history of civilisation 'may be rivaled only by the invention of the wheel.'

Much to his followers' disappointment the inventor could not be present himself for the trial, as he is currently on a lecturing tour of the northern provinces. In his place the Society's secretary, Mr. C.F. Stollmeyer, also of Germanic origin, supervised the proceedings of the day. Two grandstands were erected to seat the spectators. Adding to the festivities food stalls were set up, together with a gin palace and several beer-booths, the Satellite Ensemble on hand to provide entertainment.

For the purposes of the trial (rather than a giant sail-mill, or a waterwheel turned by a roaring tropical river), the Satellite would be powered by a small locomotive. It was loaned to the Society by one of its prominent members, Mr. Edmond Whitechurch, who also provided his country estate as the property comprising Satellite Field. The loco-motive, or Prime Mover, was moored in a stationary position with a trench dug beneath its rear wheels. Two ropes of the Connective Apparatus were attached to the wheels in such a manner that— once the steam engine was put into motion—the wheels would pull alternately upon the ropes, thence upon the Central Drum in mid-position. Two further ropes stretched from this drum to the Satellite itself on the other end of the field, one attached to either side of its large upper Vibratory Beam. The ropes therefore pulled alternately upon the beam, to-and-fro, to-and-fro, this movement regularized and transferred to a fiercely armed shaft churning at the front: thus the Satellite would advance across the earth.

As the ropes were wound multiple times about the Central Drum, the machine traveled around its axis in an outwardly spiraling track, hence its name.

Lashing rains of the previous night had softened to a light drizzle by the appointed hour, which was announced in advertisements posted throughout London. Mr. Frank, the engineer hired to construct the Satellite, together with his assistant, Mr. Tucker, determined that the first order of business ought to be disconnecting the ropes from the locomotive, and checking its operation in the fixed position. But with the first blast of steam the spectators on the field—several having already made a visit or two to the gin palace, and believing it to be the official takeoff of the Satellite—began running en masse towards the machine. Discovering, however, that the Satellite was unmanned and disconnected, they altered their course, bolting now in the direction of the locomotive, crowding quickly around it. By this point, due to wet weather, the locomotive had begun slipping from its moorings. It threatened to run out of control, eventually sliding backwards into the trench, at the bottom of which lay a fairly deep mire. So before Mr. Tucker could possibly blow off steam—so as to shut down the runaway locomotive—the churning wheels sent a great torrent of mud high into the air, like an exploding derrick, soaking all present head-to-foot.

It now appeared that the trial would have to be suspended. But the labourers quickly gathered forces, rolling up their shirtsleeves. And coordinated by the *heave-hos* called out by Mr. Stollmeyer through a large pasteboard cone constructed especially for the day's event, they hoisted the locomotive from the ditch. It was re-moored in a new position determined by Mr. Frank, on higher and drier ground, a fresh hole dug beneath it. And with a bit of impromptu ceremony, Mr. Stollmeyer descended into the trench to reattach the ropes.

Mr. Frank now donned his goggles and protective leather helmet. He climbed onto the back of his machine and took hold of the reins. Mr. Stollmeyer assumed his position behind the Central Drum (of the three men only he had a clear view of Satellite, Central Drum, and Prime Mover simultaneously), Mr. Tucker with his hand on the locomotive's throttle. At the ready signal from Mr. Frank, Mr. Stollmeyer called out though his funnel to Mr. Tucker, who applied power. Now the spectators in the stands watched the two lines of the Connective Apparatus draw taut. They observed the Central Drum rotating smoothly, clockwise-and-counterclockwise. The Vibratory Beam above Mr. Frank's head jerked roughly back-and-forth, two or three times, the Satellite lurching forward as though roaring into life.

But with the first blast of steam issuing forth from the locomotive, the spectators on the field took off running as a single body towards the machine, accompanied by a great cheer from the crowd and a burst of music from the Ensemble. And even before the Satellite could advance a few feet, the spectators had gathered around it, much to the dismay of Mr. Stollmeyer: he called out to Mr. Tucker to back down the throttle. Over the mayhem of the spectators, however, and no doubt carried by his own emotions, Mr. Tucker misinterpreted his instructions: he applied full power.

Presently the Satellite gave such a tremendous jolt that Mr. Frank lost his footing at the back of his machine. He was instantly tossed ten feet into the air, coming down upon the still-oscillating Vibratory Beam. This he managed to wrap his arms and legs around, hugging the beam like a bear, fighting for all his life to hang on. At that moment a rope of the Connective Apparatus caught in one of the pulleys between the Satellite and the Central Drum. It was instantly severed, whipping past the drum and, due to the excessive coiling, wrapping itself around Mr. Stollmeyer's leg. The rope began dragging him on his buttocks across the damp grass, in the direction of the Prime Mover. At which point several of the labourers—including a rather heavyset triangle player from Ensemble—seeing Mr. Stollmeyer in danger, flung themselves bodily atop him as he slid past, hoping to bring him to a halt. As a result not only Mr. Stollmeyer but three or four other men were dragged the length of Satellite Field—whilst Mr. Frank clutched for dear life to the wildly oscillating Vibratory Beam—before Mr. Tucker could successfully blow off steam, shutting down the runaway locomotive.

After this second breakdown there was another substantial delay whilst the severed rope was rewound around the Central Drum, then spliced together. The locomotive was re-stoked and Mr. Stollmeyer, Mr. Frank, and Mr. Tucker resumed their positions. Since Mr. Stollmeyer's cone had been crushed beyond all possible recognition or use, at the ready signal from Mr. Frank he cupped his palms around his bearded mouth and called out to Mr. Tucker. The response of the crowd and the Ensemble, this third time, was somewhat delayed. Yet even before the Vibratory Beam above Mr. Frank's head could make a half-dozen oscillations, his machine was trailed by a crowd of excited, cheering spectators. All of these men, however, had learnt a valuable lesson from Mr. Stollmeyer's buttocks-slide earlier in the day. And despite their inebriated state, they were careful to stay clear of the ropes. Mr. Tucker gently applied more power; the Central Drum rotated smoothly back-and-forth, clock-wise-and-counterclockwise; and the oscillations of the Vibratory Beam caused the Satellite's fiercely armed front shaft to turn and rip up the ground.

All were ecstatic. For almost a minute the Satellite achieved its maximum velocity of three mph, successfully tearing up approximately nine yards of dirt. Yet within seconds, perilously, even the most inebriated of the spectators had left the lumbering Satellite behind. They'd gathered before the machine, directly in the path of its fiercely churning front shaft. Mr. Frank, holding tight to the reins, pounced with all his weight upon the right side of the rudder. The machine veered sharply to the left and toppled—this time tossing Mr. Frank a good fifteen feet behind his machine, and clear of all danger—one of the ropes kinked and snapped, and a thoroughly demoralized Mr. Stollmeyer called out to Mr. Tucker to blow off steam.

Thus the trial of the Satellite was concluded. And despite the dubious success of Mr. Etzler's machine, there could be little doubt that the spectators had been treated to some rather splendid acrobatic antics by Mr. Stollmeyer and Mr. Frank, in addition to a rural fest.

3

27 Flickering Churchcandles

Marguerite left her cabin that morning walking barefoot, still wearing her thin nightdress. She took my arm as we made we way down the corridor, up the carpeted steps, out onto the forecastle deck.

Neither of us noticed the little man dangling from the rigging high above our heads. Not before he called down to us—

To slake his surst zey gave him vinegar unt gall!

We paused to look up at him, hanging there with the sun shining so bright behind his back, we had to squint to make him out. The noose tied by Captain Damphier round his waist had, overnight, worked its way up to his armpits. Now he hung there with his arms spread wide as if to embrace us—like if he was nailed to an invisible cross in truth—swaying side-to-side with the slow roll of the ship. He'd lost one of his shoes. His long beard a gnarled mess that looked like a picoplat's nest tucked beneath his chin. Mr. Etzler seemed to have soiled he trousers.

Marguerite looked at me quizzical—she'd not been there the previous afternoon to witness the fiasco. She reached into the pocket of my frock coat where she'd tucked her little book and pencil, taking them out, scribbling—

performing an experiment with solar heat?

I glanced up, then back to Marguerite—
And baked his brains-pot in the process.

We turned and continued cross the deck, Mr. Etzler calling out behind us—

Zey know not what zey do!

Now we proceeded down another short flight of carpeted steps, Marguerite's hand clasping my forearm. As we passed the window of the dining hall reserved for upper class, I glanced sideways to take in Mr. and Mrs. Whitechurch, just finishing the third course of they breakfast, the fruits-and-nuts tray. I escorted Marguerite past the galley, down the series of narrow, dim, rough plank stairs. Three flights below. At the bottom I turned the crude latch and swung the door open, directing Marguerite into the dingy hallway. Lined on both sides by other plank doors, each with its shining padlock. I shut the door behind us again, enclosing us in total darkness. Feeling Marguerite's hand tighten round my forearm, her breathing quicken beside me—

Only a few steps, I whisper.

I led her to the last plank door on the starboard side. Four doors down, twenty-three steps. I reached deep inside my pocket for my ring of keys. Selecting the proper one, I opened the padlock, swinging the door in, slipping my arm round Marguerite's waist. Directing her blindly into the storeroom. Now I detected the pungent, though not entirely disagreeable odours of mould and salt-laden moisture. Like I was smelling them for the first time. The air heavy, wet against my cheeks—slippery, cool. A soft tinkle of bilgewater someplace beneath the boards, distinct and musical as chimes. I let Marguerite's waist go and closed the door behind us, poking my fingers through the handle-hole till the padlock clicked shut.

I continued shifting round in the dark, locating my pitch-oil lamp, feeling for the box of matches and striking one against my thumbnail.

I raised the lantern up above my head. Marguerite's hazel eyes glistening as she studied the storeroom: the wooden crates of all shapes and sizes, piled in short and tall towers, contents stamped in black letters cross they tops and sides; stacks of pasteboard boxes and piles of jute sacks; pallets of horizontal-lying bottles—clear-coloured & green & blue & brown; shelves lined with tinned goods and dusty jars, parcels wrapped in coarse brownpaper.

At one side the hams hung from the ceiling, swaying back-and-forth in counterdirection to the ship's roll. Marguerite gazing over at they perfectly orchestrated movement.

All-in-a-sudden her expression changed. She reached inside my pocket for her book and pencil, scribbling something. Whilst I strained my eyes to make her letters out—

you're quite sure there're no shiprats?

I smiled—

Pssst! I say, looking round.

Calling out again—

Pssssst!

A few seconds later the large gray-and-black-striped tabby ap-peared—jade eyes with the markings of a white ascot under his chin, four seemingly oversized white boots. Striding out from behind a wall of crates. The tabby approached us, rubbing his shoulder against my trouser leg, plume of his tail brushing side-to-side.

I put the lamp down and reached to the top of the crate beside me, breaking off a piece of Swiss cheese and offering it to the puss-cat. Taking him up—

Mr. Talbot, I say. After a gentleman Father introduced me

to on a trip to Wiltshire. He showed us his photogenic process.

I paused—

I've no idea what the sailors call him.

Marguerite put her book and pencil down and reached for Mr. Talbot.

He's quite special, I say. A six-toed Chinese cat—polydactyl—the sailors consider 'em good luck. Every vessel has one aboard.

I watched her scratch under the tabby's chin, his oversized white mitten pressed against her shoulder.

Now I turned round, studying the storeroom. And throwing my weight behind a stack of three crates labeled *PORTUGAL PORT WINE*, I shoved them over behind the door, blocking it shut from the inside. I removed my top hat and placed it up on the shelf amongst the Stilton cheeses. Then I took off my coat, crossed to the other side, and hung it from a nail alongside the swaying hams. My embroidered vest. I pulled off my silk cravat and folded it into my coat pocket, rolling the French cuffs up over my elbows.

I began shoving aside several other stacks of crates, clearing a space at the centre of the storeroom. Tossing aside a mound of fragrant jute sacks labeled *INDIA DARJEELING*.

By the time I'd finished I'd worked up a sweat. Mr. Talbot had gone off behind the crates, Marguerite standing behind me holding up the lantern. I turned towards her.

Her eyes shone, hazel hair soft and delicate over her shoulders. I took a deep breath, reached for the lantern, and hung it from a nail in one of the beams. I turned to her again. Taking hold of her hand, I closed my eyes. And for the first time since we'd met on the train to Bicester, first time since we'd hidden weself in our secret place beneath the stands, four months previous, I leant forward to find her lips.

So as not to worry she aunt and uncle, Marguerite returned to her cabin to sleep the night. Likewise I returned to my own cabin. Having—for the first time since we'd come aboard—perilously skipped the previous night. Son, I didn't have no idea how my family might've reacted to my disappearance—maybe I'd scared them half to death, thinking I'd fallen overboard.

Much to my surprise I learnt my absence hadn't troubled them a-tall. It took me a good few minutes to suss out the reason why. Now I discovered my father had gotten the notion into his head I'd been hired out by Captain Damphier. Temporarily. As a ship's hand. Papee assured Mum and my sisters that I now slept in a hammock in the sailors' quarters. No doubt about it a-tall, he'd told them. Because he'd seen me heself early one morning—up on the forbidden forecastle deck, barefoot and still wearing my nightdress—hurrying to my new new duties of swabbing down the boards. On another occasion he'd stumbled cross me—all dandied-up in frock coat and top hat—scrambling towards my charge of serving dinner in the upper-class dining hall.

Son, I was just as taken aback by all this deckhand-bubball as you are. But I assure you I didn't say nothing to change my mum and sisters' minds about it. Nor Papee's neither.

Whilst the rest of them slept that night I lay on my bunk with my arms doubled up behind my head—legs folded tight like a crab—my eyes closed. Remembering. Drifting again in my familiar memoryspace.

❁

That afternoon, hidden in we secret place beneath the stands—whilst the trial of Mr. Etzler's machine was concluded outside—I lay flat on my back, my head cradled in Marguerite's lap. How I'd found myself in that position I couldn't tell you. Only that I wanted to lie there forever. Now I felt her hand caress my cheek, a moment's tenderness that will remain with me the rest of my days.

At some point during the waning afternoon I'd tipped Mr. Powell's bottle back for another swig, finding it empty. I'd looked at the bottle holding in my hand like I wasn't even sure where it had come from. Then I recorked it and tossed it aside, watching it take a slow tumble in the yellowed grass. Deeply regretting I'd ever set eyes on that bottle of whiskey. Because all-in-a-sudden I wasn't feeling too good a-tall. The grass beneath me swimming like the bench on the train, only far worse. That was when I'd tumbled onto my back, seeking the solace of Marguerite's lap. The lingering memory of her soft hand caressing my cheek.

Then I tumbled headlong into a black hole, bottomless and dreamless both.

I awoke on the cold hard ground. Alone. Unsure at first where I was or how I'd gotten there. My head pounding like a tassa-drum. I lay there another minute trying to recover myself. Attempting to act like a man, I'd behaved like a forceripe school-boy. Now I climbed up onto my feet, reaching down to take up my cap and the picnic basket. And I stumbled out onto a thoroughly trampled Satellite Field, littered with empty bottles and rubbish. The sun already disappearing beyond the distant line of sycamores, sky behind them fiery pink. Only Papee, Mr. Powell, and Mr. Frank remained on the field. They crouched round a lantern in the semi-dark, a short distance from the toppled machine, its thirty-foot scar curving out in the dirt behind it. The three men still discussing the results of the trial.

I took a seat on the ground beside Papee. And I sat there on the trodden grass a long time, hugging Marguerite's lilac scarf against my chest. The men talked quiet, occasionally interrupting they discussion for one of them to roll out a large dog-eared diagram, take up the lantern, and point out something to the other two. Papee recognised the picnic basket beside me. He passed it round, taking out a sandwich for heself as well.

But son, I couldn't have put nothing inside my churning stomach. I wasn't listening. Didn't have no idea whether this trial had been a success or not. I didn't care. The men didn't seem upset, though the jubilation they'd exhibited earlier in the day had clearly subsided. Eventually they rose to they feet, collected they jackets & papers & paraphernalia, and I took up the empty picnic basket. We set off to catch the final train.

By the time Papee and me exited the station and started our short walk home the streetlamps had been extinguished. Mum and my sisters had returned to Suffolk Dyers at noon. They'd worked a five-hour shift and were now dead asleep in they beds. As we walked I held Marguerite's scarf loose in my hand, but I wouldn't have let it go not for nothing in the world. In my other hand I carried the empty picnic basket.

We didn't talk. After a few blocks we came to a little square in the shape of a triangle, ancient oak implanted in the middle, lone sentinel of our meagre borough. Its dusty leaves were stirring gentle in the breeze, and with the dim light of an unseen moon they cast mottled shadows cross the ground. Cross my father's back as he unbuttoned his fly, bent forward at the waist to remove heself, and began splashing warm weewee against the trunk. A faint smoke rose up caressing the bark. I set the basket down and stuffed the scarf inside my pocket, stepping up beside him, taking myself out too.

After we'd finished we stood in silence another minute, before Papee spoke—

'Twill never work, he says. I've known from the start. And after today I know it better than ever.

Something in Papee's voice told me he hadn't finished—

Doesn't matter, he says. Not in the least. The only important thing is that we have something to believe in. Anathing. Only important thing is it's fervent enough to get us someplace else.

Papee stood staring up into the shadowy leaves, pensive, toetee still in hand—

I haven't forgotten, he says. Happy birthday, son.

He turned his eyes down to the trunk for a second, then over towards me. And what my father said then is something else that will remain with me the rest of my life. A tender sweetness, bitter sting—

Imagine, son, he says. A year from now, all the Tuckers together, we'll celebrate your birthday in Trinidad.

◎

I felt a pang of guilt—lying in my bunk imaging all those delicacies that awaited us in our storageroom, whilst my family consumed they horrid breakfasts in the third-class dining hall. And I determined to smuggle some of those goods out to them at the first opportunity. I stepped down and took out the bundle I'd stashed the previous evening in the space beneath Georgina's bunk. Dressing myself back in my fancified clothes, returning straightway to Marguerite.

But before we left the Whitechurches' cabin to make we way towards the bridge, in a moment of inspiration, Marguerite penciled out a note for she aunt and uncle. Leaving it there on Mrs.

Whitechurch's dressing table—

Auntie—despite my protests Dr. Worthington has insisted
upon moving me to another cabin he says with superiour
circulation of fresh ocean air—very healing!—& he can observe
the progress of my convalescence more closely

I stepped behind a wall of crates, returning with a parcel wrapped in coarse brownpaper. Tied tight with twine. I set it down on the stack of boxes beside Mr. Talbot's piece of Swiss cheese. And using Papee's penknife to snap the twine, I peeled back the brownpaper. Shaking out the first white sheet.

I smiled at Marguerite—

Ours'll be the softest mattress you've ever known!

She stooped to take a corner in each hand, me holding the opposite side. And together we ballooned the sheet high as the storeroom's low plank ceiling. With a faint exhalation of moist, patchouli-scented air, we let the sheet float back down to the floor, spreading it out simultaneous cross the boards. After that we ballooned a next sheet between us. Another soft white sheet woven from the finest Chinee silk, patchouli-oiled to protect against the assault of moths. Spreading it out careful on top.

Another sheet; and another; and still another.

Till we'd unfolded and emptied three similar brownpaper packages, each containing a half-dozen sheets. Till we'd mounted up a mattress a foot thick.

I disappeared behind the wall of boxes again, returning with a small crate making a *glassy* noise as I walked. Labeled simply—

Packed with votive churchcandles, each in its canister of bright crimson glass. We lit them one-by-one. Setting them down in they bright shields along the edges of shelves, atop the short and tall stacks of crates—a flickering rectangle round the floorboards framing our mattress-self. Till we'd emptied the entire crate: twenty-seven flickering churchcandles. Our storeroom suffused with a soft crimson glow. All round our woodsy-scented sheets, smelling like a country stream in early morning.

I stepped from out my boots and removed my stockings, balling them up and stuffing them inside. Placing my boots on the shelf beside my hat.

Now I turned to Marguerite. We looked at each other, my heart beating out a soft warm space inside my chest.

Without shifting her gaze from my eyes, Marguerite pulled the ribbon loose at the nape of her neck. She crossed her arms over her breasts, reaching towards her shoulders, gently slipping down the open neck of her nightdress. She exposed the soft skin covering her clavicles, shallow pools of crimson light collecting in the hollows alongside her shoulderbones.

Marguerite dropped her arms. She leant slightly forward, the breath of her nightdress slipping-way from her breasts, hips, thighs. And at that same moment the crimson pools of light spilt out over the ridges of her clavicles. Down over the length of her long body—a glossy film. As the soft circle of the nightdress gathered round her ankles.

She stepped out.

One-by-one the flickering votive candles surrounding our elaborate bed burnt down, sizzled, and extinguished theyself in a puff of smoke. Marguerite and I lit others. We paused to quench our thirst with sips of French champagne. Which I uncorked and we drank straight from the bottle, feeling the tickle of bubbles along the back of our parched throats. We sampled the Spanish ham. The selection of cheeses stacked high on the shelves of our storageroom, accompanied by slow sips of sherry, port, cool champagne.

There were bottles filled with green Italian olives, black Greek olives soaking in brine. Packages of cripsy water-crackers and rosemary-sprinkled biscuits. Tins of sardines and pickled herring, Russian caviar, miniature pots of French truffles and goose liver pâté.

With all of these exquisite flavours still lingering on our pallets, we tasted each other's bodies again. Until, dizzy and exhausted-out, our skins crimson with a film of perspiration beneath the glow of the flickering votive candles, we fell asleep in each other's arms. We awoke to rediscover each other's bodies, and our own bodies, and we ate and drank whilst Mr. Talbot preened heself with the same dedicated care and attention, there beside our intertwined legs atop the mattress of silk sheets.

Lying on our sides, the lengths of our long bodies cupped together, my chest pressed tight to Marguerite's back, nose buried beneath her mound of fragrant hair, I dreamt—

4

Minstrel Passage

Under cover of darkness, and not unlike a pirate heself, Mr. Stollmeyer eventually dared climb the *Rosalind*'s mainmast. He companion having hung there suspended, baking beneath the sun, for two entire days. Large silver carving knife clenched between he teeth, Mr. Stollmeyer climbed all the way up to the crow's nest at the top. He'd petitioned Papee's assistance below the mast to arrest his companion's fall. My father dutifully rounding up Mr. Whitechurch to help—and much to my own surprise, me as well. Papee insisted. The three of us standing there in the dark with one of the sailor's rope nets stretched out between us, mound of soft canvas piled beneath it as a further precaution. Mr. Stollmeyer closed his eyes against a vertigo attack, and hugging tight to the swaying mast, he reached to cut his companion down. Mr. Etzler instantly plummeting thirty-feet through the air, landing in the net easy & safe & snug-as-a-trapped-quenk. Now the three of us hurried him straightway to his cabin-suite, not even pausing long enough to give him the requested drink of water. We shifted him out the net, up onto his big four-poster bed, and Dr. Worthington—a retired physician from the parish of Bath, self-appointed ship's doctor—made a quick examination. Pronouncing Mr. Etzler unharmed with the exception of a nasty sprain to the ankle of his unshod left foot.

And now Papee sent me hurrying back up to the deck to retrieve the snakeskin shoe.

Yet it wasn't the sprained ankle, nor his general condition of dehydration, that worried Dr. Worthington: it was Mr. Etzler's mental state. The inventor now imagined heself pursued by unseen assailants, day-and-night, demons who didn't allow him no kinda rest. Mr. Etzler barking at he invisible attackers in a language that neither Dr. Worthington nor nobody else could identify with any certainty. But which Mr. Stollmeyer decided was a lost Hebrew dialect spoken by the Pharisees. On those occasions when Mr. Etzler did return to standard English, or he native German, he fell into the confusing and exasperating habit of referring to heself in the third person. So you never knew if he was describing one of his demon-attackers, or discussing he own ailments. When Mr. Etzler didn't speak in third person, he utilised the royal *we*.

Most peculiar of all, despite his lifelong adherence to a strict vegetable diet, Mr. Etzler now refused any food other than fish.

This he consumed with a ravenous, insatiable appetite, which of course pleased Dr. Worthington. On his new diet the patient's physical health showed fast improvement. And despite the doctor's questionable success, at least at the start, in scaring-way his phantom attackers, everybody felt relieved by the signs of recovery. Nobody less than Mrs. Etzler.

She, understandably, had been a wreck from the moment she husband ascended to the top of the Satellite's crate. To say nothing of when he shot so shocking into the air—*Like a circus-clown out huv a cannon!* I heard her tell the doctor. Now Mrs. Etzler appeared as placid as if the frightful ordeal had never occurred a-tall. Of everybody she was the only one unfazed by she husband's shouting, his indecipherable language, like if she'd never much understood him anyway.

Mr. Stollmeyer, I don't have to tell you, considered this Dr.

Worthington an outrageous quack. A fraudulent and most dod-
dering humbug. He ridiculed him severe, doing everything in he
power to keep the retired physician away from he comrade. He'd
have succeeded too, if not for the intervention of Captain Damphier. The captain insisting, in the very least, that the doctor
treat Mr. Etzler's swollen ankle. Of course, this Dr. Worthington
was happy for any excuse to bust out he big black bag, stuffed to
the brim with congealed medicines and antiquated instruments.
With the sanction of the ship's captain he couldn't scarcely restrain he enthusiasm to the sprain.

I don't have to tell you neither that Mr. Stollmeyer admin-
istered to his comrade heself—every time the doctor's back
was turned—from he own box lined with rose-coloured vials
of little homeopathic pills. Pressed beneath Mr. Etzler's tongue.
And each time he managed to escape the prohibitions of Mr.
Stollmeyer, the doctor gave his patient a quick dosage of powered acetylsalicylic acid dissolved in a glass of water (as an anti-
inflammatory agent and pain reliever) and twice—with the co-
vert collaboration of Mrs. Etzler—he tied his patient down to
a chair long enough to give him a proper bloodletting (to purge
the demons).

Whether it was due to the doctor's secret phlebotomies or he
comrade's homeopathic pills, Mr. Etzler's phantom attackers
became fewer and farther between. He got a good sleep. The
inventor even satisfying his wife's petitions to patiently comb
out and detangle he picoplat-beard. The patient's morale im-
proved, and before long he roucou-mottled cheeks blossomed
again, everybody pleased as punch.

That is, till the evening five nights after Mr. Stollmeyer cut
him down from the top of the *Rosalind*'s mast. On that evening

he'd organised a small gathering to commemorate he companion's recovery, held in the Etzlers' own cabin-suite. To be attended by the three men who'd assisted in the rescue operation: Papee, Mr. Whitechurch, and—once again at my father's insistence—me. In a moment of uncharacteristic benevolence, at least so far as the retired physician was concerned, Mr. Stollmeyer even accommodated Mrs. Etzler's request to invite the doctor.

That evening, as petitioned, the six of us gathered in Mr. Etzler's cabin at the foot of he bed. All with we glasses raised (champagne glasses borrowed from out the saloon, but filled by Mr. Stollmeyer with lemon-bitters), mustering as much hoopla as we sober spirits could manage. Mr. Etzler, however, didn't exhibit no enthusiasm a-tall for these festivities arranged in he honor. To the contrary, after five days of ferocious shouting, he lay in he bed perfectly placid, not saying a word.

Mr. Etzler lay on he back—dwarfed by the enormous, cloud-canopied, four-poster bed—propped up against the pillows. With the rabbit-ear corners of a white napkin tied by he wife in the manner of a bib round he neck. Directing all his attention to the plate of poached codfish in his lap, feeding heself morsel by morsel with a large silver soupspoon. Mr. Etzler didn't pause from his eating long enough to acknowledge his guests, nor even raise up his eyes from off he plate. Like he was geegeeree somebody'd steal it out from under he nose.

After several minutes—after finishing his platter and depositing the empty dishplate on the bedstand atop three others—he looked up, blinking, like he's seeing us standing there at the foot of his bed for the first time.

Mr. Etzler let loose a satisfied-sounding belch.

To which Mr. Whitechurch sounded out he approval—

Here here! he says.

By this point Mr. Whitechurch had succeeded in charging he own glass with a generous shot of whiskey out his flask—I'd seen him myself.

Well done! he continued.

Mr. Stollmeyer chiming in behind, unwittingly offering Mr. Etzler his cue—

To the restored health of our Good Shepherd! he says.

Now Mr. Etzler untied the rabbit-ears of the napkin from round his neck. He got up out the bed, still a little shaky. And speaking for the first time all evening, in surprisingly clear English (despite a lapse to the third person), he asked—

Did you not know zat he must be about hiss father's business?

With that he turned round to take up the parcel of papers from the bedstand beside his soiled plates, in addition to a small box containing his writing instruments and drafting pencils. Mr. Etzler turned round again—

Zen look for him in zee temple!

And stepping tender on his swollen left ankle, wrapped by Dr. Worthington in a white gauze—still wearing his rumpled nightshirt, one bedroom slipper on his good foot—Mr. Etzler padded past us. Cross the carpeted floor. He entered the private toilet stall of his cabin-suite, pencils and papers tucked under his arm, closing the door behind him. Now we stood there at the end of the big empty bed, still with we glasses raised, looking round at each other bobolee. As we heard Mr. Etzler turning the latch on the other side of the door.

He didn't exit the lavatory for another three days.

To date Mr. Etzler had published four widely read scientific treatises. Though unquestionably of a philosophic stripe as well, these four works were investigations of the known and know-able. That is to say, the verifiable: they spoke solely of facts. Supported throughout by careful observations and experimentations, in accordance with the rigorous strictures of the scientific method. All Mr. Etzler's previous publications dealt exclusive with the *real world*. Plain things, that can be seen with the eyes. Everywhere argued in the irrefutable language of mathematical calculation.

Despite the claims of some of Mr. Etzler's detractors, none of he previous four works were in any way tainted by what might be called *fantasy* or *fiction*. None might remotely be confused with *art*.

Not so a-tall with his next endeavour.

For the whole of those three days and nights, in self-imposed solitude, Mr. Etzler struggled with his imagination. Though not as an inventor of machines, sure to alter the course of history. Not even as a mathematician, scientist, nor university-trained engineer. Mr. Etzler struggled as a literary writer.

Because what he presented Mr. Stollmeyer with—at the end of those three days and nights of concentrated, uninterrupted labour—was the completed manuscript of a theatrical performance. It was written for two characters (two actors) and it even incorporated the minstrel tradition of blackface. The play entitled *A Dialogue on Etzler's Paradise between the West Indian Plantation Owner, 'Lord Louse,' and His Former African Slave, 'Savvy'—or—English vs. Nigrish.*

As with all of his writing in the English language, down to his letters of informal correspondence, Mr. Stollmeyer edited the text for clarity and proper usage—even in he native German Mr. Etzler's writing tended towards the archaic and obscure. Occasionally even the sublime. Mr. Stollmeyer checked the manuscript over for grammatical and spelling errors. Due to the creative nature of this particular work, more than usual care was taken to assure the fluidity of the *spoken* language contained in the *script.*

When the manuscript was combed through to both writers' satisfaction, Mr. Etzler and Mr. Stollmeyer committed the text to memory. They rehearsed they performance together. Coaching and prompting each other. And only when all was practised over and thoroughly rehearsed did Mr. Stollmeyer write out a handful of playbills, posting them throughout the ship. He even painted out a couple body-length sandwich-board placards, attached by pieces of twine over they shoulders. He and Mr. Etzler taking turns wearing them and parading about the ship.

On the awaited afternoon Captain Damphier again ordered iced lemonade for the children, rum punch for all the adults. Since this performance would be free of charge for everybody who chose to attend, he wasn't fearful of a repetition of Mr. Etzler's previous ordeal. Indeed, distractions of this kind were so few and far between in the middle of the Atlantic, the captain welcomed the event.

That afternoon practically every passenger aboard crowded weself onto the third-class deck. Due to the lack of space a number of sailors perched theyself in the rigging overhead as well. It was a clear day, without a cloud in the cobalt sky, the sun a blistering ball. Though by this late in the afternoon it had started its descent towards the sea. According to Mr. Etzler's specifications an elongated planter's chair, borrowed from out he own cabin-suite (wicker backing and concealed leg-perches that swung out from under the arms), was placed atop the Satellite's crate. Beside it a short stool belonging to the sailors.

In keeping with his character Mr. Stollmeyer costumed he-self in a khaki suit several sizes too big for he lanky frame, pillow stuffed beneath the shirt to give him a good-sized paunch. From his vest pocket dangled a gold watch-chain. He wore tall riding boots, pith helmet, and a monocle. In his hand he held a leather crop, using it to strike every now and then against his boot. Mr. Etzler, by contrast, donned a pair of shabby canvas overalls, patches stitched on both knees, with a larger one sewn in over he bamsee. He had on a soiled undershirt, fraying at the wrists, his feet bare. On his head he wore a beaten straw hat, tied with a piece of twine beneath his chin. He grayed out he long beard.

As advertised in the playbill Mr. Etzler blacked his face with burnt cork.

Accompanied by a burst of applause—together with a good amount of jeering—the two actors ascended the ladder to the top of the Satellite's crate. Lord Louse (Mr. Stollmeyer) puffing-way exaggerated with the effort of he climb, crop tucked under he arm. Whilst the elderly Savvy (Mr. Etzler) paused dramatic a couple times, reaching to he tired old back and letting forth a groan.

Savvy then assisted Lord Louse to stretch out heself on the planter's chair—legs splayed wide and riding boots cocked up on the swing-out perches, his paunch a mound atop he lap. Savvy then crouched on the stool beside him. He removed a corncob pipe from his pocket, proceeding to fill it with tobacco from out his pouch. Then he struck a match to light it, puffing gray clouds contemplative into the air.

Lord Louse cracked his crop three times against his boot—*thwack! thwack! thwack!* And the actors waited for the crowd to quiet weself.

*

Contrary to the expectations of many—or, rather, in spite of them—the response to Mr. Etzler's play was favourable. I can assure you it didn't happen easy. Nor did it happen straight-way. Son, the first few comments shouted out by the spectators crowded onto the deck—not to mention the sailors perched clamorous in the rigging overtop we heads—were not so savoury a-tall.

Mr. Etzler and Mr. Stollmeyer were *not* the most popular travellers aboard ship. Not by a long lag. They haughty manners, superiour attitudes, and frank disregard for the opinions of others, had turned a number of the passengers against them. As you can well imagine several members of the audience had come to this performance with the sole intention of heckling the actors. And they did a good job. At least for the first few minutes.

But as the performance continued and we surrendered we-self to Savvy's wit and easy sense of humour—each time he got the upper hand on a dotish Lord Louse—the antagonistic atmosphere seemed to dissolve. To disappear, slow-but-sure. And once the first few chuckles burst forth, unchecked, the laughter became quite contagious. Every time Lord Louse mouthed a silly mispronunciation. Each time Savvy twisted one of he former master's misstatements into a humourous jab. In addition, the rural speech of Mr. Etzler's character was so suited to he *own* broken English that his German infections seemed somehow to fade-way. Indeed—speaking in the language of he character, Savvy—Mr. Etzler was easier to understand than normal.

There was a part later in the play when Savvy helped Lord

Louse to get up from out his planter's chair, assisting him to bend down and try to touch he toes. Everybody responding enthusiastic to Lord Louse's antics at the edge of the crate. Threatening each time he bent over to tumble down onto the spectators below—we even called out for him to try to touch he toes again.

Son, you got to realise that what Mr. Etzler gave us in this play was a biting satire. Directed at some of those very members of he audience. Some of whom caught on good enough, others remaining oblivious—but it hardly seemed to matter. Because after a time everybody was laughing to we heart's content. Finally Lord Louse unbuttoned the patch over Savvy's upturned buttocks (the audience realising then that Mr. Etzler had blacked he bamsee-cheeks too). And when Lord Louse bent down to kiss his ex-slave's arse, actually pressing his face snugly to it and coming away blackfaced heself—so now the reversal was complete—by then we couldn't hold weself back. Not only from laughter and applause but shouts of bravo! requests for encore! And Captain Damphier was so pleased with the performance he commanded he sailors to serve us another round of rum punch. Even the French comte could be seen getting up quiet from out his chaise lounge at the far corner of the deck, offering the actors he standing ovation.

Whilst Mr. and Mrs. Whitechurch ate they breakfast the following morning, Marguerite and I took turns sponging down each other's backs. Soaking together in they big porcelain tub—filled to the overflowing with soapy hot water, brought by the steward at Marguerite's bidding. First time in my life, I can assure you, I'd bathed in anything more luxurious than a rusted zinc basin. Yet hardly had we finished our bath, toweled weself off and begun dressing, when we heard the first distinct, though slightly muffled shout. Coming from two decks above our heads.

We strained our ears to hear another shout. Then another.

Marguerite reaching for her book, scribbling—

???

I shrugged my shoulders.

By this time one of the stewards had commenced to ringing out he bell—*ca-clang! ca-clang! ca-clang!*—and before long a *louder* noise could be heard, coming from the main deck. From all parts of the ship at once. All-in-a-sudden every steward who had a bell to his charge seemed to be clanging-way, cook beating his ladle against the side of a tin pot, kitchen hands ringing out spoons against bottles. Now, up on main deck, the passengers and sailors commenced to stomping they feet and whistling— we even heard singing.

Marguerite and me hurrying to dress weself. She gathered up her skirts in both arms—not even bothering to slip on her shoes—and we took off together. Down the hallway and up the carpeted steps.

Hurrying hand-in-hand cross the forecastle deck, towards a crowd of passengers gathered alongside the windward rail. Several of them pointing out to sea, shouting.

On the distant horizon, Marguerite and me made out the faint gray shapes: two tiny islands.

It was the passenger standing in front of Marguerite who cried out first—

Trinidad! he says, pointing at the island with its triple peaks.

Then the other, smaller island beside it—

Trinidad n' Tobago!

Bollocks, countered the sailor perched in the rigging overtop our heads, hand holding to his brow against the glare—

Them there islands is the Aaa-zores!

3rd Message

21/8/10

dear mr robot:

so u asks me last night when we did get through wid all dat
amount of jooking up & shouting down de place sweet-as-shiva,
& we was relaxing lil bit after catching weself a cool, & u wants
me to tell u lil someting bout my own family here in t'dad &
where we comes from, & even though in trut i aint know 2 good
bout where we comes from meself, only as i was saying last night
dat de furst of my ancestors 2 reach here in dis island come from
calcutta pon de very FURST ship dat land wid dem indentured
east-indians, de FATAL ROZACK, & u sit up in de hilton bed
just den wid you toetee only half-hard but still standing up like a
standpipe as i say dat exclaiming out loud HOW COOL it is dat
my ancestors arrive here in p-o-s de very same year as u family
reach wid dat crazyass man etzler & he society, de selfsame year
of 1845

& i was telling u how deepra, she was my great-great-gran-maadoo,
how she meet mahun, he was my great-great-gran-paadoo, pon dat
crossing from calcutta but in fac i aint know if it was calcutta we
come from a-tall, since de history of all dem indentured east-indians in dis place reachback ONLY so far as de PORT dey disembark
from, either calcutta or madras, wid all else before dat chop off &
obliterate 4good 4ever, cause in trut my gran-maadoo uses 2 have a
tiny lil sketching dat she say pass down 2 she all de way from deepra, & even though dat sketching disappear longtime i could still
remember it good, & it was a lil stream wid some rocks & lil bamboo bridge crossing over, & if u turn de paper it write in handscript
PUNJAB 1842 pon de backside, & so i did start to think from den

DAT is where de family must have come from in de northwest part of india & we was probably punjabi in trut, since where else would dat sketching come from? & why else would deepra & my gran-maadoo have it like dat? but nobody know 4 sure

deepra was 17 when she make dat crossing from india & mahun only 18, & how dey meet was by chance 2 of dem wind up lying side-by-side pon de pallet down below in de bowels of dat FATAL ROZACK as i was saying, & deepa was sick-sick & weak wid dysentery 4 most of de whole voyage, & even though mahun scarce know she he did feed she grain-by-grain wid he own ration of daily rice & hers 2, 4 she 2 gain back strength like dat, & he give up most of he own 3 tin cups of daily water 2 keep she from dehydrating, & when dey reach in t'dad at last after 96 days of voyage from calcutta, & 41 days from de cape, & dey was BOTH near dead in trut, dey have de very good fortune 2 get hire out pon de selfsame estate in de south of de island near san fernando dat wasnt even much of a town yet in dem 1845 times, & so from de start of dat voyage cross de sea mahun & deepra never did spend not even 1 single night separate, very romantic just like hollywood-self!!!

mahun & deepra was both de same sudra caste, & dat was good & bad 2 in different ways, first it was bad since sudra was de servant caste, which is de lowest of de 4 castes after brahmin & kshatriya & vaisya, but mahun was even LOWER den she as u go hear in a sec, de lowest of de low, only people lower den he is pariahs, but dat was GOOD 2 in de sense dat since mahun & dee-pra was de SAME sudra caste dey could marry widout breaking de law, by which i mean to say de CASTE law, & deepra & mahun DID marry as u go hear, cause u might tink dat after dey reach in t'dad all dem laws of caste did no longer apply 2 de east-indians neither, & dat crossing 2 a new land & life would put everybody pon de SELFSAME level and station, but u would be very wrong mr robot & dat is 1 ting de chupidee whitepeople dont have NO FRANCIN IDEA, cause even though everyting ELSE change

4 dem indentured east-indians, de separation of caste is 1 ting dey still maintain in dem old days very stringent & rigid mongst deyself

but mahun was even lower den just sudra, as i was saying, he was a CHAMAR-sudra & dey was de leather workers who mutilate de hide of de sacred ox, but dat was bad & good again as u go hear cause dat skill of leather-working 2 make de shoes & belts & bags & such dat mahun had plenty skill in from a lil boy, even though it was looked down pon in india so bad dat even de SHADOW of a chamar pon de food of a holy brahmin would contaminate it & u got 2 throw it way & not even a potcake could eat it, but dat was a GOOD ting 4 mahun cause before long de overseer of dat estate find out bout he skills 4 making shoes, & next ting u know he take mahun off de cane-crew & put he 2 make boot 4 he & shoe 4 he wife & doux-doux & ALL de whitepeople, & paying him fa dese shoes 2 since dis kinda work didnt have no bearing pon he contracture, & soon as mahun could catch enough money from making de shoes he marry deepra in one bigass fancy MON-SOON WEDDING PON DAT ESTATE!!! & now de overseer take deepra off de cane-crew 2 & put she 2 assist mahun in de shoe-shop, so listen here what happen how de whole ting did catch like bushfire

cause furst mahun was making shoe 4 de overseer & de rest of de whitepeople pon dat estate, & in trut he & deepra was making dey daily wage by law 2 like all de rest of dem indentured east-indians, ¢25/day each & sometimes dey would get a lil ¢5 or ¢8 lagniappe from de overseer wife or he doux-doux or he daughter when she get a nice pair of shoes, but next ting u know all of dem EAST-INDIANS come 2 mahun & deepa 2 make DEY shoes 2, at ¢50 4 man-boot & ¢45 4 woman-shoe & ¢25 4 child-shoe, so just as u could imagine next ting u know word spread round 2 all of dem other estates, & mahun & deepra was making plenty shoes 4 de whitepeople, & even MORE shoes 4 de east-indians now, & before long plenty plenty dollars was wetting dey palms in trut so nex ting u know de 10 years of dey indentureship was finish-up, so deepra & mahun was entitle 2 free passage back 2 india now, or else according to de NEW law just instituted den if dey elec to re-main here in t'dad dey would receive a small parcel of land 2 put in agriculture 4 deyself, but since deepra & mahun didnt want 2 go back 2 india not-4-noting, cause dey was RICH RICH & living like king-&-queen in t'dad now, so dey choose 2 take de land dat was 5 acres each, or 10 acres 2gether, but since mahun & deepra didnt know a pum bout agriculture neither but only making shoe shoe shoe & more shoe, dey didnt want dat land in de country & so dey sell it off & take dat money plus what dey have save-up 2 buy a shop in san fernando on coffee street 2 make & sell de shoes, wid a floor on top where dey could live wid dey children dat was 3 now, 2 boys & 1 girl & ALL of dem born trinis!!!

so now mr robot u have a lil bit bout where my family come from & how we reach here in t'dad, dat i dont mind telling u as i was saying, but i was just bout 2 finish writing u out dis email dis morning 5 minutes ago when miss samlalsingh arrive 4 work & she explain 2 me how yesterday thursday when i did had de afternoon off & she was in charge, & u come inside here in de archives saying how MISS RAMSOL GIVE U PERMISSION 2 USE DIS MACHINE & copy out u copies of dat MORNIN STAR or whateverdeass it is of dis crazyass man ETZLER u say u writing u book bout, & u tells miss samlalsingh how u & miss ramsol is tight tight now jooking-down de place like pusscats most every night & miss samlalsingh know is de trut 2, but mr robot she tell u just as i instruct SHE enough times dont matter if is de QUEEN OF FRANCIN ENGLAN TUTI U JOOKING dat dont give u access 2 dis xerox machine, & i aint know who de ass u yankees tink u is, just cause u skin white like u toetee make from gold bar & u pums smell like french perfume, but miss sam-lalsingh is more savvy den dat & she see through all of u boldface lies & bullying straightway & dont let u near dis machine, not 4 hell mr robot, so listen here what i telling u, eh: u best learn some effin manners & behave uself proper & follow de rules just like everybody else, unnastan? eh? cause laws is laws & rules is rules & aint no exceptions 4 dis xerox machine not 4 u nor nobody else, unnastan?

good

so watch u francin self mr robot, unnastan? eh?

cordial,
miss ramsol
director, t&tna

ps if u want u could meet me at pelo 2nght again round 9

pss & me or miss samlalsingh would be holding 2 articles 4 u at de reserve frontdesk out de p-o-s gazette of 1845 would be of plenty interest 2 u i feel sure

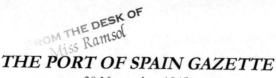
THE PORT OF SPAIN GAZETTE

30 November 1845

FIRST LOT OF INDIAN IMMIGRANTS

We have much pleasure in announcing the arrival this afternoon of the long-awaited ship, the *Fatal Rozack*, 96 days from Calcutta and 41 days from the Cape of Good Hope, with 217 coolies on board 'all in good order and condition,' as the bills of landing have it. There were five deaths on board during the passage, but the general appearance of the coolies is very healthful indeed. When our people are informed that there are countless thousands of these coolies, inured to a tropical climate, starving in their own country, and most willing to emigrate to the West Indies, it may be the means of opening their eyes a little to the necessity of working more steadily and giving greater satisfaction to their employers. Coolie provisions, also arriving aboard the *Rozack*, are available at Losh, Spiers & Co. at Richmond Street Wharf. The *Fatal Rozack* is a fine vessel of 445 tons and is manned by a crew of lascars.

Coolie provisions (very cheap) including:
> rice
> dhal
> ghee
> turmeric
> chillis
> tobacco &
> Indian hemp

THE PORT OF SPAIN GAZETTE

2 December 1845

ARRIVAL OF THE *ROSALIND*

We have the pleasure of announcing this morning that the *Rosalind* has arrived in port, 47 days out from London and 19 days from the Azores, bearing a good deal of long-awaited goods and produce. Included amongst the passengers travelling on this vessel were the first lot of 'pioneers,' 37 in number, of the Tropical Emigration Society, a joint-stock association formed in London by Messrs. Etzler and Stollmeyer, who arrived amongst their enthusiastic followers. Mr. Etzler is a self-styled inventor, scientist, and philanthropist. He is here in Trinidad not only as director and founder of his Society, but also as Consulting Engineer for the construction of the Great Western and South-Eastern Railway, Trinidad's first locomotive system which is to utilise 'wooden rails,' and which will connect our capital with San Fernando and other locations in the south. Mr. Stollmeyer, who acts as Secretary for the Society, has been a printer in London and Philadelphia. The *Rosalind* is a fine vessel of 596 tons under charge of Captain James Damphier. Newly imported articles and provisions may be purchased at Losh, Spiers & Co. at Richmond Street Wharf, including the following—

> Fine European Goods:
> > linens & silk bedsheets
> > female lingerie & hosiery
> > sherry & wine
> > champagne
> > brandy
> > votive churchcandles
> > salted hams
> > Dutch Edam
> > & other cheeses

5

The Captain's Ball

They were Santa Maria and Sao Miguel. And as the *Rosalind* drew closer, as the whitecaps settled and the ocean shifted colour from slate-gray to bright aquamarine, they revealed theyself to us in all they splendour. Because let me tell you after twenty-eight days aboard ship, only staring at nothing more solid than the empty horizon, they were something astonishing to see. First it was Santa Maria, which gave the illusion of being the larger of the two, due to its height and closer proximity. Like a hallucination it slipped past we starboard rail. And the ship made she way towards the habour of Punta Delgada, on the southern shore of the more elongated Sao Miguel. Its triple brown peaks lined up before us, one after the next. And presently on the grassy hillsides of this isle we made out numerous white *dots*—wandering about, puzzling at first. They were grazing sheep.

Pulled along uneven by a single foresail at the prow—puffing up and falling limp again like the beaten canvas itself was exhausted—the ship creaked she way into the harbour's clear lime-green water. So still that upon its shimmering surface a succession of watery rings could be seen. Issuing forth from the *Rosalind*'s hull-line. Spreading out round us in all directions. Until—at the centre of these brightly undulating rings, in a silence void of all save the distant squawk of gulls—Captain Damphier at last issued he command: the sailors dropped anchor.

Out from nowhere a yellow-sailed sloop appeared, seemingly overburdened by its cargo of brown-hued men and women, all wearing colourful costumes. Calling out to us in a language sounding like water sloshing forth from a bucket. Without warning they scrambled aboard. And even before we had a chance to suck we first breath of earth-smelling land-air, we heard they mandolins, strumming-way in our midst. Now the barefoot, brightly-ribboned dancers divided theyself up into parallel lines, stretching the length of the third-class deck. Bowing and curtsying to each other and pairing off, turning round with they hands clapping above they heads, ribbons twirling. Singing out in they water-sloshing tongue. Eventually forming a circle so wide it seemed to encompass the entire ship.

With smiling gestures the dancers encouraged us inside they circle. And led off by none other than Captain Damphier heself—spinning round expert and kicking up he heels—we followed timid behind. Next thing you know, son, we were all dancing—every man-jack and woman-jill aboard that ship! In whichever graceful or bumbling manner we spirits commanded. Laughing out loud. And in no time a-tall those tedious weeks at sea seemed distant and unthreatening as the sun sinking into the rose-tinted horizon behind we backs.

Other sloops arrived. Bearing quantities of fresh fruits and vegetables—milk, eggs, cheese—fish still flapping in they wicker baskets. Cackling chickens and fat guinea hens clasped upside-down by they wiry feet. Transforming the deck of the *Rosalind* to a raucous marketplace. The captain setting about replenishing he stock, bartering like a seasoned old housewife.

More sloops shifted alongside. And eventually smaller dinghies drifted up too. The gesturing, smiling, sunbaked Azoreans passing us up bottles of wine. All our arms reaching down to grab them up. An exotic liquor smelling strong as brandy—but tasting like a combination of the sweetest strawberries and tartest limes—for which those of us who could afford the extravagance readily tossed down we shillings. Flashing into the dinghies' wells.

Son, whilst the Azorians were allowed aboard ship, due to immigration and quarantine regulations the passengers were strictly forbidden to disembark. And in any case the *Rosalind* had already fallen behind schedule. So there wasn't time. The captain announcing that any attempt to depart ship would amount to nothing short of insurrection. He own *legal* jurisdiction to leave us behind: under no circumstances would said passengers be allowed back aboard.

Such prohibitions made the starkly weathered wharf and gray-shelled shore, the quaint village rising behind of neatly whitewashed houses with red-tiled roofs, seem to us even more enticing. At the same time there was something gentle & easy & comforting in the island's mere presence before us: its hazy solidity. The indisputable fact of its simply *being there*—only a stone's throw away—despite its dreamlike appearance. And those of us still leaning up against the rail, still gazing through the descending dark, found it difficult, almost painful, to turn we backs to it.

But son, now we all experienced a next emotion again. A growing excitement to return to we cabins, freshen weself, and don we finest apparel. Because that same evening we'd be treated to a special banquet, anticipated since the start of the voyage. Served to us beneath the stars on the third-class deck, at tables and benches already being shifted into position by the sailors. To be followed by the Captain's Ball. Because even those deckhands were freed from all duties tonight—Captain Damphier's treat—since they'd be served dinner by the Azoreans too.

Our own two adjacent cabins already a hubbub of commotion, the Tucker clan hurrying to dress weself. Georgina pulling out her clothes garment by garment, all-in-a-sudden in a serious flap—she couldn't find she lace brassiere. It'd somehow disappeared from amongst the things packed so careful beneath she bunk. Her fancy square-toed shoes gone too. Next thing Mum couldn't locate her silk stockings and garter. And Mary couldn't find her bloomers with the little pink bows at the hips.

With me standing just outside our cabin door—waiting for my own chance to dress—only wishing for a porthole big enough to disappear my bony backside through.

Now I heard Mum cry out—

Mon Dieu! she says. Un voleur a volé ma robe!

By this time Papee had finished dressing. He'd taken up his top hat. And reaching down to pull out a handkerchief he found Georgina's brassiere. Tucked in under the stack. A couple more kerchiefs balled up mysterious inside the cups. He pulled out Mary's bloomers, stuffed inside the other cup.

Finally Amelia spoke up—

Willy knows where everything is, she says. Ask him.

Willy? Mum says.

As if on command a Moroccan scythe-of-a-moon had positioned itself above the ink-black water. Laying down a milky trail cross its slippery surface. On the shore, not far away, long flat swells rolled up in resonant crashes. Receding with a glassy tinkle of shells colliding together. Meanwhile, on the deck of the *Rosalind*, the Tucker clan took we seats at a long table with two other families, the Woods and the Hemmingways. Fellow members of Mr. Etzler's Society.

Captain Damphier, wearing the kilt and leather pouch of

his native Scotland, rose to his feet at the head table. Seated between the comte and Mr. Whitechurch, he wife and Marguerite
seated in turn beside him—

'Ere 'ere! the captain says.

He knocked his fork against his glass with a set of loud
clinks—

I'd beg ye all to raise tall ye glasses. En commemorate with
me the termination o' the first en most arduous leg o' our journey!

Here everybody cheered aloud.

Eee-ditionally, the captain says, we need give thanks to our
neighbourly Azoreans. 'Oose gracious serviceability provides fer
this fine feast!

Now we all let loose a next cheer.

The captain continued—

But before we break bread, let me state that prospects peer
excellent-well in onwards fair weather. En aye-*briskly* trade, en
speedy voyage 'enceforth down to Trineedad!

At last we touched our glasses together and drank up hearty.
Everybody. Me & Mary & Georgina & Amelia & the three
Wood daughters too. All our glasses filled to overflowing with
sweet Azorean wine, though watered down some for the youngest girls.

Now the small orchestra assembled atop the Satellite's crate
commenced to blowing into they fifes, strumming they mandolins and tinny banjos. And the islanders hired out by Captain
Damphier began bustling amongst the tables, they trays laden
with food.

But even before dessert was served Marguerite and me had
sought each other out in the darkness behind the Satellite's crate.
Orchestra playing-way above our heads. A caper we'd planned

that afternoon at Marguerite's bidding—a soft retaliation against the notorious comte. Now we made we way sternward, towards that part of the ship farthest removed from tonight's banquet. Ducking beneath railings, shimmying along narrow plank bridges, climbing over piles of rope & nets & canvas sails.

Bouncing up all-in-a-sudden with a nightmarish group of passengers, a dozen in number, most of them men. Crowded into a barricaded portion of the deck alongside the starboard rail. We'd never seen them before. Not a one. The lone woman amongst them holding in she arms a toddler, the little girl staring-way into the night as stony and eerie as all the rest. She own dull eyes incongruous to her youthful face, little cap with its fuzzy red ball at the peak looking more sprightly than she did.

A most severe stench emanated from they ragged clothes, from the open hatch beside they filthy bare feet. Son, these passengers appeared to us so bizarre and disconcerting, at first they seemed *apart* from this ship and the voyage we'd undergone. Like if they'd only just been brought aboard. But these passengers were clearly, unmistakably, *English* people. As might be encountered in any basement or sewer-dwelling of the city we'd left behind.

They didn't stir. Neither did they utter a sound as we hurried past.

Finally we reached the stern railing. Facing a short stretch of dark sea, with the still-blacker shadow of the island rising behind. I lit the pitch-oil lamp I'd stashed behind the crate, raising it up, taking a good look round. This was the only part of the ship completely unknown to me. Since up till now I'd never ventured farther astern than my own cabin. But after a minute I found a hatch, hidden behind some half-barrels of sweet water, hoisted aboard by the sailors that afternoon. Ropes of a davit-and-pulley left draping against the stern.

I turned to Marguerite—

We'll make good use of this in a few minutes, I say, nodding towards the davit.

Whilst Marguerite held up the pitch-oil lamp, I tilted one of the half-barrels onto its edge, shifting it out the way. Then a next barrel. The hatch was hinged along the top, secured at the bottom by a brass padlock. I tried my keys. One-by-one. Till the lock sprung open, Marguerite smiling down at me from above the lamp. As I lifted the hatch a pungent odour issued forth, faintly familiar, and we peered together into the black hole. Making out only a rickety ladder descending into the gloom.

Marguerite down it first—she didn't flinch—handing me the pitch-oil lamp as she slipped past. When she got to the bottom I motioned for her to step back, dropping in the heavy coil of a rope ladder, thudding to the floorboards before her feet. I started down the ladder behind her, loop of the lantern clenched between my teeth. Closing the hatch overhead, my fingers feeling through the crack till I heard the padlock click shut.

We found weself locked inside a narrow, dark passageway. Ceiling not sufficiently tall for us to raise our heads. I shined the lantern forward, then behind, the passageway veering off like a rodent's underground maze. Taking hold of Marguerite's hand, I led her in the direction of the stern. But after a few steps the passageway ended abrupt in front of my face, Marguerite indicating another hatch, just below my boots. We backed up, and I lifted the hatch by its rope handle. Finally we detected the odours of close-packed animals—damp wool, urine, caca, mouldy straw— a flurry of muffled noises. Hoofs scraping against floorboards.

I shined the lantern down into the hole: at the bottom, huddled against the far bulkhead—they coal-black eyes shining up at us—we made out the comte's five remaining sheep.

Marguerite climbing down first again, already caressing one of the startled sheep by the time I reached her side. This pen triple the height of the passageway above, its ceiling several feet above our heads. Hayloft at the front. With a latticed window stretching cross the stern, heavy plank shutters latched open against the bulkheads. A faint checkerboard of light seeping in though the lattices.

I hung the lantern on a nail at the front of the hayloft, studying the pen. Facing the window, I took hold of the crossbeam above my head, raising my feet off the hay-strewn floor—hanging there, swinging my full weight against the lattice-struts. Kicking my boots. And after a few solid blows they began to give-way. I continued swinging, kicking, splintered fragments splashing down to the water. Till I'd opened the entire window, darkly forested shore of the island looming up before me.

I let the crossbeam go, looking over the water at the dark island, catching my breath. Then I turned to Marguerite—

Off to fetch the rope ladder, I say.

I climbed up and dropped it into the pen, lugging it over beside the window. And after making the two loose ends fast to a crossbeam below the opening, with a grunt, I heaved the bundle out. The ladder uncoiling as its wood rungs bounced hollow against the hull, like sticks knocking together, bottom end splashing down solid into the water.

With the first rush of adrenaline I began stripping myself. Not stopping neither till I'd stripped myself down naked.

I turned to Marguerite, finally admitting something I'd been contemplating all afternoon—

I haven't been swimming since the age of six. Not since we left Ventnor!

Marguerite reached towards me. Placing her palm flat against my pale chest.

Don't worry, I say, raising my eyes to meet hers. If I don't surface in a minute, you'll have to come in after me!

And with that I hoisted myself up onto the crossbeam again, glancing down for a second at the ink-black water. I sucked in a last breath, squeezed my eyelids shut, swung my legs out the window.

At first, with the shock of the cold hard water, my legs locked up beneath me. I felt myself sinking, immobile, down into the depths. But after the first moment of panic, first mouthful of saltwater burning inside my throat—and seemingly of its own accord—skin-water-memory returned. Taking hold of my frantic limbs: I kicked hard, my long limbs reaching up to grab armfuls of water. Pulling them down along my bursting chest. Till my head popped like a champagne cork out the surface.

I thrashed about, spitting, catching my breath. And after a minute my muscles relaxed. I began to tread water. Turning round to wave up at Marguerite, there holding the lantern fifteen-feet above my head.

I ducked my shoulders into the dark surface. Swimming round to the leeward side of the ship where the Azoreans' dinghies were tied up, somewhat haphazard. Two and three abreast of each other. I swam towards one of the dinghies on the outside, reaching up and grabbing hold of the gunwale, catching my breath, hoisting myself in.

Head low, dripping, I clambered forward, untying the line from the stern of the dinghy in front. Son, in my excitement I didn't feel even the slightest chill. The tide pulling slow, steady, drawing my dinghy sternward. And after a few seconds I sat up, adjusting the oars in they rowlocks, working my way round to the *Rosalind*'s stern.

I signaled up to Marguerite, motioning for her to climb down.

My heart giving a jump as I watched her reach to hang the lamp from a piece of broken-off lattice: she'd stripped sheself down naked too. Down to the smoothness of she burnt-sienna skin. Her arms slender in the soft light, hair loose and draping over her shoulders. As I watched her turn round and reach her foot down for the first rung. Making her way, one wood rung after the next, till I helped her step into the shifting dingy.

Marguerite's eyes flashing excited at me over her shoulder.

I smiled too—

With a bit of luck, I say, Captain Damphier won't let us back aboard!

I turned and climbed up to the pen again, pulling cross the ropes and pulley, davit stretching forth from the deck above my head.

Now I passed the belt of the harness under the first sheep's belly, snapping the eyehook in position above its back, tightening the straps. And leaning my weight into the davit above I hoisted the sheep into the air. Smooth and easy, up and out the window.

And as the orchestra continued playing at the other end of the ship, I lowered the first bleating sheep to Marguerite. Reaching up her slender arms to ease it into the dingy.

After dinner came the most anticipated event of the night's festivities. The Azoreans cleared the tables, shifting them to the front of the deck and piling them up. Only the head table remained in place, atop which they set a quantity of cocktail glasses, together with an ample bowl of the captain's punch.

Beneath the flickering stars, Moroccan moon spilling its milky trail cross the water, the *Rosalind*'s deck was transformed to a formal ballroom. And the first of the elegantly costumed couples, my father and mother no doubt included amongst them, strode out onto the floor—the seven broken hooks at the back of Mum's gown repaired at the last minute. They danced the first waltz together. Followed, a short time later, by the rest of the passengers. Not excluding Georgina and Mary, changing off to take a turn with we younger sister.

But it didn't take the orchestra long to exhaust they repertoire of sedate European waltzes. Switching to they own more energised Azorean music. And the passengers—having shed they inhibitions earlier in the day, fortified by a glass or two of the captain's punch—embraced the night and the music with scant restraint.

By the time we'd transported all five of the comte's sheep to the island, in two separate trips, the sky was already showing traces of purple on the eastern horizon. We'd watched the sheep set off on trembling legs, cautious, picking they way amongst the coarse undergrowth a few yards up from shore. Stumbling over the loose ground. Like they'd forgotten how to walk. Then, a few seconds later, we heard them bleating content as they trotted off, scampering-way to join the others.

Now Marguerite and I lay side-by-side, soaking in the shallow water. Much warmer than it had been over beside the ship. Our borrowed dinghy beached on the gray-shelled shore beside us. We looked out over the water at the *Rosalind*'s tall shadow. The vessel having swung broadside to us with the shifting tide, scythe-of-a-moon still decipherable behind her mainmast. Stars blanketing the sky. From cross the water we heard the gay music—a little tired-sounding by this hour of the morning—the occasional muffled cry of a passenger or sailor.

Son, as we lay there soaking in the warm water the *Rosalind* seemed a world away. Separated from us by a pane of glass.

All-in-a-sudden a rocket—launched from the ship's fore-deck—shot screaming into the air. Leaving behind its smoky corkscrew trail. Bursting with a loud *pap!* above the ship. It scattered a hundred bright blue sparks cross the sky, descending through the air in the pattern of an overturned, slowly opening flower. Another rocket followed behind. Exploding in its overturned flower of tiny yellow lights: red, blue, green, yellow.

The rockets screamed skyward. One after the next. Bursting and descending through the air, they overturned flowers of brightly coloured sparks. And each time they exploded a cry of delight issued forth from the passengers gathered along the rail—

Ooohhh!

Aaahhh!

And as the final blue flower dissolved into the sky before us, as it vanished-way, Marguerite and I turned to one other. Gazing into each other's eyes. Happy as we were exhausted-out.

7/9/10

dear mr robot:

i wish to broach a certain topic mr robot very important & i hope
2 EJUCATE u a lil bit 2 bout how we feel here in t'dad, & what is
de proper attitude & etiquette involved on de subject of PUMS,
cause last night when we did finish up we THIRD sweet jook 4
de night, & we was lying dere catching weself a cool & relaxing
lil bit & i was feeling so NICE in trut mr robot, so comfortable
& relaxed & i just let a good 1 fly, & stink lil bit 2 from all dem
curry-crabbacks we enjoy so much from we dinner by ganeshhouse & fresh seamoss drink, & in trut mr robot when i let dat
pum go & smelling up lil bit stink 2 as I have to admit it meself,
dat straightway u pinch u nostrils & look at me all squeezeface like
if i aint got no manners a-tall, but dat only go 2 show u mr robot
how u dont understand noting bout how we feel here in t'dad, &
what is de important HEALTH ISSUES involved on de subject
of PUMS, same as belching as a matter of fac

cause here in t'dad nobody would never cause such a fuss & make
u feel shame & look pon u all squeezeface when u let a good 1
loose, just de OPPOSITE mr robot, here in t'dad de people understand how pums is a natural organic process & nothing to feel
shame 4 a-tall being a true expression & celebration of de good-
ness of life, & mr robot why u want to hold DAT back? & not
let it show how u feel happy & content in de selfsame moment
& SHARE dat happiness wid other people 2? cause krishna-only-
know human beings come out de womb pumming & we would
all go 2 we graves pumming 2, so why u want to hide it way? & in
trut mr robot de best ting dat could happen to u in my opinion,

& de best ting dat we trinis could teach all of u stuck-up yankees is to set uself loose lil bit & free-up & let down u guard, & learn how 2 ENJOY DE SIMPLE PLEASURES OF A SWEET-SWEET PUM

dat is my hope 4 u in dis life mr robot

cordial,
miss ramsol
director, t&tna

ps see u at pelo round 9

pss & me or miss samlalsingh would be holding a article 4 u out de t'dad guardian weekly health advisement column of dr brito salizar plenty informative 4 u & prove just what i saying

LISTEN TO YOUR BODY CAUSE IT KNOWS BEST

The Guardian's Weekly Health Advice Column

Brito Salizar, MD, OBE

Today, in response to a number of inquiries expressing deep and understandable concern to arrive of late at this PO Box, October being the official opening of châtaigne season (♫ *châtaigne châtaigne, the musical fruit, the more you eat, the more you toot!* ♫) we shall consider, in some detail, the proper and healthful attitude towards 'flatulence,' or as it is called here in Trinidad in the local parley, *pumming.* Now: in a number of so-called 'advanced' societies, historically speaking, it is known that the unguarded and bold-faced expression of flatulence is widely frowned upon. This may be so. What must be understood clearly in the first instance is that these particular mores have never held any sway whatsoever for the health profession, and absolutely no subscribing to by medical science and/or practitioners of the same. They are purely societal conventions, inconvenient at worst and misleading at best, and should be dispensed with immediately.

How can we say this, and with what surety? Well, do the beasts of the field, the fowls of the air, or the fishes of the sea strain so inexplicably to hold up their flatulence? This could and should never have been so for the history of human civilisation, and sad that it has ever come to pass! In fact, the restrained or incomplete expulsion of gases from the colon is known to cause a number of health issues, psychological and psychical, e.g., premature aging and mental blindness. It plays havoc with the entire circulatory system, including the heart. Where the gases collect, joint pains are frequently encountered. There is occasional osteopathy.

Permit me to end on a personal note: Myna, my old Venezuelan grandmother, was in her last years confined to a wheelchair. This did not deter her. When the need arose she would shift her weight in her chair as best she could and lift up the appropriate buttock manually, even in mixed company. *Fait accompli*, and smiling like a young girl, she would tell us, 'El culo está contento!' ('My pumsee is happy!') She lived to 98.

6

7 Apples

It was well past noon on the following day when the passengers crept at last from out we cabins, up onto the main deck. By that time, much to we disappointment, the islands had long disappeared beneath the horizon at the ship's wake. True to Captain Damphier's predictions a brisk following trade drove the vessel smooth and steady ahead. Broad rolling swells came too, providing an extra push. The *Rosalind* making surer headway than she had since the start of the voyage.

After a day or two we settled weself begrudgingly back into the routines aboard ship. Yet now, as the *Rosalind* ploughed she way into the wide Sargasso Sea, the sun shone brighter. Temperature warmer, sky clearer, the water positively bluer. The passengers scarcely realising weself that now—as we strolled the deck or stretched out lazy in a patch of bright sun—we no longer held we dingy coats and blankets clutched round us. On occasion one of the sailors might even be seen going about he duties bareback, much to the scandal of the ladies aboard.

One afternoon the sun was shining so relentless that in addition to the sailors, a number of the male passengers reclined bareback on deck as well. Or they'd stripped theyself down to they filthy merinos. The women and girls having accustomed theyself to remaining below—despite the baking heat—fans fluttering-way in they hands busy as butterflies. That same afternoon, on the deck allotted to the third class, a row of some sort seemed to have erupted between two of the sailors. The passengers hurrying towards the starboard rail—realising there wasn't no kinda argument a-tall, but that one of the sailors had evidently spied a tiger-striped shark swimming alongside the ship.

The third-class men raising up the cry, charging towards the rail, draping theyself over.

But son, no sooner had all these men gathered at that side of the deck than several sailors perched discreet in the rigging above they heads began pouring buckets of seawater over them. Till they stood in the blazing sun soaked down to they bones.

Some laughed out hearty at the seamen's rouse. They took up a bar of soap and began scrubbing under they arms. Others became irate at the sailors' trick—*shark indeed!* But regardless of the men's approval or disapproval, this was the first proper shower any of them had partaken of in over a month. And even *they* couldn't've doubted that it served them wonderful well.

With the dispensation allotted only to lovers, Marguerite and me strolled arm-in-arm about the ship. Boldface so. Nobody said a word. Nobody even seemed to take notice. On tranquil nights we spread out a blanket in our favourite secluded spot on the forecastle deck. Lying on our backs and gazing up for hours at the glittering stars. With the same boldface abandon one night we fell asleep right there on the deck. Arms wrapped round each other under the blanket. And son, the following morning we awakened to a spectacle more marvelous than any we'd ever witnessed: the blood-red ball of the sun, black-rimmed, rising up enormous out of a fire-blazing sea.

Another afternoon, with a shock—she was supposed to be up in the parlour taking tea with the other ladies—Mrs. Whitechurch entered her cabin. Knocking on the door to Marguerite's adjacent room. With me jumping up stark naked out the bed, hiding myself behind the same door Marguerite opened cautious to address her aunt. Mrs. Whitechurch handing over a tray of tea-n'-pastries, her niece's face crimson as the pot of strawberry jam.

Still more perilous and inexplicable than this, on two separate mornings Mrs. Whitechurch entered the bathroom of her cabin-suite—she was supposed to be up at breakfast at that hour—going straightway about she business. Right there in front of us. Not even taking notice of her niece and me, there soaking in the soapy water of her own porcelain tub—Marguerite's hand clasped tight over my mouth—only an arm's reach away.

Other peculiar events occurred aboard ship. One morning Amelia woke to discover an enormous wedge of Edam cheese— edged with its crescent-skin of bright red wax—tucked beneath her pillow. That slice of cheese almost as big as the pillow-self! So heavy Amelia had to strain to take it up, her fingers trembling to peel back the paper and break off the first bite.

Another morning all three of my sisters awoke to find colossal slices of cheese, of three distinct varieties. On still other mornings they discovered tins of sardines and smoked salmon, boxes of water crackers & sugar biscuits. Pots of corned beef & herring & goose liver pâté.

Early another morning Mum startled everybody with a piercing shriek. A big box of crackers and three tins of caviar beside she pillow.

One of those same unending afternoons, calm & quiet & mildly breezy, Marguerite and I lay reclining on the foredeck in a patch of sun. Marguerite reading in she book by Benjamin Disraeli, a novel titled *Sybil or the Two Nations*. Me reading my own book with its bright-coloured plates—a present from Marguerite—my first introduction: *Hummingbirds of the West Indies*, by Sir Eardley Holland.

Papee strolled over, so casual and unassuming at first I didn't even take in my own father—

Afternoon, Miss Whitechurch, he says, touching his hat for Marguerite.

She was lying, at that particular moment, with her head propped against my chest. Me sitting up so startled I almost sent her reading glasses pelting over the rail—

What is it, Father? I ask, embarrassed.

Papee looked away—

Only a small matter, he says, waiting a beat. Only that I've asked the family to join me for a short confab. Before dinner. In our cabin.

He paused—

I'd like you to attend as well, Willy.

Papee paused again—

That is, he says, barring duties to Cap'n Damphier!

And with that Papee touched his hat once more for Marguerite, striding off across the deck.

I entered my parents' cabin at the petitioned hour, Papee sitting on a lower bunk, the rest of my family crowded round. On his lap, over Georgina's shoulder, I made out the pasteboard box— only then did I realise we'd been at sea six weeks already.

Papee looked up, seeing me enter—

Most excellent! he says.

I crouched to the bunk beside Mary.

Now Papee pulled the piece of twine loose from round his

box, lifting off the lid, placing it on the mattress beside him. And we all leant forward, peering inside. Of the twelve apples, five had withered to crinkly brown balls, with splotches of mildew the colour of oxidised copper. Papee removed these first, placing them careful on the overturned lid. The remaining seven apples looked ripe & red & rosy enough. Perfect even. Papee removed these ripe ones, shaking off the straw, passing them out one-by-one to Mum, each of the girls, then me. Giving the additional apple to Amelia.

A single apple remained in the box, belonging to Papee.

Straightway Amelia raised one of the shiny red apples up to her mouth—she was about to bite into it when Papee stopped her short.

Just a moment, Amelia, he says.

He cleared his throat—

I'd like to propose . . .

Papee started over—

I'd like to ask each of you to give me your apples *back*.

Amelia's jaw dropped.

Papee continued—

I'd like to propose that you offer them up to a group of passengers—aboard this very vessel upon which we travel—who're in greater want n' need of them than we are. Considerably greater! I'm referring to the steerage passengers. Of whose existence you may not even . . .

He broke off again—

You see, just this morning, together with Mr. Etzler and Mr. Stollmeyer, I made a visit to the stern where these steerage passengers are lodged. And there we three witnessed a scene of such depravity—the likes of which I've little comparison.

Papee looked round at each of us—

You must believe me that these unfortunate passengers are deserving of this small . . .

Straightway I reached my apple forward. Placing it back inside the box. After a few seconds Mum reached over to do the same. Eventually Georgina, Mary—and finally Amelia, tears in her eyes—returned they apples too.

Most excellent! Papee says.

He replaced the five withered apples back in the box, topping it over.

Already I'd turned to leave, ducking my head to exit the cabin door. I heard my father's voice behind me—

Willy, I'd like you to come along.

Box tucked under his arm, Papee now led me towards the stern. Arriving a few minutes later at the barricaded section along the starboard rail, same decrepit passengers standing there, staring-way at nothing—

Evening, Papee says, cheerful as he can manage.

They didn't give him no kinda response a-tall.

Papee turned to me—

Just here, he says.

He indicated the open hatch beside they bare feet. Papee continued down the ladder, me following behind, descending into a stench that was palpable as a blast of hot air. I struggled to breathe. My eyes burnt as if in reaction to some noxious gas.

Now I peered into the dark, blinking. But all I could make out was a sea of eyes. Staring straight back at me. Then, slow but sure—with the sombre light entering through the hatch above my head—I began to decipher the place.

Separated on both sides into upper and lower levels, each with little more than three-feet of headroom. The plank flooring on both tiers divided up by crude railings—into what looked like animals' pens, five-to-six-feet square—each allotted to a family. But son, even the sheep's pen was a substantial improvement over this place. The passengers, most of them naked to the waist, clutched at they ragged clothes. Majority of them women and children, lying or crouching or kneeling on burlap-covered straw mattresses. Bursting through in places, buried under mounds of stinking bedding and piled-up clothes. Only then did I notice that all along the spaces between the straw mattresses—along the passageways and gathered in each corner—were thick, black, putrid puddles. Oozing side-to-side with the roll of the ship. Dripping down through cracks between the boards.

I was cognizant of a low, deep, groaning sound. Faintly aware of a slow, crawling movement. Towards Papee and me. Filthy hands reaching out to grab the apples. Me standing there with my left foot still perched on the last rung of the ladder—like I haven't decided yet whether I'm coming or going.

All-in-a-sudden, in the dim light, I recognised the woman kneeling on the mattress just beside me. Holding in her lap a little girl hardly more than three years of age. The child's eyes staring back blank and stony into my face.

I stepped down and reached my hand round Papee, taking up the last remaining ripe apple. Turning and holding it out to the little girl. I recognised her red cap, fuzzy ball at the peak— with the faint shine of the apple in my hand, they're the only two splotches of colour. Only signs of life.

The little girl didn't move. Eventually I got on my knees before her, setting down the apple for a moment atop the mattress. I reached for the girl's little sticky hand. Prying her wiry fingers loose one-by-one. Fixing them one-by-one round the apple.

The following afternoon the sun-blistering sky turned ebony-black in a matter of minutes. Jagged fiery forks sundered the air. Followed by sharp, heart-wrenching crashes. So loud they shook the deckboards beneath our bare feet. Now we watched a solid white wall approaching from the distance. Suddenly pelting the ship with stone-hard pellets of rain. And in rapid succession our world changed colours from blue, to black, to solid impenetrable white: tall white waves pounding the ship, thudding down atop the deck. And no longer could we distinguish white sky from white, featureless sea.

Below it was as if the ship had been turned topside-down. Chairs, benches, tables lay toppled. Every piece of furnishing not bolted down. Buckets, suitcases, boxes, and canvas sacks. Scattered about. Tin plates & cups & eating utensils—every object not locked inside a cupboard—tumbling from the shelves to the plank floors. Rolling back-and-forth. All in constant motion, shattered glass everywhere.

We stumbled about like drunkards. Throwing weself onto our bunks, arms wrapped round the mattress like if we were clutching to life itself. All activities aboard ceasing, beginning with meals. Since there wasn't no way for the cook and stewards—seasick theyself—to prepare and distribute food. Even hand out cups of water. And almost any food or drink taken in came straight back up, so better to remain without. All our throats and bellies burning from the constant dry-retching.

Three days and three nights it lasted. When only Captain Damphier and his first mate remained on deck, lashed to posts behind the helm. Even so it seemed impossible the swells didn't sweep them overboard. Three days and nights when the captain and his first mate lived as if beneath the sea, rather than on top.

Then—as abrupt and unprecipitated as it had departed from

us—the pleasant, torrid, tropical weather returned.

Still, it was a good few hours before the first of the battered passengers could venture up from out we cabins. Yet it wasn't the sudden stillness that drew us above. Not the eerie quiet neither. Not even the hot sun baking the steaming boards. Not so a-tall. It was something else: a sudden uproar erupting *somewhere* aboard ship—riotous or celebratory or what nobody at first seemed to know. Till word began to circulate amongst us that, in truth, terra firma—*land!*—had been sighted off the port rail.

Yet those passengers who had the energy to hurry over to that side of the deck only found theyself staring-way at a flat sea. At a bright and empty horizon. No land visible a-tall. And it wasn't till the true explanation began to spread round the ship— one mouth to the next—that we came at last to understand the reason for all the uproar. What it was all about. But son, even this explanation seemed to us, at that moment, as hard to imagine as the prospect of sighting land itself.

It had to do with the steerage passengers.

Apparently, those passengers had awoken that same morning—only an hour or two after the storm subsided—to find in each of they family-pens a white silk pillowcase. A dozen of them. Maybe more. Wherever-the-arse these pillowcases had come from, nobody knew. Nobody had the remotest idea. But even more peculiar than the appearance of all these silk pillow-cases theyself, was the fact that in each of them—like a Christmas package—the steerage passengers discovered a salt-cured Catalonian ham.

Another balmy, star-filled night, Marguerite and I fell asleep again in our secluded corner of the forecastle deck. Arms wrapped round each other under the blanket. With me waking first the following morning, just as the sun had begun rising up out of the fire-blazing sea. I was about to turn and wake Marguerite when—at the other end of the horizon, the *Rosalind*'s slow-dipping bow pointing straight at it—something else arrested my attention. Like a black splotch, stuck to the surface of my own eye.

I sat up, throwing the blanket off, climbing onto my feet. My two hands grasping tight to the wood railing, staring out over the choppy sea. There, several miles off the bow—unmistakable—an island. Its three green-black peaks rising up out of the azure water.

But son, what startled me more than this sight was the ship's eerie silence. The fact that no cry of the sighting had been sounded a-tall. Yet clearly the captain—or his first mate, or whoever else had they hands on the helm at that moment—had seen the island too. Because the ship was pointed straight-as-an-arrow at it.

Maybe he'd decided to give the passengers a few more minutes' sleep before sounding out he cry? maybe he'd chosen to study the spectacle in private a while longer—this island so calm & serene & so unspeakably itself—before announcing it aloud? The same contemplative turn-of-mind with which I stood there now. Studying it. Staring cross the water at the triple-peaked splotch of darkest green.

I stood another minute. Then I turned my eyes to Marguerite, still asleep at my feet. She lay on her back, her face turned to the side, a few moist strands of hazel-coloured hair draping cross her cheek. Stirring soft in the breeze. The blanket had slipped away from her shoulder. It had pulled the neck of her frock down too, morning sunlight pooling up in the shallow depression along her exposed clavicle.

I paused a moment. Then I got down on my hands and knees, pressing my lips to it. To the edge of that tiny pool. Like I could drink it up. Like that little pool of light could quench my thirst. Marguerite smiling, stirring from out of she dreams beside me.

5th Message

21/9/10

dear mr robot:

i so HAPPY 4 you in trut mr robot cause listen hear what happen
how yesterday tuesday afternoon was miss samlalsingh 1/2 day
off, & i here in de archives all alone wid not a person in de place 2
check out none of dem old newspapers nor oldbooks nor noting
else a-tall, wid me only sitting here so BORED-out-my-bones dat I
was just wishing maybe u might arrive uself to do some more of
u research pon dis man ETZLER 4 dis book u say u writing, & i
say well let me take a lil looksee meself in dat journal you name
de MORNIN STAR, & see if maybe i could find anyting would
be of interest & useful or maybe a reference 2 u mother surname
TUCKER someplace dat you might not have see it yet, but i have
a very PECULIAR habit mr robot, sometimes i likes to skip to de
END of a story & read it ASSBACKWARDS towards de front,
so i go to de very last number of dat STAR and commence 2
reading de story backwards like i say but wasnt noting 2 much of
interest dat i could tell & soon enough i was falling asleep again
feeling bored wid dat journal 2, & i start to skip backwards some
more reading faster till maybe 2 or 3 numbers in from de back, &
den in #32 all-in-a-sudden just like dat my finger fall pon someting in trut!!!

i find a LETTER mr robot dat write out by must be you OWN
great-great-gran-paadoo MR WILLIAM SANGER TUCKER
after he did arrive here in t'dad & write back 2 englan 2 de editor
of dat same journal address 2 he FRIEND POWELL, cause dat is
how de editor name, & dis letter is
publish in de journal 2 cause from what i could tell just scanning

it lil bit dis letter describe in full details bout some estate up pon
de north coast wid some bigass long name call CHAGUABARRI-
GA or someting so, dat it was sounding lil bit familiar 2 me in trut
but i cant remember where i see dis name be4, but i say it MUST
be de place where dis man ETZLER go wid all he english people
and u family 2? cause why else would it be publish in dat journal
like dat? & dis letter is saying how de estate was & what animals
dey got in de forest & fish in de sea & what crops dey plant, all
kinda peas & plantains & groun-provisions & everyting else like
dat u could want 2 know right here in dis same letter!!!

so mr robot i cant WAIT 2 show it 2 u & i would be holding it PER-
SONAL in my office at de back of de archives, cause dis is surely
de most important & exciting piece of news & HISTORICAL
ARTIFAC u find yet 4 u research pon u family here in t'dad, & i
want to see de look pon u face when u read it

cordial,
miss ramsol
director, t&tna

ps i would be holding dis photocopy 4 u in my back office just
as i say & wearing my dental-floss panties 4 u & me 2 celebrate
2gether 2!!!

II
On Land
2 December 1845

7

Arrival

Under the late afternoon sun the sea had already changed colour. From that sombre slate of open water, it had turned a cripsy beryllium-blue. In the glaring distance gulls and raucous kingfishers went about they business. Awkward pelicans dropped out the sky in cannonball-splashes. The *Rosalind* hugging tight to the island's rugged north coast, a ridge of serrated mountains rising above we heads. Sailing alarmingly close to rock-shorn cliffs, past jagged inlets and wider, beach-encrusted bays. They names pronounced aloud for us from a dog-eared seaman's chart by Captain Damphier—*Madamas, Chaguabarriga, Morne Poui, Blanchisseuse, Macqueripe.*

Out from crevices between the rocks graceful coconut palms sprouted, as if in boldface defiance to gravity's laws. Dense tropical forest lined the promontories like an animal's pelt, right the way up to the loftiest peaks. Now the ship rounded Corozal Point, when all-at-once the three teeth of the Dragon's Mouth jutted up before us—*Monos, Huevos, Chacachacare.* Beyond these three steppingstones, in the hazy distance, the mountains of Venezuela. Highest peaks lost amongst the clouds.

The ship sailed through the Boca de Monos, past Scotland Bay to port, the water changing colour again to a murky emerald-green. As we entered the Gulf of Paria—fed, miles away on the South American mainland, by the alluvial flush of the River Orinoko. Yet hardly had we time to glance round again when the imposing structure of Fort San Andrés stood glowering at us, cannons mounted round the periphery above like sawed-off wagon spokes. And stretching out into the bay farther still—a giant's great stone finger—the mole of Kings Wharf.

The *Rosalind* creaked her way round it. Slipping into a quiet, almost hidden bay. Suddenly alive with ferries, white-sailed sloops, rowing pirogues. All scuttling amongst the larger vessels at anchor here. And as the sun dropped behind the mountains of the Northern Range, those same mountains we'd first perceived from out at sea on the opposite side of the island—opposite side of the world it seemed—now we got we first ever sightings of our destination: this modern capital of the colony, crown of the West Indies, the town of Port-Spain.

But hardly was it more than a glimpse. A fleeting impression. Cut off by the velvet curtain of night. The surrounding hills closing in, one crowded cluster after the next, as if in ordered succession. They tumbled down atop the town—*Laventille, Belmont, Maraval, Montserrat.* Sails aflutter, in a shock of total darkness, Captain Damphier at last issued he command, sailors scrambling like ghosts towards the bow. And presently we heard a splash followed by a rumble of rusty chain so foreign to our ears, we couldn't scarcely identify it.

Much to our regret customs officials could not be contacted to clear the ship till morning. Yet the majority of us stood trans-fixed before the rail. For still another hour. Staring away at noth-ing. Nothing more than the afterimage of a pasteboard town fading fast from out our eyes. Because all that remained were its diverse scents—wet earth & cooksmoke & baking pitch & putrefying morass. All subdued by the heavy dampness of night. Nothing but a half-dozen hucksters' flambeaux reflecting at us in wavering lines cross the still water.

The weary travellers succumbing at last to the exhaustion of our long day. Wandering below for a subdued and surprisingly haphazard evening meal, most of us still too emotionally wrung even to eat. And after draining a quick cup of cool water, we descended below to our cabins. Determined to rest up for the event of going ashore in the morning—first time we'd set foot on solid ground in nearly seven weeks.

The Tucker clan snoring-way in a matter of minutes. All of us excepting me. Because I lay there in my bunk, head resting atop my folded arms, half-asleep. Drifting again in my familiar memoryspace. My daydream night-place.

❂

The sky already turning a faint purple as I arrived back to our East End borough from Knightsbridge, my heart still beating fast. Skin still crawling like a line of batchacks up my spine. Completely exhausted. Having followed the Whitechurches home after they meeting, in secret, just as I had planned.

And after hiding in the shadow of a horse chestnut tree for still another half-hour, a candle had shone in a second-story window. The curtains were swept aside, and Marguerite appeared. Son, I went to her. Just as I'd intended—at least I made my most valiant try. Moreover I'd managed, *somehow*—without a single word, written nor spoken neither—somehow I'd convinced Marguerite to forego her steadfast convictions for the sake of love.

She'd agreed to come with me—with us—to Trinidad!

As I approached my own basement home I listened to Dyers' clocktower sounding four times in the distance. I descended from the street. Only to find my family assembled round our kitchen table, even at this hour. And *not* for breakfast neither. All still wearing they nightdresses.

My family sat silent, blankfaced, candle flaring up in they midst.

I didn't know what to think. Where-the-arse to carry myself. So after a pause I took a seat on one of the benches too, between Georgina and Mary.

Finally Papee spoke up. Addressing nobody in particular—

No way we can afford six passages, he says. Not *six*.

Another minute of silence. Now it was Mary who spoke—

But Amelia, she says, would travel at half-fare, wouldn't she?

Doesn't matter, Mum answers. We couldn't afford five-n'-a-half passages either.

She looked at Papee—

Not after purchasing a full share in the Society for each of us. Even Amelia! Shares your father believed would guarantee his delegation as Mr. Etzler's agent. In which case we'd've *all* travelled to Trinidad at the Society's expense.

Papee interrupted—

I'd hoped that after my efforts on the Satellite with Mr. Frank . . .

But his voice broke off.

Mum continued—

Now, not only are we stuck here in London, we've no reserve.

Another minute of silence. It was Mary who spoke—

Couldn't we sell off our shares of the TES then, n' pay for our passages that way?

No one would buy them, Papee answers. The entire Society's overinscribed. TTC as well. Everybody scrambling to offload. Our shares, at the moment in time, are all but worthless.

Hopeless, Mum says, as though she's correcting him. As though she's marking down the final full stop at the end of the sentence. End of discussion.

I didn't know what to think. How to comprehend this piece of news: now that Marguerite had decided, finally, to come with us to Trinidad, it seemed that my family—I—wasn't going noplace a-tall.

I rose up to my feet, slow, leaning forward onto my hands to steady myself. Feeling the wood pressing up soft and warm through my handpalms. All-in-a-sudden my head spun. My vision went blurry. I fought to find a focus, looking round at the faces of my family, one-by-one.

Then I found my voice. Or *it* found me—

Fuck Jesus, Joseph, and Mary, I say.

Swallowing—

What are you people talking about?

❖

All-in-a-sudden I heard a loud rapping on both our latched-back cabin doors together. Sitting up so startled I bounced my head against the ceiling, hard. For a moment I didn't know where I was. Then I recognised Mr. Whitechurch's voice.

Mr. Carr, he was saying, n' Captain Taylor!

I heard Papee—

Whom?

Why, Mr. Etzler's two agents—Carr n' Captain Taylor!

Whereabouts? Papee asks.

Whereabouts, my darling William? *Whereabouts?* Why— aboard ship—that's where! I do mean *here*, William. Been parleying with Etzler, Stollmeyer n' me these past two hours together!

Papee paused a long minute. Sussing all this out—

Well isn't that grand! he says at last, his voice sleepy still, still subdued.

Grand indeed! says Mr. Whitechurch. Etzler's called for an assembly of the entire Society. Every member aboard ship. Including the wives n' children. Even at this late hour.

He paused to swallow a breath—

I do mean *now*, William!

And presently Mr. Whitechurch shoved his head inside we own cabin. Rattling the door handle, startling us, his voice suddenly booming—

Up up up my young lad n' lassies. We've all of us a jolly *congress* to attend!

The night, which had earlier felt so thick and obscure, was now considerably brighter. Stars swept the sky. A three-quarters moon had positioned itself above the ship's mast. Pitch-oil lamps were dispatched, and the thirty-seven pioneers assembled weself on the third-class deck. Some already wearing they tropical costumes—canvas jerseys and trousers, tall boots and wide-brimmed straw hats—prepared for a moonlit trek into the rainforest. Others, like my own family, still wearing we tatty nightdresses. Feet bare against the deck's salty, still-warm boards. Mum with her nightrobe wrapped round sheself and Mary both, against the damp of the tropical night. The Tucker clan taking our place behind the others, Papee hoisting Amelia atop he shoulders to see over they heads. Moffie perched in turn atop my sister's back.

With me standing there pressing up onto my toetips, looking round for Marguerite. Son, I couldn't find her not-for-nothing. Neither Marguerite nor she aunt. And now I wondered if Mr. Whitechurch, in all his excitement, had neglected to inform the members of he own family about the meeting.

After a couple minutes Papee put Amelia down. He took

hold of her hand and led her to the front of the crowd, crouching to one knee beside her. I was just about to turn and leave—
having decided to go rouse out Marguerite myself—when I was
stopped short by the arrival of our two leaders. Both they faces,
above they freshly groomed beards, a reflection of the serious
business at hand. They made they way through the crowd, ascending to the top of the Satellite's crate. Followed by a pair
of unfamiliars—because none of us had seen these latter two
before. Both filthy and scruffily dressed, olive-hued stains in the
pits of they arms when they raised them up. Both wearing five-
day-old beards—the one blond, other gray. Both shockingly red-
faced—either burnt by the sun, or they'd just stepped from out
the local pub. Or whateverelse went for such establishments in
this place. The younger and taller of the two wearing a battered
straw hat—so now I couldn't help but recall Mr. Etzler's own
costume for Savvy—the gray-bearded one with a threadbare
seaman's cap.

And son, when the breeze shifted in our direction, we took
in they rough scents.

The fact is these two looked rather like vagrants. Even to
us—unwashed, ungroomed seafarers—the majority not having
partaken of a proper scrubbing in over a month.

Mr. Etzler first to address the crowd. With the three taller
men standing behind him, peering at us awkward overtop he
head—

Ladies unt gentlemen, he says. Fellow members huv zee
Tropical Emigration Society! It gives me great pleasure to introduce our two agents—Mr. Carr unt zee Captain Taylor!

Here, with an ample gesture of his upraised arm, jacket unbuttoned to reveal his crimson vest, Mr. Etzler indicated the two
men.

He continued—

For zee past sree months zey haff prepared for our arrival. Unt zee wonderful news, my good ladies unt gentlemen, is zat our Society is now in possession huv a home in zee tropics! Zee exact details huv which my comrade, Mr. Stollmeyer, will now inform you in full!

A second burst of applause followed. Mr. Stollmeyer stepping forward, chest inflated, smartly groomed beard tussled by the breeze. Mr. Etzler retreating behind his back.

He cleared his throat—

Let me begin with a bit of background, Mr. Stollmeyer says.

The crowd letting loose a subdued groan. As we prepared weself for a lengthy—if not painfully tedious—preamble.

Mr. Stollmeyer explained how our agents had been sent out from England to petition from the Trinidad government a parcel of freehold land. It was understood that such parcels were available to enterprising Englishmen simply upon the asking.

Mr. Stollmeyer's voice changed tone—

Ladies n' gentlemen, he says. Upon these and other related matters *all* of us were quite blatantly misled. That is to say, we were openly, and somewhat underhandedly, *deceived*.

Here a general murmur of disappointment issued forth from the crowd. Laced with the first few frightened gasps.

Mr. Stollmeyer raised up his hands, open-palmed in the manner of an itinerant preacher, by this gesture quieting us down.

He explained how our two industrious agents, upon landing here in Trinidad, had petitioned a meeting with the Director of the Colonial Office, a certain Mr. Reginald Johnston. This gentleman only confirming for our agents what they'd already determined for theyself aboard ship, simply by studying the map: that *no* tracts of free government land remained available for emigrants. Be they Englishmen, or any nationality a-tall.

Again a general grumble of disappoint. Again Mr. Stollmeyer raised up his hands.

He explained how our diligent agents, undeterred by such formidable news, decided to rent a pair of donkeys. Upon these animals to cross the entirety of the island to its farmost eastern shore. Where they were informed land was selling cheap. This trip—passing through wild savannah and coarse jungle—was to have taken a day or two. Yet it wound up consuming more than a week—serving no purpose whatsoever, other than a waste of valuable time!

After a pause, during which the crowd again expressed we disappointment, Mr. Stollmeyer continued—

Our good agents were not able to find a single estate within range of their meagre purses. They then proceeded . . .

Here Captain Taylor stepped forward. Boldface so. Much to everybody's surprise. He cut Mr. Stollmeyer off in midsentence—

Mr. Docket n' Miss Bly, he says.

Until this point neither the captain nor Mr. Carr had dared interrupt our leader's impassioned speech. Now, somewhat taken aback, Mr. Stollmeyer turned to the captain—

To whom are you referring? he asks, his voice subdued a half-notch.

Why, our two arses, the captain says, smiling peculiar. You disremembered to remark that they names 'us Mr. Docket n' Miss Bly!

Visibly irritated by this intrusion—since he no doubt considered these details irrelevant—Mr. Stollmeyer stared at the captain a few more seconds. He turned to his audience again, taking up his extended oration.

Mr. Stollmeyer explained how, at this point in they quest, the agents returned to Port-Spain. They'd now determined that the most efficient means of exploring the island would be to charter a small vessel and guide. Since surely they'd make swifter progress should they continue they explorations by sea. A sloop was subsequently chartered . . .

Captain Taylor interrupted again—

Miss Bee, he says.

Mr. Stollmeyer paused, turning once more—

Thank you, Captain, he says. I believe you've already told us the names of your bloody arses!

The captain blinked. As though to fend off the assault of Mr. Stollmeyer's voice—

The sloop, he says, 'us called the *Miss Bee*. You neglected to mention how she 'us named.

After another pause Mr. Stollmeyer turned and continued. His tone betraying his own vexation—

On a sloop named the *Miss Bee*, our diligent agents set out upon their daily expeditions . . .

The captain interrupted again—

May-nard, he says, this word coming out in a distinct hiccup.

Mr. Stollmeyer looked him in the face—

What is it *now*, Captain?

The sloop, he answers, 'us under the charge of Cap'n *May-nard*—again the hiccup.

Mr. Stollmeyer went on—

Having surrendered the faithful Mr. Docket n' Miss Bly. And embarking upon a sloop called the *Miss Bee*, under charge of a certain Captain Maynard, our good agents now set forth upon their daily seafaring expeditions.

Mr. Stollmeyer settled into his previous ramble. He explained how our agents then proceeded inland from they various coastal landings to examine still other properties. Travelling farther and farther from the capital. First along the island's west coast, as far south as the pitchlake at La Brea. Then the rugged north coast—along which, Mr. Stollmeyer informed us—*we* had travelled ourselves this very morning aboard our own *Rosalind*.

Yet every expedition led only to bitter disappointment! With the pioneers—meaning *ourselves*—due to arrive at any moment, the agents began to fear that no suitable property might be procured in time. Indeed, it appeared that the first lot of eager pioneers—meaning *us*—would soon disembark in Trinidad only to find ourselves completely and utterly *homeless!*

Here Mr. Stollmeyer raised up his hands. Quieting the fearful murmurings of his listeners.

And yet, he continued, the tide was about to turn! As you shall all presently hear. For scarcely a fortnight ago, on the majestic north coast of this fair isle, our industrious agents met with the good fortune of examining still another estate. This property was sufficiently expansive for our purposes. Most significant of all, it was the first estate examined by our agents that fell within reach of their meagre pocketbooks!

This property—which, unbeknownst to us, we sailed past ourselves this morning aboard our own *Rosalind*—was subsequently purchased. In haste our agents hired a handful of peons to assist in clearing the brushwood, so that our first food crops might soon be sewn. To drain a rather oppressive mangrove swamp, so as to render our property immediately more healthful. And upon the elevated portion of its picturesque and most idyllic bay, the sturdy foundations of our modest cottage have now been laid out—

In other words, says Mr. Stollmeyer, our first tropical *home!*

It was these very labours that our agents left off this morning when—in a flap, spying through their eyeglass—they observed our happy *Rosalind* scuttling past. The agents hailing Captain Maynard, who'd coincidentally arrived the previous evening, bearing fresh supplies. And so it happened that our good agents—most anxious to see us and relate to us their cheerful news—set off on the *Miss Bee* directly in our wake behind us. Having arrived at this port within the hour of ourselves!

At this point, as though Mr. Stollmeyer had finally given Captain Taylor his queue—which, of course, he had *not*—the captain stepped forward again. This time to the very edge of the Satellite's crate. Crimson-faced and smiling—

Belly-a-mud, he says.

Now Mr. Stollmeyer spoke out bold from behind him. In no quiet tone of voice neither. He was, by this point, far beyond the limits of his patience—

Inebriated fool, he says. Pie-eyed nincompoop! Will you kindly . . .

Belly-a-mud, the captain repeats, then takes a breath. Chagu-abarriga, he explains. It's Español. And *War-ra-hoon*. What means *Belly-a-mud*.

With this pronouncement Captain Taylor, still perched at the front edge of the crate, a dozen feet above our heads, re-moved his tattered seaman's cap. Proceeding to wipe it cross his perspiring brow. Revealing to us—with something of a shock—his perfectly round baldhead. Shiny and topped over with a cir-cular patch, like a bright white bowl. The cap preventing the sun from colouring this portion of his scalp the equivalent crimson of his face. A shiny white bowl that seemed, in truth, like the only clean part of our captain's person.

He replaced the cap, bowl disappearing again—

Belly-a-mud, he says. *Belly-a-mud! Belly-a-mud!*

The captain paused, stumbling forward a step, accompanied by a cry of alarm from the women gathered below. Causing several of the men standing near the front, including Papee, to shove forward. Past the women and children. Holding they hands suspended above they heads.

And son, this was a good thing too. Because now Captain Taylor smiled his peculiar smile one last time. He removed his cap to wipe it cross his brow—white bowl appearing and disappearing—and he pitched forward. Down off the crate. Into the waiting arms of the men gathered below.

By this time the cries of alarm had escalated to shrieks of panic. Women and children shoving back, the men laying out Captain Taylor cross the salty deck.

At which point Mr. Etzler shoved forward heself, shouting out from atop the crate. Shaking a disdainful finger down at the sprawled-out captain—

'Ese drunk! he shouts. Blind drunk!

Which had the curious effect of silencing us all in one—every manjack and woman-jill gathered on that deck—turning in confusion to gaze up upon our leader—

Douse em down wiss a bucket huv water! he orders. It's perfectly clear zat ziss blathering imbecile is PISS-ARSE-DRUNK!

Another silence followed. During which Papee—kneeling now at the captain's side, his ear pressed tight to the old man's chest, two careful fingers probing at the artery along his neck—raised up his head. Calling out to Mr. Etzler—

On the contrary, he says. Our Captain Taylor is *dead*.

28/9/10

dear mr robot:

you is a effing shitong mr robot, is what you is!!! all night long 2
of we jooking-down de place like no 2morrow, & u playing so
innocent, never mind dat jooking was sweet 2 bad & i can only
admit how much i was liking it 2, my tuti still pulsating & twitch-
ing & smoking-up lil bit so nice dis morning when i reach here in
the archives & miss samlalsingh come running 2 tell me furst ting
what take place yesterday thursday afternoon during my 1/2 day
off, how you did come inside here toting U OWN PERSONAL
XEROX MACHINE, wherever-de-FRANCE u get it from, & u
tells miss samlalsingh how i give u EXPRESS PERMISSION to
bring dis machine inside de archives like dat, & u tells she how
MISS RAMSOL SAY u could copy out as much of copies as u
want to do u research 4 dis crazyass man ETZLER & dis book
u say u writing, even though of course miss samlalsingh know
straightway dat is only another 1 of u boldface lies & bullying
& SCHEME IS SCHEME U SCHEMING SHE again to copy
out u copies, & she tell u NO EFFIN WAY MR ROBOT!!! but u
carry u bigass machine inside de place regardless & plug de plug
& commence to copying out u copies

but miss samlalsingh tell me how before de furs 5 copies come
out from u machine, or maybe de furs 2 numbers of dat MORN-
ING STAR, whilst she was bawling down de place hysterical
like i instruct her to do in perilous situations like dat to SHUT
DOWN DIS BLASTED MACHINE STRAIGHTWAY MR
ROBOT!!! & miss samlalsingh tell me how furs ting before u
know it ALL de visitors in de archives commence 2 queuing up

straightway in a long long queue wid all of dem people only fighting down each other now 2 copy out DEY copies pon u machine,
& dey was all shouting dat if some blasted-foreigner-yankeeass-
whiteman could copy he copies den DEY COULD COPY
DEY OWN COPIES 2, & before de furs 5 copies of dat STAR
come out u didnt have no choice a-tall but let miss roses to copy
out she copy of recipe 4 guava duff out last saturday gazette,
& mr hosien want 2 copy out he copy of sunday-horseraces-
paddocks-lineup from de standard, & michael antony want to
copy out a next article from some bigass oldbook he got, & earl
& marlon & caz & lawrence & all de rest of de wotless crew, &
u had 2 let dem copy out dey copies 2 mr robot, cause if not u
would have pon u hands a RACE RIOT 4 EQUAL & FAIR USE
OF DE PHOTOCOPY MACHINE IN DE T&T NATIONAL
ARCHIVES

so in trut mr robot i aint know how much of copies you manage to copy out yesterday afternoon, dat i can only suppose not
much more den de furs few numbers of dat MORNIN STAR,
cause u had to let all de rest of dem people 2 copy dey copies
2, & den miss samlalsingh say u had to put in more ink, was so
many copies dem people was copying, and den dat xerox start to
smoke-up from overheat-exhaustion just like my tuti did wear-out
and break-down last night from all de jooking, so before u know
it was 5 oclock time 4 de archives to close & u didnt scarce get
through 5 numbers of dat STAR, & after longlast wid all she
shouting and bawling miss samlalsingh could pull de plug pon
u machine & shut it down, but i say it serve u yankee-francin-
whiteass right

so mr robot u best listen good good 2 me & hear what i tellin u,
eh? & dont try dat one again, u unnastan? eh? cause laws is laws
& rules is rules and NO PERSONAL PORTABLE PHOTO-
COPY EQUIPMENT allow inside, & u know it good enough,
even though in trut according to miss samlalsingh dat machine u
was toting wasnt so small a-tall a-tall, but she say it was BIG as

a BARREL of BABASH BUSH-RUM, wid u redface straining hard like u making a caca now 2 carry dis machine, dat me & miss samlalsingh couldnt HELP weself from laughing lil bit at dat 1, & i hope it give u a HERNEA mr robot, just so long as it don't ruin de jooking equipment, cause DAT would be a shame in trut

cordial,
miss ramsol
director, t&tna

8

Disembarkation

As Kings Wharf remained congested with packets off-loading the first class—and the morning slipping away fast—Papee made arrangements with a fisherman, hailed over to the side of the *Rosalind*, to row us ashore in his small pirogue. Now we climbed down a rope ladder, one after the next, stepping cautious into the rocking rowboat. A sailor tossing down we hastily prepared bundles of belongings. Wrapped up in blankets and tied tight with twine. They contained the things we'd brought along for the voyage. All our other possessions packed into the trunk in the hold, to be forwarded to our place of residence after a day or two. Exactly what this place might turn out to be, none of us knew. Not even Papee. Because prior to the previous night, when Mr. Carr and the deceased Captain Taylor had informed us of the state of our 'cottage' at Chaguabarriga—a dozen bamboo poles stuck in the mud—all of us, including Mr. Etzler and Mr. Stollmeyer, had expected to arrive in Trinidad to find *some* kind of accommodations. For this reason the agents had preceded us to Trinidad with the Society's funds in they pockets. So despite all of those interminable days and nights aboard ship—only dreaming about this very moment when we would, finally, set foot in Trinidad—none of us, not even Papee, had thought scarcely a moment beyond it.

I can assure you it wasn't the enchanting moment we'd envisioned neither. The fisherman rowing us ashore perched atop a mound of mullet he'd spent the morning seining. Some

still alive, occasionally flapping up they tails in little explosive
fits—like a cornered batimamselle beating her wings against
a screen. Finally, with a crunch, he beached his pirogue on
the gravelly shore. Now, one-by-one, we jumped down from
the pointed bow, bundles clutching under our arms. Bracing
weself against each other as we traipsed awkward up the steep
embankment. All our knees and ankles wobbly for the first
few steps. Like we'd forgotten how to walk. Son, I could only
recall the comte's sheep—we were *them* now—stumbling up
the seafront.

Yet hardly could we reach the boardwalk at the top when a
handful of bareback young boys approached. Surrounding us,
smiling, grabbing our bundles from out our arms—

Me to tote dis load for you, suh! one says.

Please feh carry dis parcel, mis'ress! says another.

And before we could utter a word in response—even if we
had understood the boys' singsong—each of them had hoisted
a bundle up atop he head. Holding it balanced with a single
spindly arm, or no arm a-tall.

They led us onto the wide-open expanse of the Plaza de
la Marina. Lined on both sides with dusty almond trees. Son,
they're not there again, those trees. But in the old days we used
to call it Almond Walk, so prevalent were they round the periphery. At one end, facing the bay, we saw the hard stone structure
of Customs House, with the harbourmaster's office inside.

The boys leading us over to the nearest patch of shade. They
took down they loads to rest a minute, passing round a corked
bottle of water. Papee searching his pockets for something. We
didn't know what it could be. Eventually he produced a folded
slip of paper, opening it out careful, showing it to the eldest of
the boys.

This same boy squinching up his brow, staring down at the piece of paper—

Vin-*cent!* he calls out. And the smallest and skinniest of the boys jumped up and hurried over.

Vincent squinched his brow in a similar manner, head cocked to the side, staring at the note holding in Papee's hand. Then he took the piece of paper heself—raising it up to the sun like he's verifying a bank-bill—slowly mouthing out the words.

Yessuh! he says at last. Only a lil temporary cumbruxion. Everyting undah control, suh!

He paused, smiling up at Papee—

Me knows de house good-good, suh. Numbah nineteen Duke Street—Mastah Johnston res'dence. Scarce fifteen minutes footin from here!

Son, only then did I recall the prime minister back in England—suddenly it seemed so far away—sitting behind his big disheveled desk. Writing out that address with his delicate fingers.

Now the boys hoisted they bundles up atop they heads again. And Vincent led us off like the Pied Piper, Papee's note holding out before him like if it's a map.

He directed us round the perimeter of the plaza, in and out the patches of shade cast by the almond trees. Turning up onto Abercrombie Street, off to the side of the Customs House. Now we entered the metropolis of the town itself: a careful checkerboard of treelined boulevards, each laid out parallel or, like Abercrombie, perpendicular to the sea. With a fresh breeze off the bay filtering along it. The street itself paved over in a thin layer of pitch, softened by the sun at this hour. So with each step we felt its surface sinking a little beneath our boots, waves of heat rising up. Yet our porters walked over the hot pitch barefoot, without even a flinch.

They turned right after a block onto Queens Street, tall tower of Trinity Cathedral rising up before us. But not before we crossed Chacon could we view the building from in front like it was meant to be seen. Only then could we take it in, in a single breath—the gothic-styled tower and intricate front façade, modeled after Westminster Hall itself. Son, I don't have to tell you how there isn't another church in the West Indies—nor few others elsewhere in the world neither—could give you that kinda impression. That feeling inside you stomach of soaring splendour.

Eventually we turned and continued down Fredrick Street, entering Brunswick Square, sidewalks radiating out the middle like a giant ship's wheel. Sir Woodford's statue standing there at the centre like if he's Ulysses heself.

Following Vincent's lead we veered left, proceeding down the main walkway to the middle of the square. Passing beneath Sir Woodford's upraised sword. Now we veered right at a forty-five-degree angle, turning east onto the walkway bisecting the square, leading us onto Upper Prince Street. Which we followed for another three short blocks, crossing Henry and then Charlotte Street.

We passed the first private homes—sparse, inward-looking, constructed in the Spanish style. They thick stone walls enclosing musty courtyards. Further along we saw the more modern, timber-built, French-style homes. Erected on groundsills, with deeply shaded galleries at the top of elaborate filigreed stairs.

Only a few pedestrians out walking the streets in the midday heat, the town still adhering to the old Spanish custom of an afternoon siesta. Even the potcakes lay sprawled in patches of cool shade, paying us little mind as we walked past. Even as Amelia stooped beside each one to give it a patting.

A block beyond Charlotte Street Upper Prince Street inter-
sected George Street. From there we could peer slightly downhill
to the public market, beneath a handful of carrotroofs. But at
this midday hour the market appeared all but abandoned. Now
we turned left onto George Street, for the slight uphill march of
a single long block. Walking perpendicular to the shore again,
cool breeze blowing against our backs. Finally coming to the
intersection of George and Duke streets where—turning right
again behind our porters—we saw the first ostentatious, notice-
ably wealthy homes. Set a good distance back from the road.
Surrounded by lush foliage. And only a few hundred yards beyond the crossing, scarcely fifteen minutes from the time we'd
left the harbour—though to us it felt like we'd been wandering
through the town all afternoon—we arrived at our destination:
#19 Duke Street, the Johnstons' residence.

Entr'acte
7 September 1881

Cumbruxions

My father paused here a moment. He reached into his pocket for his old-fashioned watch, attached to his vestcoat buttonhole by its long goldchain. That same watch that had once belonged to Mr. Whitechurch—and had somehow been passed down to my father—but he hadn't reached that part of his story yet.

He clicked it open. Then he stretched the watch forward, into the glow of the pitch-oil lamp, studying its face—

Twelve o'clock already.

My father clicked the watch shut and slipped it back into his pocket, taking up his cigar box—

Son, I have a map somewhere inside here, showing you just how the old town was looking in those days. Because I don't have to tell you it's changed up plenty since then!

He paused, looking over at me—

Once, when I was giving somebody this story—I can't even remember who-the-arse it was—I marked out the exact path we walked through old-time Port of Spain that afternoon. With a red pencil. The Tucker clan following young Vincent like a string-of-squids. Walking from the old Plaza de la Marina, up the hill to Mr. Johnston's house on Duke Street.

My father turned to his box again. Ruffling through the papers.

I sat trying to imagine what the city must have looked like. Back then, when my father first saw it, at fifteen years of age. That first night when he arrived from England.

The incoming tide held the *Condor* steady, her stern still facing the shore. It hadn't turned yet. Neither the tide nor the ship. I looked up at the moon, standing there above the dark mountains, cut with a knife down the middle into a perfect half. So somehow you saw the moon's other side, even though that half was caught in the earth's shadow and blanked out completely. You saw it—like a kind of reflection—even though it wasn't there. Plenty stars in the sky.

All-in-a-sudden Captain Vincent appeared, shaking us from out our solitude. Striding forth from the dark shadows by the side of the wheelhouse. My father and I turning together, startled.

The captain cleared his throat—

Ah-ham!

He approached us with a half-full bottle of rum tucked under an arm, stack of three tumbler glasses holding in his other hand. Still in full uniform, even at this late hour.

Look the devil-self! my father said, putting down his box. *I was just telling R-W here about you!*

The captain came to a halt before us. My father turning now to give me a sly wink—like if *he'd* orchestrated this appearance of Captain Vincent, at this particular moment, to coincide with the telling of his tale too—

You know who Captain Vincent is, don't you, son?

It must've been clear from the look on my face that I didn't have a clue.

Well, he said, *he happens to be that same bareback young boy who met the Tuckers when we arrived here in Trinidad. Thirty-six years ago it is now.* My father turned to point his chin over the water. *Right there on that boardwalk at the top of the shore. The same young Vincent who directed us to Mr. Johnston's house.*

My father turned back to the captain—

Though it looks like he's putting on a little bit of a paunch these days, eh, Vincent?

He smiled at my father—

I was hearing some kinda ole-talk giving out behind here. I figured it couldn't be nobody but you, Willy. At this damn hour!

The captain crouched to take a seat on the deck between us, reclining against one of the coils of rope too. He recognised my father's briefcase, there beside the pitch-oil lamp—

Like you boys having youself a business meeting!

He uncorked his bottle and poured us out a finger each, the three of us taking up our glasses, touching them together, firing them back.

We sat in silence a few seconds, feeling the soft burn of the rum at the back of our throats, contemplating the moon and the handful of lights that remained tinkling round the curve of the bay. With the two brighter lights at the end of Kings Wharf reflecting at us over the water.

The captain rose to his feet again, yawning—

You boys could tief Bazil time if you want, but duty calling pon me fore-day-mornin!

With that the captain reached down for his bottle and poured himself out another finger. But he didn't drink it. He turned and walked to the edge of the deck, tossing the rum cleanly over the stern. So quiet we heard it splash down below into the water—

Sleep good, ole lady! Don't give me no cumbruxions tomorrow, you hear?

He came back and set his bottle and glass down at my father's feet, turning on his heels and striding off towards the wheelhouse again, disappearing into the shadows.

After a minute my father took up the bottle and poured us out another finger. We touched our glasses together and fired them back.

Then he reached to his feet again for his slightly battered cigar box. With me still studying the extra empty glass sitting there at my father's feet, cupping its neat little fistful of light. Like an invitation. Or a promise.

My father took up a folded and ragged-looking piece of paper from his box. He opened it out, careful—

Here, he said—

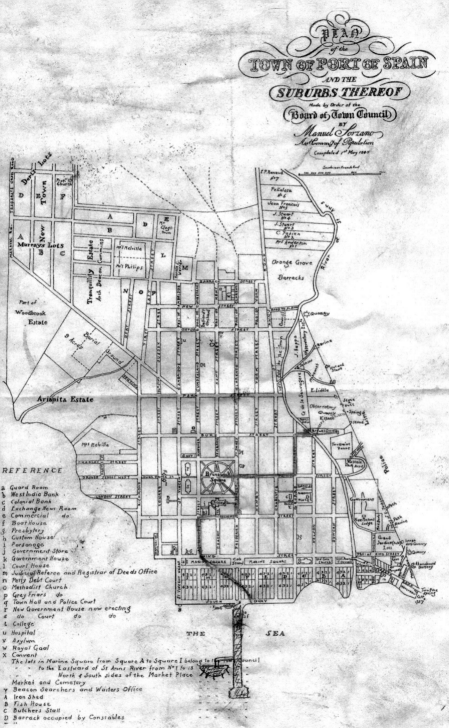

PLAN
of the
TOWN OF PORT OF SPAIN
AND THE
SUBURBS THEREOF
Made by Order of the
Board of Town Council
BY
Manuel Sorzano
Ass Commis of Population
Completed 1st May 1845

REFERENCE

a Guard Room
b West India Bank
c Colonial Bank
d Exchange News Room
e Commercial   do
f Boat House
g Presbytery
h Custom House
i Parsonage
j Government Store
k Government House
l Court House
m Judicial Referee and Registrar of Deeds Office
n Petty Debt Court
o Methodist Church
p Grey Friars   do
q Town Hall and Police Court
r New Government House now erecting
s   do   Court   do   do
t College
u Hospital
v Asylum
w Royal Gaol
x Convent
  The lots in Marine Square from Square A to Square I belong to the Town Council
   "   "   to the Eastward of St Anns River from No 1 to 13
   "   North & South sides of the Market Place
  Market and Cemetery
y Beacon Searchers and Waiters Office
A Iron Shed
B Fish House
C Butchers Stall
D Barrack occupied by Constables

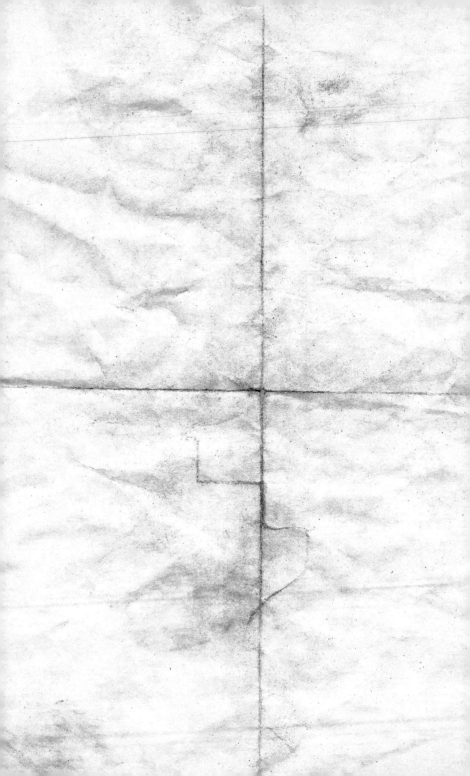

We passed between the two wrought-iron gates, left propped wide-open. Now we followed our porters down the long drive, gravel crunching beneath our boots. Carefully manicured gardens at both sides. At the end of the drive a roundabout circled the trunk of a mammoth tree, perfectly symmetrical. It stopped us in our tracks, this tree. We'd never seen nothing like it before. The thick lower branches stretching out horizontal, covered over in lush lichens and lacy ferns. Brightly blooming orchids and bromeliads sprouting from the forks of each branch, a giant mushroom-cap of leaves overtopping the massive trunk. Son, not even the grandest oaks back in England, the loftiest pines, could raise up a finger to this tree!

Behind it stood the Johnstons' home. Modest in size, though highly elaborate in the island's French style. Its roofed-in front gallery framed by gingerbread fretwork, potted ferns hanging at intervals between the posts. Our porters coming to a halt at the bottom of the steps, shifting they loads to the ground. Now— having directed us successfully to our destination—Vincent returned Papee's slip of paper. Like if it's a ticket he needed to get inside the house.

Papee stepped up onto the front gallery, the main door left open like the front gates, only a rusty screen blocking the entrance. Papee attempting first to sound the brass knocker, managing only a silent, awkward shifting back-and-forth of the big door. Flustered, he proceeded to scratch his fingernails cross the screen, two or three times. Making a startling set of racket.

Papee removed his straw hat, holding it behind his back, navy ribbon round the brim dripping down. And after a second a woman appeared, opening out the screen door with a rusty squeal. Revealing to us a hefty figure clad in black down to the flooring, starched white apron tied up round her waist. Beneath the frock's hem we saw her yellow toes peeking out.

Vincent was the first one she addressed, which struck us as odd enough—

Best carry you lil bamsee round to de kitchen, hear, Vincen? she says. Let you mummy give you one good cut-tail. Runnin roun de place since foreday-mornin, n' bareback too!

She steupsed—a long loud suck-teeth.

Now, in a more reserved tone—yet speaking as though she's known him all his life—she addressed Papee—

Come come come, she says. Mastah Johnston been waiting pon you all geegeeree since yestaday-evenin-self. Soon as news come de *Rosalin* reach!

She turned again, looking down the steps at the rest of us—

Come, *every*body. Toute famille! Leh-me run wake Mis'ress Johnston, fix all-you-all up wid some nice cool guavajuice!

In the same breath she addressed Vincent again. Altering her initial instructions—

Vin-*cen*, you hurry you bamsee quick-quick to Mastah Johnston office. Tell him de Tucker family done reach. Tell him dey waitin pon he up to Samaan Repos.

Now she addressed the other boys—

N' de rest of you whatless scoundrels, carry dem bundles in de back. Let Vincen mummy give you each a fie-cent. Fix you up wid a piece of hot dinner!

We took our seats round the settee in the front parlour, waiting for Mr. Johnston to come from his office at Brunswick Square, Mrs. Johnston to descend from her bedroom. According to Berty—as we now learnt the housekeeper was called—she'd been taking her siesta. Meanwhile, Berty brought us out a tray of icechip-tinkling glasses of guavajuice.

Mr. and Mrs. Johnston arrived at the same moment, approaching the parlour from opposite sides of the house. All of us standing together—a small confusion following, everybody turning this way and then that to shake each other's hands. Papee pronouncing each of our names two times in succession.

They introduced theyself as Reg and Heather. Mr. Johnston resting his hand cordial on Papee's shoulder—

William, he says, Sir Robert's instructed us to give you a good welcome.

He paused—

N' we shall endeavour to do our very best!

Lunch followed in the Johnstons' formal dining room, served by huffing Berty. Fricassee chicken & fried plantains & steamed christophene. Little mounds of rice shaped like overturned bowls, leaves of shadowbenny pressed in at the top. Soursop ice cream for dessert. All these flavours new and exotic to us—and I couldn't tell you how *good* they were tasting neither—after our weeks and weeks aboard ship. Only at the end of we lavish meal did the cook, Vincent's mum, make she appearance. So that we all can sing her our lavish praise.

Now, under Mr. Johnston direction, we went for a tour round the grounds. Mr. Johnston offering Papee a cigar, lighting up one for heself as well. So now we were followed by they puffs of smoke. Floating up amongst the tall trees. At one side of the house he showed us the vegetable garden and orchard. Then Mr. Johnston led us between two cedar trunks at the back of the property, into the entrance of a hidden path. Winding down the hill in several switchbacks, passing beneath thick wet forest. At the bottom we stepped out from under the canopy of leaves, into hot sun again. Arriving at the banks of St. Anns River.

In the late afternoon the water was coloured a gilded olive-green, deeply black in the shadows of the overhanging trees. Long limbs reaching down like fingers scratching at the still surface. We continued behind Mr. Johnston, along a path that followed the river upstream another hundred yards. We crossed over, stepping careful from one boulderstone to the next, the women and girls with they skirts bunched up in they arms. We climbed the bank on the far side by another steeply switching path, Mr. Johnston directing us first to the Stone Quarry—and after another still more strenuous climb, to the Observatory at the peak. Right the way up at the very top.

Winded, we turned round to look down over lower Port-Spain. Past the La Basse, with its handful of cobos circling per-petual above. All the way down to the bay in the distance—a dazzling blue.

And amongst the ships at anchor there, like toy boats, we made out our tiny *Rosalind*.

The sky already turning a soft pink as we arrived back to Samaan's Repos. The temperature, even at this hour, still considerably warm. We'd worked up a good thirst—though by now we'd accustomed weself to the tropical heat. Mr. Johnston led us first to the small grotto at the side of his property, with a siphon splashing down into the pool beneath it. And we each took a turn hopping onto the boulderstone at the centre of the pond, leaning forward to drink from out our cupped palms. My sisters shrieking with the first touch—the water so cold it burnt our fingers and lips.

We wandered round the house again, up the front steps, onto the wide gallery. Now followed a moment of awkward confusion, the Tucker clan looking round at each other bobolee. Not knowing what to do next, where-the-arse to go: all-in-a-sudden our afternoon had come to an abrupt halt.

Mr. Johnston turned to Papee—

One moment, he says. Whilst I go n' fetch . . .

But he interrupted heself—

Heather, now where did I leave that blasted key? Twice already today I've misplaced it!

He looked round at Papee again—

Some small arrangements I've taken the liberty of making on Prime Minister Peel's instructions. And, I daresay, the Crown's expense. A small home, round the corner from here on Charlotte Street—I trust you'll find it suitable.

He paused, padding the pockets of his shirtjack—

If I can just find that confounded key!

It was Mum who broke the silence now, smiling at the flustered look on Mr. Johnston's face—

Reg, she says. I've a feeling you and William are going to get along très bien.

Only Vincent remained in the kitchen at the back of the house. Berty sending him straightway to round up the others. And after a few minutes they'd formed they train again, smiling Vincent out in front. Ready to lead us off to #7 Charlotte Street.

A small, French-style house, considerably more modest than the Johnstons' own. But son, I don't have to tell you that this house was bigger and fancier than any we'd ever lived in. Including our country cottage at Ventnor, much as I remembered it. Of course it's long gone, that little house halfway up Charlotte Street—knocked down to make space for something bigger— even before you were born.

But in those days it stood five steps up from the street. Furnished by its previous tenants, Mr. Johnston's former secretary and his family. With a settee in the front parlour, two tall wicker chairs, a writing desk with another chair. Three small bedrooms behind. Mrs. Johnston had seen to it that all the coconut-fibre mattresses were made up with fresh linens, Mary and Amelia smiling up at the mosquito nets funneling down from the ceiling. At the rear of the house was a screened-in porch with a dining table and benches. Behind it—five steps down—a small garden with only weeds at present. Two paths cutting through to the back corners. Standing in one, the little kitchen, privy in the other.

Having shown us the house, Mr. Johnston took his leave. Reaching out to shake our hands one-by-one. And clasping his arm round father's shoulder he asked him to stop by his office in the morning. After we'd settled in proper.

He left us standing there, in the small front parlour, all our twine-tied bundles occupying the settee and chairs. Like they were our first houseguests. We watched the screen door clap shut behind Mr. Johnston. And he started up Charlotte Street again, into the falling dusk, surrounded by his little band of porters.

Papee took off his straw hat for a brief wave through the window. Then he turned round to embrace Mum, holding his hat behind her back, its navy ribbon dripping down. And in silence, one-after-the-next, slowly, the rest of us approached. First Amelia. Then Mary, Georgina, me following behind. We wrapped our arms round our parents' backs, and round each other. Still too stunned to smile. Listening to the little house creaking round us.

9

A Second Departure

Mr. Etzler and Mr. Stollmeyer refused to attend the small ceremony for Captain Taylor, held the following morning at Lapeyrouse Cemetery. Only a handful of members showed up. Though our poor attendance was due mostly to the difficulty of getting word round to the group, since we'd now scattered weself like a flock of frizzlefowls to every corner of Port-Spain. Papee and me the last two mourners to arrive. Having learnt of the funeral rites completely by chance, and only a half-hour beforehand. Walking through Brunswick Square on we way to Mr. Johnston's office, we'd happened to notice the announcement penned by Mr. Carr, plastered with laglee to the pedestal of Sir Woodford's statue.

Our little group consisted of seven men. With the addition of Mr. Bundron's young nephew, Billy Sharpe, and Mrs. Hemmingway, the sole woman present. For the occasion Mr. Carr had managed to bathe, shave, and dress heself in a suit borrowed from Mr. Hemmingway. The suit's owner, however, was substantially shorter, so the jacket-sleeves rode several inches above Mr. Carr's thin, bramble-lacerated wrists. Trousers exposing his knobby ankles above he stockingless brogues. Mr. Carr insisting upon wearing his battered straw hat—his 'West Indian wife,' as he affectionately called it—so despite all his efforts, he still looked like something of a vagrant.

The headstone wasn't finished yet. Only a bouquet of wild flowers lay on the ground at the head of the reticular hole, kiss-me-nots and cacashats picked by Mrs. Hemmingway on she way to the cemetery. The casket sitting to one side, pile of dirt at the other. Under Mr. Carr's directions we lowered the coffin into the hole by two ropes passed beneath it. Each then taking a turn to toss in a spadeful of dirt—mixed with rockstones that tumbled down in a heart-wrenching clatter onto the lid of the cheap coffin—everybody flinching together with the fall of each shovelful.

Now Mr. Carr attempted to say something by way of religious formality. Deterred not only by he own pent-up emotions, but the fact that—like everybody gathered there excepting me, due to Mum's influence—he didn't subscribe to no kinda spiritual persuasion a-tall. Except maybe socialism.

Following a lengthy and uncomfortable silence Mr. Carr managed to mumble a few words—

So long, old mate, he says.

He turned to Mrs. Hemmingway, who took him into her arms. Mr. Carr bent to press his head against her shoulder—they difference in height somehow exaggerated by the miniature suit—and he proceeded to weep like a child.

Meanwhile, two shoeless and shirtless gravediggers—sitting on a tombstone nearby, busy sucking the seeds of two mangoes—hurried over to finish filling in the hole. It took them a few minutes. Patting down the pile of dirt with the backs of they shovels, outlines of the seeds still visible behind they puffed-up cheeks.

By this time Mr. Carr had recovered heself. He centred Mrs. Hemmingway's bouquet of cacashats over the mound of dirt. Bowing his head. And he turned to lead his little band of grim mourners down the line of tombstones, in the direction of the exit.

It was my first burial.

Who should Papee and me find sitting before Mr. Johnston's desk when we arrived at his office at Brunswick Square but Mr. Whitechurch! My heart giving a skip to see him sitting there. His cane with the shining panther-handle balanced against his knee. Son, I hadn't heard a word about Marguerite, nor she aunt and uncle neither, since we'd disembarked from the *Rosalind*. Mr. Johnston and Mr. Whitechurch getting up together to greet us, everybody exchanging handshakes that turned to backslapping bear hugs, myself included.

Mr. Whitechurch was deeply distressed to learn he'd missed the rites for Captain Taylor. The very subject Mr. Johnston addressed, once we'd seated weself before his desk. He told us how shocked he'd been to read, in all the local papers, accounts of the circumstances under which Captain Taylor had lost his life. He was talking about the estate itself—Chaguabarriga. The descriptions of which he'd found worrisome indeed—

Little surprise, he says, that your men managed to get hold of it for a pong-n'-a-song!

But Mr. Johnston had decided to take matters into his own hands. He'd examined the deeds of sale for this estate, discovering a clause written in by Mr. Prescott—the gentleman responsible for selling the property, who resided on the adjoining estate. Only Englishman, far as Mr. Johnston could tell, who lived on that rather desolate stretch of the north coast.

According to this clause Mr. Prescott had guaranteed to provide food and shelter in his own home—here Mr. Johnston quoted the document from memory—*for up to a dozen members of the Tropical Emigration Society, until such time as they may become situated on their own property.*

In any case, Mr. Johnston was determined to make sure that this Mr. Prescott lived up to his promises—

Let me assure you, he says. You'll find accommodations of *some* sort in this chap's home. Together with the other men going out with Mr. Etzler. Because surely he's not ruthless enough to take along the women n' children!

Mr. Johnston went on in a similar tone. But I wasn't listing. I didn't want to hear another word: I was busy turning over in my head what he'd just finished telling us. And I assure you I wasn't liking it too good neither. Son, before that moment in Mr. Johnston's office, I'd never imagined that Papee and me might be going out to the settlement alone. Without Mum and my sisters. Had we made this lengthy journey cross the Atlantic, with such travail, only to separate weself soon as we reached the other side?

But what Mr. Johnston said made proper sense. And that wasn't all. Not by a long lag. Because now I realised something else. And the *other* thing distressed me even more than the idea of separation from my mum and sisters: now I understood that Mr. Whitechurch would most likely be going without the remainder of *his* family too. That for the time being at least, Marguerite and she aunt would remain in Port-Spain. Wherever-the-arse they happened to reside at the present moment.

Mr. Johnston went on talking, me sitting there struggling hard *not* to listen. Not to hear him. Because I'd heard enough for the time being. I'd heard enough already.

But it couldn't've been more than a few minutes. Because next thing I realised Mr. Johnston was excusing heself. Saying he regretted having to cut our meeting short—

Unfortunately, he says, I'm already late for an appointment with Governor McLeod.

Papee and Mr. Whitechurch thanked him for all the trouble he'd taken on the Society's behalf.

Nonsense, he says. I'm paid quite handsomely for such trifles!

And upon saying good-bye he offered us still another kindness. A gesture that managed to lift even my own distressed spirits a moment. Mr. Johnston extended an invitation to both our families—all the Tuckers and the Whitechurches together—to come round to Samaan's Repos one evening soon for cocktails and dinner. He'd check with Heather to find out which evening suited her, and he'd send word.

Yet my spirits plummeted just as quick with Papee's enthusiastic response—

We'll raise a glass or two to our bon voyage. Since surely by then we'll be all set to sail off with Mr. Etzler!

But after a week we still hadn't dined at Samaan's Repos. I still hadn't heard a word about Marguerite neither. Only that the Whitechurches were staying with a French family named de Boissiere, amongst the earliest and most prominent settlers on the island. They lived at the Champs Elysées Estate, in a place called Maraval Valley. Located, far as I could tell, a good distance outside town.

For the whole of that exhausting week Papee and me, together with a half-dozen other men, spent our days struggling to refloat the submerged Satellite. Captain Damphier arguing from the start that the barge onto which he'd been ordered to off-load the two-ton crate was inadequate to keep it afloat. Captain Maynard—who'd chartered the barge on Etzler's orders—saying the same thing. Yet Mr. Etzler had insisted that his numbers proved a barge of those dimensions, with that specific buoyancy-coefficient, was adequate to transport *three* of he Satellites.

After securing the crate to the gunwales of the undersized barge, Captain Maynard had the good sense to tow it behind the *Miss Bee* to the eastern corner of the bay. Just to the west of the bocas of St. Anns River. A spot where the current deposited a substantial mound of mud and sediment. And in this shallow place, fifty yards from shore, he'd left the barge anchored overnight. Till he received further instructions.

By the following morning both barge and Satellite had sunk to the marshy bottom. With the upper few feet of the crate still visible above the ripples, waterline at high tide neatly bisecting the word ~~SATELLITE~~ cross its middle.

Our group of rescuers consisted of the same men who'd shown up for the captain's burial (excepting Mr. Carr, who'd returned to Chaguabarriga alone). Every morning we gathered at Park Street, in the home Mr. Etzler had rented for heself and he wife, cross the street from the Stollmeyers' residence. And every morning Mr. Etzler presented us with some new strategy he'd thought up overnight to accomplish the task. As though Mr. Etzler *enjoyed* the challenge this predicament had landed atop he head. For which, it goes without saying, he heaped all the blame on Captain Maynard and Captain Damphier. And the more frustrated we became in we various attempts to refloat the sunken machine—reporting back to Mr. Etzler at meetings held in his parlour each evening—the greater became our leader's enthusiasm. The more outlandish his instructions.

Son, from the first moment Mr. Etzler and Mr. Stollmeyer had set foot in Port-Spain, they'd launched a veritable blitzkrieg on the island's wealthy populace. Attempting to win them over to the cause of the TES and TTC, in addition to they railroad company. And yet—far as any of us knew—not a once during that week did either gentleman make the five-minute walk down to the wharf to take a look at the half-sunk Satellite for theyself.

It was Captain Maynard who eventually devised a sensible strategy. He moored the *Miss Bee* parallel to the sunken barge, and utilising a wench-and-pulley rigged through the boom of his mainsail, he hoisted the unfastened Satellite off the bottom. Now we watched it rising slowly into the air, deluge of rust-red water sifting out though the cracks between the boards. A thick cloud forming in the water round us, like a softly breathing patch of tomato soup.

Captain Maynard then set the crate down on another barge, this one adequate to float the load. And utilising his pulleys and hand-wench—secured this time to a furry casuarina standing on the shore itself—the sunken barge was dragged at high water as far up onto the bank as possible. When the tide receded we bailed it out and floated it easy enough.

Whilst all of this strenuous Satellite-rescuing activity was taking place, several hostile arguments erupted between Mr. Etzler and his most disgruntled members. These pioneers demanding that he lay down straightway for they return voyage to England. Meanwhile they insisted that he pay for all they food and lodging *for however long we remain shipwrecked up this stinking arsehole of Port-Spain!* All they pleas, to be sure, falling on deaf ears. Mr. Etzler refusing even to grant them an audience. And only after busting down the door of he house on Park Street—at knifepoint, according to rumor—were they able to talk to him a-tall.

A handful of these same members had taken up residence at Le Palais Cramoisi, the most luxurious boardinghouse in town, located on Kings Street. There they treated theyself to lavish meals and drink, all on Mr. Etzler's chit. Of course, when payment was not forthcoming they were promptly tossed out into the street. One member, a fancy gardener named Mr. Bisbeal—after three days of drunken, riotous behaviour—arrested and thrown in prison. He then demanded that Mr. Etzler pay all he fines and bail. Mr. Etzler informing the police constable that never before in his life had he heard of any such *Monsieur Imbécile.*

Hardly had the TES arrived in Trinidad a week when three other prominent members—Mr. Cooper, Mr. Perry, and Mr. Whidden—announced they were severing all ties with Etzler's Society. Not-for-nothing would they consider going out to that mosquito-infested morass at Chaguabarriga *only to drink swampwater and eat iguana-stew!* Mr. Whidden, a trained chemist, set sail with his wife and children on a ship bound for New Orleans. Despite Mr. Etzler's efforts to confiscate they luggage and have the family arrested before they went aboard.

But Mr. Perry and Mr. Cooper had no intention of leaving Port-Spain. They found lucrative employment in town. Mr. Cooper engaging heself to a local firm as a professional *cooper* (according to Mr. Etzler the first occupation to pop into his tiny brain). Mr. Perry, on the other hand—though he'd contracted heself to the TES as a blacksmith—found employment at an engineering firm. According to his own boasts, at a salary of eighteen dollars a week, plus a horse to ride upon. At this news in particular Mr. Etzler fumed. He vowed that before it was too late he'd force Perry to refund the Society every farthing for his passage out—

If zis nincompoop is an engineer, he grumbled, zen I am a zebra! Unt whatever salary zey *do* pay him is zat much huv our own money srown away on concupines unt rum!

In addition to Mr. Etzler and Mr. Stollmeyer, the group who'd signed up to go to Chaguabarriga consisted of eleven men. There were also three women and five children, including Mr. Bundron's nephew, Billy Sharpe. Because for these women and children the option of remaining behind in Port-Spain did not exist. By this time they were all but penniless.

Concerning our impending departure I could find only three minor consolations: that the pioneers would have a proper roof over we heads, and proper food, thanks to the intervention of Mr. Johnston; that our departure had been postponed five additional days, so we could spend Christmas with friends and families in Port-Spain; finally—and most important of all so far as *I* was concerned—that our much-delayed invitation to dine at Samaan's Repos, all the Tuckers and Whitechurches together, had been changed to a Christmas dinner. In addition to we bon voyage.

At last, after waiting almost three weeks, I'd be reunited with Marguerite. If only for a single night.

Much to everybody's surprise Mr. Etzler and Mr. Stollmeyer readily agreed to the five-day delay. Without a word of protest. There was even some talk of postponing our departure further—till after Old Year's night—but few in the group could restrain they excitement to get to Chaguabarriga for so long.

Until such time as our group would be ready to depart the Tucker clan had taken in Mr. and Mrs. Wood, together with they three young daughters. If not they'd've been forced to live in the street. Mary and Amelia hardly able to contain they disappointment at having to give up they new beds, together with the magic of the mosquito nets—for the time being they spread blankets on the floor in the parlour, whilst the entire Wood clan occupied they room. And in any case Mary and Amelia were so excited to return to school after two years' absence—they'd been accepted into St. Joseph's Convent, the Catholic girls' school—that they scarcely said a word. Georgina, who'd been enterprising enough to find employment at a bookseller, had the smallest bedroom of the Tucker home all to sheself. Of course, from that first evening we'd arrived at the little house, Papee and I had shifted aside the dining table on the back porch. We'd strung up a hammock for me to sleep in for the time being. Till we'd be ready to go.

The final decision, agreed to by general vote at a meeting held in Mr. Etzler's parlour, was to set sail early on the morning of Boxing Day.

5/11/10

dear mr robot:

i only got 1 ting to tell u, so LISTEN GOOD: u best haul u tail
& go back home to new york or wherever is de francin place in
amerika u comes from, cause u say u cant take it no more, u goin
mad, all u want 2 do is copy out a few copies 2 make u research
4 dis book u say u writing bout dis crazyass man ETZLER, but u
cant do it, u just cant do it, u done try everyting & every scheme
is scheme u could tink of & plenty bullying & more bullying &
noting work, noting a-tall, 3 months now u trying & STILL no
photocopies, & u say how dis place t'dad is de turd-world & we
is all backwards living here dat we dont know noting bout noting a-tall, but i could only tell u DIS mr robot: TENEGRITY &
IMPETUOSITY is what we got aplenty here in t'dad dat u never
bounce up de likes of noting like DAT before in amerika, cause
rules is rules & laws is laws & when i say NO photocopies allow
inside de t&t national archive i means NONE, no matter who u
is & what tuti u jooking even if it is de director MISS RAMSOL
OWN, & if u cant write out u notes wid pencil & paper like everybody else den 2 francin bad 4 u mr robot!!!

& i could tell u someting else: i got a good mind to tell my brothers how u do, cause if raj and lil buddha only FIND OUT would
be proper hell to pay, i could tell u dat mr robot, how u did try &
subjuice me only to gain access to dis machine, & how u succeed
sure enough but ONLY in de subjuicing part, & not de photocopies part a-tall a-tall, & soon enough 2 of we was jooking
down de place like no tomorrow & i could only admit how much
i was loving it 2, but den mr robot U FIND OUT sure enough

how SWEET is trini-east-indian-tuti-in-trut, & nex ting U CANT
GET ENOUGH NEITHER, same as me, & u say 1 ting 4 sure
dey aint got NOTING like DAT in amerika, dat east-indian-t'dad-
tuti-ting, & soon as we start to jooking down de place like dat u
forget every scheme u was scheming & bullying u was bullying
to try to get u hands pon dis xerox machine, & all u want is jook
jook & nex jook again every night 2 of we shouting down de place
like wild pusscats, & nex ting like u forget everyting else, book-writ-
ing & ETZLER & all de rest, & only jook is jook u want to be
jooking so sweet every night same as me, but now u say u done
had enough, u OVERSATURATE & cant take it no more, & if u
cant copy out u copies u give up and goin back home 2 amerika,
& i say in trut mr robot dat would be very sad 4 me & i got a
good mind 2 tell my brothers lil buddah and raj how u do

cordial,
miss ramsol
director, t&tna

ps u say u dont want to see me never again (less u could make u
copies) but if u change u mind u could meet me at pelo round 9
same as usual

pss & i would make sure 2 be wearing dem dental-floss panties u
love & LOOK how many articles i have waiting 4 u at de frontdesk

CAPTAIN'S DEATH LINKED TO INSALUBRIOUS ESTATE PROPERTY

Trinidad Guardian, 4 December 1845

The *Guardian* reported yesterday on the death of Captain John Taylor. As has now been revealed the captain arrived in our colony three months ago as an agent of the Tropical Emigration Society, under the auspices of Mr. J.A. Etzler. The exact cause of death, as provided by Mr. Etzler himself, was 'the direct result of drinking three coconut waters, whilst in a state of extreme agitation and exhaustion.' This had occurred several hours earlier at Chaguabarriga Estate, located on our north coast, where the captain was stationed. Together with his fellow agent and companion, Mr. Carr, and a handful of peons, the two men had undertaken the strenuous labours of clearing several acres of brushwood, and attempting to drain off the pestilential waters from a low-lying section of the estate, working daily beneath the sun for twelve hours at a stretch. This work they had persisted in for nearly a fortnight. To quench his thirst the captain drank continuously of the only water available on the estate, that taken from the swamp itself, and the aforementioned coconuts. For his sustenance, rather than adhering to a strict vegetable diet, as did Mr. Carr, the captain prided himself in

partaking of animal food cooked by the peons, principally grilled iguana and stews of the indigenous bush rat known as aguti.

Following his grueling work sessions Captain Taylor insisted upon retiring to the rotted-out hulk of a schooner washed up onto the beach, and in this entirely unventilated place, he sought shelter. Mr. Carr made his own camp beneath a tarp nearby. It was apparently so hot inside the schooner by the end of a day's baking that the captain was able to brew his ginger tea without resort to a fire. For the previous several days he had suffered from nightly bouts of fever. Mr. Carr would discover him sequestered in his secret abode, huddled under an old blanket, shivering, his skin stone-cold to the touch despite the oppressive heat. For these conditions Mr. Carr attempted to treat his companion from his box of homeopathic pills, the captain insisting solely upon his seaman's remedies. According to Mr. Etzler, 'Aught other than a jigger or three of the devil's own strong rum. Of this fine medicine he treated himself in ample avail!' Mr. Etzler concluded the interview in saying: 'Clearly the captain's death can be blamed on none other than himself. For after such selfish, intemperate, and irresponsible behaviour, it's a great wonder the foolish old billy goat lasted as long as he did!'

For the greater part of his life Captain Taylor had commandeered every manner of vessel sailing between London and the South Pacific. He was renowned amongst his fellow seamen as an officer of utmost capacity and experience. This was his first visit to the West Indies. The captain died at age 72, and he is survived by a wife and nine children, all residing in the Eastcheap district of London.

DEATH OF CAPTAIN TAYLOR

POS Gazette, 3 December 1845

Chief of Police Derek Adderly boarded the newly arrived *Rosalind* early this morning so as to investigate the death of Captain Taylor, who had apparently arrived to this island several months ago, and had gone aboard late last night. The *Gazette* interviewed Captain Damphier, commander of the *Rosalind*: 'Captain Taylor came aboard my vessel at some point during the wee hours, without my knowledge or consent.' Indeed, Captain Damphier was only made aware of his presence aboard at approximately 3 AM when—in response to a cry of alarm sounded by one of his sailors—he rushed from his cabin to the aft-deck. There he discovered two of his passengers, Mr. Etzler and Mr. Stollmeyer, in the final stages of their attempt to dispose of Captain Taylor's body in the waters of the bay. They had tied him up in a large canvas sack which, curiously enough, they intended to weigh down with a valuable teapot and a large tureen of solid silver.

Captain Damphier made swift work of arresting the two men, and of confiscating the aforementioned articles of silver. He held Mr. Etzler and Mr. Stollmeyer shackled wrist-to-wrist around his mainmast, until early this morning when he sent for the chief of police. The *Rosalind*, however, was officially *still at sea* (the ship hadn't been cleared, her landing papers remaining unfiled), in which case Constable Adderly, as he informed Captain Damphier directly upon arrival, held no jurisdiction.

Nonetheless Captain Damphier and the police chief interviewed a number of passengers, including Mr. Tucker, who vouchsafed that Captain Taylor had died before his eyes of natural causes. Written statements to this effect were taken down. Captain Damphier was admittedly pleased as punch to brush his hands of the entire sordid affair. He was anxious to proceed with the details of clearing his ship and seeing his passengers safely ashore. Indeed, he was just preparing to do so when five other passengers stepped forward: two presented Captain Damphier with receipts of purchase—officially signed and stamped by Mr. Etzler—for the silver teapot, and the three others for the valuable tureen. These five passengers claimed to have paid for the articles in full, but had yet to collect from Mr. Etzler, and now *all* riotously claimed ownership.

THE TRINIDAD GREAT EASTERN AND SOUTH-WESTERN RAILWAY, WITH A BRANCH TO THE HARBOUR OF PORT-SPAIN

INITIAL DEPOSIT £50 PER SHARE
PROVISIONAL COMMITTEE:
GENERAL DIRECTOR & CONSULTING ENGINEER,
J.A. Etzler, Esq.
ASSOCIATE DIRECTOR & SECRETARY,
C.F. Stollmeyer, Esq.
BANKERS,
COMMERCIAL BANK OF LONDON,
OFFICES OF THE COMPANY: *No. 29 Strand*

THE ISLAND OF TRINIDAD, renowned for its fertility, the richness of its productions, salubrity and elasticity of its luxuriant climate, is about to partake of the prodigious advantages of Railway Communication, which all of its agricultural, commercial, and maritime circumstances so admirably demand.

A most enterprising Company in London under the above Title offers to construct, entirely at its own expense, a Railway through localities judiciously selected for their proximity to Ports, Towns, and Cultivated Estates, presenting neither engineering difficulties nor entailing any serious outlay of Capital. There is little doubt but that the proposed Line will be enthusiastically embraced by the public—both in Trinidad and here in Britain—inasmuch as it embraces features of a super-eminent practical utility. Of which the following details wholly exemplify: —

The Railway shall commence at the harbour of Port-Spain, the capital of the island on the North-Western coast, running through various towns and districts to Arima in the East, thence to San Fernando in the South. The island of Trinidad contains 2,400 square miles, or 1,536,000 square acres, affording great scope for the introduction of Railway Communication to this Richest and Most Fertile of all West Indian Colonies.

It is the intention of the Company to provide for the colonists the increased advantages of the Wooden Railway, which has been so thoroughly tested by our esteemed engineers in the neighbourhood of London. And which, in point of economy, comfort, durability, rapidity, and safety, must be apparent to any person who has given the subject consideration. More especially so in Trinidad, where timber in inexhaustible quantities—adopted not only for our Rails, but other purposes as well—may be obtained at trifling or no expense whatever.

The important question connected with this subject, however, is the durability of the material of which our Rails shall be composed. Beech Wood has been chosen in England, but Trinidad presents ever-exclusive advantages, since many other kinds of Woods are met there harder than Iron, and in the tropical climate far more durable.

Indeed, Gentlemen of esteemed engineering talents have painstakingly studied, analysed, and established that with engines properly constructed, Wooden Railroads possess advantages superiour to Iron in four essential points: they are 1. cheaper, 2. more durable, 3. far more comfortable, 4. altogether much safer. Now, as to the first consideratum alone, it should be seen that the difference in price between the proposed materials, Iron and Wood (notwithstanding freight), will be so great that the Wooden Rails utilised by our Company forms a desideratum of unrivaled significance.

On this point and all others the opinions of our eminent engineers, Messrs. Etzler and Stollmeyer, may be consulted at the Office. These experienced Gentlemen will soon depart for Trinidad, whereupon landing they will make an immediate survey of the intended Lines, of which it is already known with greatest assurity that they present no engineering difficulties whatsoever. From a commercial point-of-view, the island of Trinidad will soon become to the Americas what England is to Europe, and therefore ultimately THE WORLD'S GREATEST MARKET for the interchange of the most valuable productions of the East and West. The enormous fecundity of its soil, its gigantic and magnificent vegetation, its rich plantations and highly elastic atmosphere, here combine to crown Trinidad THE WEST INDIAN PARADISE. Her resources are in fact inexhaustible, the annals of no other place on earth presenting such an extraordinary increase of Cultivation, and consequent production of exploitable WEALTH.

To wit, an arrangement has already been made with the Tropical Emigration Society here in London, consisting chiefly of highly experienced English Artisans and Labourers, soon to depart for Trinidad as well, in consequence of which the Company will render available the services of said Members of the Society for the construction of our Railway GRATIS, without the expenditure of a single penny! So that no, or at most very few, African or native Laborers will need be hired away from the cultivation of the Sugar Estates, and so deplete our resources.

FORM OF APPLICATION FOR SHARES

To the Provisional Committee of the
Trinidad Great Eastern and South-Western Railway:

Gentlemen, — I request you will allot me _____ Shares of £50 each in the above Co., and I hereby undertake to accept the same, or any less number you may allot me, and to pay the Deposit of £1 per Share thereon, and to sign all necessary Deeds when required.
Dated this day of 1845.

Your name in full_____

10

Chaguabarriga

As we approached the wharf it became more and more obvious—the closer Marguerite and me drew—that the small band of people waiting there were distressed about something. It was obvious from the looks on all they faces. From the women's languished gestures. The men's muffled curses. Of course, I could only assume that this something—the *source* of our group's collective concern—was none other than me and Marguerite. How could it be otherwise? Not only had we disappeared since the early hours of the previous evening, it was a scandalous matter for the two of us to be associated a-tall—under any but the most innocent circumstances—none one of which occurred to me at that particular moment: a boy of fifteen and an eighteen-year-old woman. And even more significant than this was we differing class rank. They had a right to be scandalised too. So exquisite was the night we'd spent together, sheltered only by the big-leafed bozee majo trees of the forest. But son, I'm not yet ready to tell you about it. Not as yet. That single night we'd spent together since our arrival in Port-Spain, finally, after our long wait. You just going to have to hang on a little bit for that one.

Our overnight disappearance also explained Papee's absence amongst the group. Since no doubt he was out searching for us right now—perhaps with Mr. Johnston as well?—because I couldn't find him there amongst the farewellers neither. Mr. Johnston promising at our Christmas dinner he'd be here bright-and-early this morning to see us off. Both men probably occupied at this very moment trudging through the woods behind Samaan's Repos, scouting the hillside below the Observatory, foraging the banks of St. Anns River. Shouting out our names. Searching for Marguerite and me.

Much to my own surprise nobody seemed especially relieved—nor newly outraged neither—as we stepped arm-in-arm past the wrought-iron gates at the entrance to the wharf. As I escorted Marguerite cross the jetty towards the members of our families. Nobody even seemed to take notice. Only young Amelia gave us a brief wave as we walked up—she smiled suspicious—the only one remotely interested in our shocking interlude. Marguerite bending for Mrs. Whitechurch to give her a distracted-looking good-morning kiss on the cheek. As though she aunt was so consumed by other, more significant matters, that our tardy arrival on the jetty, our scandalous overnight disappearance, hardly amounted to nothing a-tall.

Mrs. Whitechurch turned from her niece, pointing her chin up at me—

Well, isn't *this* lad the early rooster? she says.

And that was the extent of the reception they gave us that morning.

Only after listening to the agitated voices round us a few more minutes could we begin to decipher the cause of the morning's calamity. It seemed that the two individuals who'd not shown up on the dock, and had kept the rest of us from setting sail—the two conspicuously absent members of our group who had the others so distressfully up-in-arms—were none other than our two leaders: Mr. Etzler and Mr. Stollmeyer.

Now we began to wonder, along with everybody else, where could these two possibly be.

Eventually Papee and Mr. Johnston were pointed out in the distance. Wading through the waves of heat rising at the farthest corner of Marine Square. Hurrying towards the wharf.

Our group assembled anxious before them, both men red-faced and in a sweat. Papee raising up his two hands asking for quiet. In one he clutched a piece of paper that looked like some kinda official document—a summons from the chief of police?—the word WARNING stamped conspicuous cross the top. Clearly visible through the page in large inverted capitals.

Papee announced, in a loud voice, that they'd just returned from Mr. Etzler and Mr. Stollmeyer's residences on Park Street. Where urgent enquiries had been made.

He paused, slowing down his speech some—

According to what we've learnt from Mrs. Stollmeyer, he says, her husband set off at the crack of dawn this morning. Pushing a wheelbarrow in the direction of the La Brea pitchlake. In the far south of the island, some twenty miles from here.

He paused again—

As I understand it, Mr. Stollmeyer has gone to this remote location on official business of the TTC. Since he's about to construct the first of his Floating Islands, and intends to coat its bamboo hull with pitch taken from the lake.

A number of uneasy murmurs arose from the crowd.

Papee continued—

On the other hand, it seems that our Mr. Etzler has set off for a far more *distant* destination.

Here Papee was compelled to raise up his hands again, paper flapping in the breeze, begging for quiet—

It seems that Mr. Etzler has departed on a ship bound for South America. For the city of Caracas, in the country of Venezuela.

Papee waited a few beats for us to swallow this down—

According to *his* wife, Mr. Etzler set sail three days before Christmas. Unbeknownst to any of us. His objective, apparently, to petition from the Venezuelan government a parcel of freehold land. This property—according to what Mrs. Etzler has just informed me—to constitute the Society's *Main Grant*. Whatever Mr. Etzler means by such a term, because his wife couldn't tell me.

Papee halted a few more beats. He shifted to a tone that sounded, at one and the same time, subdued yet still more incredulous—

What I mean to tell you is that *neither* of these gentlemen *ever* intended to accompany us to Chaguabarriga a-tall. Indeed, for quite some time, both have had very different itineraries. Whether-or-not such travel plans were devised in secret—deceptively—I cannot rightly say.

With the uproar that followed our group seemed to lose sight of that conspicuous, official-looking document still clutching in Papee's hand. That is, till Mr. Whitechurch, standing towards the rear, questioned him about it—

And what of that notice you've got there, William? he asks.

Papee turned towards him—

This? he says. Raising up the paper as if he'd forgotten it heself. Inverted WARNING flashing at us anew from the top of the page—

This document was given to me by Mrs. Etzler, as instructed by her husband, prior to his departure.

Papee looked down, studying the page—

Evidently it's a letter written by a certain A.L. Gomez. Whom I take is a local attorney representing Mr. Etzler. In any case, the letter is addressed to *us*—that is, to the members newly disembarked in Trinidad. It says something to the effect . . .

Here Papee cleared his throat, reading from the paper itself—

. . . that any and all attempts to remove, transport, or convey said Satellite from the immediate environs of the township of Port-Spain, without express written consent from its rightful owner, J.A. Etzler, who remains in full possession of all pertinent patents and licences, &c., &c.—shall hereby constitute an unmitigated act of larceny punishable to the fullest extent of all binding British, Spanish, and Maritime laws.

Again a pronounced protest. Again it was little Mr. Whitechurch, perched on toetips to peer over the members gathered in front, who interrupted the clamour. He asked for permission to examine the letter heself. Papee handing it over to the woman standing before him, with a little train of passes till the document arrived at Mr. Whitechurch.

We all turned anxious towards him. Watching Mr. Whitechurch remove from his vestcoat pocket a crystal monocle attached to a goldchain, fix it in place, and squint down through his single bloated fisheye at the letter.

A minute later he looked up, giving us an oversized fisheye-blink through the monocle. After which we watched the lens drop from out his eye, dangling on its long chain. Swinging back-and-forth and flashing beneath the sun.

Mr. Whitechurch raised up the document in both hands, high above his head. Holding it there suspended a moment before us. He ripped it in two; then he ripped these two pieces again in two; and two again.

With a little celebratory flourish he tossed the eight fragments into the air. High above his head. As we watched the breeze carry away the pieces of paper like a distant flock of gulls. Out over the sparkling waters of the bay.

Son, despite my tardy arrival I was first to board the transport. Since I needed to take advantage of its small cabin to change my outfit, still wearing my fancified clothes from our Christmas bon voyage the previous night. I scrambled to dress myself in my tropical costume. Reaching up the disheveled bundle to Mum just as the ferry pulled-way. Standing there on the wharf with my three sisters, Mr. Johnston & Mrs. Whitechurch & Marguerite. All with they hands raised high above they heads, cheering, waving good-bye.

Captain Maynard wasting little time off-loading our luggage onto the deck of the *Miss Bee*. The vessel awaiting us anchored out in the bay—barge bearing its colossal crate floating off her stern, now with a two-week-old mossline bisecting the ~~SAT-ELLITE~~ cross its middle. To make up for our tardy departure, added to the considerable disadvantage of having to tow the heavy-laden barge, Captain Maynard set sail as soon as he bos'n could haul in the anchor. And before long we were hurtling past those towering cliffs, leaving behind us the larger, more recognisable bays.

We soon arrived at a stretch near the middle of the north coast that became suddenly indistinct. Mangrove-fringed. The water shallowing and growing calmer, shifting to those lighter tones of sandy greens. The bays and coves smaller, still more numerous—tiny inlets caught between stone clumps and patches of gnarly mangrove. The most challenging part of our journey being the pinpointing of Chaguabarriga itself.

Each time we sailed past a stretch of sandy beach, to the delight of the children, Captain Maynard raised a faded pink conch up to his lips. Blowing into the crown through bulbous cheeks.

Eventually, as the *Miss Bee* glided past still another patch of gray sand, and the captain sounded his conch, a tiny white flag appeared in the distance. Fluttering-way. Beckoning to us over the brilliant green mass of mangrove. Just at the base of the jagged mountains.

All-in-a-sudden Captain Maynard turned his sloop about, tacking back a short distance. He tacked again—and letting loose his mainsail and jib in the same breath, the captain eased his vessel into the shallow, crystal water of a tranquil bay. Two hundred yards from shore he turned about a last time, up into the wind, bowsprit pointing straight out to sea. Bringing the *Miss Bee* and her charge behind to a swift and simultaneous halt. Sails loudly aruffle. His bos'n reaching out over the bowsprit to toss in the anchor.

Moments later a small rowboat appeared, seeming to coalesce from out the bright clumps of mangrove theyself. East of the little beach. It came rowing steady in our direction. And moments later we made out the man working the oars, his battered 'West Indian wife' perched as ever atop his head—he was our own Mr. Carr!

There was, of course, insufficient daylight remaining for Captain Maynard to transfer us to the Prescott Estate. Located on another of these sandy coves a couple miles up the coast. And in any case the pioneers had already sounded out our demand—in a single voice—to be taken ashore immediately. So anxious were we to set foot on our own property. We'd come too far, and were far too excited, to wait till morning—devil-be-damned where we slept the night!

Mr. Carr much taken aback to learn that for the time being, rather than remaining with him there at the settlement, we'd reside at the Prescott Estate. Nonetheless, Mr. Carr had to admit—brushing aside his personal feelings for that unsavoury gentleman—that the plan for us to stay beneath Mr. Prescott's roof for the present time seemed sensible enough. In particular the women and children. Yet it disheartened him to think some of us wouldn't wish to remain with him at Chaguabarriga—

A handful of the men at least? he says. A wee little show of camaraderie?

At which point Mr. Whitechurch, rucksack perched already atop his back, spoke out bold for the rest of us—

Nonsense! he says. We're all anxious to go ashore and see what you've been up to. So let's shake a leg, shall we?

Indeed! Mr. Carr answers, all but beaming.

Within minutes he set off with the first boatload, including Papee and me. He rowed us over to the small beach, landing us atop a raised stone pathway at the centre of the patch of sand. Like a natural jetty, formed on purpose by Mother Nature for our own convenience. And whilst Mr. Carr returned for his second load, we wandered off towards the hulk of a bark washed up onto shore. So camouflaged by creepers we hadn't seen it from out on the bay—Captain Tailor's schooner, as the Port-Spain newspapers had christened it.*

But Papee and me soon left the others to take a short walk up the beach. The tide fully in, so before long we found weself picking our way amongst the rugged boulderstones. The gnarly trunks of dried-out driftwood weathered to a stark white. Forging our way along—our boots already wet and caked in sand— till the thicker mangroves cut us off.

Papee stopped beside a tall boulderstone, caught between a couple mangrove clumps. Its underside encrusted with sharp barnacles, alive with a swarm of scrambling crabs. Now he re-

---

* Referred to throughout by the pioneers as 'Captain Taylor's schooner,' the name of this beached vessel, painted on the stern plate and still discernable (it is listed among the property's *accoutrements* in the original purchase deed), was the *Miss Ellen*.

moved his pocketknife, opening it out. Papee used the blade to pry off a piece of the rock, crushing the sample in his fist. Watching the fragments fall to the sand before his boots—

Roman cement stone, he says. Same as I remember from the Isle of Sheppey.

Papee wiped his hand against his trousers. Then he wiped the blade, folding it closed and putting it away. He turned to climb up atop the boulder itself, eight-to-ten-feet above the beach, me following a step behind. And together we surveyed the bay from this vantage point, gazing out over the sparkling water.

Mr. Carr had just landed his third load. The pioneers stepping anxious from out of his rowboat, onto the stone jetty. I glanced back over my shoulder, watching Papee remove from his breast pocket a stub of pencil and a small notebook, spined along the side.

I saw him print the word *CHAGUABARRIGA* in hard capitals cross the cover. Then he opened out his booklet to the first page, sketching a quick map—

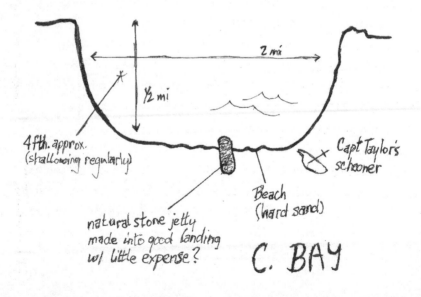

When we got back to the beach Mr. Carr was landing his final boatload. Then, without explanation, he set off rowing again. Disappearing mysteriously behind the clump of mangroves to our right. But only a few minutes later we heard Mr. Carr's excited voice behind us. Turning together to see him hurrying through the line of sea oats at the top of the beach, waving his West Indian wife. His trousers soaked up to his knees, boots caked in black mud—

I've moored our dinghy in the lake, he says, out of breath. Now let me show you round our handsome little estate!

Mr. Carr turned, leading us along a sandy path that wound through the sea oats, his wet boots sloshing up in front. Soon we entered a grove of graceful casuarinas, breeze whistling through they needles high above. The path veering left, changing from loose sand to hardened dirt, then softish mud. And we arrived alongside the lake Mr. Carr had mentioned a moment ago—his rowboat moored a dozen yards off the shore, tied to a mangrove branch.

But son, this wasn't the picturesque *lake* we'd all envisioned. Not by a steups. This was a morass—its bottom a thick, black, ugly ooze—and when the breeze shifted in our direction we got a whiff of its sulfurous stench.

The children pinched they nostrils. Adults surveying the scene with expressions of horror.

Mr. Carr explained how the lake formed a perfect natural anchorage, safe in all weather, even *huracanos!* He had plans to dig it out deeper—important for health reasons, he explained—and the mud removed from the bottom could be used to fill another low-lying area to the other side of our compound. Which, Mr. Carr informed us, presented a rather serious risk of flooding at high water—

One of the minor inconveniences of living in paradise, he says. That bloody swamp has flooded up on me a couple of times already!

Unaware of the gasps coming from the women and children—not to exclude a couple of the men—Mr. Carr continued smiling. Pleased as punch with heself. He removed a handkerchief from his back pocket—the rag so soiled it was almost as black as his boots—proceeding to swab his perspiring face and neck. Neither of which appeared a good deal cleaner than the rag.

He turned round, pointing ahead, filthy kerchief dangling from his hand—

Our handsome little compound's but a few steps away!

Mr. Carr led us farther along the path, rising beneath our boots, changing from mud to hard-packed dirt again. Passing through another pleasant grove of widely spaced trees—sea grapes & almonds & spindly coconut palms—the ground covered over by a thick padding of leaves.

A moment later we found weself standing at the edge of a circular clearing. A hundred yards in diameter. With a tall bamboo pole set at the centre and highest point, tattered white strip fluttering at the end. And now we identified the little flag we'd seen earlier from out at sea, appearing at the sound of Captain Maynard's conch. A few yards behind it we observed a dead cookfire, with an enormous cast-iron pot suspended above it from a tripod of bamboo poles. Nearby the pot a long table—seemingly built from planks of salvaged wood—sawed-off logs at both sides for benches. The table itself tucked under a widespread almond tree. But what attracted our attention most was a number of small crocus sacks hanging from the tree's outstretched limbs—foodstuff suspended from the reach of crabs

213 ⋈ Robert Antoni

and wild animals, though of course we couldn't have known this yet—like a madman's version of a Christmas tree.

Mr. Carr pointed his rag in the direction of the table—

Our kitchen n' dining facility! he says.

Off to its far side we now observed a rather puzzling structure. Three parallel lines of bamboo poles—six-feet tall and spaced about the same apart—sunk into the ground. At the end of this structure was a series of bamboo cross-braces, tied with vines to the tops of the poles, above them a covering of palm fronds. Crudely thatched together. Son, it looked like a goat's pen, lacking only the picket fence round the perimeter. Except for the fact that two hammocks—obviously intended for humans to sleep in—were slung under the piece of thatch at the end.

Mr. Carr confirming for us what we'd already begun to fear—

Our humble little cottage!

And even before we had a chance to swallow this down—with a surge of fright rising inside our stomachs as we took them in—three men appeared. Running from out the bush behind the cottage. Charging straight at us.

On seeing them Mrs. Hemmingway turned to bolt in the opposite direction, held back only by she husband.

These three men barefoot, they legs coated to the knees in black mud. Stark naked saving what looked to us like crude loincloths. Tied round they waists with pieces of rope. One of the men tall, thin, ebony-black. The other two short & squat & brightly redskinned—they oval faces with fringes of coarse hair cut straight cross they foreheads. With these latter two, as they charged towards us, shouldering a bamboo pole from which hung a large animal of unknown identity, its hide covered over in orange bristles. Fierce fangs protruding from its pointed snout, thumping mercilessly cross the ground. With a number of long spikes—presumably arrows—projecting at various angles out its sides.

The three men came to a halt before us, they chests breathing in-and-out. Whilst Mr. Carr, still smiling, placed his arm affectionately round the black man's shoulders—

Let me introduce to you my three helpmates, he says. This is John. And these two other gentlemen are Esteban n' Orinoko.

He nodded to the two men shouldering the animal—

They've all three been busy working like troopers. Alongside me and our unfortunate Captain Taylor!

Now the three men smiled on cue. The two Amerindians turning they eyes timid to the ground.

Finally Mr. Carr gestured with his filthy rag at the suspended animal—

And what have we here? Seems you lads've been busy hunting us up some supper!

It was the black man, John, who answered—

Qwenk, sir. Wild pork. Cause Rinoko n' Steban go cook he up in a nice stew!

And with that Mrs. Hemmingway—with a solid *thud*—dropped to the ground in a faint.

11
Pepperpot

After Mrs. Hemmingway had been revived, and Mr. Carr had given her a drink of water, it was decided that the women and children should sleep the night aboard the *Miss Bee*. Captain Maynard had earlier offered them use of his own cabin—in addition to the other guest cabin—saying he'd be happy enough sleeping in a hammock on deck beside his bos'n. Now we decided that the women and children should take they evening meal aboard the *Miss Bee* as well, from stores brought with us from Port-Spain, still to be unloaded. Indeed, everything seemed to be settled amicable enough. That is, till Mrs. Wood requested that she husband accompany her and they three daughters for the night. Now a fierce argument rose up from Mr. Spenser and Mr. Hemmingway. Demanding that they be allowed to accompany they own wives too. At which point young Billy Sharpe, almost in tears, announced he felt the onslaught of a stiff *meegraine*. He required his medicines that remained aboard ship.

Following a heated discussion—including several rather nasty threats—a much-embarrassed Mr. Carr announced that he was willing to transport *only* the women and children, in addition to young Billy, back to the *Miss Bee*. The other gentlemen, he said—in manly fashion, and without further complaint—would sleep with the rest of us right here in the compound.

Mr. Carr set off rowing his loaded-up dinghy again. In the meantime John took the men out to inspect the gardens, whilst Orinoko and Esteban dedicated theyself to slaughtering the quenk.

John led us along a path that continued at the back of the compound. Passing through another pleasant grove of sea grapes and spindly coconut palms, reaching they ragged heads up above the canopy into patches of bright sun. The ground turning rocky, vegetation sparse, interspersed with clumps of crabgrass growing along the declivities. We gazed up at the forested mountains looming before us, about a half-mile ahead. Seeming to rise straight up out of the flat ground. It was this bramble-covered strip of flatland, running roughly east-west at the base of the mountains, that had been cleared to plant the gardens.

They occupied four to five acres at present. The rocks taken out piled in neat low walls, separating the various plots. Towards the rear, in a long mound, we saw the jumble of gnarled brushwood uprooted in clearing the ground. Drying, waiting to be torched.

Obvious—even at first glance—that these gardens had been laid out by a most meticulous hand. Each plot a perfect rectangle of red or brown or ochre-coloured earth, varying in size, each demarcated by its low stonewalls. With the newly planted seedlings spaced at equal intervals, none as yet taller than a few inches. Neatly printed signs, indicating a variety of sweet peas, stood at the heads of this first group of smaller, more compact plots— *SNOW PEAS, BROAD BEANS, FRENCH LEGUMES, COW-PEAS*. A larger plot, its shootlings more widely spaced, contained *WEST INDIAN PIGEON PEAS*. Another *YAMS* and *IRISH POTATOES*. Still another *GROUND PROVISIONS*, subdivided into *CASSAVA, EDDOES, ARROWROOT*.

John turned round to face us, smiling—

All de ground provisions, he explains, is planted pon dis side excepting greenfig. Cause Mr. Carr did insist pon putting dem ovah by de fruits horchard.

Bordering this first group of plots stretched a dry riverbed, the ground etched-out and pebble-paved, reaching towards the mountains—

Dis dry bed, John tells us, go make a good 'nough river when de rains come. Soon-soon!

It formed a natural division, in Mr. Carr's elaborate layout of the gardens, between the vegetables and the fruits.

Now John brought us to the other side of the riverbed. To an unlabeled plot he called the *coco-nursery*, containing a number of large, brown, half-buried coconuts. Spaced about a foot apart. Each with its bright green shootling unfurling out the crown. Another more expansive plot contained a quantity of miniature, yellow, dried-out-looking stumps. Planted at separations of three-feet—*PLANTAINS*. This field, according to John, was Mr. Carr's pride and joy. Subdivided into five varieties—*SWEET PLANTAINS, RED BANANAS, SICKEEAFIGS, GREEN-FIGS, CAVENADISH BANANAS.*

By this point we'd worked up a good thirst. John led us over to a single spindly coconut palm—it seemed to be growing at random at the back of the plantains field—laden with nuts. And presently we had the pleasure of watching him climb up using his *bicycle*—a loop of rope circling his waist and the palm's trunk—cutlass clenched tight between his teeth. John leant backwards into his bicycle, circling round-and-round the trunk as he scampered up, chopping down a thick bundle of nuts. He descended to make short work of preparing them for us to drink.

Now we rested in the patch of shade cast by the lone coconut palm, enjoying our unexpected treat. Grateful to John, marveling at the industry of our Mr. Carr: so much he'd done already, in so short a time.

Mr. Spenser drained out his nut, addressing the group—

And without a Satellite to assist him. Imagine what *we'll* accomplish, soon as our machine's up n' running!

Aye, aye! we answer together.

We were further impressed with Mr. Carr when we arrived back at the compound. From stores still to be unloaded from the *Miss Bee*, he'd brought back a hammock for each of us. These eight hammocks already strung up in a most ingenious fashion. Amongst the eighteen bamboo poles of our humble cottage.

Dusk was upon us, and we couldn't have been more pleased.

By this time the compound was infused with the aromas of Orinoko and Esteban's stew. And shouldering the bubbling cauldron as they'd previously done the quenk, they shifted it off the flames. Proceeding to ladle out the steaming stew onto wide balisier leaves, utilised for plates. Everybody squeezing weself round the dining table, eating with our hands, by the light of the still-blazing cookfire. Some of the men returning to the pot three and four different times.

Only the two non-flesh-eaters amongst us did not partake of the stew. They were Mr. Carr and—much to Papee's surprise— he own son. Because I hadn't touched a morsel of meat since the *Rosalind* had departed the Azores. Not another paper-thin slice of acorn-fed Catalonian ham. Mr. Carr preparing a dinner for us of boiled yam and mashed greenfig. Which I can assure you we enjoyed as much as the other men did they own dinner.

A pleasant breeze kept the sandflies at bay. And just as we were finishing up our meal—and the deeper dark descended upon us—a three-quarters moon appeared above the rim of trees, overshadowing our small compound. The night all-in-a-sudden bright as day. But softer, cooler, more sheltering.

Only one ingredient remained to make us feel even more happily arrived at Chaguabarriga. And Mr. Whitechurch provided it. He reached beneath the dining table to retrieve his canvas rucksack, which none of us had noticed up till now. Rising to his feet at the head of the table—

Gentlemen, he says, I've been withholding from you a small secret. In regards of which it now gives me great pleasure to share.

He paused—

My only regret is that our good host, Mr. Carr—who's gone to such great lengths to prepare for our arrival—is of the *spare* sort himself!

Now Mr. Carr produced a smile as ample as Mr. Whitechurch's. In response to which the rest of us added a collective—*'Ere, 'ere!*

Mr. Whitechurch continued—

But tonight we shall forego our host's admired fastidiousness. And hope, likewise, that he shall pardon us our wee indulgence.

With that Mr. Whitechurch removed from his satchel two bottles of Irish whiskey. Holding them up before us, a bottle shining in each hand—

Gentlemen, welcome home!

Later that evening, by the light of the still-smouldering cookfire—after Papee and me had helped weself to a sup each of Mr. Whitechurch's whiskey—I watched him reach into his breast pocket to take out his journal again, scribbling various notes—

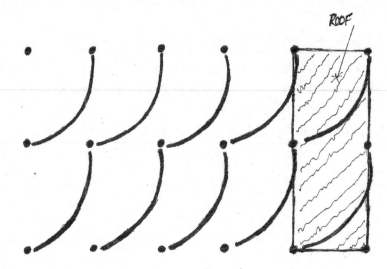

ROOF

COTTAGE (incomplete)

PEPPERPOT

Method:

1) chop quenk into large chunks, including bones (scrape skin free of bristles)
2) add cassareep & water & bring to boil
3) add vegetables, bird peppers (pricked), cinnamon stick, sugar, shadowbenni
4) salt & pepper to taste
5) boil one hour

Description:

Ancient Arawak recipe utilizing cassareep (fm. grated bitter cassava) as method for preserving meat. If added in excess this cassareep is poisonous to point of fatality. If used in proper measure, however, it prevents the meat from spoiling once the pepperpot is brought to a rapid & complete boil every 24 hrs. More meat & vegetables may be added so long as daily boiling routine is kept up.

Some Caribbean pepperpots, Orinoko tells me, over 100 years old.

That first morning at Chaguabarriga, after a leisurely arousal, we ate a hefty breakfast of still more pepperpot. Topped off with the dregs of Mr. Whitechurch's bottles—

Nothing to fear, gentlemen, he says, bouncing sprightly on his toes like he'd slept the finest night of his existence. There's a good deal more cherub's-piss where *that* came from!

After convening for a short meeting, Mr. Carr presiding as chair, we determined that our first order of business ought to be transferring the crated-up Satellite ashore. Thence to the locality of Mr. Carr's gardens: our Satellite must be put to work for us at the first opportunity.

By this point we had considerable experience manoeuvring about the obzockee two-ton crate, having rescued it once already from the harbour at Port-Spain. Mr. Craddock—a fancy milliner by trade, and self-taught scholar of the ancient world—devised the plan.

Our Satellite would be moved using the same method that the ancient Egyptians, in the third millennium, utilised to transport great blocks of stone vast distances to construct the pyramids. That is to say, by dragging our crate over tree trunks—in this case bamboo poles—placed beneath it as *freewheeling rollers*. Over which our crate would travel with a minimum of effort.

Mr. Wood raised a polite objection. That perhaps we should stick closer to our Egyptian model—and use solid trunks as opposed to bamboos, which are hollow, susceptible to crushing and snapping.

He was silenced in the same breath.

Mr. Craddock went on to explain that once the barge was floated at high water as close to shore as possible, a bridge of two bamboos would connect it to the natural stone jetty at the centre of the beach. Then a number of shorter bamboos would be laid down transversely cross the bridge, in such a manner that our crate would glide over them *as if upon greased wheels*. After our Satellite was transferred onto the jetty—hence dry land—the bridge would be reassembled on the ground before the crate as it rolled its way steady towards the gardens *like a species of movable railway track*.

Mr. Craddock concluded—

Mark my words, gentlemen. We'll have that Satellite up n' running afore our evening pepperpot!

We set weself eager about the task. Using Mr. Carr's rowboat—in addition to Captain Maynard's tender, lowered from the deck of the *Miss Bee*—we towed the barge, crate lashed down atop it, over to the small beach. All this accomplished by early afternoon when, according to plan, the tide was approaching full mark. The barge beached and moored into position fifteen short feet from the stone jetty. Now two long bamboo poles—cut fresh by Esteban and Orinoko from a patch growing alongside the sweetpond—were laid down to form the bridge. Shorter bamboos crosswise to act as rollers.

A hand winch, also loaned to us by Captain Maynard, was secured to a casuarina growing a short distance above the beach. The rope passing through it made fast to the crate via a series of block-and-tackle, just as we'd done so successful in Port-Spain. And in little more than a couple hours—without scarcely any effort a-tall—our Satellite was winched off the barge, out over the bamboo rollers. Out onto the middle of the bridge.

It stood there before us a full minute, suspended, hovering in midair.

But now we began to notice something else: our bridge seemed to be *bowing* slightly under the crate. Nobody said a word. Not a one. We simply stood there, trousers soaking in the shallow water up to our knees, staring at the bridge cokeeeyed. Whilst Mr. Hemmingway—who'd just taken his turn on the winch—commenced to cranking the crank with all the life he had in him.

To no avail. Because a moment later we heard the loud *KERRRACK-CAKKK* as the bamboos comprising the bridge snapped in two—rollers flying up into the air—our Satellite dropping with a great splash into the water. Accompanied by a *THUD* as it settled to the sandy bottom, at a depth of three-feet, bamboo rollers splashing down at our sides. Now we began to notice that familiar ooze, seeping out through cracks between the boards. As a thick, tomatoey, gently breathing cloud took shape in the crystal water round us.

By this time it was late afternoon. Leaving us little choice but to abandon our Satellite soaking in the shallow water, return the empty barge to the *Miss Bee*, and regroup first thing in the morning. Of course, by the time we managed to tow the barge out to his sloop, Captain Maynard informed us—much as we'd already begun to suspect—that insufficient daylight remained to transfer us to the Prescott Estate. Which seemed all for the best. Because we were so exhausted after our long day, even the short voyage up the coast seemed too strenuous an effort. Wanting only to retire to we compound and rest up little bit. That is, after helping weself to a couple more bottles of Mr. Whitechurch's whiskey.

But Papee didn't even give me a chance to relax myself with the other men that afternoon. Earlier I'd spied a russet-breasted hummingbird feeding on some white flowers, all the way down by the beach. I'd wanted to look in my book and try to identify him. But Papee was anxious to survey the remainder of Chaguabarriga—that part of the estate that extended beyond Mr. Carr's gardens—which we hadn't inspected yet. So whilst the other men lounged about happy inside they hammocks, treating theyself to a well-deserved sup of whiskey, and Orinoko and Esteban added more quenk to the evening pepperpot, Papee and me set off behind John into the mountains.

We started out along the dry riverbed, dividing the orchard from the vegetable plots. Easygoing for the first half-hour, the ground rising gentle beneath our boots. Then, all-in-a-sudden, it angled up before us almost vertical. We abandoned the dry bed, John leading us along a path that cut sideways cross the flanks of the mountains. Weaving its way between giant trunks of cedar & bois cannot & spiky boxwood. Purple-skinned balata trunks that John called *bullyboy* trees. Others he called *bittah* trees—raising his cutlass up to chop a wedge of the bark for Papee and me to touch we tongues against. Squinging up our faces at the harsh taste.

John laughed at us—

Same as how he tie-up you mout, just so dat bittah swill does keep-way erry kinda varmint. Good wood to make furniture, me could tell you. N' build strong house!

Papee turned towards him—

And what of boat-building? Good wood for the hull of a ship?

Egn-egn, John shook his head. Cause he plenty *weighty*—heavy too bad. For build boat you does use de bois cano. O' de bois gri-gri.

We rinsed our mouths out with a swallow of water from Papee's canteen. And we continued climbing. Another half-hour. Picking our way along the sideways-sloping path. Then it turned up, so steep we had to scale the cliffs on all fours. The air cooler, drier. Now the path turned sideways again, and we passed before a series of dark echoey caves. Receding into the rock walls. John explaining that in these caves the oilbirds built they nests—

We does call dem *diabotins*.

Eventually we reached a place where the trees opened up into a small plateau, looking down from the top of the first ridge. Running roughly parallel to the contours of the coast. Two other mountain ridges rising up parallel behind our backs. We took our seats along a fallen log at the back of the clearing—three of us sitting in a line like schoolboys—catching our breath. Taking a swallow of water from Papee's canteen, as the feelings of vertigo settled theyself inside our stomachs. Taking in the view.

Below us stretched Mr. Carr's gardens, a neat quilt of red & ochre & brown, covered over in tiny green dimples. A short distance beyond them we saw the circular clearing that was our compound, looking like a child's abandoned game of matchsticks in the dirt. Tiny white flag fluttering-way at the centre. And near the middle of the splotch of gray beach—just off the stone jetty—the child's discarded matchbox itself. Looking so small and innocent, scarcely capable of frustrating a dozen men the entire day.

Stretching off in alternate directions from both sides of the bay (east and west), we saw the mangrove swamps. The drinking-pond to this side, deeper salt-lake at the other. Our compound as though squeezed between the two. Beyond it all the sparkling bay. With the toy-sized *Miss Bee*—empty barge bobbing off her stern—floating placid in the middle.

We sat a couple more minutes. Watching the sun slip behind the mountains, lighting up the horizon a startling crimson. Bleeding upward into fiery orange, azure swirls amongst the pink-dusted clouds.

In a vaps I got up to walk to the edge of the cliff. Climbing atop a small promontory, like a lookout platform. Papee following behind me a minute later.

We stood before the precipice, looking down, tingling sensation rising inside our stomachs. As though our feet were dropping out from under us.

I listened to Papee's breathing. Quiet behind my back—

Mum n' the girls would've loved this, I say. But the person I was thinking about was Marguerite.

He didn't answer for several seconds—

Imagine Amelia, he says. She'd be swinging off the cliff!

She'd give us a fright, I say.

And after pause—

Amelia would've got on fine with the Wood girls, don't you think? They'd've had a fine time together?

But Papee didn't answer. Like he hadn't heard.

By now the bright crimson had faded from out the sky. Fiery orange all cindered up. I turned to climb down off the precipice, seeing that Papee had taken a seat on the rock floor behind me. He'd taken out his journal and the stub of pencil, and cross two open pages he was busy sketching out a map—

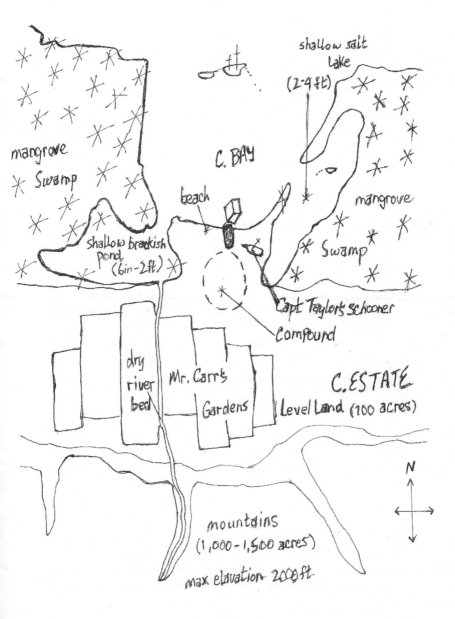

LETTERS FROM MR. STOLLMEYER & MR. ETZLER
TO THE MEMBERS OF THE TES & TTC
STILL RESIDING IN ENGLAND
The Morning Star, No. 28, 21 February 1846

We deem it of utmost importance to lay before our readers the following just-received correspondence. The first, from Mr. Stollmeyer, is addressed to the whole body of shareholders. The second, penned hastily by Mr. Etzler to the Directors, contains propositions some of which were alluded to in his last letter. In all of these correspondences we find suggestions and subjects introduced that are worthy of our deepest and sincere contemplation. For it now seems the time has come for us to decide whether our leaders have their own best interests at heart, or those of ourselves and our friends who struggle on alone at Chaguabarriga.

—Thomas Powell (editor)

28/12/45

GENTLEMEN—

By my last I informed you that I was about to commence construction of the first of our floats, to be comprised of bamboos bound together with vines, the whole encoated with tar taken from the La Brea pitchlake in the south of the island. My good news, Gentlemen, is that these much-anticipated labours are already nearing completion! As you know Mr. Etzler has travelled to Caracas on urgent business of the TES, the precise nature of which is to secure in the name of our Society its much-needed Main Grant.

But prior to his departure Mr. Etzler and I together contracted a local welder, a native by the name of Senor Smitty, to construct vari-ous parts of the machinery that shall comprise our NAVAL AUTOMATON, the engine run by the power of waves alone that shall drive our float. (The combination of these parts is, in the opinion of the inventor, the subject of a separate patent from those already taken out. Therefore, to guard against imitation and piracy, Mr. Etzler is compelled for the present time to keep it in his own mind a secret.) Senor Smitty's parts, then—with the addition one or two not yet revealed to him as a further security—shall be mounted together in strict privacy by Mr. Etzler upon his return. And not even I shall be permitted to witness their assemblage! As I expect him back here with me in Port-Spain within the week, I can assure you in the greatest confidence that it shall only be a few days more before the two of us will undertake the first SEA TRIAL of our finished float, with its attendant wave-machinery!

In my last correspondence I informed you that as the entirety of all funds at our disposal were expended during the passage over, and in our members' settling in here in Port-Spain, whatever subsequent monies have be laid out for the building of our float, as well as the contracture of Senor Smitty and purchase of his required materials, have come from the combined pocketbooks of Mr. Etzler and myself. We do not mind this in the least. But please note that until further funds are sent the float and its attendant wave machinery belong exclusively and entirely to us. Again, we are not bothered by this in the slightest. Our sole purpose is to demonstrate for you the ABSOLUTE ADVANTAGE of floats over hollow vessels, and wave machinery over conventional sails or steam engines, and once FULLY AND COMPLETELY convinced of this FACT, you may commence to pouring your coins into our coffers just as fast as they may be poured forth! For you have our solemn promise, as honest men, to build for you as MANY floats as you may care to purchase, to be at your desideratum driven by our Naval Automaton, at which time Mr. Etzler and I shall request for ourselves nothing in return but 10% of profits from said enterprise. But Gentlemen, I ask you, why wait even another day to rein in your profits? Send us your money NOW so that we may go to work for you immediately!

On this subject it appears that you have 200 shares of the TTC still available, and might sell off more, and thus in a short time raise as much as £4000. The passages and provisions of ourselves (being the first lot of emigrants sent out) cost as you will recall £7s10 each: therefore 400 passages would cost £3000. For that sum you may have a FLEET of 36 floats at your disposal! Each 5 feet thick (or they may consist of two, each 2½ feet thick and separable as desired on occasion (=72!). The passages and provisions would therefore not cost more than £1000—which is the totality of expenses for transit of 400 persons on FLOATS—¼ the expense of ordinary vessels! The difference would be your own clear gain (£3000!). You may do the math yourselves, Gentlemen, and draw your own conclusions. You need not take my word on these matters. And yet afterward, when our enterprise is done and finished, the floats will remain your property forever. Indestructible floats that will last as long as any man's life, and be ALONE the means to raise our company to grandest opulence. Therefore, if the majority of you have now understood the true nature of floats with wave machinery to drive them, and it is your desideratum to have them at the earliest possible opportunity, and see straight to your clear profits, NOW is the time to send your money and put us to work!

I remain, your honest companion and associate,
C.F. STOLLMEYER

* * *

30/12/45
SIRS—& those of you who would feign be called FRIENDS—

My Satellite has been stolen from me! The culprits? The undeniable roguish curs? None other than YOURSELVES. If still you count (as I do not!) those—former—members of our Society who have gone so skippingly off to Chaguabarriga, our money ringing in their pockets to see them along their merry way, as HONEST men and TRUE associates of this, our heretofore grand and most auspicious TES. For I deny them! And henceforth do proclaim to sever all ties with that ATROPHIED ORGAN of our great and one-time noble enterprise. My friends, if your left hand is found to taketh from your right, what shall you do but cut it off? This for my own part I have done already forever. I shall not rescind, never (unless my Satellite is returned to me immediately).

This is the disheartening news that reaches me from my companion, Mr. Stollmeyer—the theft of my Satellite!—here in this foreign city of Caracas where, as I have dutifully reported to you already, I have come not for my own purposes, but on urgent business of the TES to secure from the Venezuelan Government our Main Grant. In this endeavour already I have made great progress. Not the least of which is verification of my earlier suspicions that in this country may be achieved a thousand times what is possible in that small, most unneighbourly, and already overpopulated island of Trinidad. Yea, a thousand-thousand times! Friends, my question for you is this: Will you join me? Or shall I be forced to reap my reward in achieving all of these glorious things for humanity alone? Shall you turn your backs, as I have done, on those dishonest and self-serving thieves who have gone off so slouchingly to Chaguabarriga—where they remain still, utterly ashamed and in hiding—and constitute with me a NEW society of BETTER men in a more hopeful and promising land?

Our first mistake was to place any confidence in the likes of a Mr. Carr and a Capt Taylor. Who chose them? Where did they come from?[*] For clearly these two are incompetent and small-minded, most supreme of selfishness (witness for yourselves the death of one of them already!). Men lacking in both the character and vision necessary to act in a responsible manner, since how else could they throw away monies—not belonging to them, not in the least, but placed in their hands in good faith and trust!—on such a stench-hole as Chaguabarriga? The greatest part of which is ought other than miserable and uninhabitable morass? My friends, the damage has been done. Money tossed away like leaves in the wind! Never to be found again for a million years!

Here, in this most Democratic country of Venezuela, good and fertile land may be had for free (according to their ancient Castilian laws of emigration which I have examined) or very nearly so. The land is dry and mostly level, pleasantly rolling hills in the higher, cooler altitudes. There is as much here as may be desired, for little more than the asking (or a trifling farthing or two). I have with me the modest funds obtained from Mr. Rake's cutlery, placed in my charge to do with as I saw fit and proper (all of which has been sold off except a handful of knives and forks and a single teapot of which the Venezuelans have expressed some interest), and with these meagre monies I propose to purchase for myself and Mr. Rake and those of you who care to join us—should you but say the word!—an estate called Santa Magdalena, here in the locality of Baranjas, just a few miles south of the capital town of Caracas. This property is unmeasured, but said to exceed 70,000 fanegas! Gentlemen, I can only assure you of this: A man might gallop upon his steed for 3 days and nights without rest and still not gain a fair glimpse of its farther side! There are already buildings enough on this estate (formerly utilised by peons and cowboys) which, with some minor renovations, will house 30-40 of our persons most admirably. This in addition to the main house where I propose to

* We find these questions posed by Mr. Etzler incomprehensible, since we had never met nor heard of Mr. Carr or the unfortunate Capt Taylor until he introduced them to us. TP, ed.

reside with my wife (just as soon as I am able to settle the affairs of the TGE&SWR and other pending matters in Trinidad). There is not a finger to be lifted, only the gleaming brass door handles to be turned! Only to fold back the handsome Indian spreads and slip between the sheets!

Gentlemen, I wait to hear from you on this matter. Will you join me in constituting a new and better society here in Venezuela? Not composed of thieves and petty men? (I will get my Satellite back from them one way or another, of this you may rest assured. For imagine what WE shall do with it here!) You need only say the word and I shall be healed. I, who am more sinned against than sinning! Our former TES promised you one solitary acre for every £10-share of that joint-stock company (a puny acre we now know consists of nothing more than miserable morass). Yet in this, our newly composed Society—the MANIFESTO of which shall be drafted and sent to you via the next post—I hereby pledge ONE HUNDRED acres of the most luxuriant Venezuelan farmland, fertilised by the sweet dung of roaming herds of fatted cattle from time immemorial, for your same £10-share investment! You may come here immediately and take up residence in a fine house on your own property. Or you may entrust me with your purchase only to reap your sure profits, until such time as you see fit to join me.

My fellow Directors still in London, one final word: You do wrong to limit this business to the members of the TES and the TTC. No. You must draw in others! Many others! Even Capitalists and Money-Lenders where you see the chance. Even Jews. (I mention this only in case you should have any difficulties in raising the funds quickly.) For time, my friends, is the LEAST affordable commodity when greater profits may be made!

—to be continued at next mailing—

I am, in haste, your trusted servant & true friend,
J.A. ETZLER

12

Black Vomit

The following morning, after rising a good few hours later than we'd proposed—after our customary hefty breakfast—we gathered on the beach to plan out our strategy for the day. Son, something stopped us in our tracks: now we saw that the entire bay—stretching as far as the spot where the *Miss Bee* and her charge floated serene at anchor, two hundred yards from the beach upon which we stood—had changed colour overnight. It was tinted that startling magenta you find beneath the severed skin of a Seville blood orange—the whole bay purple-red, one side to the next.

We stood speechless, boobooloops, staring at the rust-tinted water. Our soaking Satellite the cause. Like some kinda natural phenomenon—beautiful and alarming at the same time—we just couldn't shift we eyes from it.

Eventually we huddled together for our meeting. Taking a good deal longer than we'd expected, Mr. Carr again presiding as chair. Our problem, of course, was that standing directly between the shore and our crated-up Satellite stretched the seemingly insurmountable obstacle of the stone jetty. Rising a good five-feet above the level of the sand, a foot above the surface of the water at full tide.

Clearly we had but two options. We could move our Satellite round the jetty, in order to get it up onto the beach, or we could somehow move the crate over it.

After several hours of heated discussion, with a handful of

not-altogether-idle threats—tensions escalating with the freshly retrieved bottle of Mr. Whitechurch's whiskey—we came at last to a consensus. We elected the latter option. That is to say, we'd move our Satellite *over* the obstacle of the stone jetty, but by way of *tumbling*.

Mr. Wood, who conceived the plan, used his forearm to wipe an ample page clean in the sand, his pointer-finger as a drawing-pencil. He illustrated this tumbling action for us, later copied by Papee into his notebook—

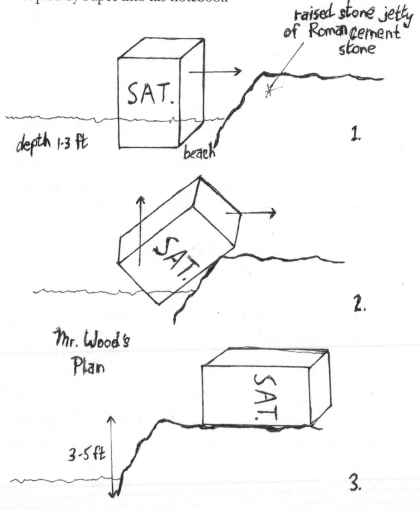

By this time the tide was receding fast, leaving our Satellite sitting on the rust-stained sand in but a half-foot of water. Much to our favour. So after winching—and simultaneously shoving—our crate a strenuous half-dozen feet closer to the stone jetty, we secured ropes round the top part. Using Captain Maynard's hand winch to slowly pull the crate over. Simultaneously raising up the back edge off the sand with bamboo levers.

After several stressful hours of shoving, jostling, and winching—not to mention a good deal of rather nasty cursing—our tumble was achieved. In but a split second, without any forewarning a-tall, the front side of our crate dropped down with a tremendous *BOOD-DOOM* onto the stone jetty. Followed by a soft, almost musical *ping-pa-ding-ping* of loose metal pieces colliding together inside the box. The falling crate almost crushing little Mr. Whitechurch beneath it, there still pulling against one of the ropes.

We looked round at each other silent, booblooops again. Hardly believing it had taken us the entire afternoon to accomplish nothing more than the Satellite's tumble. Because by this hour the sun was descending behind the mountains at our backs. So once again, exhausted-out, we decided we'd accomplished enough for the day. Retiring, content, back to our compound.

Thus it took us the whole of our second day to complete #2 of Mr. Wood's plan. With the whole of our third and most strenuous day so far at Chaguabarriga—taking turns one after the next on Captain Maynard's hand winch—dedicated to accomplishing #3.

It was already approaching noon on our fourth morning when Papee—as usual the first to stir from out his sleep—stretched his foot down from his hammock to detect a peculiar *wetness* with his toes. His nostrils simultaneously assaulted by a vile, sulfurous stench.

He sounded out a cry of alarm.

The rest of us awakening, startled, looking round to see that overnight our compound had been flooded over by several inches of putrid-smelling water. Only a handful of still-dry patches poking out here and there above its mirrored ink-black surface. Including the mound at the centre of our compound with its bamboo pole, tattered flag fluttering listless above.

Son, the only thing I could think about was my hummingbird book—I'd fallen asleep with it here inside my hammock, otherwise it would surely've been ruined.

On the previous night a sinister moon had risen up above the compound. A blue moon, according to Mr. Carr. Yet that moon was coloured a most decisive *green*. So were the lot of us—we just couldn't find no escape a-tall from its eerie rays. Even as we sealed weself up inside the bananaskins of our hammocks.

Surely that moon had something to do with all this water?

At last Mr. Carr spoke up, offering a kinda confirmation—

Extreme high tide, gentlemen, he says. I'm afraid she comes round every full moon. Raising up the pond o' sweet water to our west, salt-lake to our east. The both o' them meeting up precisely *here*.

With that Mr. Carr spat into the mercury-tinted water, sounding more pestered than perturbed. The rest of us staring at a few sad ripples radiating from his splotch of phlegm.

Mr. Carr adding as an afterthought—

Though I've never before seen her nearly this high. With a bit o' luck she'll recede again in a wee few hours!

Mr. Carr swung heself round to step down cautious from

out his hammock. Dressed, same as the rest of us, in his merino vestshirt and tatty drawers. He bent over, fumbling beneath
the murky water, locating his boots and stepping invisible inside
them, one-by-one. Then he retrieved his trousers and canvas
jersey from someplace beneath the water, wrung them out, and
spread them cross the rope of his hammock to dry. He pulled
on his soggy West Indian wife, wiping his forehead and shaking off his hands. Mr. Carr went off wading through the water.
Dragging his invisible boots. The rest of us assuming he'd gone
in search of a dry spot to use the toilet.

But he returned in a matter of minutes. Only now he came
running towards us in a panic—great splashing lunges—muddy
trail following behind in his wake.

He came to a halt. Mr. Carr looked shaken—on the verge of
tears—his sunburnt face now the same mouldy-blue, cadaver-
ous colour as the rest of his gaunt body—

Gentlemen, he says, breathing hard, his face and chest dripping. She's risen up high as the gardens! All my hard work—my
weeks n' weeks o' clearing n' digging n' planting!

Mr. Carr swallowed, his chest heaving—

We've got to do something to hold her back. Or drain her
out!

Now he looked round at us, desperate. At all our sleepy,
stonefaced expressions—

We've got to do something to save the gardens!

It took us a good few minutes to mobilise, despite Mr. Carr's
urging. We went off traipsing through the shallow swampwater,
dragging our invisible boots, dressed in our merinos and tatty
drawers. After a considerable effort we arrived at Mr. Carr's gardens, only to confirm for weself what he'd already reported.

The water high as the low stone walls demarcating the northern edges of the plots, commencing to spill over them, into the newly planted fields. Some of these plots already flooded halfway up. Most distressing of all, a number of newborn, bright-green sweet pea shootlings had already been uprooted. They lay before us, floating cheerless as orphans on the black surface.

Mr. Carr dropped down to he hands and knees in the muck. Making a frustrated attempt to replant the shootlings in they former holes beneath the water. But after a few seconds they floated back up.

Mr. Carr stood, shaking he hands dry. Looking round at us with the forlorn expression of a wounded potcake. He led us along the front border of the flooded gardens, crossing over the previously dry riverbed, already a few inches deep. Mr. Carr called for a quick meeting on the high ground atop the plantains field. Beneath the solitary coconut palm John had bicycled up on our first afternoon at Chaguabarriga—already that day seemed donkey's-ages ago.

This time, as opposed to the coconut palm's cool shade, we stood in a patch of welcome sun. Warming weself and shifting leg-to-leg in little hops of our soggy boots. Like awkward warblers drying off they feathers after a summer sprinkling.

Meanwhile Mr. Carr, in the most persuasive language he could summon, laid out his twofold plan of attack—

First, he says, the previously dry riverbed bisecting gardens—and forming a natural runoff in the event of flooding—must be dug out considerably *deeper*. Second, the sea inlet feeding the drinking pond to the west of the compound must be closed off—with a chagua-packed stonewall—the swamp on that side subsequently *drained*.

Here Mr. Carr paused to catch he breath. The rest of us only staring at him confuffled, stonefaced—we hadn't even woken up proper yet, much less to worry we heads deciphering-out his plan.

After a minute of silence Mr. Wood raised a polite objection to the second phase of Mr. Carr's strategy. He pointed out that by cutting off and draining the brackish pond, we'd effectively be depleting our only source of drinking water.

Mr. Carr assured him that the brackish pond had already been contaminated with seawater. And in any case, he explained, with the onset of the rainy season, soon to be upon us, we'd have a veritable river flowing through the gardens. Providing us with more drinking water than we'd ever need. And much *safer* water than we were presently consuming out the pond.

Now Mr. Carr crouched down, taking up a short stick, scratching out an illustration of his plan for us in the dirt—

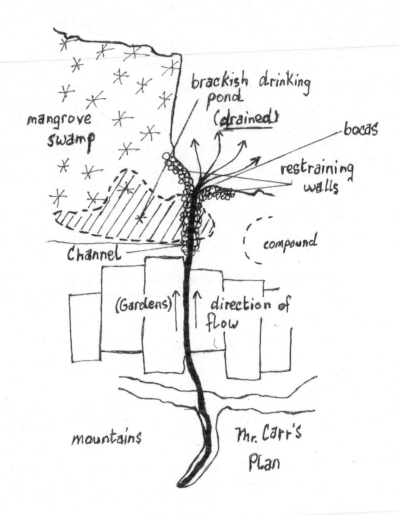

According to he strategy the stones needed to construct the seawalls—and the bulwarks we'd build on both sides of the proposed channel—could be obtained easy enough by deconstructing the walls dividing the gardens. Those walls, Mr. Carr pointed out, were merely decorative. All we'd need to do was shift the stones. Half of us, he explained, could dedicate weself to this job. Whilst the remainder commenced to digging out the channel.

Mr. Carr looked up from his elaborate plan, pleased as punch with heself. Only to confront all our puzzled, still-confuffled faces. Still shifting leg-to-leg like warblers in our soggy boots.

Yet despite it all, Mr. Carr smiled. For the first time on that eventful morning of our fourth day at Chaguabarriga—

Gentlemen, he says, which of you would like to volunteer for which task?

True to Mr. Carr's word the floodwaters did not recede that day. Nor the following. On the contrary, the water inundating the newly planted gardens seemed to rise higher. Yet only a handful of us assisted Mr. Carr in he efforts to save them. They included Papee & me & Mr. Whitechurch. Also Mr. Wood and Mr. Hemmingway, together with they wives and children when they came ashore. John assisted as well—Orinoko and Esteban stuck in they mountain village till the path drained-out.

The other pioneers took up residence on the beach. This they discovered was the driest area of the estate north of the flooded gardens. Following Mr. Craddock's lead they took they hammocks down from the inundated cottage, retying them beneath the grove of casuarinas a hundred yards up from shore. There, and on the beach, was where they congregated during the day. Sleeping the nights in the hulk of Captain Taylor's schooner, which they found was dry & protected & comfortable enough.

Collecting up as much wood as they could find, the defector-pioneers built a large bonfire there on the beach. They attempted to bust apart the Satellite's crate and use those boards too, but Mr. Frank had done such a sound job constructing it that they soon gave up. They moved the cast-iron pot from the waterlogged compound, setting it down atop the flames. The pot still containing a quantity of fresh turtle-stew, the animal harpooned by John just off the beach, early the previous morning whilst the rest of us were still asleep. This stew the defectors consumed with the last of Mr. Whitechurch's whiskey, ganging up on Captain Maynard to get they hands on the final bottles.

Meanwhile the rest of us dedicated weself to constructing restraining walls round the western shore of the bay. In hope of staving off the still-rising floodwater. The short walls surrounding the inundated gardens were disassembled quick enough, stones dragged cross the flooded ground on a sled of John's design: a wide plank with skegs and a loop of rope attached at the front to form the yoke, two of us fitting weself inside shoulder-to-shoulder to drag it along. Another group—these under the direction of Mr. Whitechurch—busied theyself digging out the riverbed running through the gardens. Continuing onwards with they bulwarked channel all the way to the sea.

But son, I couldn't begin to describe for you how disagreeable were these labours. Undertaken in the most miserable conditions imaginable. Our waterlogged clothes filling up with every manner of muck and debris, whilst leeches and other unseen tropical insects festered upon our blood. Yet after nearly two days, according to Mr. Carr's notched stick, the flood had not receded an inch.

Then, in the late-afternoon hours of our second day, we were distracted by a soft though clearly discernable *sucking* noise. Coming from someplace we couldn't pinpoint. Now we looked round at each other perplexed, the sound growing bolder—broader—till it achieved a slow-and-steady *hiss*. All-in-a-sudden, before we scarcely had a chance to take it in, a wave three-feet tall came busting down the bulwarked channel. Almost flushing little Mr. Whitechurch, caught standing in the middle still holding his shovel, out to sea with it!

In a matter of minutes the whole of Mr. Carr's gardens were drained. Just so. In a single breath. Only a few shallow puddles remained, turned to flaming mirrors by the setting sun. And by the time we managed to drag weself back to the compound—even refusing a seabath at the beach to avoid a nasty confrontation with those deserters—we found that our clearing, too, had drained out dogbone-dry.

Yet no sooner had we eaten our supper—and flung our bone-weary bodies inside our hammocks—when the rains began. Not the gentle, soft, pleasant kinda sprinklings we'd grown accustomed to, coming in the early-morning hours. That syncopated *pac-pac-pac* of fat raindrops falling on the wide sea grape leaves, whilst we lulled half-asleep inside our hammocks. This was a deluge: it pelted us all night long. Hard, steady, punctuated only by bouts of thunder and lightning. All of us huddled together beneath the piece of thatch at the far end of our cottage, arms wrapped round each other for warmth.

Towards daybreak it tapered off, finally coming to a halt. The morning sun appeared huge and hot, as we tumbled one after the next into our waterlogged hammocks. Steam rising up round us from the sopping dirt. All of us snoring-way almost before we could shut our eyes. Our dreams transporting us to that other, safer side of the sea.

◈

Papee had overseen production at Stevens Millworks, the largest paper manufactory in all Britain, for nearly a decade.

Ever since he'd moved our family from the Isle of Wight, back to East London. Because at that time Papee had been taken on by Mr. Stevens to fit out his new mill—a paper manufactory the likes of which nobody'd never seen before. Papee designed and built the mill's fourdrinier machines. For nearly a decade he'd kept them running—it was due to Papee's innovations that those machines achieved record speed: fourteen yards per minute.

In those days my father was renowned amongst papermakers, and not only in East London.

Then, when Britain was hit by the nationwide shortage of cotton rags, and even the queen's beggars learnt a new fashion—that of going about the kingdom bare-arsed—it was Papee who made the switch to timber as the raw material for pulp. He was the first one to do it. And not just mulberry neither: a variety of woods and other plant substances—even grasses—that Papee travelled the English countryside in search of and experimented with to determine they precise beating-times and techniques—

Paper's made in the beater, he always boasted. And there isn't a papermaker in all Blighty knows the beater better than me!

In those days Papee used to take me along on some of his trips to the countryside too. But once Mr. Stevens and his foreman had all Papee's collected knowledge at they disposal—and they'd already made good money selling off his secrets to the other manufactories—he was rendered redundant. Just so. Now my father was called in only on occasion. When one of the fourdrinier machines broke down, or the mill met with some other calamity. And it was fortunate for us, I suppose, that one of those same emergencies happened to coincide with the finish of the Satellite's construction project with Mr. Frank. With its final crating-up in preparation for our departure. Because now

Papee could pocket some of the funds necessary for our trip to Trinidad.

During those days he directed the biweekly meetings of our own East End branch of the TES heself. That is, unless Mr. Etzler or Mr. Stollmeyer showed up, which was rare as they focused they energies on the more lucrative branches. Mum and the girls generally went along to Papee's meetings too, even after a full day at Suffolk Dyers. But son, despite that I didn't have any responsibilities a-tall excepting my studies—which by that time I'd learnt easy enough to ignore—I didn't give a pum about those meetings. If Marguerite wasn't going to Trinidad, then I didn't want nothing to do with none of it a-tall.

Then, one night as I lay in my bed, half-asleep, I got an idea. I could attend one of the meetings—not in we own district, but in Knightsbridge. Where I knew the Whitechurches were members. I could deliver a note to Marguerite via she aunt. A note persuading her to come with me to Trinidad. Suddenly it all seemed clear and simple and easy enough—like if the feat was accomplished already! All I had to do was convince her that love meant more than her moral values. That her stern principles didn't amount to nothing compared to the stirrings of she own heart.

I sat up in my bed five nights straight struggling to compose this note. X-ing it out and rewriting it and X-ing it out again. I went through dozens of slips of paper. Ripped in two and crumpled up and tossed into the corner till they piled up tall as the mattress-self. Till inevitably, unavoidably, I came to understand the truth: writing is impossible. It's *unbearable*. The difficulty of writing down anything a-tall. With any kinda accuracy, or meaning, or any kinda worth. Any kinda *content*. And son, during those five sleepless nights I came to understand something else: the depth of my admiration for Marguerite.

She had learnt to live with her condition, so well. She had turned a holdback into a strength. That was everything and it was nothing a-tall. There was something else, something more integral. Deeper, simpler, more profound: her honesty, her unflinching personal integrity. And yet she was so kind and gentle.

Son, during those five sleepless nights I learnt to care for her deeper than I could bear.

Now I realised I had to go to her. In person, somehow. I had to attend the TES meeting in Knightsbridge, and when it was done I had to follow the Whitechurches home. In secret. Till I discovered where Marguerite lived. Then I had to talk to her.

It was my only chance, only hope. Somehow I had to give my heart to her in *words*. And if I couldn't write them down— if it was impossible to get them down on a blasted piece of paper—at least I could speak them to her aloud.

◈

All-in-a-sudden we were shaken from our sleep by Mr. Carr's shrill voice. Coming to us from the gardens. Grudgingly, we rolled out of our hammocks. Making our way towards him. Finding Mr. Carr sitting there like an emaciated Buddha—his legs folded beneath him—in the midst of a plot of sweet peas. With a river of bright clear water washing down the bulwarked channel behind him.

But son, this flood came at us from the opposite direction. From a thousand different sources high up in mountains. Not from the sea behind our backs. This flood came at us controlled, untainted, serviceable. Mother Nature, bent according to our own collective will and design. Offering up her gifts. We'd achieved it *not* with the aid of machines, effortlessly, but by our own hands and our own hard toil. Most significant of all we'd achieved it together.

And now, together, we reaped our well-deserved reward.

As if by instinct—and without a word spoken between us— we stepped from out our soggy boots. Stripping off our soiled drawers and ragged merinos. Mr. Carr standing in his plot of sweet peas to do the same, in addition to doffing his soggy West Indian wife. Six pale Englishmen and one ebony-black African. We climbed over the bulwark of stones, wading out into the cold clear water in the middle of the channel—a startling four-feet deep! And now, together, holding hands and hooting like badjohn-schoolboys, we threw weself in. We abandoned weself to the water. Letting it carry us for three-quarters of a mile, right the way out to sea.

But when we swam round to the beach and climbed up onto the sun-warmed sand we found it deserted. No fire burning beneath the stolen cast-iron pot. The hammocks previously tied between the casuarinas all taken down. For a moment we stood there looking round at each other chupidee. Then, as if in answer to the question we hadn't even formulated yet, we heard the sound of Captain Maynard's conch behind us—*baaaaah!*

We turned round to look out cross the bay at the *Miss Bee*. Which had escaped our notice up till now, all our attentions focused on those deserter-pioneers. Now we saw that after a delay of six long days, Captain Maynard's sloop was at last ready to sail off to the Prescott Estate. Her bright mainsail and jib already flapping loose in the breeze. Deserters packed up and aboard.

The seven of us stood there naked, lined up on the beach, warming weself in the sun with our hands cupping over our shriveled-up stones. Staring cross the water at the *Miss Bee*. And son, now we realised something else. Something rather vile: those dissenters had taken Mr. Carr's skiff. Without any discussion a-tall. Conceivably they'd need it to get back to the estate—to visit us, perhaps daily, and aid us in our labours, our group endeavour. But they'd taken it without warning, no boat remaining for us a-tall. Because there it floated, two hundred yards away, tied off the stern of the empty barge. The barge in turn tied off the *Miss Bee*. With the three vessels lined up one behind the next in order of diminishing size.

Leaving Mr. Wood and Mr. Hemmingway with no choice but to take off swimming again. Straightway, naked as they were. If they had any chance of catching up with the *Miss Bee*—not to mention they wives and children—before they set off for the Prescott Estate. And after a few minutes they were taken aboard, embraced by they waiting families, blankets wrapped round them for decency till fresh clothes could be retrieved.

Only five of us remained now at Chaguabarriga: me, Papee, Mr. Whitechurch, Mr. Carr and John. Standing there on the beach warming weself in the sun. Watching from a distance as Captain Maynard's bos'n stretched heself out over the bowsprit to haul in the anchor. We watched the *Miss Bee* turn broadside to us, her bright sails filling with the gentle onshore breeze. And she started off, hobbling out the bay, her two smaller charges hobbling behind like a family of floating pelicans.

Not till Orinoko and Esteban arrived later that same afternoon—smiling and bearing a crocus sack stuffed to the brim with pheasants they'd hunted down for the evening meal—did we realise the full significance of the occasion: it was Old Year's night. It hadn't occurred to us not till now. The pilfered cast-iron pot scrubbed clean right there at the beach, returned to its rightful place above the cookfire. And Orinoko and Esteban set about preparing they lavish meal. To which Mr. Carr contributed a single ingredient that, in point of fact, did not rightfully belong to him. It was the property of our deceased Captain Taylor. Mr. Carr had kept it a secret all this time, waiting for the appropriate moment. Because now he rolled from out its hiding place beneath a clump of sea grapes a half-full half-barrel of the finest West Indian rum.

Of this liquor Mr. Carr did not partake heself. With the exception a short calabash cup raised with the rest of us at the stroke of midnight, according to Mr. Whitechurch's golden pocketwatch.

Standing to his feet at the head of the table, Mr. Whitechurch slipped his watch back inside the pocket of his green velvet vest. And taking up his own cup, he begged us for a moment's indulgence. Mr. Whitechurch offered a toast, saying that never before had he felt happier nor healthier—

And barring only my dear wife and niece—'oom I hope are enjoying as splendid an Old Year's fête as we are tonight—never've I known such affections as for these six gentlemen gathered round me at this table! So let us bless this ground, and offer thanks for a new life embraced together. Here in this, our cherished new home!

Tears in he eye-corners, Mr. Whitechurch knocked back his calabash cup.

It was late the following morning, a good hour after breakfast—whilst me & Papee & John were taking our daily seabaths down at the beach—that Papee sent me back to the compound to check up on him. Since, as we all suddenly realised, Mr. Whitechuch hadn't risen from his hammock that morning to take he breakfast with us.

But I couldn't find him not-for-nothing a-tall. Calling out his name at the compound, proceeding to the gardens, and calling out his name again. In the distance I made out Mr. Carr & Esteban & Orinoko, over by the plantains plot, crouching together in the dirt. I shouted out for Mr. Whitechurch again. But oddly enough it was Mr. Carr who stood and doffed his hat, crouching back to the dirt.

I shrugged my shoulders, returning to the compound, calling out for Mr. Whitechurch a last time.

Suddenly I breathed a sigh of relief. There he was, sure enough, in the most logical place—the only place I hadn't looked proper yet!—fast asleep inside his hammock.

I hurried towards him, there at far end of our cottage beneath the piece of thatched roof. I reached my hand into the shadow of the hammock to take hold of his shoulder and shake him awake—maybe a bit too abrupt, a bit too harsh. Watching Mr. Whitechurch sit up slow and unsteady. His trembling hands groping for the sides of the hammock, swinging gentle back-and-forth, back-and-forth.

Son, my heart gave a jolt: now I saw that his face was stained a most repugnant *yellow* colour. Most unnatural—because I'd never seen nothing like it before. The colour saturated all *through* his skin. Unlike the film of slimy sweat covering it over. Mr. Whitechurch staring up at me through bloated-out eyeballs. Stained the same frightful, same hideous yellow.

But son, it was like if he's seeing a stranger standing before him. Like if he doesn't know who-the-arse I am a-tall.

Then I saw a flicker of recognition. Floating up from somewhere in the depths of his hideous yellow-stained eyes. And now he leant forward, towards me, shoving his head over the side of the hammock. Reaching his face towards me at the end of his long yellow clean-neck-fowl neck. And for some peculiar reason I can't explain, now I felt like he wanted to *kiss* me. Just so. And for some peculiar reason I'm *embarrassed* by it. By this sudden show of unmanly affection.

I jumped back a step.

But son, Mr. Whitechurch didn't kiss me. He didn't kiss me a-tall. He coughed twice, spewing forth a small puddle of vomit. A small puddle, lying there on the dirt before my bare feet. Shaped like a dagger: it was the colour and consistency of molten tar.

11/11/10

dear mr robot:

i so sorry!!! cause i was sittin dere in pelo waiting 4 u so long &
den i did start to getting vex 2, vex & sad both, so i txt my brothers pon de cell & tell dem come carry me home, & nex ting lil
buddah and raj come inside pelo & dey see me sitting pon de bar
& looking so forlorn most in tears, & dey asks me straightway,
what happen wid u, lil sis? & nex ting u know i tell dem everyting,
de whole long story come spilling out, bout how u did subjuice
me just to try & copy out u copies but still i stick by de rules no
matter what, cause laws is laws & still i wouldnt give u de copies
but take proper advantage of all dat sweet jooking sure enough,
cause i aint no fool mr robot, but now u say u vex & cant take it
no more & want 2 go back home in amerika jook-&-run

raj say OH-HO!!! he say JOOK-&-RUN?! francin-yankeeass-
whiteman want to JOOK-WE-LIL-SIS-&-RUN?! & right den lil
buddah chime in behind he 2 saying sis, i didnt just hear you say
JOOK-&-RUN?! please dont tell me my ears didnt just perceive u
saying JOOK-&-RUN?! not JOOK-&-RUN?! & nex ting u know
lil buddah & raj bolt from inside pelo out de door & no way i
could hold dem back neither, cause dey was in a RAMPAGE on
de search 4 u now in de hilton or wherever dey could find u mr
robot, & i did know dat would only mean plenty plenty trouble
2, so onliest ting i could do is knockback de rest of my rumcock-
tail & hurry hail a maxitaxi & go home fast as i could to wait 4
dem, & soon as my brothers reach home i ask dem U FIND MR
ROBOT? & raj say, give he 2 blue-eye, & lil buddah say, buss mr
robot nose, & i say what u do dat 4? how u could buss poor mr

robot nose and give he 2 blue-eye? & lil buddah say sis, u dont say
JOOK-&-RUN & ask WHAT 4? not JOOK-&-RUN, so i ask,
well where mr robot is now? & raj say, must be de hospital

so mr robot i was feeling so bad when i hear bout this beating raj
and lil buddah give u, i rush furs ting down to dat mergency room
& dont even tink to change from out my panties i was wearing
special 4 u 2, dem dentalfloss ones u love so much & say dey aint
got noting like dat in amerika neither, dats how bad i was feeling
mr robot, & then de nurse tell me u was only a lil bit rattle wid
no broken bones but only de blue-eyes and buss-up-nose, & she
give u de discharge, but now in trut i was more distress den ever
mr robot, cause u wasnt dere dat i could explain everyting & say
how sorry i feel, & i go back to pelo & u wasnt dere neither, & i
check de hilton & u wasnt dere neither, & now i was going mad, i
just dont know what i could do i did feel so terrible, & onliest ting
i could promise u mr robot, if u come in de archives dis morning u could make a few, only a FEW photocopies mr robot, but i
know dat few would be enough to make u heart feel glad

cordial,
miss ramsol
director, t&tna

ps plus mr robot we would be private back in my office where de
machine keep

pss & i would still be wearing dem 4 u 2

psss & plus i find 2 more articles de furs i know u would love, de
2nd from plenty years later bout u family, i tink maybe de selfsame R-W TUCKER u name 4???

INVENTORS NARROWLY ESCAPE
DROWNING IN SEA TRIAL OF NAVAL AUTOMATON

Trinidad Gazette, 7 January 1846

Yesterday afternoon at Maracas Bay a crowd of animated observers, together with a handful of unruly hecklers, gathered beneath the sun in bleachers erected especially for the occasion to witness the much-anticipated sea trial of the Naval Automaton. This contraption, purportedly fuelled and powered by waves alone, was designed to drive a unique craft called a Floating Island. According to the boasts of its inventor, Mr. J.A. Etzler, the resulting craft (Naval Automaton + Floating Island) would be 'capable of crossing the Atlantic in the cheapest, safest, and most comfortable manner in five days or less.' It would soon supplant all other outmoded models of 'hollow' vessels presently traveling the sea.

The proceedings of the afternoon were met with some delay when a number of the spectators refused to pay the admittance fee of $5 per adult, and $3 per child. As advertised this fee permitted them entrance to the stands, in addition to the privilege of observing the spectacle of the Naval Automaton 'in full action.' The fractious individuals congregated on the beach in front of the stands, claiming their entitlement to do so, refusing to move off even when threatened by Mr. Etzler himself. Tempers flared under the hot sun, resulting in a further confrontation between the inventor and the Police Constable, whose opinion favoured the crowd. The situation grew still more volatile when several angry spectators, having paid the admittance fee, demanded their money back. But everything was settled amicably by Mr. Stollmeyer, the inventor's associate, who removed his leather helmet and passed it amongst the rebellious beach crowd collecting $2 each.

Finally, after a lengthy speech delivered by Mr. Etzler through a large pasteboard cone, in which he recounted the many attributes of his invention, the craft (hidden beneath a tarpaulin at water's edge) was unveiled to a burst of applause. Derogatory hisses were heard as well, together with a generous amount of laughter, since the advertised 'futuristic' craft scarcely looked more novel or sophisticated than the river-raft of a half-tamed Warahoon living up the Orinoko.

The craft's hull consisted of liana-bound bamboos, with a small carrot-roofed hut (intended to provide shelter in the event of nasty weather) situated towards the rear. At the front of the thatched hut, above its low entrance, a large posterboard sign was affixed containing a seaman's chart of the Atlantic Ocean. In the lower left corner of this chart our tiny island of Trinidad could be seen, with the somewhat larger isle of Grand Britannia on the upper right, a red line traversing the blue void so as to connect the two, indicating the operators' course of travel over the next five days.

Behind the hut, attached via rowlock to the stern of the craft, was a wide-bladed oar, presumably the steering mechanism.

Two large paddlewheels could be seen on either side at the front (as though the Warahoon had attempted to convert his river-raft into a crude, pedal-powered paddleboat). Located between these two wheels, at the very centre of the raft, was a wooden box with the letters N-A-V-A-L A-U-T-O-M-A-T-O-N painted across its four visible sides, in addition to the mysterious symbol: 回 * A fiercely toothed iron shaft protruded from the top of this box, projecting fifteen feet into the air, passing through the float's bottom and extending another three feet below the raft. It was welded to a wide steel platform below the hull (the platform's size roughly 2/3 the surface area of the raft). This platform was raised into the *up* position, the craft resting atop it on the sand, with a three-foot gap-space between the platform and the bottom of the raft. Thus the craft seemed to hover slightly in the air above the sand, the only possibly 'futuristic' attribute of its appearance.

At the rear of the box was a crank which, in the words of the inventor, 'serves to lower the platform into the still water beneath the waves' undulations, so that once the mechanism is engaged, the upward vertical thrust exerted upon the hull will be captured and transferred to the shaft driving the paddlewheels, thus converted into a horizontal propulsion.'

Between the box and the hut sat two tall operator's stools, fastened to the floor of the raft, complete with seat belts. At the front was a flagpole with a white banner, its purpose to warn slower vessels to take heed and clear out of the way. Dangling from the lower portion of the flagpole was a four-foot-long bunch of green bananas, intended to serve as sustenance for the operators during the five days of their journey.

For the sea trial Mr. Etzler had engaged the assistance of Captain

Jerry and his mailboat for the purpose of towing his craft off the sand and into the water, thence out to sea. Mr. Etzler and Mr. Stollmeyer, wearing their leather helmets and safety goggles, strapped themselves onto their pilot stools and gave the thumbs-up signal to Captain Jerry, waiting 50 yards off the beach with a towline attached to the craft. An emotional crowd then watched as the captain engaged his engine. But the steel platform below the hull dug into the sand, preventing it from being dragged off the beach. Captain Jerry applied more power: the platform only dug deeper into the sand. Finally the captain applied full throttle, and amidst a cloud of smoke and an uproar coming from both the crowd and the mailboat's engine, the craft was yanked with a great splash into the water, the operators fortunate to be wearing their seat belts and safety helmets.

Captain Jerry then backed down his throttle, and he towed the raft slowly out into the calm water of the bay. When the craft met with the first gentle undulations, 100 yards from shore, the thumbs-up signal was again given by the operators, and the craft was turned loose. Those spectators resourceful enough to have brought along their binoculars and lorgnettes, now raised them to their eyes.

They watched as Mr. Etzler leant forward on his tall stool to turn the crank and lower the steel platform (now hidden beneath the craft) deeper into the water. Slowly the fiercely toothed shaft became shorter and shorter. When it had disappeared completely, Mr. Etzler threw a lever beside the crank, then he sat upright again on his pilot's stool. At this point the copilot, Mr. Stollmeyer, took hold of the steering mechanism.

Excited spectators stared through their binoculars and lorgnettes, offering a running commentary. But for the first few minutes the craft, pointed towards the open sea by Mr. Stollmeyer— bow-first into the gentle, oncoming waves—seemed only to drift backwards, rising and falling gently as it floated over the swells. After a few minutes the craft commenced a visible bouncing action on the surface of the water. This motion gradually increased, until the raft appeared to be jumping up and down, sending out large splashes from each of its four sides. Until this point no forward progress had been noted. But no longer did the craft seem to be drifting backwards either. Slowly but surely the paddlewheels began their visible churning, and the bouncing craft seemed to move gradually forward. This continued for fifteen or so anxious minutes, as the craft progressed slowly out to sea, bouncing its way towards the first whitecaps. Even those spectators without binoculars, and those who'd previously derided Mr. Etzler in the foulest language, could now be heard cheering him on.

As it encountered the first white breakers the raft bounced still higher off the surface of the water (whether this was to due to the onrushing waves or the craft's machinery was unclear). But as the first large waves broke over the bow, and her forward momentum increased, the craft seemed to dig into the water—in great, lunging jolts—driving itself deeper and deeper each time. Suddenly, as it encountered still another tall white crest, the raft disappeared alto-gether beneath the surface. A moment later the operators strapped to their stools disappeared beneath the water as well, then the pointed tip of the hut's carrot-roof, last of all the fluttering white banner.

Spectators and hecklers alike could be heard uttering cries of serious concern. They stared through their binoculars at the spot where the craft had gone down.

Eventually, after several stressful minutes, the two operators were seen once more, splashing and flailing about amongst the waves. Captain Jerry immediately turned his mailboat about, making his way towards them. Thus the sea trial was concluded, with Mr. Etzler's Naval Automaton gone to join the esteemed company of Davy Jones's locker.

DIRECTOR OF TRINIDAD TRANSPORT COMPANY NAMES SON AS MAJOR SHAREHOLDER

Trinidad Guardian, 7 May 1898

After forty-eight years at the reins Mr. William Sanger Tucker today retired from his position as head of our largest shipping and lighterage company, the TTC. He has named his eldest son, Robert William Tucker, known to many of us as 'R-W,' as the company's new Director and majority shareholder. The TTC owns and operates a fleet of nine lighters and three tugs. These vessels transport sugar, cocoa, copra, and other manner of agricultural produce from San Fernando and locations in the south to the capital, and they carry back supplies needed on the estates. The TTC also supervises a steady stream of traffic from the islands of Tobago, Grenada, several ports of costal Venezuela, and most recently Barbados.

Tucker Senior got his start in the business of transportation soon after his arrival to Trinidad from London, at the young age of fifteen. At that time he began the operation of the island's first 'omnibus,' a carriage drawn by a donkey along an unpaved track that delivered its passengers between Port of Spain and Arima. Indeed, no public transportation had existed in Trinidad until Mr. Tucker advertised in our own *Guardian* of 27 March 1846: 'To commence on Monday morning Mr. William Tucker most respectfully informs the Public that he has established an omnibus for the purpose of conveyance of passengers and parcels to-and-fro Arima, starting from Losh, Spiers & Co. at Richmond Street Wharf Mondays, Wednesdays, and Fridays, and from the Arima Hotel on Coffee Street Tuesdays and Thursdays.' Popularly called the 'Van,' it took about a day to make each leg of the journey, the charge for passengers being ¢10 per mile.

Mr. Tucker claims never to have grown bored on these daily expeditions, since they allowed him the opportunity to make frequent stops along the way in pursuit of his hobby of collecting and stuffing hummingbirds. Mr. Tucker is also amongst Trinidad's first experimenters in the art of photography, the plates and exhibits of his hummingbirds sold on the side to field naturalists and nature enthusiasts. The Van not only enabled Mr. Tucker to support his mother and three sisters, but after only five years he had set aside sufficient funds to put a down payment on the first TTC lighter, a sloop of twenty-one feet with sails and a small steam engine, marking the beginning of what would in short measure become a successful shipping empire. This first schooner Mr. Tucker captained himself for many years.

The announcement of Tucker Senior's retirement comes on the thirty-seventh birthday of his son, R-W, who has worked in the business alongside his father since the age of eighteen. He is himself a licenced ship's captain.

13
Flies

We tended to Mr. Whitechurch the whole of that afternoon. Watching him alternate between sessions of violent chills—he skin cold, teeth chattering—and bouts of feverous sweats. And I couldn't tell you which one was worse. Mr. Whitechurch wrapped up in the old blanket belonging to Captain Taylor, retrieved by John from out the schooner on the beach. We wrapped him up like a mummy. Then we pulled the blanket off. Then we wrapped him up again. The hideous colour of he skin and eyes remaining constant, fixed. Till the sun descended below the rim of trees sheltering our compound, and under the glow of the flickering pitch-oil lamp his face turned yellower. More repugnant. But I couldn't tell you, son, because I couldn't hardly bring myself to look at him.

Mr. Carr used Mr. Whitechurch's watch to time his bouts of fever & sweats & the lapses between, doses of powdered acetylsalicylic acid dissolved in a calabash with water, the little blue homeopathic pills pressed under his yellow tongue. Then, towards midnight according to Mr. Whitechurch's own pocketwatch, he stretched his clean-neck-fowl neck over the side of the hammock. He coughed twice. Spewing forth his second puddle of black vomit. Afterward—much to everybody's surprise—he seemed better. Plenty better. Chatting-way enthusiastic & smiling & even giving us a good joke. Like if his fever was past now. Like if Mr. Whitechurch had returned to he previous, good self.

Then he let loose a long sigh, closed his yellow bloated-out

261   ROBERT ANTONI

eyes, and he slept quiet and peaceful like that for the rest of the night.

The following morning he was still sleeping docile as a baby, his temperature stable and normalised, when Papee suggested we make a short excursion up the coast. Him & John & me. Because what was the point in all of us sitting there watching Mr. White-church sleep? Especially since he seemed to have recovered hes-elf? Mr. Carr promising he wouldn't stir from the old man's side.

There was another small bay a mile or so west of the settle-ment called Guanimita. It was part of the property, and Papee wanted to inspect it. Son, I couldn't have cared a pum—far as this Guanimita was concerned—but I was getting antsy. I want-ed to *do* something. Anything. Same as John and Papee.

The tide dead-low, so we could make we way up the shore with a minimum of effort. We'd be back in no time a-tall. Yet it took a good hour of trudging through the thick black mud to get there. Our boots soppsing, heavy as bricks after our first five steps past the beach. Because Papee and me would've surely been better off barefoot like John, but our English footsoles were still too tender. And let me assure you of this: Guanimita wasn't nothing much neither, once we got there. A little indentation in the mangroves scarcely seventy yards deep. Nothing but a small catchment filled up with the same stenching chagua-mud we'd been trodding we way through for the previous hour. No beach a-tall—not like Chaguabarriga had—nor nothing else neither. Only mud. Papee didn't even bother making a drawing of it inside he journal. That's how insignificant was this Guanimita. But the worst part was that now—when we turned round again to head back up the coast—the tide was coming in. Fast. So we didn't have no choice a-tall but to climb over the thick arching mangrove roots, forging we way along. Slow & tedious & tiring enough.

It took us probably another two-three hours to get back. But I couldn't tell you for sure since we didn't have Mr. Whitechurch's watch with us to check the time. And son, it was a good while too—*before* we reached back to Chaguabarriga—that we saw the birds. Circling ominous over the compound. Four of them. Turning they slow ragged gyres through the bright liquid sky. Suspended a few hundred yards above the sun-glittering trees, above our tattered flag. It was the first time Papee and me had seen them congregated like that—other than over La Basse in Port-Spain—but we didn't say nothing about the cobos. Neither Papee nor me. John didn't mention them neither.

What was there to say?

Papee first to stomp up anxious off the beach. His boots and trousers wet and muddy up to he knees, same as me. He led us along the path through the grove of furry casuarinas—only that afternoon I didn't like the melancholy sound of the breeze whistling through they needles. I didn't like it a-tall.

We found Mr. Whitechurch alone. Unattended. Much to our surprise. Lying there quiet in his hammock same as we'd left him a few hours before. Even from the distance we could see his shaggy head—bony neck protruding over the side of the hammock at an oddish angle—his face illuminated by a slice of sun. And even from the distance it shocked us to see his deep yellow colouring again. But son, what struck us as still more disconcerting as we approached Mr. Whitechurch was he eyes. Because we realised he wasn't sleeping a-tall—his eyes were wide open. Only now they didn't appear yellow as before. They looked like dark slits. Slashed into a piece of sackcloth. Like if he eyeballs were missing altogether—dug from out they sockets!

A pair of cobos crouching ragged and stoop-shouldered on the piece of thatching above his head. We approached stomping the ground, *hard*, scaring them off. Watching the cobos lift up swift and silent—*voop voop voop*—and with three wide flaps of they ragged wings, they sailed up to join the others.

At that same instant something terrifying occurred to me. Horrific: that in his enfeebled condition, Mr. Whitechurch had been too weak to fight off the birds—they'd blinded him, pecked out he eyes!

Yet when we got to Mr. Whitechurch's side we saw that his eyes were intact. And they were open—wide, wide open. Though the surfaces of both eyeballs seemed to be covered over with some kinda gelatinous, greenish-black, slightly irides-cent substance. Slightly *flickering*. But not in any way a living & seeing & functioning eye ought to flicker.

Only then did we realise that the surfaces of both Mr. White-church's eyeballs were covered over with a film of miniscule, flickering, greenish-black flies.

Papee stepped up quick to brush his hand through the air before the old man's face. Brisk. Two separate times—at first I thought he was trying to *slap* Mr. Whitechurch awake! John and me watching him bend over to blow into each of his eyes. Care-ful. Shooing-way the flies. Those same flies rising up and drifting off in a small, tumultuous-looking cloud. A couple of feet off the ground. Like if the air itself was boiling up before us. Drift-ing off towards the low sea grapes.

Papee picked out two or three more that remained. Pinching them dead, flicking them away between his thumb and forefin-ger. Then he glanced back over his shoulder at John and me, summoning our assistance. We each took hold of a thin, bristly leg, whilst Papee grasped Mr. Whitechurch from behind, under his hairy armpits. And together we lifted him up and out the hammock, over to the dining table, laying him down atop his back. His body hadn't stiffened up yet—though his neck held the same awkward clean-neck-fowl twist to it—even out the hammock. Mr. Whitechurch laying there with his one ear pressed tight against the table. Like if he's straining to listen through a door.

All his skin the same hideous colour, including the whites of his eyes now that they were exposed again. And son, laying like that in the middle of the long table, wearing his merino and tatty drawers, he looked even smaller than usual. Like a potbellied schoolboy, all ankles & knees & hipsbones & protruding knotted-up wrists.

Papee searched the ground for two small smooth rockstones. Twisting Mr. Whitechurch's head round, so his face looked straight up from the table. But when Papee let it loose his neck twisted back into its former clean-neck-fowl position. Papee then took hold of both his bearded-over cheeks, turning his face right the way round to the other side. With an awful creaksing noise I felt *crick-crick-crick one-two-three* right the way up through my *own* spinebones. Papee held his head firm like that a minute, his other ear straining to listen through the door. Then Papee released, and Mr. Whitechurch's neck remained more-or-less straight, his face looking up. Like now he's contemplating the bright almond leaves glittering high above.

Papee blew-way the few flies that had settled again. And one-by-one he pulled down Mr. Whitechurch's eyelids, weighing them closed with the small rockstones. He twisted Mr. Whitechurch's arms round, smoothing out his knotted-up wrists, fixing his hands crosswise over his patch of woolly chest hair. With the bottom of Mr. Whitechurch's soiled merino rising up to expose the half-moon of his soffee, rounded, slightly pock-eled belly. Deep indentation of his navelhole staring up at us like a third yellow eye out the middle.

Papee walked round to the other end of the table, bending to press and hold Mr. Whitechurch's knobby ankles together. He stood, taking in a breath—

Willy? he says, quiet.

Sir, I answer, my own voice coming out creaksing as Mr. Whitechurch's neckbones.

See if you can find Mr. Carr out by the gardens, will you?

I nodded my head, turning, hurrying off.

Because son, let me tell you I was happy enough to unstick my eyes from Mr. Whitechurch's geegeeree corpse. Happy too bad! But after hurrying along the path a minute or so, I came to a slow halt. Realising I'd clean forgotten my destination. Wher-ever-the-arse I was going to a-tall. I shook my head, trying to fling the cobwebs loose. All-in-a-sudden I couldn't recall the name of the kind gentleman we'd just finished laying out atop the table.

Not *Carr*, I think—he's the man I'm going to look for. Out by the gardens.

Now I heard a smooth, almost rhythmic *scrapesing* sound of metal-against-rock. I turned to abandon the path. Wandering aimless in the direction of the noise. A few haphazard steps later, in the hard ground beyond the pigeon peas plot, I found Mr. Carr. Already knee-deep inside he hole. Tossing out shov-elfuls of ochre-coloured dirt and fist-sized rockstones. A low, loose mound along one side of the hole. And under his West Indian wife I could see that Mr. Carr was weeping—tears wash-ing down his sunburnt face, the whole front of he canvas shirt soppsing with them.

Mr. Carr didn't even notice my approach. I stood there above him another minute. Watching him work his shovel. My mind a blank slate, head heavy as a bucket of water I'm struggling to keep balanced atop my shoulders.

Then, slowly, it dawned on me what Mr. Carr was doing.

I lurched forward, grasping hold of the shovel by its handle. Pulling it away. Nearly yanking Mr. Carr clean out he gravehole along with it!

All-in-a-sudden I couldn't hardly see beyond the tears burning inside my own eyes. I looked down at Mr. Carr—

You can't put him here, I say. You *shan't!*

And after another pant—

Mr. Whitechurch needs to return to his wife and Marguerite!

I raised the back of the shovel up above my shoulder. Trembling in the grips of my hands. Fully prepared to bludgeon Mr. Carr cross he pate with it.

Then, through my wash of tears, I saw the mound of ochre-coloured dirt. Rising. Flying up to press itself enormous and gritty against my face.

◈

Unnoticed by the Whitechurches I slipped past the Royal Court Theatre on the eastern side of Sloane Square. Having followed them home after they meeting, in secret, just as I had planned. Now I hid myself in the shadow of a streetlamp along Cliveden Place, still lit in the early evening. I watched a doorman, summoned by the old couple, step from out a building designated by its shining bronze nameplate as *Eaton Mansions*. The doorman holding his lantern up for the Whitechurches to enter. He shut the door behind them. And a minute later a window lit up on the second landing. Faint. A few seconds later the window beside it lit up too.

I waited patient in my hiding place. Till both lamps were extinguished again, a good few minutes later. Then I crossed the street and began making my way, shadow-by-shadow, round the sides of the building. It formed the shape of the letter U. With a small courtyard tucked between the arms. I leant against a brick wall at the back, waiting for my eyes to adjust to the dark. Making out a stone birdbath at the centre of the courtyard, beside it a single horse chestnut tree, already losing its leaves in autumn.

I crossed over and hid myself behind the trunk.

On the second floor—corresponding more-or-less to where the lights had appeared on the other side of the building—I noticed one of the windows slightly ajar. I stared up at it. Son, for some reason I can't explain, I felt a peculiar attraction to this particular window. Something physical. Tingling up my spine-bones like a line of crawling bachacks. Without taking my eyes off it I crouched down to sweep aside the dry leaves beneath the tree, the eyelashed half-shells of the fallen horse chestnuts, scratching blind in the hard dirt. Till I'd scraped up a handful of small rockstones.

Now, reckless, I began pelting them up at the slightly opened window.

I listened to the sharp *pings* one after the next, watching the rockstones bounce off the thickly bevelled panes. But nothing happened. No response from nobody a-tall. I reached down to grab up one of those same big horse chestnuts—pelting *it* up at the window—smacking against the pane with a loud *braps!*

Son, all-in-a-sudden the window lit up. But faint, coming from deeper within the room. My heart pounding inside my chest like a caged zandolee. A second later the curtains were swept aside—the two window-leaves swinging open with a single, sharp, rusty screech—and like the soft inhalation of a breath, Marguerite appeared. Her hazel hair loose and draping over her shoulders. Face lit from below by the candle holding in her hand.

Son, I wanted for all the world to call out to her: now my voice stuck-up inside my throat like I'd swallowed laglee. I wanted to give her some kinda signal: I couldn't even raise up my hand.

After standing like that a full minute—unmoving, *both* of us—Marguerite stepped backwards into the depths of her room. Blowing out the candle. The window darkening again.

I leant against the chestnut tree, catching my breath. Brushing the sleeve of my patched-up jacket across my beaded-over forehead—agonised, defeated, swallowed-up inside. Eventually, I crossed thorough the shadows of the small courtyard, till I stood directly below Marguerite's window. Peering up at it in the dark, some twenty-or-so-feet above my head.

Ivy had once covered the brick wall, twisting between the chinks, weaving its way up. Now the vine was dead and leafless. I reached to take hold of the thickest part—bracing my boots against the wall—hoisting myself up.

Reaching, grabbing, pulling myself higher. And higher still.

Till I'd got to within an arm's-reach of the sill—an arm's-reach!

All-in-a-sudden the vine pulled loose. In three punctuated sections—*voop, voop, voop*—and I tumbled backwards to the hard ground. Flat on my back with a loud *humph*. Inhaling a crust of gritty dirt.

I lay there on my back—winded, panting—length of the vine still clutching between my fists. Struggling to breathe—my lungs on fire, burning, spitting out the grit.

I couldn't open up my eyes. Wouldn't *dare* open them, thinking I was surely dead. And if not dead then paralysed from the neck down. Because I couldn't suck a breath.

Eventually—agonisingly—my breath returned. And when I'd managed, slowly, to open my eyes and look up, I found Marguerite again. Standing in the frame of her window, lit candle holding in her hand.

I sat up, blinking, shaking the stars loose. Watching a wave of relief pass over Marguerite's candle-lit face. She smiled, and after another minute she put the candle down on the sill. Marguerite disappeared, returning to the window a few seconds later with her small white book, her writing pencil.

She daubed the lead three times against her tongue—her smile no longer one of simple relief, but joyful, playful—and she scribbled out a word. With the same flourish she tore the page loose, tossing it into the air. She repeated the gesture. Again & again & again. Daubing & scribbling & ripping out the page.

Till seventeen pieces of paper floated in the dark air. Seventeen pale-white moths, fluttering, descending slowly towards me.

Already I was on my feet, running behind the slips of paper. Grabbing them out the air one-after-the-next. Breathless again, I stopped to look up at her, clutching my slips of paper—Marguerite's words, not my own, holding tight in my hands—and at that moment, in my beating fifteen-year-old heart, she appeared not simply beautiful, but radiant.

Yet it lasted only a moment. Because quick like that she took up her candle from off the sill. She blew it out, the window darkening again.

But son, something in all this had revived my spirits. I couldn't tell you what. Not as yet. I turned to take up the last slip of paper, there on the bare ground before my boot. And I hurried cross the courtyard again, round the U-shaped building, clutching at my slips of paper.

The streetlamps on the other side of Cliveden Place had been extinguished by now. I hurried towards the nearest source of light, I didn't know what it was—*something* glowing in the direction of Sloane Square—bright in the distance. And a few seconds later, across the three wide marble steps of the Royal Court Theatre, beneath the flaming torches of the marquee, I spread out my seventeen slips of paper—

sweet I mind Trinidad & that

decided we two changed have will

my together Willy travel go

◈

It must've been a couple hours later when I woke up. I didn't have no idea. Only that the hard sun had dipped beneath the rim of the trees sheltering our compound. At first I didn't know where-the-arse I was—I'd thought I was back in England! Then I recognised John's face. Leaning in over my hammock, holding a cup of water against my lips. Tiltsing it back slow.

I coughed, trying to swallow—

Wha . . . ?

Boy, John says, smiling. You catch one good fit o' de malkodee, hear? Pass out cold-cold. Mistah Carr carry you ovah he shoulder all de way back from de gardnens!

I looked round the compound. My eyes settling on the dining table, on the figure of Mr. Whitechurch reclining there on his back. Fully dressed now, but in the clothes he'd had on when we first arrived, including his green velvet vest. I could see a flash from the chain of his goldwatch disappearing into his breast pocket, a flicker of leftover sun reflecting off the gold St. Christopher medal round his neck. The rockstones weighing down Mr. Whitechurch's eyelids had been removed, his white beard combed out and detangled. Even from a distance I could see that the hideous colour seemed to have drained-out some from his face. His cheeks rosy again, playful—like he'd just knocked back a calabash of rum. Only his boots, severely torn—one sole dangling loose in an ugly black gaping mouth—seemed to speak for the previous eight days. They looked like the boots of a bedlam beggar.

I turned my eyes back to John—

Where's Papee? And Mr. Carr?

Dey still out by de gardnens, he says. Got to finish digging-out Mistah Whitechurch gravehole, you know!

I sat up, anger washing through me hot again—

We've got to get him back to his wife n' Mar— Back to his wife n' niece. It's only proper!

I swallowed—

Doesn't anybody realise they have to *see* him? they would want to *be* with him?

John waited a few seconds—

Ain't no way to get he far as Port España. Less you aiming to tote he ovah de mountains youself!

He paused—

Mailboat don't pass for ten days. And Cap Maynard don't come again for more den fortnight.

John smiled, shaking his head—

Mistah Whitechurch can't wait for dat, Willy-boy. He bound to find he res' place inside de groun!

I looked into his face another minute. Then I laid back in my hammock again, quiet, reaching to take the cup from him. Swallowing the remainder in a single mouthful.

A few minutes later Esteban and Orinoko arrived, speaking softly with John. But for me it was like listening to a group of voices talking way off. Then I heard them set about preparing dinner.

Sometime after that Papee and Mr. Carr returned from the gardens. And seeing supper was almost ready, they continued down to the beach to wash up. Now I swung my legs round, letting them hang down from out my hammock. Sitting there a moment—my feet planted on the ground, feeling it pushing up soft and cool through my footsoles. I went down to the beach to splash some cool water on my face too.

The six of us ate our evening meal together. Sitting there at the same dining table with our balisier plates and calabash cups surrounding Mr. Whitechurch. Son, I found all this disconcerting—disrespectful to the old man. Then I realised something else. And this *other* thing upset me even further: someone had stolen Mr. Whitechurch's pocketwatch. His gold St. Christopher medal from round his neck. Because I couldn't find them a-tall! And son, this thiefing-business had me so vex, for several minutes I couldn't even swallow down my dinner.

Then, after a time, my anger began to wash-way. And I began to warm up a little better to this idea, this gesture of a final meal in the company of Mr. Whitechurch. Especially when Mr. Carr, seated now in Mr. Whitechurch's place at the head of the table, tossed out the water from his calabash cup. Replacing it with a short draught of rum.

He stood to his feet, raising up his cup—

To a grand old gentleman, 'oom we shall all dearly miss!

'Ere, 'ere, we say together, quiet, touching our calabash cups. Even over Mr. Whitechurch heself.

When our meal was finished we stood together. And the six of us took up Mr. Whitechurch. Me grasping one shoulder and Papee the next, John and Esteban holding they hands clasped beneath he pockeled potbelly, whilst Mr. Carr and Orinoko each took hold of a spindly leg. By this time his body had stiffened up substantial. So we hardly disturbed the position he'd rested in so peaceful a moment before atop the table.

We carried him out to the gardens. Followed, high above— because I kept glancing back over my shoulder to see if they were still behind us—by the ragged birds.

Whilst the others finished covering up Mr. Whitechurch's grave, Papee and me set off on a short hike into the mountains. Our second excursion for the day. Papee saying he wanted to search the forest for two tall gri-gri trunks, suitable to replace the masts of Captain Taylor's schooner. Something-or-other, because he never mentioned those trunks again after we'd left the gardens. We didn't say nothing a-tall for the longest time, in the way of the forest. Plodding our way between the towering trees, cutlasses out swiping at vines draping down before us. A thick layer of leaftrash covering the ground beneath our boots, muffling our footsteps. Occasionally we passed patches of mist that had gathered at the bases of the thick trunks, ankle-deep—like small flat clouds—Papee and me kicksing them up as we passed through. Eventually we reached the place where the path turned vertical, and now we scaled the rockface on all fours. Then it turned again, cutting sideways cross the mountain, Papee leading me past the series of dark echoey caves.

Suddenly, like if he'd caught a vaps, Papee stopped. Turning round to face me. Speaking for the first time since we'd started out—

Let's see if we can find those *diabotins?* he says. Those oilbirds John mentioned?

He paused, studying my face—

What do you say, son, if we take a look?

I shrugged my shoulders. Trying to recall whatever-the-arse kinda birds were those *diabotins*—and wondering how would we see them anyway? inside the darkness of these caves?

The first two stretched back only ten-to-fifteen-feet. Barren as the skullcap of a baldheaded old man. A handful of zandolees scampering cross the green-gray walls.

We had to enter the third, smallest-looking cave through a narrow porthole-like opening. Two- to three-feet wide and the same distance above the ground. Our cutlasses left stuck in the hard dirt outside. We stretched our arms out straight and ducked our heads, squeezing weself in, like diving through a hoop. Papee first and then me. Scrambling up from off our bellies once we'd found weself inside. We saw that this cave opened up and fingered off, but we didn't have no idea how far at first. All we could know for now was that we were standing upright. That this front part of the cave could at least accommodate we full statures. Ten degrees colder inside than out, a coldness made the more palpable by the heavy humidity. We stood there, unmoving, a full minute. Just listening to each other breathing. Waiting for our eyes to adjust to the dark. Now—slow to begin with, then fast—this underground cave-world began to take shape before our eyes.

First thing we noticed was the white flooring. Covered over with a chalky kinda paving, two-to-three-inches deep—*guano*, though we hadn't identified the substance just as yet. We could also discern a slight echoing *slurrrup-pup-pup slurrrup-pup-pup*—water dripping into a puddle someplace. Though we couldn't find the drip nor the puddle neither. All-in-a-sudden—very slow, then fast-fast—it dawned upon us that the entire ceiling of this cave was *alive*. Breathing. Undulating above our heads in a peculiar, splotchy kinda movement. Like the inside surface of the water when you gaze up at it from underneath.

We saw that this entire cave-ceiling was covered over with a congregation of tiny bats. All hanging upside-down by they invisible feet. All trembling, hugging they folded-up wings in miniature gabardines clutched round them. All moving together—jittering, fidgeting, wriggling in they peculiar kinda aggregated, syncopated, breathing movement. And son, let me tell you, *thousands*-is-thousands of bats covering over the ceiling of this cave! With all they thousands of tiny black beetle-eyes, thousands of tiny black mouse-ears, thousands of tiny black picoplatt-beaks.

And we began to perceive with our *inner* ears—at the bottom-edge of this cave's profound silence—the low, squeaking, *tit-tit-tittering* of all these thousands of bats. All conversing they bat-conversations together!

Papee pushed forward. Parting the air before him like a velvet curtain. Shoving his way into the cave a few more powdery steps. With me pressing tight against his back, following behind. He chose the fork branching off towards our right—this one narrower, deeper, taller. Yet after a few shuffling steps we were compelled to duck our heads beneath the living ceiling of bats.

Straightway—like he wasn't even pausing a second to reconsider this thing!—Papee got down on his hands and knees in the thick paving of guano. Me doing the same despite my reluctance just behind. And we recognised for the first time the awful *stench* of this blasted guano, because it hadn't found our nostrils not till now. But much as our nostrils were flaring all-in-a-sudden to life, we couldn't perceive nothing a-tall with our eyes yet. *Feeling* our way slow and cautious through the velvet curtain of moist cave-air—Papee crawling forward a few inches farther at a time, then stopping to let his eyes readjust—me crawling & stopping & readjusting reluctant behind.

Through the jelly-thick blackness before us, plastered to the low walls at the back-end of this particular finger of the cave—like they were constructed from the same chalky white guano, in addition to a fistful of twigs—we began to recognise something looking like birds' nests. Though we hadn't seen the diabotins perching above them yet. But sure enough, slowly, we started to make them out. Crouching hunched-over on the ledges—*big* birds, between the size of a kiskadee and a cobo—coloured the same brownish-green as the cave-walls. Same filthy brownish-green as the cave-ceiling of living, fidgeting, breathing bats.

And let me tell you son, now we understood why they called these birds *diabotins*—little devils—because they didn't look like no kinda birds a-tall. Or only partly so. Like if these diabotins were some kinda cross between a bird, a river-agutee, and a mongrel-cat.

Above they fiercely hooked beaks were huge, obscene, clouded-over eyes. Surrounded by agutee-lashes. Hideous whiskered cat-faces. All with they little chests thrusting forward, heads pulled back. And soon we made out the most frightening feature of all—they scarlet, gaping, mucus-dripping mouths.

There were five-six of them. Perching on the cave-ledges in the darkness above they nests, staring straight at Papee and me.

But *not* looking at us through they oversized, clouded-over eyes: because somehow these birds were staring at us through they scarlet-dripping *throats*.

We'd only been in this branch of the cave a few seconds. Everything dead still up till now—dead silent—though these bloody diabotins' mouths were wide-open. All-at-once they began kicksing up a tremendous screeching ruckus. Echoing off the cave-walls. So loud and piercing it pained us inside our ears.

In the midst of they wild hullabaloo, all of them lifted off they cave-perches together. Hovering. Side-flapping the stagnant air with they large bat-like wings. Hovering before us in the furious wing-flapping cave-air.

In addition to they piercing screeches, we began to hear the sharp metallic clacks of they echolocation—*clack-clack, clack-clack, clack-clack*.

All-at-once, all-of-them-together—and without giving us any warning a-tall—these diabotins flew straight at Papee and me. Straight towards our faces with they hovering, screeching, clacking diabotin-flight. And before we could even duck our heads they'd brushed past, all five-six of them, clacking and screeching they way towards the cave-door behind our backs.

Son, I couldn't tell you why my fear was delayed—I couldn't explain to you the logic of it a-tall—but now, not the moment before, a terrible *fright* overtook me. Because all-in-a-sudden I was trembling like a blasted mamapoule. Scared out my skin—I couldn't think of nothing more than to hurry my little backside to hell *out* from this cave, fast as I could hurry it!

I shifted round on my hands and knees with a few quick sideways-shuffling movements. Crawling and dragging myself cross the guano-carpeted floor—rising up onto my feet the same instant—stumbling the last few frantic paces towards the dimly lit, porthole-like door.

I ducked my head down, stretching out my arms, diving through. Like diving through a flaming hoop.

The sky was already dusking over a deep purple as I lifted my face off the hard dirt outside. Lying on my belly beside our stabbed-in cutlasses—spitting a mouthful of grit, swallowing a breath of clean air. But straightway I pulled myself up onto my feet again, stepping from out Papee's way, as he was only a pace behind.

We stood side-by-side, hands bracing on our knees, bent over. Panting. Catching our breath. And for some peculiar reason both of us straightened up together, turning round together again. Looking back in through the cave-entrance. That same dark porthole through which we'd just fled, just escaped.

And now, son, the most extraordinary thing of all: like we'd pulled the cork from a colossal glassbottle. Now—in a single, collective, fluttering rush—the bats commenced to exiting out they cave-dwelling behind us.

Before us. All these thousands-upon-thousands of minuscule bats. All-at-once. All-of-them-together. Flying up round us with they great rush of tiny, fluttering wings—and it was as if we were being lifted up off our feet with them! Even though our feet remained planted firm and solid atop the ground. As if Papee and me were being *elevated* together. Up into the cool, purple, just-dusking-over sky. Together with all this multitude of wings flapping round us. To such extent that I reached out quick to grasp hold of Papee's hand—because if I didn't hold onto *something*, these bloody bats would surely carry me away with them!

Yet somehow we didn't feel nothing a-tall. Nothing but the rush of air. Lifting us up without our feet leaving the ground. Because not a single batwing even braised against our forearms—necks—cheeks—foreheads—not a *touch*.

I have to tell you something else, son. Another thing not so much extraordinary as inexplicable. Because to this the day I can't explain to you the logic of why it happened. Papee and me were standing there like that, holding hands, staring back into the cave-opening with all these thousands of tiny bats streaming up out they cave-door like the cork pulled loose from the colossal glassbottle. Streaming up all round us. I shut my eyes, squeezing them tight. Holding onto Papee's hand and squeezing *it* tight too. Just sensing the exhilaration of all these bats fluttering round me, my own living, fluttering, exhilarating skin.

And a moment later, like I'm hearing it from outside my body, from outside my own panting, exploding breast—like if it's the fluttering bats *theyself* I'm hearing now—I hear my own fifteen-year-old voice. Repeating over and over. Shouting out into the rage of fluttering wings—

White Church! Missterr Whiite Churrch! Miiisssterrrwhiiite-churrrrrch!

14

Captain Taylor's Schooner

Papee had selected and marked off with a chalky rockstone two gri-gri trunks during our excursion of the previous afternoon—I hadn't even seen him do it—suitable to replace the schooner's snapped-off masts. These two trunks, with John's aid, we set weself to felling the following morning. It didn't take us no time a-tall. The second trunk *booming* down with the startling catastrophe of knocking from out her perch a female red howler monkey. Unseen by us high above the canopy-crown. We watched her drop from out the sky. Clutching her baby tight against her breast for the entire unending duration of that treacherous fall. But with her final brutal bounding against the hard forest floor, the baby was flung forcibly out her arms. *Smack* against the side of a cedar trunk. Some five-or-six-feet from where she lay.

I dropped my hatchet in the same breath, running to take the baby monkey up. Reaching its long woolly arms round my neck—the warmth of its tiny handprint lingering on my cheek a moment as I bent to lay the baby down beside its mother. Now I stepped away, the baby scrambling of its own accord back inside its mother's arms. Taking hold of her once more round her waist. But the mother didn't stir. A-tall. She simply lay there, unmoving, perfectly still with her wide sad eyes unblinking, dull-looking, staring up at us.

We thought her dead.

Then we watched with stifled breaths and beating chests as

281 ～ ROBERT ANTONI

the mother rolled over in the leaves and started-way. Dragging her ill-twisted, severely damaged leg behind her. Comforting her startled baby by suckling it up gentle against her tit—like a human infant—whilst struggling at the same time to drag her crumpled-up leg behind her. Amongst all those deading leaves & creepers & snaggling doux-doux vines. Away from such violent intruders as we personified to the full. Off to the quiet safety of the deeper forest.[*]

Son, it pained our hearts to watch it happen. To such extent we couldn't even speak to express our hurt. We didn't say nothing a-tall till long after we'd toted those gri-gri trunks out the jungle, past the compound to the schooner's side. Sized & cut & cleaned & shaved them both smooth as the twin cheeks of you own backside. Woodcurls floating down like giant snowflakes to mingle amongst we bare toes in the sand. Both mast-poles stripped of every manner of bark & branches & protruding knots top-to-bottom.

We set them aside to weather a few days. Before we'd raise them up and slot them in.

All this accomplished to Papee's satisfaction—and it still being early morning—he stood on the beach a minute, studying the lie of the wrecked schooner in the sand. Sussing out our next move. John and me resting in the shade nearby.

I watched Papee dragging from out he trousers' pocket a shining goldwatch. Like if it's the most natural gesture in the world for him to be doing this. Like if he's been doing it he whole bloody life. The watch attached to its long goldchain like a sleeping mappapee coiled up in the depths of his pocket.

---

[*] During the early settling of Trinidad and parts of South America a strain of 'jungle' yellow fever, carried by red howler monkeys, was transmitted to *Haemagogus* mosquitoes that lived only in the upper canopy of the rainforest. The virus, found to have an incubation time as short as seventy-two hours, was passed to humans when the tall trees were cut down.

Papee snapped the cover open. Turning the watchface up cool-cool to examine it. Goldchain dangling down like a fuse ignited by the bristling sun.

A second later I was on my feet. Grabbing hold of Papee's shirt-neck in both hands. Tight as vicegrips between the clutches of my trembling fists—

Bastard! I shout into his face, spittle flying. Bloody thief! You're the one who stole Mr. Whitechurch's watch!

Papee remained calm. Unconfuffled. Looking slightly down at me according to the slope of the sand. His head back-tilted, lips assuming the shape of a mocking smile. And let me tell you he smile only enraged me further.

Out my eye-corner I saw him slide the watch and mappapee-chain back inside his pocket. He waited a minute before answering, my fists still clenching his twisted-up collar. Trembling against the sides of Papee's bullmoose neck—

Son, he says, calm, quiet. I'll have you know Mr. White-church *willed* his watch to me. And I intend to keep it a good long time in his memory.

Papee paused a second, waiting for me to swallow-down this—

That's what he informed Mr. Carr, he says, still looking over his chin at me. And almost with his dying breath, according to Mr. Carr, he gave explicit instructions that I was to keep his pocketwatch until one day, I should pass it on to you, Willy.

Papee's smile broadened now—

And one day, son, I trust that you shall treasure it just the same!

I let my fists loose from his collar. Stumbling a step backwards, down the slope of the beach. Then another step. Wiping my wet hands down the front of my suddenly sweated-up shirt.

We remained like that a full minute. Standing there, staring at each other.

I felt a drop sliding down the back of my neck, down over three ridges of my protruding spinebones. A sandfly buzzed beside my ear. Settling & falling silent & sliding its tiny dagger into my skin at the top of my jawbone. Just below my ear. Stinging like it's on fire. Yet I refused to swat it away.

Finally Papee broke the silence—

Now, he says, marking down the final full stop and the end of the sentence, end-of-discussion. I was just about to inform you n' John that our next task shall be digging the schooner out her hole. And propping her up in a bamboo cradle. Because we need access to the entire hull, you understand—including the keel, where I suspect she's woefully rotted-out 'neath her venerable copperplates.

I was still angry. Still vex. No doubt I was still emotional over the female howler and her baby. No doubt I missed my *own* mum and sisters at that moment—no doubt I missed Marguerite more than I could say. Aside from the fact that I was already growing exasperated with this schooner. With Papee's sudden obsession to make her seaworthy in but a single breath.

I turned my eyes from him—

Sir, I say, looking down at my ankles above the sand—at my mosquito-bitten, blistered-over, whitee-pokee-penny-a-pound ankles—

Won't you be needing more slaves than John and me to accomplish that?

A vile statement. I regretted it the instant it took shape inside my mouth. Especially with John standing there, just beside. The words sticking to my tongue like the juggers of a pommerack fruit.

After a few seconds Papee turned his eyes back the schooner, still smiling his mocking smile—

A sound strategy, he says, that's all we're wanting!

He turned round to face me again—

We shall have to think one up together. Directly following lunch.

It took us three days to dig the schooner out of the sand. Prop her up in her bamboo cradle. Only Papee never doubted a moment that we could do it, only he believed from the start. Mr. Carr & Esteban & Orinoko assisting us some, but hardly a-tall. Mostly they dedicated theyself to replanting the washed-out gardens. Understand, repairing this schooner was Papee's project. He own personal endeavour. Papee didn't *want* too many people fussing-up round him, tripping under his feet, getting in his way. Only John and me.

The schooner lay half-buried on her starboard side, ten paces into the crabgrass and tall sea grapes. Lying there with her prow pointing down the slope of the beach, aiming straight at the sea—as though, on the day of her ultimate calamity, she'd drifted up onto shore stern-first. According to Papee she'd been lying there a good five-six years at least. We dug right the way round her rotted-out, worm-eaten hull. Deeper on the starboard side towards which her tilt was directed. Propping her up with bamboo poles as we proceeded. But son, we didn't just toss the dug-out sand aside. Not so easy a-tall. Because Papee insisted we pile it up in a mound before the schooner's prow—just in front of her—like we were purposely building up a tall barricade between this schooner we intended to refloat and the very sea upon which we intended to refloat her. Which didn't make no kinda sense to me a-tall, nor John neither.

We did it regardless. Following Papee's lead. Shoveling the sand into a buggy and wheeling it over to where he indicated. And let me tell you it wasn't no kinda breezing effort a-tall, wheeling this buggy filled with sand cross the beach. We did it regardless, following Papee's instructions. Taking the task in turns: shoveling & wheeling & busting a break between.

When he'd returned to Port-Spain Captain Maynard had left his tackle-blocks and winch with us. And these we made good use of to drag the schooner body-and-soul up from out her hole. Securing the winchlines to nothing less than the crated-up Satellite itself—lying there tumbled onto its side atop the stone jetty—fifty yards distant. Our perfect anchor-hold. Only practical purpose that Satellite would ever serve: dead weight. Tying off the other end of the winchline direct to the schooner's prow, still sound enough to carry the load of the vessel dragging behind. Despite that prow's state of dilapidated, dripping rust.

Slow but sure—in a series of minuscule, creaking, jerking movements—we winched the schooner up from out her hole. Inch-by-inch-by-inch. Careful at the same time to work her up level as we proceeded. Winching her out her hole and purposely up on top the mound of loose sand, the same mound we'd just finished piling up before her. But son, now we were dragging her down the slope of the beach, gravity aiding us, much as it appeared we were hoisting her straight up into the air. All of this thought out and calculated careful by Papee. And next thing we knew—before we could even take in how it happened—we had that schooner standing atop the mound of loose sand, as if atop the crest of a giant wave. Not only that, but dead-level.

Third thing we did was dig out all the loose sand from beneath her bow again. From all round her rotted-out, delicately exposed hull. But this time the loose sand dug-out considerably easier and swifter. And in the midst of all of this careful re-excavation, Papee orchestrated the construction of the cradle beneath her. Bamboos knotted together with lianas—each pole angled strategic & braced & cross-buttressed—all the while minding to keep her balanced and on the level.

Three days. Three of the longest, most strenuous days I care to remember. But when we were done, and there the ancient bark stood before us in her elaborate cradle—appearing twice her previous size and almost rejuvenated already—we couldn't hardly recall how Papee'd directed us to do it.

Next morning he revealed to us a small satchel he'd brought with him from Port-Spain—we hadn't seen it up till now—containing a handful of tools: a pair of augers, jigsaw, hammer, several scrapers. To which Mr. Carr contributed the hatchets and a couple more hammers. But son, it wasn't the schooner we set weself to working on first. Not as yet. Because that morning, satchel of tools in hand, Papee led us first to the Satellite's crate. Sitting there atop the stone jetty, our winchlines still knotted in a web round it. Mr. Frank had built that crate from the finest-grade cedar—sturdy, solid, rot- and insect-proof—only reason it had lasted this long.

Papee looked back at John and me, standing there on the jetty, hands shading our brows against the glare—

Perfect wood for shipbuilding, he says. Or ship*repairing*, as the case may be.

Papee knew exactly how to disassemble that crate—he'd assisted Mr. Frank in building it. Not a single nail had been used. Not a one. And within a few minutes Papee pounded out a dozen dowels from the lid—now its side. The heavy lid dropping down with a loud *brum* to the rock floor.

287 ✺ ROBERT ANTONI

John and me saw that Mr. Frank had lined the inside of the lid with several layers of canvas. Designed to protect the Satellite from rain seeping in through the top—since, of course, he could never've suspected the real danger lay in seawater invading the crate through its bottom. That canvas still in perfect condition. The only thing inside the crate left undamaged by the saltwater. Only thing worth salvaging—aside from the pulleys and ropes of the Connective Apparatus, which Papee intended to make good use of too.

He folded the canvas into three packets—

We've got ourselves a mains'il here, he says. Perhaps a jib as well.

Papee busied heself disassembling the lid. Knocking out the dowels and taking it apart board-by-board. John and me toting them over beside the schooner and piling them up. Next Papee disassembled the crate's three exposed sides. Then the bottom. All those boards toted over and piled up beside the schooner. The only part of that crate he left intact was its single side—now below—with the indecipherable mangle of metal sitting on top, rusted to a brilliant orange.

It was now dusk, and John and I had built a neat pile of boards four-feet tall. We were exhausted—not so much by our efforts of disassembling the crate, as by the accumulation of four days' work without a break. So much so that the following morning—the morning of our thirteenth day at Chaguabarriga—we made the strategic error of sleeping late. Till almost midday. Even Papee. Not a one of us stirring from out our slumbers till we smelt the smoke.

It took those pioneers three tedious hours—rowing theyself in Mr. Carr's overloaded dinghy—to traverse the two-mile stretch from the Prescott Estate. Most of that distance, however, they didn't even row. Since they found it all but impossible to make any headway against the current. They let the dinghy drift ashore, several of them jumping out. Attempting to shove the skiff as best they could up the coast.

But most of this shoreline wasn't sandy beach, or even rock—it was irregular mangroves. And most highly irregular mangroves at that. A vast profusion of snarls & snags & ragged indentations, beneath the arching roots only pestilential muck. The same muck they stumbled and sludged they way through. So by the time those pioneers arrived at Chaguabarriga, three long hours later, not only were they exhausted-out, but the entire boatload of them—men, women, and children—were soppsing head-to-foot. Coated high as they waists in the thick, nasty, stenching chagua-muck.

Immediately upon landing they washed theyself off with a quick seabath. Just as they were—boots, hats, and all. Then, so as to warm and dry theyself, they built a bonfire there on the beach before the schooner. A big bonfire. Utilising as fuel— as you have no doubt already guessed—the most convenient wood to come to hand. Son, half the pile had already gone up in smoke by the time Papee & John & me smelt it. Making our sleepy way down to the beach. Only to find those pioneers sitting in they defeated-looking semicircle before the fire—bright orange flames rising up tall as the topmost-tip of that schooner standing behind them. Because let me tell you this was one hell of a bonfire those pioneers built with Papee's boards.

Mr. Carr detecting the smoke from the gardens, arriving at the beach a moment behind us.

Now a row broke out between Mr. Craddock—the leader in all this—and Papee. As you can well imagine. But *not* over his pilfered pile of timbers. Throwing me into the same confusion as everybody else: they quarrel was over the decrepit schooner sheself.

Understand, Mr. Craddock claimed that the schooner belonged to *him*. He own personal property and private abode. Despite that for the previous five days he'd resided at the Prescott Estate—

So what right, he shouts, does this Tucker son-o'-a-bitch have laying a bloody finger on her for any reason a-tall!

Papee stood there confused. Enraged. Not saying a word. He simply stood there, staring at Mr. Craddock, his fists clenching and unclenching over and over—like if the air's made from dough he's kneading up to bake bread.

At that point Mr. Craddock stepped forward. Not towards Papee, but sideways, towards the blazing fire. Reaching down and dragging out the longest board, end of it in flames. He raised it up slow, threatening Papee. But before he could swing his flaming timber at him, Mr. Craddock turned round, raising it up still higher. Swinging not at Papee, but the nearest bamboo brace of the schooner's cradle—BRAPS!

Nothing happened. Nothing a-tall.

He swung his board again—BRAPS! Again—BRAPS! And with his third violent swing—trail of the timber's fiery arch ablaze in all our eyes—he knocked the brace loose.

The entire bark wobbled. Like a drunken humpback whale. Then she began to sway side-to-side. Slow. Bamboos supporting her portside beginning to give-way. Not snapping—bending back-and-forth—with they twisting, slithering kinda motion. Like live snakes. Like if these blasted bamboos suddenly had a mind of they own. Slithering and squirming theyself loose from the grips of those lianas holding them bound.

The schooner stood before us a last second. Now she steadied sheself—appearing to rise up still higher into the air—and she pitched forward. Like she's pelting down off the top of a tall seawave. Her rust-dripping prow nosediving straight down into the sand—BROOM!

We felt it in our footsoles, this jolt from the schooner's nose-dive. The entire beach rebounding beneath us in a single rever-berating shock.

Then stillness. Silence. Nobody moved a muscle.

A few seconds after this our eyes began to shift again—from the now stationary, almost comical-looking nosedived schooner, back to Mr. Craddock. Still standing there holding his timber, the end smouldering-out. Issuing forth little puffs of black smoke.

Once again we took in the soft hissings-and-poppings of that bonfire still flaming up in our midst. Beginning to die down too.

Mr. Craddock stumbled before us, tottering, yet remaining atop his feet. His face vacant. And we watched the smouldering timber drop from out his hands. The burnt end splintering off as it landed, tossing out a small fistful of sparks. Tumbling over the rippled sand at Papee's feet.

Son, now I recognised something else for the first time. Something that struck at me like a stiff zobell cross the back of my head. I recognised that familiar colouring of Mr. Craddock's face. Same familiar uninhabited stare in he hideous, yellow-stained eyes. Because all of this had happened so quick, I didn't have a chance to take it in not till now.

Mr. Craddock stumbled another step forward, down the slope of the beach. He dropped to his knees in front of Papee, like he's kneeling down before him. We watched his head drop down too, slow, like his neckbones have been replaced by a rusty hinge.

Mr. Craddock spewed forth a thick black puddle onto the white sand.

He raised up his head again, dribble of pitch trailing down from one corner of his mouth. Down alongside the protruding veins of he scrawny neck.

Mr. Craddock's head dropped slow on its rusty hinge—and as if he's trying to mimic the gesture of that same schooner behind him, he nosedived into he own black puddle.

Nobody dared approach him. Not for the duration of a long minute. Kneeling there with his skinny bamsee pointing straight up in the air, face pressing just so into his puddle of vomit. Mr. Craddock and the schooner behind him frozen contrapuntal into the same nosedived position, mocking each other.

Papee took a step forward, crouching to the sand before him. He took hold of Mr. Craddock's shoulders, rolling him to one side, then onto his back. Cradling Mr. Craddock's head with the same gentle motion, guiding it onto his lap.

Now Papee leant forward, over him, using the tail of his canvas shirt to wipe the vomit and caked sand away from his face and neck. With all the care and deliberation of a midwife sponging down a baby after birth. Mr. Carr came running with a glassbottle filled with drinking water, holding it up to Mr. Craddock's cracked yellow lips. Tiltsing it back for him to swallow a few sips, rinse out his mouth.

Papee turned to summon my assistance, John's as well. And together the four of us took Mr. Craddock up, carrying him back to the compound, laying him down in the nearest hammock.

As he was burning a high fever, Mr. Carr set about preparing a dose of acetylsalicylic powder, dissolved in a calabash with water. Giving it to him to drink.

But Mr. Craddock refused—rum, he wanted only rum.

This, of course, Mr. Carr denied having. Causing Mr. Craddock to curse the lot of us as villains and lying scoundrels. He began to struggle in the skin of his hammock, violent, fighting-up the four of us together. All four struggling together to hold him down.

Eventually, in the midst of this, Mr. Craddock threw his head over the side of the hammock. Spewing the ground with pitch again. Which had the fortunate effect of subduing him some—or frightening him into submission. Because once he'd finished—and Papee'd cleaned his face again with a damp rag—he drank down the dosage of acetylsalicylic acid without a fight. Then Mr. Carr gave him two blue pills from a vial in his little box, pressed under his tongue, which Mr. Craddock complied with too. Calm & quiet & amicable enough. To such extent that Mr. Carr acquiesced into giving him a short calabash of rum. He swallowed it down in three gulps, tossing the cup aside.

Mr. Craddock remained like that a minute longer. Sitting up in his hammock. And after babbling a set of nonsense about Greener's Grove—a wee pint o' lager n' Mauger's mince-n'-raison pie—he dropped back into his hammock again. Out cold unconscious.

We left him under the care of Mr. Carr. By this time Orinoko and Esteban had arrived at the compound. They set about preparing an early dinner for everybody. Yet when Papee & John & me got back to our toppled-over schooner, we found those other pioneers already loaded up. Preparing to set off in they dinghy again. Understand, prior to this episode on the beach they hadn't the remotest notion that Mr. Craddock was ill—any more than Craddock heself seemed to've known. And this sudden discovery alarmed them to such extent all they wanted was to get theyself away from him & Chaguabarriga & the rest of us as fast as possible. Back to the Prescott Estate.

Not even remaining with us long enough to take they dinner. Son, they didn't suggest bringing Mr. Craddock *back* with them neither. Not for a steups. Now, of course, they had the current coming from behind, shoving them up the coast. So they return trip wouldn't cost them hardly any effort a-tall. Nothing more than an oar rowlocked at the stern to steer them along. And almost before Papee & John & me could raise up we arms to bid good-bye, they'd disappeared again.

Much to we own surprise it didn't take us hardly any effort to get our schooner braced back up in her cradle. A single hour's easy toil. Again we utilised Captain Maynard's winch-and-blocks, tied off this time to a horizontal sea grape limb, stretching across just above her prow. John climbing the tree in two ticks to make fast the lines. This time we did winch her straight up into the air—the foremost part of her bow anyway—and after an hour's breezing work our task was done.

It was whilst eating dinner that evening that Mr. Carr informed us of something else. Something that struck me with a serious shock. Though I couldn't even be sure of my own suppositions yet. And in any case I kept them quiet to myself.

According to Mr. Carr a government surveying vessel had dropped anchor in the bay early that morning. The captain coming ashore in search of potable water. And Mr. Carr told us he'd been more than happy to oblige him. This captain was on his way back to Port-Spain, and so Mr. Carr had placed in his trust a letter composed by Mr. Whitechurch in he final hours. Addressed to his wife and niece. In addition to that gold St.

Christopher medal the old man had seemed most anxious for them to have.

Son, Mr. Carr narrated these events for us calmly enough—between sips of water from his calabash cup—yet as he spoke I felt my heart beating right the way up through me.

Mr. Whitechurch wasn't even a Roman Catholic—he was a bloody High Protestant!—so where-the-arse did he get that St. Christopher from? Yet the medal's significance—patron saint of travellers—seemed obvious enough: it was meant to safeguard Mrs. Whitechurch on she journey back to England.

It *did* seem inevitable that with the old man gone, Mrs. Whitechurch would want to return to whatever family she and Marguerite had remaining there. Because now I realised I didn't have any idea—I'd never even thought to question Marguerite about it. But regardless of any family they might or mightn't have, Mrs. Whitechurch would no doubt need to return to London: she'd have to settle she husband's estate.

Why-the-arse should she remain in Trinidad anyway? what did she have now to keep her there? Worst of all—I understood with a jolt—Marguerite would need to accompany she aunt to England. And what of Marguerite's own anger—directed possibly at *me*, having convinced her to come so far only to have her uncle perish in the bush?

I tried my hardest not to think about it. Not to consider it further. And in any case we were so occupied with our labours over the schooner I hardly had energy leftover by the end of our long days to contemplate it. Even if I'd wanted to. Yet I couldn't close my eyes at night without seeing the flash from that St. Christopher medal. Dangling now like a noose round my own neck.

From that day of Mr. Craddock's incident we slept right

there on the schooner's deck. Suspended above the moon-bathed beach by her bamboo cradle. Three of us sleeping side-by-side together—Papee, me in the middle, John at my other side—the unfolded parcels of canvas spread in three separate layers to make a mattress. Comfortable enough to sleep on. And time as night arrived we could've slept anyplace we lay down we heads.

After that incident with Mr. Craddock Papee refused to stray far from the schooner's side. For any reason a-tall. Like if that cumbruxion of Mr. Craddock's making had *spooked* him or something. Like if it was Papee's duty now to defend the schooner—though whatever-the-arse he felt he needed to protect her from I couldn't tell you. Not Mr. Craddock, because we found him dead in his hammock the following morning. That is to say, Mr. Carr found him. But even with Mr. Craddock gone and out the way, Papee became even more obsessed over the schooner. Something more penetrating and consuming than whatever need he felt to make her seaworthy again. Something more disturbing. More alarming to witness at close hand. Like if Papee's own survival—the survival of *all* of us—was somehow dependent on how fast he could breathe-back life into this ancient bark. Some kinda arse-backwards race not to the finish, but the starting line. Redrawn right there in the sand.

We had to dress Mr. Craddock back in his vomit-soiled clothes to bury him. But in a profoundly different way than we prepared Mr. Whitechurch, prior to carrying him out to the gardens to lay him to rest. Mr. Craddock was of a different stripe.

According to Mr. Carr he'd spewed up pitch several more times that night. One moment his yellow-stained skin was burning up with fever, next it was stone-cold, his body trembling in a fit of ague. Mr. Carr covering him over with Captain Taylor's blanket till the chills passed. Then he pulled it off. At one point, approaching dawn—so Mr. Carr told us—Mr. Craddock found the strength to get up from out his hammock. And after helping heself to a calabash spilling over the brim with rum, he stripped heself down naked. Slow & careful & methodical beneath the billowing moon. Folding each garment of he ruined clothes like they'd just come from a Kings Road tailor. One-by-one in a neat pile atop the dining table. His last remaining seven shillings in a little shining stack balanced on top.

He lay heself down on he back on the cool dirt. Right there in the middle of the open space at the centre of we compound. Just beside the mound with its tattered flag. Just so—stark naked with the moon spilling down atop him, arms spread to each side in the posture of a crucified Christ.

After he'd expired Mr. Carr had moved him to the dining table. Yet this time the spectre of death lying there hardly affected us a-tall. Nothing more than a mild nuisance, a duty to be performed. And son, as we dressed Mr. Craddock and carried him out to the gardens that morning—as we dug the hole beside Mr. Whitechurch, swung him down and topped him over again—all we felt was a sense of relief. All I can recall feeling.

We were back to work on the schooner in the blink of a hour. Working till evening without a pause. Till the time came for us to tumble down onto our canvas mattress again, tumbling again into our distant dreams.

❁

Papee and me sitting together in the tavern of our East End borough—two of us alone at the long table at the back—Papee ordering fried eggs & bacon & buttered toast. Breakfasts we subsequently devoured like prisoners out the gaol. Eating with our hands. Wiping up the yolks of our eggs and bacon grease with pieces of ripped toast. Till our plates shone like if they'd been scrubbed.

Papee then led me round the corner to the barbershop. Where he proceeded to have his head shampooed, his hair trimmed. The barber laying him back in the big chair to lather and shave his face. Then—much to my own surprise—I substituted my father in the chair for the same lavish treatment. Minus the shave. First time in my life anybody other than Mum or Georgina had cut my hair. And nobody'd never shampooed it neither since I was a bloody tyke.

Now we went off to the tailor's shop. And during the hour that followed Papee and I were measured-out for matching frock coats—single vents at the back according to Papee's specifications—pinstripe pants, embroidered waistcoats, white linen shits with French cuffs and silk cravats.

Whilst the tailor and his two assistants busied theyself with all this—at a couple other shops—Papee purchased new dress boots and stockings, tall stiff top hats that resounded like tassa-drums when you rapped on them, pairs of soft white button-up gloves. For both of us.

All on credit—you can bet you tail—like everything else purchased by Papee that morning. The whole business so sudden and so bizarre—so far removed from reality—I'd long given up trying to suss out where the *funds* would come from for all these inexplicable extravagances. Beginning with the absurdity of we eggs and bacon for breakfast.

Only after we'd departed the tailor's shop for the second time that day—both wearing our fancy new outfits with the transformation so complete, already my former self felt like a distant cousin—only then did Papee offer me an explanation. The semblance of an explanation.

He put his arm round my shoulders. Round the shoulders of my new frock coat with the single bloody slit at the back—

A summons to Government House, he says. It arrived late last night for a *William Sanger Tucker.*

He paused—

The truth is, your mother and I are clueless as to what it means.

Now he smiled—

We don't even know if it's addressed to me, son. Or to *you.*

Papee paused again—

Of course, we assume the summons was sent for me. But your mother and I have decided, nonetheless, that you should come along.

And following a breath he added—

As the only male representative of the Tucker clan after me.

It was several long minutes before I could absorb the fact that the haughty-mannered gentleman seated at the other side of the enormous, disheveled desk—dressed like us excepting our gloves and top hats, the latter of which we'd no doubt have doffed if we weren't so thoroughly unnerved by all this—was the PM.

He had the distracting habit of breathing out noisy through his nose. After a minute, without looking up, he cleared his throat—

You may thank your man *Etzler*, he says, like if he's talking to the piece of paper still holding in his hands. For the arrangement of this meeting.

He tossed the paper aside. Raising his long nose up to Papee and me. His little black beady eyes—

And the *con-se-quences* of it, he says. Mr. Etzler believes that it is in our interest—that is to say, in the interest of the government of Great Britain—to become *fis-cal-ly* involved in this enterprise he's about to embark upon in one of our colonies. And it may well be. It may well be.

Now he looked at Papee—

Mr. Tucker, I can assure you only of this: at Christ Church College it was my privilege n' distinction to win a double-first not only in classics, but also mathematics n' physics. So let me cut to the chase here. I have taken the time to peruse the man's book, which he titles *Paradise*. I've examined, at some length, the plans for his Satellite.

Here the prime minister shook his head, simultaneously raising up his small, delicate, impeccably clean hands off his desk. Folded as if in prayer, thumbs crossed, pressing the sides of his pointer-fingers against his lips. Closing his eyes—

'Twill never work.

And after another long pause—like if he was sussing all this out right there in front of us—the prime minister cleared his throat again. He looked at Papee—

Let me come to the point, Mr. Tucker. Our government, by my authority, has seen fit to send you, together with your family, out to Trinidad as its especial *rep-pre-sentative*.

He waited a beat—

Make no mistake about it. I am fully aware of your recent clash with the authorities—along with your colleague, Mr. Powell—for your so-called *Chartists*. Fully aware. I know you very narrowly avoided Newgate Prison yourself. Yet in our opinion such passions *better* qualify you for the obligations we are about to place in your capable hands. It shall be your duty, therefore, to act as go-between for our government and those British citizens about to accompany Mr. Etzler out to Trinidad. You'll report to us on any and all matters you may deem important. This done by way of Mr. Johnston, Colonial Secretary n' Agent General of Emigrants, to whom a letter of mine has already been sent in your regard. And with whom you shall acquaint yourself immediately upon landing in Trinidad. Moreover, it shall be your duty—as especial *rep-pre-sentative* of the British government and Her Majesty the Queen—to keep a watchful eye on Mr. Etzler.

Finally a pause. But it's Papee and me who suck in a breath, not the prime minister—

It is my understanding, Mr. Tucker, that Etzler was jailed himself and later sent packing from his native country of Germany. I am further informed that scarcely a year ago, creditors at his heels, he fled forcibly from the United States as well. Indeed, an emotional treatise of not-inconsiderable length has just reached my desk, warning the *world* against the man! It was penned by an American gentleman of whom, frankly, I am ignorant. Though I'm told he's somewhat renowned in literary circles—a certain Mr. Henry David Thoreau.[Δ*]

Here the prime minister cleared his throat for the umpteenth time—

To conclude, this man Etzler may be a genius—as he's so apt to proclaim himself—but it is my profound fear, Mr. Tucker, that he is dangerous.

I turned to look at Papee. For the first time since we'd entered the prime minister's office. First time since we'd taken our seats before his desk. Because now I couldn't help myself. But I couldn't read nothing in Papee's face a-tall, only that he looked confused—

Do you mean to say, sir, that I am to be contracted by the Crown to *spy* on Mr. Etzler?

The prime minister didn't answer for several seconds—

Call it what you will, Mr. Tucker. Call it what you will.

Already he'd turned his nose to the document lying on the desk before him—

Now, he continues, like if he's talking to the paper again. Let me be the first to wish you n' your family *bon voyage*.

⟨◇⟩

A strange gurgling, *choking* noise. I sat up startled on the canvas mattress, looking over at Papee. Then I turned to John—

Wake up! I say, crouching over him.

John opened his eyes slow, staring up into my face—

Egn? he says.

Then, after a breath—

Boy, like you see diab!

Papee, I say.

Egn?

Papee!

Finally John sat up. He shuffled round on all fours, both of us kneeling together over my father. Lying there on his back with the moon spilling down so bright we could see him clear as day. The dull reflection in Papee's eyes. Wide, wide open. But both his pupils were turned back so only the whites showed.

Except they weren't white a-tall. They were yellow. Purple veins crawling all through. Like two bright yellow marbles, pupil-less, snagged up in they little purple nets. Papee's face covered over in a hundred tiny drops of sweat. Beaded-up. His teeth clenched tight-tight together.

I reached to feel for his pulse—searching at the side of his bullmoose-neck for the thick protruding vein there—my two fingertips probing, pressing. Except I'd never done this thing before in all my life. I didn't even know what-the-arse I was meant to be feeling for.

And in any case Papee's pulse was racing so fast, it had turned into something solid. Unfeelable. Uncountable. Or no pulse a-tall. His skin so hot it stung my fingers.

John steupsed. He shoved me out the way—rough—reaching to grasp hold of both Papee's shoulders in the grips of his strong hands. Shaking him. Rattling Papee against the unpinned boards of the deck beneath us. Like stones in a tin bucket, rattling right the way up my own spinebones.

Finally Papee gasped, sucking in a short breath. Followed by a single long exhalation. His teeth slowly unclenching, lips flapping loose, spray of sweat flickering off—a soft nimbus, floating over Papee's mouth beneath the moon.

But he didn't wake up. Not now. Not yet. His eyes didn't turn round inside they sockets not-for-nothing neither.

I turned to John—

Look, I say.

I grasped hold of the sweated-up strip of canvas. Pulling it away from the lower part of Papee's thighs—

Look! I say again, the only word I can think of, only word I can shape my tongue round.

I nodded my chin down at him.

Beneath Papee's pale drawers—on the pale, moonlit canvas—he was lying atop a puddle of shite.

Only it was too black to be shite. Proper shite.

LAST LETTER FROM MR. ETZLER TO ALL MEMBERS OF THE TROPICAL EMIGRATION SOCIETY

The Morning Star, No. 31, 12 March 1846

Ladies and Gentlemen:

I write to you with a heavy heart. A battered soul, shunned by mine own people, slandered against by those same persons who hastened to call me prophet, genius, patron saint of all who labour and toil. They hound me to the quick, brute ruffians in the shape of honest men. My crown is metaphoric, yet its thorns prick as true. My blood floweth as red! For if—as a certain ASSASSIN EDITOR who proclaims to speak for the MAJORITY has put it down in our own fair *Star*—'the Society now wishes to sever all ties with the likes of Mr. Etzler,' then my answer to you, Mr. Powell, is this: Let it be so! Let me cease from this moment forward to rent the hairs from this white head, and wish you Godspeed along your way, and beg leave and liberty to do the same. Fear not, gentle people, I shall not trouble you again.

What a heinous crime it was in me to renounce all profits for myself, whilst offering at the same time to TEACH, free of charge, those willing to LISTEN and LEARN, affording thereby the means to live a life of leisure, accompanied by every pleasure and luxury known to humankind. How wrong of me to place all of this within your easy grasp! What a terrible sin to offer for every £10 share of your investment in our TES an acre of your own private land, 1/2 to be cultivated within the first year by my Satellite GRATIS, with all the best foodstuffs plus the requisite houses to live in—1/2 of those profits to be devoted to the shareholders for your own purposes as you saw fit, the other 1/2 dedicated according to my and the Co.'s directions. This celebrated union to be above all labour forever, beyond any care or unpleasant preoccupation for its physical wants: one hour's easy gardening per day, or not, to be accompanied by song and music, with utmost cleanliness, simplicity, and elegance in dress. Your passions to consist of cheerful, inoffensive conversation—lecturing, reading, innocent amusements. All tending to a contemplation of the means by which to increase the wellbeing of our kind, individually and universally, every day a feast of pleasure and utility! To make of you and your children and your children's children TRUE princes and princesses. A new tribe of humanity, reigning in dominion over the earth!

Be not afeared, my children, for no one shall make such an offer to you again. Since no one but myself is capable of offering and fulfilling such a promise.

Are you not ready, then, to lift the stone to stone that 'execrable tyrant'—as the butcher editor of our *Star* has named me—that 'diabolical dictator' who proposed to perform all of this tedious business himself, and leave to YOU all the benefits? How unpardonable in him to have the WILL to execute his plan without suffering any others—no more slaves but insensible machines of iron and wood!—whilst pledging at the same time the patent rights for my own machines as SECURITY in the same undertaking? Did I not constitute the organ of TES myself to be the sole paymaster for my own inventions, all things to be the profit of said shareholders? Did I not declare myself to be content with the mere crumbs that might remain, after all expenses were defrayed according to my plan? I do not want to TOUCH the other monies, nor would I soil my hands in the fingering of them! So I am at complete remiss to discover how I could contrive to enrich myself by embezzlement, swindle, or any unfair means—so accused by that perfidious editor of our little *Star*.

And yet, to have been shackled hand-and-foot to the likes of a Capt Taylor and a Mr. Carr! Who against my every plea and instruction hastened to purchase at all hazards for £1000 of your dear money, 100 or 150 acres of useless undeveloped woodland, with a large mangrove swamp in their midst detrimental to health and life. Then, against all my advices, to the complete disorder and utter mischief of his OWN petty contrivances, Mr. Carr (his colleague, the Capt Taylor, having suffered already the consequences of his own selfish behaviour!) proceeded to take to Chaguabarriga a shipload of your pioneers, with tender children and women amongst them, before they knew whither they were going, and where they remain still—shipwrecked, lost, utterly destitute. And not only that: to have stolen my Satellite! Pilfered most vilely from under my own eyes, only to take with them to this miserable place! (I charge Mr. Carr above all others in this vicious crime.) And yet the villainous Powell has the audacity to call ME a thief! The stolen machine is with them still, for all eyes to bear witness—and to what utility? for what purpose? lacking my expertise to set the Satellite to work? My dear people, who can save them? Who can help Chaguabarriga now? Their lives are surely doomed!

For even as I write this letter, my pen is interrupted by the melancholy news just delivered by a certain Capt M'Cullum, a surveyor in the employment of the Colonial Government here, whose vessel happened to touch at Chaguabarriga Bay but a few days ago: the death and burial of Mr. Whitechurch, one of our most prominent and cherished members! His bereaved wife and niece, who remained behind in the safety of this port, are shattered out of all perceptions. Their only means of fleeing such shocking and devastating news is to return to friends and relatives in England at the first opportunity. Our humble Mr. Whitechurch may be the first (barring Capt T. who is of little consequence here), but I assure you he will not be the last! Others will surely follow, many others—women and children too—ere they quit this unhealthy place! You may mark my words in that.

I can stand by no longer and watch it happen. My conscience cannot bear it—though I am perfectly faultless in the undertaking, since you have as ample written proof my own chastisements of this enterprise at Chaguabarriga

from the outset. For this very reason, as you know yourselves, I hastened to Venezuable in him to have the WILL to execute his plan without suffering any others—no more slaves but insensible machines of iron and wood!—whilst pledging at the same time the patent rights for my own machines as SECURITY in the same undertaking? Did I not constitute the organ of TES myself to be the sole paymaster for my own inventions, all things to be the profit of said shareholders? Did I not declare myself to be content with the mere crumbs that might remain, after all expenses were defrayed according to my plan? I do not want to TOUCH the other monies, nor would I soil my hands in the fingering of them! So I am at complete remiss to discover how I could contrive to enrich myself by embezzlement, swindle, or any unfair means—so accused by that perfidious editor of our little Star.

And yet, to have been shackled hand-and-foot to the likes of a Capt Taylor and a Mr. Carr! Who against my every plea and instruction hastened to purchase at all hazards for £1000 of your dear money, 100 or 150 acres of useless undeveloped woodland, with a large mangrove swamp in their midst detrimental to health and life. Then, against all my advices, to the complete disorder and utter mischief of his OWN petty contrivances, Mr. Carr (his colleague, the Capt Taylor, having suffered already the consequences of his own selfish behaviour!) proceeded to take to Chaguabarriga a shipload of your pioneers, with tender children and women amongst them, before they knew whither they were going, and where they remain still—shipwrecked, lost, utterly destitute. And not only that: to have stolen my Satellite! Pilfered most vilely from under my own eyes, only to take with them to this miserable place! (I charge Mr. Carr above all others in this vicious crime.) And yet the villainous Powell has the audacity to call ME a thief! The stolen machine is with them still, for all eyes to bear witness—and to what utility? for what purpose? lacking my expertise to set the Satellite to work? My dear people, who can save them? Who can help Chaguabarriga now? Their lives are surely doomed!

For even as I write this letter, my pen is interrupted by the melancholy news just delivered by a certain Capt M'Cullum, a surveyor in the employment of the Colonial Government here, whose vessel happened to touch at Chaguabarriga Bay but a few days ago: the death and burial of Mr. Whitechurch, one of our most prominent and cherished members! His bereaved wife and niece, who remained behind in the safety of this port, are shattered out of all perceptions. Their only means of fleeing such shocking and devastating news is to return to friends and relatives in England at the first opportunity. Our humble Mr. Whitechurch may be the first (barring Capt T. who is of little consequence here), but I assure you he will not be the last! Others will surely follow, many others—women and children too—ere they quit this unhealthy place! You may mark my words in that.

I can stand by no longer and watch it happen. My conscience cannot bear it—though I am perfectly faultless in the undertaking, since you have as ample written proof my own chastisements of this enterprise at Chaguabarriga from the outset. For this very reason, as you know yourselves, I hastened to Venezuela to explore and investigate the possibilities of a Main Grant there. In that also I fulfilled my promise, and so much more. Wherein the accusations then of an executioner editor—'Mr. Etzler was sent out from London to obtain for the TES a tract of 70,000 acres of government land, and he failed to do so.' Did I not find at Baranjas, close to the capital town of Caracas, an estate called Santa Magdelena, to be had at little or trifling cost to our Society? a tract of the most fertile farmland known to exist in this hemisphere, unmeasured, but said to exceed 70,000 fanegas? Nearly TEN TIMES the original amount proposed and promised by me according to the bylaws of our TES. But all of our funds having been heedlessly thrown away on Chaguabarriga, I had no recourse but to apply to you for more. And even with that money not forthcoming, I offered to purchase the estate MYSELF by my own means, plus what little I had remaining from the sale of Mr. Rake's cutlery, with the invitation to you to join me under the auspices of a newly RECONSTITUTED Society (see my manifesto!), but since you chose willfully not to hear and answer my plea, with not a farthing sent, not a scrap thrown before a dog, I was once more to infernal desperation forced to abandon my plan! all my dreams dashed! cast once more upon barren ground!

And now, cursed and despised for all my efforts, shunned for time ever after by the very Society for which I laboured to conceive and give birth, what course have I but to turn my back? I am poor, penniless, alone. I can do nothing here in Trinidad. Nor would I wish to associate myself any longer with the inhabitants of this place—the wealthy white Englishmen and Frenchmen, I mean!—for they are most profound in their stupidity, a closed-minded, racist bunch—ignorant, childish, brutish as boors. Our TGE&SWR is ruined, that enterprise for which Mr. Stollmeyer and myself were sent out to this island, and would have installed here. Parties of the rival railroad have made certain our destruction and loss for their own gain, we have been declared bankrupt, and I must perforce leave Mr. Stollmeyer behind to pick up the broken pieces, before he can come and join me.

To speak nothing of the blatant misrepresentation and backbiting accounts given of the sea trial of our Naval Automaton! To expand out of all conceivable recognition a minor technical complication of our Connecting Apparatus—a mere glitch!—whereby the power exerted upon the submerged stationary platform would be transferred to our wave machinery, so simply remedied! so easily fixed with a few minor adjustments! So much ado about nothing! For which ignorant fool, my dear Ladies and Gentlemen, would demand perfection of an UNTRIED machine? Wherefore then the trial in the first place? And yet to have strangled with brutish grasp and the stroke of a murderous pen the hopes of so novel an invention! A machine that would surely have revolutionised the concept of ocean travel forever! (In this I charge not only Powell but the idiot publishers of such rubbish as passes for periodicals on this backwards place!) Those editors and Mr. Powell have written as if they had the power of the old SPANISH INQUISITION behind them—they would outdo any inquisition that ever existed! The damage has been done, never to be undone. All those enthusiastic shareholders of our TTC have run away, their purses shut, tails between their legs—that Co. declared bankrupt too, dissolved away into nothing.

But out of the ashes a new phoenix arises: READ MY MANIFESTO! For it has appeared in its entirety in the two preceding numbers of the *Star* (nos. 28 & 29), and the assassin editor (TP) would not dare touch a WORD of its pain and simple truth! According to my manifesto, a new TES shall be reconstituted in the United States, where I go now to secure and perfect my inventions. There I will search to see if people can yet be found (I mean intelligent people) to combine together for the greater salvation of themselves and all our race (I mean the human race)—from ignorance, stupidity, slavery, and their faithful companions of misery and degradation, moral and physical—a union of rational beings on the basis of well-ascertained facts with common dictates and prudence. For my own part I want only free men, and no slaves of labour, unteachable of higher things than slave-business, slave-virtue, and slave-wisdom or cunning—therefore my manifesto! My plan was and is of strictest economy, with circumspection and SCIENCE. In the Harmony Society of Pennsylvania I have a few friends yet (they are familiar with me and my writings, they have examined the plans of my Satellite, they eagerly await my arrival). And I have a friend still in Mr. Roebling. And in Mr. Rex. They shall assist me. We shall yet see glorious things. I am myself again. That the Society once fettered me, and spoiled the easiest plan ever conceived of for the wellbeing of humanity—but all of this is only suspended.

Future correspondence, prepaid, will reach me in care of my lawyer, S.S. Rex, Esq, Philadelphia.

—J.A. Etzler

15

An Ancient Arawak Trace

For the first few nights following Papee's seizure he didn't exhibit no signs of the fever a-tall. Nothing. Nothing John nor me could detect anyway, and Papee seemed all but oblivious heself. Understand, the symptoms of this sickness only revealed theyself *after*. That much we'd learnt from Mr. Whitechurch and Mr. Craddock. By the time anybody saw the telltale signs—the jaundiced skin and eyes, bouts of fever followed by cold sweats, the blood-infused vomits and diarrhoea—by the time anybody recognised any of that, the victims theyself were already beyond remedy. What-ever-the-arse *that* might be.

During those days Papee seemed stronger than ever. More bull-minded. Hardened in he tenacity to refurbish the old schooner and make her seaworthy again. Like if that first episode hadn't even happened. Like John and me had dreamt it up. Because even the frightful colouring of Papee's skin and eyes had faded by the following morning. Washed away clean.

A relief, I suppose, to the extent that neither John nor me never said nothing about it. Not to each other and certainly not to Papee. *Don't say nothing and it won't be true.* And when Mr. Wood arrived in Mr. Carr's dinghy on the fifth morning following Papee's attack—reporting that the fever was spreading like bushfire amongst the pioneers at the Prescott Estate—we assured him all of us were fine—

Healthy n' happy as a basket o' hog plums, Mr. Carr says.

A much-distressed Mr. Wood stood before us on the beach.

His eyeballs sunk deep inside they sockets, like marbles shoved into a clump of clay. Asking Mr. Carr for his little box of homeo-pathic pills. Pleading with him. Only hope, Mr. Wood claimed, to save his wife and daughters. All four of whom were suffer-ing something dreadful with this disease. Till Captain Maynard came in a fortnight's time to transport the lot of them to the government hospital in Port-Spain. Because it wasn't only his wife and girls. Mr. and Mrs. Hemmingway were ill too. And young Billy Sharpe—that poor lad couldn't scarcely raise his head up off the pillow!

Mr. Carr handed over he box. Straightway. Without a flinch. Instructing Mr. Wood as to the complete which-what-where-why of them: coolants & spleen-ventilators & blood-thinners & anticoagulants. Mr. Carr handed over the last of his acetyl-salicylic acid too. Those final few thimblefuls of white pow-der shaking at the bottom of his little brown glassbottle. And even when Mr. Wood suggested leaving half the powder back, a handful of the pills, a select few—just in case, God forbid, this bloody fever should strike at one of you lads!—Mr. Carr shook his head. No-no. Wouldn't be necessary.

Even Papee refused—

Our lot's good-as-gold, he says. It's Mrs. Wood n' your daughters in need of those med'cines!

We hurried to shove him off in Mr. Carr's dinghy, wading him off the beach a few yards into the dim morning chop. Mr. Wood setting out rowing back to his wife and daughters, little box of vials rattling atop his lap. Four of us waving good-bye.

During those days we laboured over the schooner harder than ever. Papee hardest of us all. Twelve hours at a stretch some days, breaking off only to eat. To catch a cooling seabath.

Papee's pile of timbers disappearing steady before our eyes, the ones that remained after that bonfire. Son, I watched them go with a mixture of longing and fear. Because half of me wanted those boards to be done with—at least then we could hold-up. We could stop to catch we breath. The other half feeling a kinda comfort in our endless, mindless toil. The circularity of it. To such extent that I began to picture the three of us and our schooner standing at the centre of a swirling cosmos. The sea a vast lukewarm soup swimming round us. We were its motion— we'd established it & we maintained it & we would usher in its end—the termination of which had me geegeeree as oblivion itself: the finish of Papee's woodpile.

Where we'd get more boards from he never suggested. He didn't need to. Because somehow, soon as we neared the bottom, that blasted woodpile started regrowing itself. Every time we took off a board. Every time we turned we backs to it! Because the more of those worm-eaten rotted-out planks we ripped from the bottom of that hull—coming off in our hands like pulverizing-pasteboard, like layers of compressed-sackcloth disintegrating between our fingers—the more boards we pulled from that woodpile and dragged over beside Papee, the bigger it grew. Papee fitting in the replacement boards as precise as a jig-saw puzzle, a patchwork quilt. Skills he'd learnt during his years on the Isle of Wight.

Son, the more of those boards we used up the more we found.

The patch of white sand beneath the hull became carpeted over with woodcurls half-a-foot thick. Crunching beneath our bare feet like leaves in autumn. Wafting back-and-forth & rat-tling together & spiraling round in little eddies when the sea breeze blew. Papee's hands and my hands covered over with blisters. Till they became raw, unrecognisable, misshapen things. Bulbous. Beef-red. The whites of John's palms turning whiter. More transparent—a pair of medusas sucking the life out of the shaver's knobs.

We'd hardly fallen asleep that night when John and me were shaken awake by Papee's coughing. Hawking. Both of us sitting up together. Papee lying atop the canvas mattress belly-down, his face turned away—rasping, over and over.

But after a minute it stopped. Papee went silent, like he'd fallen back asleep. Then he shuddered a last time, head-to-foot— his throat making a peculiar retching kinda noise, like if he was straining to spit something up. This same something expelled finally from out his mouth. Papee turning his head to the side with a slack-jawed barracuda-belch onto the canvas: a globule of blood-infused mucus. The size and shape of a baby's clenched fist, five little fingers fused together round it. Like some kinda smallish internal organ, lying there translucent on the white canvas. Quivering through with moonlight. Still connected by a thread of saliva to my father's lips.

But now he lay there placid again, his eyes shut, breathing soft.

John and me looked at each other relieved—that seemed to be the last of it.

Then, a minute later, we watched Papee rise up off the canvas mattress. Onto his hands and knees. Remaining on all fours, his bamsee sill draped-over by the ghostly strip of canvas. His eyes wide open now. Staring down beneath him at the quivering globule. Studying it, intent, with his whole body—Papee's particular way of looking at things. Of taking in the world.

After another minute he reached his right arm forward, slow

313 ⋈ R^{OBERT} A^{NTONI}

and purposeful, pressing the full weight of his handpalm down on top. *Grinding* the globule into the canvas. Swiveling his palm side-to-side like a footheel grinding out a smouldering zoot.

Papee sat back onto his heels again, examining his soiled palm. He wiped it clean against his merino vestshirt in a single rust-coloured swipe—like the aftermath of a sharp stick chooking him between the ribs. He leant forward onto all fours again, the canvas strip still draping over his heels, still clinging. Shifting round elephant-wise, crawling off in the opposite direction, away from John and me. Slowly cross the raw sunbleached deckboards, towards the starboard rail.

For the first few feet the ghostly strip dragged behind. Eventually snagging on a nail, Papee crawling out from underneath. Stopping only after he'd gained the farthest reach of the deck. A reverberating *brammn* as his head butted-up against the rail— as though, if not for that rust-dripping barrier, he'd've crawled straight off it.

Papee remained there on hands and knees. Peering over the schooner's side. Son, I felt sure he was going to vomit. The thing I'd feared most for five days and nights—that black pitch. But it didn't come. Not yet. Not now. Papee simply knelt there, on the sunbleached deck, frozen beneath the moon like a polar bear at the edge of his block of ice. Studying the procession of pink salmon swimming past.

John turned to look at me again. We looked at each other. Not knowing what-the-arse to do—go to him? let him alone?

We watched Papee reach to grasp hold of the rust-dripping rail. One groping hand and then the next. We saw him pull heself up onto his feet, standing there a moment—bent over, hands still grasping the rail, his back turned—tatty drawers and merino awash in moonlight.

He let the rail loose and stood up straight, raising his leg simultaneous into the air. Up over the railing. Standing there poised just so another second, his leg suspended over the rail, hands outstretched to each side like a circus bear feeling out his balance atop a ball.

He stepped forward. As easy and purposeful as striding off his morning porchstoop at #7 Charlotte Street. And we heard the solid *thuff* of his body landing in the sand below. We felt the unpinned boards beneath us exhale a breath.

I was down the ladder first, John behind, scrambling over to Papee's side. Lying there on his back with the upper half of his body stretched out cross the sand, his feet and legs buried under a mound of curled shavings. Papee's face aglow beneath the moon—docile, serene-looking, relaxed. Lying there perfectly still, perfectly placid.

Except out from the corner of his mouth a tiny stream of pitch flowed. A thin living black line. Clean. Continuous. The razor-edge of white moonlight flowing along inside it. A thin mappapee snake, sliding out from between his lips, cutting diagonal cross his cheek. Down over the sweep of his bullmoose-neck.

We knelt in the sand at either side, John and me, just watching this line of pitch. Flowing. How long I couldn't tell you. Papee with his eyes wide-open but unseeing—because John passed his hand before them with no response a-tall—staring up sightless at the bright moon.

Eventually, inevitably, the line of pitch drew itself out, becoming thinner. Till it looked like a length of filthy kitestring. Then it reached the end, snapping off, disappearing into the sand without a trace.

John and me knelt there silent another minute. Listening to

the waves breathing in and out a few paces down the sand. The papery prattle of breeze-stirred sea oats behind us. John grabbing at a sandfly buzzing beside his ear. Pinching it dead, silent. He shifted back onto his heels, looking at me—

Come nuh, he says, his voice subdued. Leh-we carry you papee up to de compoun. We could tend to he better dere, you unnastan. N' Mr. Carr could give he dose o' de white powder.

He paused. With me only thinking—but there isn't any bloody acetylsalicylic powder left, because Mr. Carr's given it all away, all his box of homeopathic pills!

John continued—

Soon as you papee could shake-off dis malkadee. Come back in conscient. And me go boil he up some good strong bush-tea feh cleanse-out he blood. Cool it down.

We sat staring at one another. Several seconds. Then I reached to grasp hold of both John's shoulders. His skin moist and hard-soft in the grips of my hands—

We've got to get him back to town, I say, slow.

John gave me a look like I gone vie-kee-vie—

Egn?

Home. Back to Mum and my sisters. To the government hospital in Port-Spain.

He steupsed—

Boy, don't talk foolishness for me now! How we go manage dat?

I looked at him. Several more seconds.

He steupsed again, turning from me—

Now make haste n' help me carry you papee up to de compoun.

Mr. Carr was awake and on his feet even before we could swing Papee into the hammock beside him—

Bloody Christ, he says. Tucker it is now!

As we lay Papee inside the hammock, his skin suddenly felt hot. *Scorching*. Like it was boiling beneath the surface. His face covered over in tiny beads of sweat, like bubbles rising up to the top.

I snatched at a piece of cloth—a discarded drawers slung over a sea grape limb—using it to swab his cheeks and forehead. Down round his neck and over his broad shoulders. Papee's merino plastered against his chest, expanding and contracting with each breath. The tiny parallel ribs of the cloth showing through.

John turned away, distressed. Starting over to other side of the compound to prepare his bush-tea.

From somewhere out of the shadows Mr. Carr produced Captain Taylor's old blanket. So many holes it looked like a bloody cobweb. Spreading it over Papee and tucking it round him.

I watched a few seconds. Then I grabbed hold of Mr. Carr's forearm, pulling him erect, away from Papee. Jerking him round—

Feel his bloody temp, will you, he's *boilin!* He's not in need of no fuckin blanket!

Mr. Carr looked into my face. Several seconds. He gave me a weak half-smile—

That's enough, lad.

Papee's skin already covered over with tiny beads of sweat. Again I swabbed him dry. Except now, all-in-a-sudden, he felt *cold*. His teeth clattering together like loose sinkers in a boatbilge.

Mr. Carr looked up—

Good, he says, smiling. Good sign, that! Your father should be with us again shortly!

He said it as if Papee'd stepped into another room. In a sense I suppose he had.

I reached to continue swabbing him dry, the rag flipping out my hand—*clop* into the dirt. But when I bent down to grab it up it was coated over in grit. Upon straightening I felt dizzy. Like I was about to pitch a faint. The rag slipping out my hand, *clop* into the dirt again. I turned and stumbled off in the direction of the dining table. But I stopped and turned round, trudging back a few paces to my hammock. Reaching in and grabbing up my book—all its pages stuck together by now, tearing-way when I tried to pull them apart. The book almost unreadable, all the words smudged, plates blotched. How would I read it in the dark anyway?

I grabbed it up nonetheless and stumbled towards the dining table. All-in-a-sudden it seemed so *distant*, an island away, my legs taking forever to get me there. And I slouched down onto the bench, my head cushioned atop my folded arms. Atop my ruined book.

After a minute, out my eye-corners, I began watching John. Over near the cast-iron cookpot, slightly out-of-focus. Like if I was seeing him inside a dream. I watched him another minute. *Not* preparing his bush-tea, but building something. Some kinda structure? a frame of some sort? Four bamboo poles crossed together to make a #-shape. Tied tight with twine. John busy wrapping the twine round & round & round in a series of double helixes. One at each of the four joints where the bamboos crossed. The two shorter poles about five-feet long, two longer ones about double they length.

What the arse? I think.

Then I understood: he was building a giant kite. What the Trinidad boys called a *madbull-slinger*. Long tails tied with razor-blades, pasted with ground-glassbottle.

Epic battles at Quayside! I think.

Then I shut my eyes.

◈

The Whitechurches had arrived at the Johnstons' home a few minutes before the Tucker clan. Since Mr. Whitechurch would depart with Papee and me early the following morning—and since Maraval, where the Whitechurches were staying, was an hour's drive by coach from the port—they'd taken a suite for the night at Le Palais Cramoisi. With a separate room for Marguerite.

Mr. Whitechurch turned to Papee, reaching to place his hand atop his shoulder—

A night of deprivation to get me ready for the bush! he says.

For the previous three days, since the Johnstons' invitation had arrived, I'd contemplated little more than how Marguerite and me could escape from this Christmas dinner. To someplace private. Where, I had no idea. Nor when. But as it turned out the chance for us to make our swift clean skedaddle didn't take no time in arriving a-tall. Because we hadn't hardly finished our plum puddings when Marguerite's aunt got up from her place near the head of the table. Making her way round to where I was seated, catty-corner to Marguerite.

She stopped beside me, the top of her head barely reaching past my seated shoulder—

Willy, she says, our host's been telling us about a popular lookout station. Not far from here. Mr. Johnston claims it's the very best place to view *le couch-soleil*, as our charming islanders like to say . . . I take it you're familiar with the spot?

I nodded my head in the affirmative—despite that I didn't have no idea what she was talking about. Then I remembered—the Observatory on the other side of St. Anns River. Where Mr.

Johnston had taken us that first afternoon.

Mrs. Whitechurch glanced over at her niece, but it was me she continued to address—

I was thinking, Willy, that per'aps you'd like to show Marguerite the place? You shall have to hurry, but you're sure to witness a splendid sunset!

At that same moment something else occurred to facilitate our exit even better: another troupe of parang singers arrived at the Johnstons' door. Third group already for the afternoon. Each of the singers strumming a quarto, scraping a grater, or shaking a pair of shackshacks. Each wearing some kinda outlandish hat. And for the third time that afternoon the dinner party jumped up, making a bolt for the foyer to hear them sing. Accompanied by Berty and—hurrying from out the kitchen with a bottle of rum to *dulcify* the musicians—Vincent's mum.

Everybody excepting Marguerite and me. Because we made a bolt in the opposite direction. Through the vacated kitchen, out the screened back door. And a minute later, hidden in the little grotto at the side of the property—spout of water cascading into the pool beside us—we embraced each other.

Son, we never did climb the hill to the Observatory on the other side of St. Anns River, so as to view the sunset on that Christmas day. Neither did we sleep the night in Marguerite's room, adjacent to the Whitechurch's suite in Le Palais Cramoisi. We wandered aimless along the river awhile. Eventually crossing the line of boulderstones to the far side.

On one of my solitary, stolen jaunts through the forest in search of hummingbirds—they seemed especially populous near the river—I'd discovered a small swimming pool. Branching off from the main stream, hidden behind a rock wall. Further concealed by towering bois cano, big-leafed bozee majo trees, spiny boxwood. That afternoon, as I followed the bank, I'd heard shouting. Coming from someplace behind the trees—I couldn't make out where. But the shouting sounded playful, accompanied by laughter, and I'd become curious. Picking my way between the boulderstones and tall trees, I'd stumbled upon the pool, several young boys swimming & splashing & having theyself a time.

They waved, and I spoke to them a minute. One telling me what the spot was called—*poo-dee-tra-dee-sell-boo*—pronouncing the name in his rhyming singsong. Laughing as I made him repeat it again and again. Till I understood—peu d' tranche d' ciel bleu.

Now, standing beside the river not far from the same pool, I told Marguerite about it. About the friendly boys.

She reached for her little book and pencil, slipped into my coat pocket when we'd made our bolt from the dinner table. Marguerite daubed the lead against her tongue—

I should like very much to go there for a swim

I turned from her, peering downriver—

I'm not sure, but it can't be much farther ahead—we may have to do some rummaging through the bush!

She scribbled again, smiling—

then we shall have to do some rummaging!

We soon found the place. A gap in the forest canopy had allowed the sun to fall onto the shallow pool. It had warmed it for us all afternoon. Now the same sun, hidden behind the rim of trees, filled the air by indirection with a softish amber light.

We left our clothes where they fell. On a patch of errant par'-a-grass beside the pool. Marguerite in first, wading a few steps into the green-gold, thigh-deep water. Raising her arms up to a point above her head and diving, clean-and-smooth, two smooth clean strokes beneath the water.

She surfaced amidst a glassy ring.

❁

Mr. Carr shook me awake—

Come, lad, your father's asking for you.

It took me several seconds to recognise where I was. To climb off the bench onto my feet. Stumbling behind Mr. Carr, bending over into the shadow of the hammock. Waking up with a jolt: Papee's face stained all through with the hideous yellow again. His eyes bulging, bloated to double-size. Caught up in they nets of tiny purple veins.

I had to fight to keep from turning my head, from looking-way.

Papee grasped my arm, pulling me down, closer to him. Near enough to smell his stagnant, coppery breath—

Something important to tell you, son. A *secret!*

Sir? I stammer.

The beater, he says. The bloody beater! Doesn't matter how you dolly-up the fourdrinier machines—beater's still the beater n' don't let anybody tell you any different!

He paused—

Heart-of-the-matter, son. The thing itself! Cloth-rags or chaff-tatter or whatever else you choose to pulp. But here's the docket—*cellulose.* Bloody lignin! secondary xylem! And not just mul'bry, my boy, not just mul'bry a-tall! Any wood will pulp if you beat it proper—beech, ash, birch. Good old everyday horse chestnut. Larch. London plane. You mark my words—the day'll soon come when paper shall be made from trees. Trees, Willy, trees!

I couldn't listen. Couldn't bear the sight of my father's eyes. The smell of his coppery breath—

Sir?

You shan't forget, son. Eh? You heard it from your father first!

Just then Mr. Carr stepped up to save me. Leaning in beside my elbow. Holding the rim of a calabash cup against my father's leathery, yolk-coloured lips. Tiltsing it back slow.

Papee let my arm loose. Drinking. I watched him drink.

And at that moment it dawned upon me—like some kinda revelation—that John was fast asleep in the hammock beside us. Snoring out loud.

All-in-a-sudden I was vex, thinking—why's he not making his bush-tea? and isn't that Mr. Carr's hammock he's sleeping in?

Papee gulped down the water. I watched the soft knob of his throat sliding up-and-down. Up-and-down under its tight, goose-pimpled, yolk-coloured sleeve.

And I slipped away. I turned my back to my own father. For the second time. Because I could no longer bear the sight of his eyes.

Thinking—once more time to make you a bloody Judas!

I trudged across the island of the compound again, back to the dining table. Slouching down onto the bench. My ruined hummingbird book.

❖

We slept the night atop the mattress of our discarded clothes, coarse par'-a-grass pressing through the cloth against our bare skin. My proper English frock coat with its single vent at the back as a cover.

Not waking the following morning till the sun stood peering at us over the ridge of bozee majo trees, reflecting off our small swimming pool like a burning mirror. Stirring us awake. Still, we didn't rush. We dressed weself slow, tranquil, like we weren't in no kinda hurry a-tall. Me helping Marguerite to step inside her scout-boy boots. One after the next. Watching her bend over at the waist to pull the laces tight over the tongue—a quick bow, double-knotted. One shoe after the next. But son, it was as if the mechanism of forming those two little bows with her slender fingers—mindless and effortless both—was something utterly unique. Marvelous. Something I'd never witnessed before. So complex and mysterious I couldn't possibly retrace the steps of making those bows in my mind. Like Marguerite had invented it. Right there and then. Like nobody'd never done it before. None of this.

She stood and looked at me. I took her hand, and we made we way slowly along the bank, upriver, to the place where we crossed over the line of boulderstones.

But when we got to the other side we didn't continue up the hill, back to Samaan's Repos. We turned, and I led Marguerite in the opposite direction. Down. Towards the bay. Following the footpath along the bank for another half-hour. And after a short while the river opened up into her wider bocas. The bank became muddy—it smelt of rotting leaves—and the tall trunks beside us turned to marshy mangrove, smooth red roots arching up out of the water. And we left behind us forever all those bright overhanging trees, reaching down they long limbs to scratch at the still surface.

Soon enough we were crossing Marine Square, between the two lines of dusty almond trees. Towards Kings Wharf, walking beneath the blazing sun. In the distance, tied along the jetty, we made out a handful of harbour-ferries. A small group gathered on the pier before one of the boats.

I turned to look over my shoulder—out over the sparkling bay—searching for the *Miss Bee*. But what enabled me to identify Captain Maynard's sloop was the barge tied off her stern, its giant crate lashed down to the gunwales. In the distance, beneath the blistering sun, it looked like a flaming matchbox.

Now I recalled the little box tucked inside my own pocket. Slipping my hand under the lapel of my frock coat, feeling its edge hard-soft through the smooth lining. But I didn't take it out. Not as yet. I waited a minute more. Till we got near enough to identify—amongst the people gathered there—Mr. and Mrs. Whitechurch. Mum and my three sisters.

I came to a slow halt, turning to Marguerite—

I've a small gift, I say. But I want you to wait till we've gone before you open it.

I paused—

Nothing fancy. A little keepsake. Till we get back.

I smiled, best as I could manage. And reaching into the breast pocket of my frock coat, I took out the little box, *buttons* inscribed cross the lid. Pressing it into Marguerite's hand.

❀

Mr. Carr shook me awake. For the second time—*third?* Not saying nothing. Just setting his calabash cup down on the table before me. Gesturing towards it with his gray-stubbled chin. Vanishing just as quick behind my back.

I slept again.

Yet somehow, from the depths of my sleep, I recalled the cup—I remembered Mr. Carr shaking my shoulder, setting his cup down on the table before me. I watched him gesturing his gray-stubbled chin at it. But I couldn't be sure if *that* wasn't my dream, this the waking part? I couldn't be sure which side was which. And I remember telling myself, even within the confines of my own dream—you're asleep now dreaming of a cup of water waiting for you to wake up and drink it—and somehow, from the depths of my sleep, I managed to wake myself.

Not before I'd swallowed it halfway down did I realise it was filled with rum. I choked, coughing, spitting it back up. Rum spilling down my chin, soaking my already sweated-up merino. Tiny rings of fire searing round my nostril-holes.

Thinking—Mr. Carr's been feeding Papee rum?

I raised the cup again. Draining it dogbone-dry.

*

When I opened my eyes I found Esteban and Orinoko. Sitting at the dining table before me. John and Mr. Carr at my sides. All four of them with they heads bent low over they balizier-plates, eating a breakfast of boiled mashed plantain. Chips of fried cassava for spoons to scoop it up.

I felt peculiar. Everything looked peculiar, like I was still asleep. Like I was seeing the world through water—all the air thickish, sluggish, its cast over objects dull. Yet at the same time oddly shiny. Everything perceived as if from a slight distance. A small separation. Like feeling the touch of you own skin through numbed, tingling fingers: you don't fully exist. That's how I'd feel for the next two days and nights—numbed, half-asleep. Not till two days later would I fully wake up.

I watched them eating another minute, the sight of that gooey mashed plantain turning my stomach. I'd never felt so thirsty in all my life.

Suddenly I remembered Papee. I sat up straight, turning on the bench, staring at Mr. Carr—

He's *dead*, I say. My own voice startling me, coming out low, harsh, coarse.

Mr. Carr looked up from his plate, white disk of cassava poised in the air like the priest's communion bread—

No, lad, but he's not doing well. Not so very well a-tall . . . Now take some sustenance, son. You'll need it for your journey.

It took me several seconds before I could respond to this—

Journey?

But it was John who answered. With me turning to my other side to look at him—

We go carry you Papee home, boy. Jus' like you say youself—back home to you mummy n' sistahs!

A long beat before I could respond again—

A *ship*, I say. Your kite's signaled a boat? your madbull-slinger?

John looked at me, smiling, shaking his head like I gone vie-kee-vie again—

No boat, boy. You ent hear me say we go *carry* you Papee home? Tote he ovah we shouldahs sure 'nough! Cause dey a ole Arawak trace crosses ovah de mountains. I nevah see it, but Steban n' Rinoko know it good. Lead we clear from here to Port-España!

John bent back to his breakfast, not saying nothing more. I was too thirsty—my head was paining me too bloody much to study it out now—to try and make sense of what he'd said.

And it was whilst dipping out my second cup of water from the rain barrel a minute later that I spied John's madbull-slinger. Propped against the side of the almond tree.

John had stretched a hammock over the # -shaped bamboo frame. He'd wrapped the hammock round the poles and fastened it taut, round all four sides of the rectangle. The pole-ends sticking out at the top & bottom & sides.

But I still didn't have no idea what it was.

III
Home
18 January 1845

16

Flow

We set off well before the heat of midday. Time as the sun was high overhead we'd be shaded beneath the forest canopy. Esteban and Orinoko toting out in front, John and me behind. Each pair around the same height. This way the stretcher toted tilted-down—enabling Papee to see where we were taking him—with a kinda built-in forward momentum, instituted by gravity. And since the upper part of Papee's body was heavier, his weight carried more-or-less evenly distributed. More-or-less. Each of us with a strip of canvas folded into a pad to cushion our shoulders, extensions of the shorter poles resting snugly cross them, our necks fitted into the opposing Js where the bamboos crossed. This way we could grasp hold of the crosspoles for more stability, ease the weight off our backs. Or we could walk with the crosspoles resting on our shoulders just so for a short while—arms swinging free-and-easy at our sides, giving them a little rest. Shacking down the blood.

So ingenious was John's stretcher that for the first few minutes, toting Papee over level ground, it felt like no kinda effort a-tall.

Mr. Carr following us as far as the top of the gardens. Talking the whole time, breathless, like he'd eaten parrot. Offering encouragement and consolation to Papee, issuing instructions to John—

Soon as Tucker's safely delivered, you must go straight away to Cap'n Maynard. Don't tarry, hear? You'll find his office on Kings Street, cross from the Customs House. Inform him we've many sick members at the Prescott Estate—most desperately ill!—have him come in the *Miss Bee* at once to collect them.

We were walking alongside the stream's embankment, just beyond the gardens. John nodding over his shoulder to Mr. Carr as we went. Soon we reached the place where the stream narrowed and seemed to shallow-up at the same time, where we'd cross over. But John directed us instead to the shade of a tall poinciana tree, telling us to set Papee down—

Leh-we catch lil rest fore we start de climb in trut.

It made me vex—we hadn't been toting Papee any time a-tall. None of us were tired yet! I wanted to cover some ground. Make a good headway. Then I understood John's intensions, four of us leaving Papee alone with Mr. Carr.

We walked a few yards down to drink from the stream. Time as we got back both men were dripping in tears.

We hoisted Papee aloft again, Mr. Carr stumbling beside us the last few steps, grasping Papee's hand over my shoulder—

Chin up, old man!

Then his hand slipped-way, as the four of us trudged into the shallow stream. Leaving Mr. Carr behind. I imagined him standing there, tears washing down his sunburnt face, beneath his battered West Indian wife. But I never turned to look.

I was the only one of us wearing my torn leather boots. My longsleeve canvas shirt and long trousers. Papee's other three stretcher-bearers barefoot & bareback & wearing only they severed-off shorts. Belted round they waists with bits of rope. We'd dressed Papee back in his trousers before shifting him onto the stretcher. But he still wore the same filthy merino, reddish-brown stain leaking out his ribs, Captain Taylor's holeefied blanket still wrapped round him. When we stomped up out the stream my pants were soaked high as my thightops, boots soppsing, heavy as bricks. Yet by the time we ducked into the cool shade beneath the canopy of leafy trees—a few minutes later where the thicker woods began—already my boots felt dry. Dry as they were ever going to get in the humidity of that rainforest.

The first part of the path felt familiar enough. I began to worry about what we'd do with Papee when it turned vertical, before we reached the caves. How would we get him over that? Yet hardly had the thought passed through my mind when we arrived at a different junction in the path. One I'd never seen before—a fork, one branch continuing west, the other angling north, rising up over a short hill. Bordered on both sides by tall balizier. With a few swift swings of they cutlasses, Orinoko and Esteban led us between the thick clumps. We trudged up-hill another hundred yards. All-in-a-sudden the balizier opened up—with a blast of cold salt-soaked air—and we bounced up face-first with the bright blue wall of the sea. Sparkling, right there in front of us—like we could reach we hands and touch it.

But that sea was already a half-mile below.

Just then the path curved round west again—it dropped out from under our feet—and over my shoulder I caught a final, inadvertent glimpse of Chaguabarriga: the bright blue belly-of-the-bay with its stretch of gray beach curving round the bottom, stone jetty like a navelhole fixed at the centre; Captain Taylor's schooner off to one side, propped up in its bamboo cradle—that schooner we'd laboured over so furious, so long it seemed; in from the beach a bit the small circle of sticks that was our compound, then Mr. Carr's gardens, all those neatly dimpled patches of brown & red & ochre; with the vast emerald expanse of the jungle framing it all, swallowing it whole. A flash, a green breath, gone forever.

We toted Papee over those mountains. Over the *top* of them. Along the ridge that formed the knobby backbone of the Northern Range, running roughly parallel to the coast. Like an almost-straight crease protruding cross the top of a square of metal—the island of Trinidad. An ancient Arawak trade route, according Esteban and Orinoko. Stretching along the top of the tallest of three mountain ridges, running roughly side-to-side across the top of the island. Connecting one coast with the next: two separate seas.

When the trail wasn't wide enough Esteban and Orinoko cuttlassed our way through. They blades, holstered to they rope belts, out quick-as-an-eyeblink. Swinging before us. Like the twin propeller blades of a tugboat pulling her arse-backwards, spinning out in front. When we encountered a stream we put Papee down to rest weself and drink. Soak our canvas-pads in the ice-cold water. And if Papee was awake and clear enough I'd stoop to hold the canteen against his cracked yellow lips. And Papee would drink too.

Orinoko and Esteban constantly scouring the forest for things to eat—wild fruit, I suppose, but all they found was coconuts. Tall spindly trunks stretching they shaggy heads above the canopy-crown, into splotches of bright sun. Esteban or Orinoko climbing up without they bicycle to assist them, cutting down green nuts for us to drink. Brown nuts for the hard, dry meat. Only once did we stumble across a cocoatree left behind from some some abandoned estate. Overgrown by bush. Nothing left of that ancient cultivation but its dilapidated cocoashed, the single squat tree. Deep purple pods hanging right from the trunk like a woman's breasts. We split them between our fingers, scooping out the cottony meat—slurping it up—spitting out the shiny black seeds. Till we felt sick with it—all that oversweet, perfumey flesh. The forest floor at our feet like a little graveyard of broken pods, shiny seeds.

We hoisted Papee aloft again.

Only once did he make us stop to set him down—we were trudging along the ledge of a steep ravine, couldn't hardly find a place wide enough. And soon as we lowered Papee to the ground he ordered us all away. He waved us off—all excepting me. We thought he'd lost his head again. Not so a-tall—it was one of those moments when Papee was clearest.

After the others had stepped-way, he reached up to grasp hold of my hand. Drawing me close—

Willy, he says, I want you to promise something. I need you to swear it.

I stooped to one knee, bending over him, smelling his coppery breath.

Papee ran his tongue over his cracked eggyolk-coloured lips. He swallowed—

Should anathing happen to me, I want the rest of you to remain here. You n' Liz n' the girls. All together, understand?—here in Trinidad. Because we've come too bloody far to go back now!

He paused, swallowing—

Mr. Johnston'll help out. Of that we can rest assured.

I thought he'd finished. For a full minute he didn't say nothing more. Then he started up again—

Now swear it. Say the names. I need you to pronounce them aloud.

My eyes burnt. I could feel the tears welling up. And for some reason it made me vex, ashamed, because I didn't want to weep before him. Not now. I couldn't speak neither.

Names, he says. I need to hear the names.

Now my tears did come. Like a dam busted loose—

No, Papee, I say, best I'm able. None of that kind of talk!

But all-in-a-sudden *he* was vex. All-in-a-sudden my father was irate with me—

Don't trifle, boy!

I swallowed, almost a sob—

All right, I say. Fair enough. We'll not go back to England— course we'll not, neither you nor any of us!

Say their names, he repeats, like he's not listening. Pronounce them aloud for me to hear!

Mum, I say quick, quiet, still unsure of what he wants.

Elizabeth, he corrects. Say Elizabeth.

I took a breath—

Elizabeth.

Go on!

Georgina.

Good.

Mary. Amelia.

I paused—

Willy, I say at last, through my tears. Me—Willy.

Finally Papee let my hand loose. I got up off my knee. And I turned my back to him for the third time, embarrassed for my bloody tears. My fists clenched tight, trembling at both sides.

I stood looking down over the deep ravine—over all those rolling, gray-green, mist-enshrouded hills. Going on and on. Crouching they way towards the sea.

Till I heard Papee behind me—

Now, he says. *Now* you can call those good chaps back!

We crossed over the first two shorter ridges—up & down & up & down & up—till, as I say, we reached the top of the third and

337   ROBERT ANTONI

tallest one. The ancient trade route. We never passed though Esteban and Orinoko's tiny mountain village of Brasso Seco. The trail forking again, circumventing it just to the west. But just at that point we did encounter the only other person we'd see for the entire hike. An old Pañol-Warahoon woman, shawl draping over her hunched shoulders. Her face like a wrung-rag. Sitting beside a stream on a fallen trunk, smoking her clay pipe. Her two beady eyes following us side-to-side as we passed before her, like she's watching at a set of jumbies.

Suddenly Esteban called out, proud and excited both—

Eh-eh, Granny!

Then to us—

Look me granny dey! He nodded at her over his shoulder.

All right! the woman answers, her gray head already lost in a puff of smoke.

And son, at that same moment something happened inside me. Inside my chest. A flood of warmth that had nothing to do with any of this, this toting of Papee over those mountains. Unless it had everything to do with it? I couldn't tell you. I don't know myself. Only at that same moment Esteban and Orinoko came alive to me. They became real—*not* a dream, figures from out a dream, caught up inside a dream—and all-in-a-sudden I became overwhelmed by my own emotions. Tears rolling down my cheeks for the second time in under an hour.

As if that was the signal—that white puff from Esteban's grandmother's clay pipe—just then we ascended into the clouds. As we turned due west to follow along the trade route. Already it was early afternoon. We'd been toting Papee four-and-a-half hours—covering only the first four-and-a-half miles. But now we no longer marched steeply up-mountain, through thick forest. We passed open brush, shrouded with cool cloud-mist. Till we ascended *above* the clouds.

And just as we rose above them the sun appeared full and strong in our faces again. So bright we couldn't hardly see the ground passing beneath our feet. We didn't need to. Because now it was mostly flat, unobstructed. Despite an almost imperceptible rise that wouldn't taper till we reached the top of El Tucuche Mountain, a full six hours' march away.

But already I felt the strain deep into my back like a knife-stab.

Flow: the only word I can think of to describe it. Or what happens to it, what that pain becomes. Because time, space, the body moving simultaneous through them—that vessel that holds the pain, its privileged container—they all go away. They disappear. Till there's nothing else. Till nothing else remains: only that pain. Till that pain becomes its own momentum, its own prime mover.

Or maybe it was simply the sun that dragged us along. That enormous sun appearing, as I say, just as soon as we stepped from out the clouds—as soon as we stomped those clouds down beneath our feet. Because all-in-a-sudden there it was again, closer and bigger than we'd ever witnessed. That sun gave us new energy. It pulled us along as we walked towards it—as that same sun drew itself away—out over the bosé-backs of those mountains. So we marched a stretch of several hours without stopping a-tall. Without setting Papee down a once to rest we-self. Because walking straight into that sun like that we didn't need to rest. We didn't need to drink.

Then the bottom edge of the flaming ball began to go black. A blue-black harsh and penetrating as the fire it filled up. All-in-a-sudden the bottom half was eaten-way—and the sun left us even faster, till only a chip remained. Then that chip extinguished itself too. And we felt the sting pull loose from out our throats.

But now it was night: cool, crisp, smoky-gray. Unbearably loud with all its magnitude of pulsating insects, its multitude of nocturnal animal-noises, its screeching & clacking & *wee-what-weeing* night birds.

We toted Papee into the night. Tireless. Till the ice-white moon rose up from behind where we knew the sea was hidden. Till exactly midnight according to Mr. Whitechurch's pocketwatch—because Papee could read it, that's how bright the moon was. Son, you could've read the *Star* by that moon! At exactly midnight we reached the top of El Tucuche Mountain. Highest point of the whole island.

Slowly, imperceptibly, we started down. Down through the layer of clouds whilst it was still night. Down though thick forest, tall trees, bush: Maracas Valley and Santa Cruz Valley. And still it was night. And just as the sun started to rise again behind our backs, we started into the low cocoahills behind Port-Spain. The ground painted that artificial pink of hard rock candy. Yet beneath our feet its surface was spongy-soft.

Now we found weself gazing out over the sleeping city. Like it had always been there. Unchanged for a thousand years: a ragged, breathing, sprawled-out animal. And beyond the city the sea.

We marched down out of those low cocoahills. Into St. Anns, Cascades. Now we followed a proper path—a proper dirt road—except this road upon which we marched was devoid of human travellers. Un-peopled. All the world asleep. All the world excepting the five of us, because now we were wide awake.

Before we knew it we passed the first sleeping shack—or it passed us—and slowly more shacks appeared. They passed us by. Then the shacks turned to larger slumbering boardhouses. Then concrete, masonry-walled houses. Houses with proper front yards and proper yards behind. And the soft brown dirt road beneath our feet changed to hardened pitch before we realised. Then we were marching down Charlotte Street—the very first named street that we encountered—me issuing directions to the others like if we were out taking a morning stroll—

Just ahead, I say. Just ahead. Just ahead.

Till at last I pronounced the single word with a finality that came from someplace outside my body, like somebody else was saying it, thinking it—

Here, I say. Here. Just here.

We turned between the two vaguely familiar rusted gate-posts. Before the vaguely familiar little white boardhouse at #7 Charlotte Street. Turning in as cool & easy & unspectacular as if we were ducking between two clumps of balizier bush. Esteban and Orinoko mounting the three short steps of the stoop, with John and me still standing outside the gate. Still in the street. And Orinoko leant forward a little, bowing down his head a little, and he reached out shy and unastonished as the rest of us to knock on the door. We heard him knocking. All-in-a-sudden standing in one place, still, but still marching.

17

When Bazil Call

Amelia, the youngest, answered the door. Wearing her ruffled nightdress, flowerprint of sleep cross her blushed cheek: Amelia took one look at us and shut the door again straight in we faces—*bram*.

She opened again after a second, cautious, her single pale-gray eye peering past the doorcrack—

Dada? she says, pressing up onto her toetips to see over Esteban's shoulder.

Amelia, Papee answers, his voice strained, scratchy. And as my father pronounced my sister's name, I felt a hollow space opening up inside my chest.

Now began that awkward jostle of the four of us. Several frustrated seconds—like this was the most complicated predicament we'd faced for all these hours of toting and marching—before we came to the collective conclusion that the door wasn't sufficiently wide to admit the stretcher. Suddenly Orinoko's cutlass appeared—instinctive, flashing above his head—like the doorframe's a balizier bush he's about to chop from out our way.

Sweet Jesus! Amelia cries. She shuts the door again—*bram*.

Back up, I tell the others. We've got to carry him in *off* the stretcher.

Now the four of us shuffled backwards a few steps, Amelia opening the door a third time. Esteban and Orinoko stumbling off the porchstoop in three successive drops, backwards through the rusted gateposts. We set Papee down in the middle of the street. Then I reached under his wet armpits to take him up, his head cradled against my chest. And Orinoko—at this particular moment, of all others—Orinoko had trouble reholstering his cutlass: he tucked the blade quick between his clenched teeth, taking hold of Papee's legs under his arms. Two of us toting him in through the gateposts again. Captain Taylor's holeefied blanket still wrapped round him, corner sweeping the ground.

By this time Mum & Mary & Georgina had awakened too. Four white nightdresses crowding the doorframe, stares of panic in all they flushed faces. Particularly as Orinoko advanced towards them, Papee's legs tucked under his arms—this half-naked Warahoon bearing his cutlass between his clenched teeth. They parted to let us pass. Mum leading Orinoko through the parlour, down the narrow hallway to her bedroom at the back. Orinoko and me creaksing over the floorboards, the entire little house shaking on its groundsills beneath us. Toting Papee into the small, dark, cool bedroom. Shifting him up onto the white mattress that seemed to me big and broad as a boat.

I'd heard my parents conversing together—greeting each other even before we could get Papee inside his room—though I was unaware of what they were saying. Both they voices calm & quiet & unemotional. Like they'd been separated only a few minutes, not twenty-three days. In contrast to the tears I could already see flashing on my mother's cheeks. I watched her brush them away with the sleeve of her nightdress, sitting on the bed beside Papee. Leaning forward to strike a match and light the candle on the bedstand.

In the flickering yellow light I saw Papee searching inside his trousers pocket for Mr. Whitechurch's watch. Reaching cross Mum to set it down on the bedstand beside the candle, gold-chain spilling over the side like prayer beads. Fixing the watch with its face tilted up so he can read it. I saw him fumbling inside another pocket, removing first the notebook, then a little roll of papers tied up with fishing-twine. Setting them both down atop the bedstand beside the watch.

The notebook I knew good enough—the roll of papers I'd never seen before. Though I recognised my father's cramped script curving cross the exposed sheet, wondering when he could have written it, what these papers might be: a letter to Mum? Papee's last will and testament?

My attention diverted back to Mr. Whitechurch's watch, its crystal catching the flash of Orinoko's cutlass as he reholstered it behind me. I listened to the watch's clear, sharp ticking—like I was hearing it for the first time—*tac tac tac* in little pebbles ricocheting off the board walls. Squinging up my eyes to make it out—*5:47.*

Papee took hold of Mum's hand. Pressing it against his chest, against the brown stain on his filthy merino.

She hadn't even looked me full in the face yet. Till now my mother had only been able to take in Papee.

I turned—

Come, I say to Orinoko, quiet. And I led him out the room. Closing the door behind us.

Georgina & Mary & Amelia wrapped they arms round me as soon as I entered the parlour. All four of us hugging up together. I felt they cool, soft arms—yet the thing I was most aware of was my own stench. I smelt myself and I smelt Orinoko standing behind me. I could smell John and Esteban all the way out in the street.

Now I noticed, over Mary's shoulder, that all along one side of the parlour were thick bolts of brightly coloured cloth. Piled perpendicular, stacked up tall as the ceiling. A solid *wall* of them,

an array of textures and colours: multiple shades of blues &
yellows & reds & greens. Mum and my sisters' handiwork, no
doubt—they'd set up a dyers' workshop right there in the house.

After a minute I stepped back, looking at my three sisters.
All three still too shocked and confused, for the moment, for
tears.

Georgina, the eldest, spoke first—

How ill *is* he?

I looked at them, trying to think how best to answer this—

The truth is that we don't know. I s'pose the doctor'll have to
answer us that. We don't even know what he's suffering from—
jungle fever, black vomit—plenty of names for the illness nobody knows anathing about!

Already I felt I'd said too much, though I knew I hadn't told
them nothing a-tall. I knew I didn't *know* hardly nothing to tell
them, even if I'd wanted.

He looks so *ghastly*, Mary says.

And Amelia—

Why's he that loathsome colour?

I turned my eyes to the floor—

There're others in worse shape, I say, trying to soften it
some. Mrs. Wood and her daughters . . .

I felt like I was digging myself inside a hole. And after another uncomfortable second I changed the subject. Addressing
the three of them together again—

We've got to eat. What've you got to feed us? Anathing a-
tall?

I was aware of pronouncing the *anathing* the same way Papee did—twice in the space of a couple breaths—but I couldn't
pause to contemplate it now.

It was Georgina who answered—

I'll run to the corner shop. I'll have to wake Miss Odette.

And with that she turned round to grab up a white kerchief sitting on the shelf, tucked under a book and knotted round some coins—I heard them rattle together as she took them up. And in the same breath she was out the door, barefoot, wearing only her thin nightdress—

Go in, please, I heard her tell John and Esteban outside. You must go in!

A second later John entered, timid, Esteban a step behind. They stood together in a corner of the parlour, not knowing what to do, they discomfort almost palpable. And I wondered how this could be—how a-tall?—after what we'd been through together? I watched John studying the settee a few seconds, like he was contemplating whether or not to sit on it. He crouched to the flooring, sitting atop his dusty heelbacks.

I reached down to touch his shoulder—

Come, I say, remembering the dining table at the back. Nodding to Esteban and Orinoko.

I led them down the short corridor—four of us trodding lightfoot as we could manage but creaksing up the floorboards nonetheless—past my parents' bedroom to the little screened patio behind. John and me sitting on the bench at one side, Esteban and Orinoko facing us.

All-in-a-sudden I felt a warm wave of déjà vu—like the four of us were back sitting at our dining table in the compound, beneath the almond tree. Sacks of foodstuff hanging above us like a madman's version of a Christmas tree.

But that feeling was blanked quick enough by another memory: one of me sitting here at this same dining table, not so long ago. Though a decade seemed to have passed since that night. Carefully dissecting my first hummingbird. I recalled Papee stepping out onto the gallery the following morning—almost at this same hour—I could feel him standing behind me. His breath warm against the back of my neck, watching me work. Studying the little bird over my shoulder.

Georgina returned with a brownpaper sack containing a dozen hopsbreads. Warm from out the oven. And I took in the smell of fresh-baked bread for the first time since I'd left—so thick and doughy it made me retch. Yet my mouth was watering just the same. In her other hand, together with the pouch of coins, Georgina held a thick chunk of guavacheese, wrapped in oil-spotted waxpaper.

She set the things down on the table. Meanwhile, Mary went to the kitchen in the yard to collect a knife and the corked bottle of drinking water. Amelia taking down glasses and porcelain plates from the cupboard in the corner—I marveled at the unspoken efficiency with which the three of them coordinated all this.

With the same efficiency Georgina prepared and served us breakfast: two hopsbread-and-guavacheese sandwiches each, peripheries of the thick purple-brown slices of cheese encrusted with granulated sugar. Glittering in the soft morning light. John and me inhaling our sandwiches—despite the shock of sweetness—soon as the plates were handed to us. I was embarrassed by the noise we made consuming them. Then we drank a couple glasses of water each, served to us by Mary.

Georgina prepared a breakfast plate for Papee too. She carried it to the bedroom and knocked on the door. I heard Mum's voice, then the door closing again.

Esteban and Orinoko ate slower. Finishing only the first of they sandwiches, ripping off neat squares of brownpaper from the sack to wrap the other. Now I noticed they peculiar method

347 ▷ ROBERT ANTONI

of drinking without touching the glasses against they lips—I'd never seen this before, never seen them drink from nothing but a calabash cup. Dropping they heads back and pouring the water out careful inside they extended jaws.

As I contemplated this John rose, handing Georgina his plate, empty glass balanced upside-down in the middle—

Thank you, Miss Tucker, he says, like she'd given him a feast.

Then he nodded his head to my sister—a small, formal bow—and turned towards me—

We goin' in search for Cap'n Maynard.

Now he smiled—

No time for skylarkin!

All-in-a-sudden I didn't want them to go. All-in-a-sudden I was desperate, afraid for them to leave us—

What the hell! I say. You don't want to bid farewell to Papee?

Then I realised I didn't know what I meant by this *farewell* myself.

John steupsed. Smiling still—

Willy-boy, he says, you Papee go recover heself good 'nough. Soon as dat doctor come from de hospital to fix he up!

And with that the three of them were gone. Down the corridor and out the front door, Esteban and Orinoko carrying they wrapped-up sandwiches.

I got up too, hurrying back to the parlour again, watching them through the front window. Three bare, muscular backs, side-by-side together. One tall, narrow, ebony-black; the other two squat & broad & reddish-brown. Walking into the sun like a single retreating figure, snipped from a sheet of tin.

After a second Georgina brushed past, out the front door too. Carrying the sack with the remaining hopsbreads, the remaining chunk of guavacheese.

I watched John stop and turn round to take the sack. And I watched him smile and bow his head to my sister again.

That morning—sitting on the parlour-settee whilst Mum and my sisters tended to Papee in the back bedroom—that morning I did something for the first time which, inevitably, I'd take up as a lifelong habit: I slept with my eyes open. Just so. People find this thing peculiar. All I can say is from that morning we'd brought Papee home from Chaguabarriga, it has become a regular habit for me. The way I take my naps during the day. Sitting up with my eyes open.

How long I slept like that I couldn't tell you. Maybe an hour? maybe two? But at some point I became aware of Mum's voice—

Willy, Willy dear.

I could see her standing before me, slightly out of focus. Yet I couldn't respond—my lips felt stuck together. I couldn't make them work. My hand heavy as a brick atop my lap—I couldn't raise it up.

After a struggle I managed to mumble something—

Wha?

Mum stared at me a few more seconds. Then she reached to hug me for the first time since I'd arrived, settling onto the settee beside me, still holding my shoulders—

You were sleeping like one of those jumbies the Grenadians talk about. Your eyes wide-open.

I sat trying to remember something, my head heavy atop my shoulders—

How's father? I say at last.

But almost before I can get this out I realised I didn't want to know. Now I was afraid for what she had to tell me.

Resting, she says, as I exhaled a breath. But he's so *hot*, burning such a fever!

Until this point my mother's voice had remained calm, steady. She looked at me again—

That detestable colour of his skin!

And now she broke down, all-at-once. Like the pivotal stone pulled loose from a crumbling wall—

William's beautiful blue eyes—so swollen, stained that dreadful colour! Those frightful blisters on his buttocks!

I stared at her—

Blisters?

She nodded—

I found them cleaning him up. Removing his trousers. A terrible, horrid open sore on each . . .

She broke off, and I decided the sores must've come from the way Papee's bamsee chafed against the bamboo braces of the stretcher. I couldn't think of any other cause.

Mum removed a white kerchief from the sleeve of her nightgown, folded into a small roll—at first I confused it with Papee's little roll of papers, the one he'd fished from out his pocket and left on the bedstand. She pressed the opened-out kerchief against her cheeks—

He defecated on himself, Willy.

I swallowed, remembering the night on the schooner's deck, Papee lying atop the ghostly canvas. I shook the image off—

You've sent for the doctor?

Georgina's just gone. I've given her all the money I have . . . I know those two doctors at the government hospital. The ones available to the general public—maybe if Dr. Bradford's there? the Englishman? But that Frenchman—Dr. Blanc! He doesn't make house visits for the likes of us. 'Less he's paid in advance.

The fact that I'm French myself only makes it worse—*souris d'église* we are to him!

She paused—

Bleed 'em blanc is what they call him here.

Mum pressed the kerchief against her cheeks. I reached and put my arms round her, feeling her shoulders trembling though the nightdress.

After a few minutes Georgina returned, rushing into the parlour. She now wore a pale green frock and white sandals. Her face flushed a bright pink, in contrast to the white kerchief tied round her hair—

He won't come! Claims he's too busy—there's not another soul in that waiting room! *No house visits for pauper patients*, he told me. I tried giving him the money, he wouldn't take it. Told me to have Father come to the hospital if he wants treatment.

Dr. Blanc? Mum says.

Georgina nodded.

Did you inform him your father's not strong enough to get out of bed? less still to walk crosstown to the hospital?

Now there were tears on Georgina's cheeks—

Of course. But the nurse informed me Dr. Bradford would be at the hospital soon. At least we can place our hopes in Dr. Bradford!

I pulled myself up onto my feet—slow, a bit wobbly—turning round to look down at my mother again—

We'll have to carry Father to the hospital ourselves. We've carried him this far, a short trip crosstown won't be anathing a-tall.

Then I realised something—

They've taken the bloody stretcher!

Georgina was standing behind me. And after a few moments of silence I heard her voice. Calm, collected—

They didn't, she says. It's just outside. That man—John—he's left it propped 'gainst the side of the house.

Five of us toted Papee now. Me behind, in the middle, Mary and Amelia at either side. Georgina and Mum out in front. We didn't hoist him up atop our shoulders—weren't strong enough for that—we carried him at waist-height. Which, in point of fact, seemed more awkward and difficult. Yet we didn't set Papee down a once to rest weself. Not a once. Despite that it seemed to take us forever to get to that hospital. Walking beneath the hot sun down Charlotte Street, crosstown on Duke, turning on Cambridge Street and following it up to the hospital.

Mum and the girls wearing fresh frocks. But I remained in my tatty, filthy clothes, my ripped-up boots. Still stenching to high heaven, to bloody hell. Mum had at least sponge-bathed Papee—she'd dressed him in fresh drawers and a fresh merino—but she couldn't find a pair of clean trousers. Mum even tried putting him into she *own* nightdress to go to the hospital, but Papee refused. He demanded that she dress him back in his ragged pants.

Mr. Carr's old blanket had been replaced by a clean cotton one—dyed by Mum and the girls a clear sky-blue—tucked round my father.

Near noon by the time we reached the hospital. Five of us stomping our rounded shadows into the pitch. By this time there *was* a queue of patients stretching out the door, waiting to see the doctor: we didn't have no choice but to get into line behind them.

But son, we didn't have to wait long in that queue, sun beating down atop our heads. Because soon as those other patients got a good look at Papee, they parted to let us pass. Straightway. It came as a shock to me—like I'd seen Papee for so long in this condition I'd grown accustomed to it.

I listened to a Creole woman fleeing the queue—

Fevah? Fevah? Is only de *cholera* could give he dat kinda colour!

And another—

Dem's de eyes of Bazil-self, *oui fute!*

Once again it took us several seconds of awkward jostling in front of the hospital door before we realised we'd have to carry Papee inside off the stretcher. We set it down on the paving outside and took him up again, all of us together. But soon as we got him halfway through the door the crowd of patients hurrying to vacate the waiting room forced us back. We stepped aside to let them pass.

Then we pressed in.

Bouncing up a French nurse in a starched white gown and headdress, her face showing the same shock as all the others. She turned to lead us down a dark corridor, to a tiny operating room at the back. And we all shoved in, all six of us together. Laying Papee atop a worn table hinged cross the middle, with the two leaves turned down to make a flat surface. In one wall there was a small window with spiderweb-encrusted jalousies. Harsh shadows of burglarbars outside. A tall rusty cabinet propped against another wall.

The nurse spoke from the door, addressing Mum—

Chacun doit partir maintenant!

I didn't have no idea what she'd said, but the girls understood. They tucked the sky-blue blanket round Papee, kissed him one-by-one, and filed out.

I looked at Mum—

I'm not leaving.

She didn't answer. Several seconds. I could see her strength

of character—I knew it good enough, I'd known it all my life—
but as I stood there before her in that little operating room, at
that moment, it was as if I was seeing it for the first time—

I shall deal with this Dr. Blanc, she says. I've dealt with him
before. You've done your part, Willy. Now go and rest yourself.

I left, reluctant.

On my way back down the corridor I passed the French
nurse, then this Dr. Blanc heself. I knew him straightway—a tiny
man, hardly reaching past my shoulders, his baldhead so shiny
it glowed in the dim light. Big walrus-moustaches and a gold
monocle flashing up at me—

Merde, he says, shoving past.

In the waiting room I found my sisters sitting on the single
bench. Not a one of those other patients had returned—that's
how startled they were. And now, all-in-a-sudden, I felt the exhaustion. Descending like a bucket of warm water poured overtop my head. Dripping off my numbed fingers. I stumbled past
my sisters and slumped down to the flooring in a far corner.
Sitting up against the wall, my legs stretching out straight before
me, my ripped-up boots. But my eyes remained open, watching
at my sisters' three backs. And after a few seconds my vision
went blurry.

❁

That night, after only a week in Port-Spain—and having
struggled the entire day with the other men rescuing Mr. Etzler's
half-sunk Satellite—I was awakened by a distinct, though
slightly subdued buzzing noise. Accompanied by a soft breeze
across my forehead. Then I heard a succession of three quick
zoops, followed by a violent *thwack* against the screen. Not twelve
inches from the side of my face.

I lay there dazed, still half-asleep, my eyes closed. Fighting off my curiosity. Then I rolled out of my hammock, wearing only my drawers and merino vestshirt. Stumbling out the back screened door and hearing it clap closed behind me. Down the three steps. The night moonless, lit only by a profusion of streaming fireflies. Yet as soon as I looked over towards that corner of our little yard—where I slept several feet above on the other side of the screen—I spotted the tiny creature. Lying on the freshly turned dirt. Just beside the ginger cutting Papee had planted in the half-shade of a groundsill.

All-in-a-sudden my legs felt energised. I hurried the few paces over and got down on my knees in the moist dirt. Even in the dark I could make out the emerald-glittering breast, little sapphire head twisted backwards at an angle I knew was unnatural. I saw the black dot of an eye, still glossy with life. But what drew my attention most was the tiny pulsating heart. Swelling up and contracting beneath its shining emerald shield. And son, as I watched the little breast moving in-and-out, in-and-out, I heard my own chest. Beating out the cadence for this tiny creature.

I knelt another minute, looking at the little bird. Then, as gentle as I could manage, I took her up. Shorter than the length of my middle finger. I carried her into the porch, screen door clapping behind, setting her atop the dining table. Then I took down the pitch-oil lamp from its hook and lit it, bringing it over.

I sat watching the tiny movement within the bird's breast. Swelling up and contracting, slowing more and more. Till it stopped altogether. Eventually, exhausted, I outed the lamp.

How long I slept again I couldn't tell you. Maybe I never fell back asleep a-tall? All I can say is that after a time I found myself wide awake. I rolled out of my hammock and went back to the table, relighting the pitch-oil lamp. But before I sat down—without any clear notion of my own movements—I went over to the sill at the other side of the porch. Taking up Mum's small sewing box.

I sat on the bench, examining the bird once more. This time, as I took her up, I didn't feel no trepidations a-tall about touching her. First I twisted her tiny sapphire head back round to its natural position. When I'd brought her in her head had quivered slightly inside my palm, loose. But already the neck was stiffening, tightening.

I realised I had to do this thing quick—whatever-the-arse it was I was going to do, because I still didn't know myself—before the creature stiffened up altogether.

I took her up again, squeezing her between my palms. Holding her little head in the proper position. And she more-or-less retained that posture. Now I laid her careful on her back, stretching out the undersized wings at each side: they recoiled, but not altogether so. I opened Mum's box and took out the pincushion, removing two of the pins. Pressing them through the apices of the wings, fixing them to the plank table. One pin at either side of her little breast. Using two more, I tacked down the tail.

I moved by instinct. All I had to go on, really, was the method I'd observed two or three times over the past few days. Watching fishermen at the wharf—or mongers at the fishhouse—gutting they catch.

Mum had two pairs of scissors in her box. One tiny, the points slightly curved like a nail-scissors, and a larger pair. I took up the small one and blew on the fuzzy feathers at the base of the abdomen, just at the top of the tail. I watched them separate, till I found the bird's vent. This was where I inserted the point of the small scissors, tip curving up, lifting a little and making a short incision. Sufficiently shallow so I didn't cut no deeper than the delicate skin.

But the process felt awkward. Like I was all thumbs.

I put the scissors down to search through Mum's box again. Amongst the various spools of thread, the wad of cotton wool and other paraphernalia, I found a little wooden box with the word *buttons* written in Mum's script across the top. Lifting off the lid, I found a thimble and a pair of tweezers, crowded in amongst a dozen different sized & shaped & coloured buttons. I turned the contents over onto the table—a neat little square—put the empty box aside.

Holding the tweezers in my left hand I used them to lift the skin a bit, pulling it away from the little body. With the pair of scissors in my right hand I made a shallow incision, slow-and-smooth. Up across the little abdomen. All the way to the base of the neck: a single clean cut. Then I lifted the severed skin and stretched it to both sides of the little breast. The tiny rib cage—various internal organs assembled inside—lying glossy and exposed before me.

Utilising Mum's sewing instruments, with a patience that surprised even me, I dissected out the bird's innards. Organ by organ. Then I packed the hollowed-out cavity with bits of cotton wool. Tearing them off the wad in fragments, moistening them with saliva, and rolling them up into tight little balls. Twelve-to-fifteen of them—because I was concentrating so hard I couldn't stop to count them out.

From Mum's pincushion I selected a large sewing needle, threading it with a length of coarse thread. Working the tweezers again with my left hand, I lifted the edge of the emerald-feathered skin at the base of the neck. Pressing the needle through—tougher and more resistant than I'd expected. Then I passed the needle through at the other side of my incision. And I pulled the two sides together over the rib cage, now packed tight with cotton wool, and tied my first suture: a simple double-knot. Snipping off the excess thread at each side. Suture by suture, I joined the skin together over the bird's abdomen, working my way down towards the tail, in a direction opposite to my original incision. Seventeen sutures in all. Because now I did stop to count them out.

Son, I would guess that I worked on my little bird for maybe an hour? maybe two? I had no way of knowing. Time seemed to flow and fold in on itself as I sat working. I wasn't even aware of the yellow morning sunlight already sifting in through the screen—pooling up on the plank table like spilled water. Just beside my elbow. Making the pitch-oil lamp at my other side redundant. The table strewn with all the various objects from Mum's sewing kit: the small piece of cloth with the piled-up bird's innards, tidy square of buttons, the little empty box.

I removed the four pins and returned them to Mum's cushion. Now, holding the bird in both my cupped palms, I pressed the wings gentle against her body again. And after a minute I lay the bird down on her side, reaching my arms up above my head. Stretching. Leaning back on the bench to examine the result of my labours. A few minutes later Papee arrived, wandering out onto the porch behind me, also wearing his drawers and merino vestshirt. He looked over my shoulder a long minute. Studying the little bird. But I didn't turn round. I sat there feeling his presence behind me, his warm breath on the back of my neck.

Then he leant forward over the table, raising up the little glass of the pitch-oil lamp, blowing it out.

❖

Sometime later I became cognizant that the waiting room was filled with patients again, a man sitting on the flooring at each of my elbows. So many people it took me a full minute to realise Mum was there in the waiting room now too—sitting with my sisters on the bench—they four backs turned towards me.

At first I took this in calmly enough. Then I pulled myself up onto my feet—feeling like I was about to pitch backwards to the flooring again. Pressing past the other patients. Over towards my mother and sisters. I looked down at them, at Georgina and Mum's flushed faces. Mary and Amelia's cheeks glistening with tears.

I reached down to grab hold of both my mother's shoulders. Tight. Shaking her—

You were meant to stay with him!

She looked up. And although the colour seemed to have drained from her face, her strength of character remained. It reassured me a little—

They forced me out. They demanded—else they refused to treat him. Said it wasn't fit for a woman to witness the procédé.

It took me a few seconds to respond to this—

What *procedure?* I ask, loud enough to make the other patients turn round. Staring. All they faces blank.

I haven't a clue, she says. But Dr. Bradford's with him now— at least we should be able to trust Dr. Bradford!

She paused—

We *have* to, Willy. Nous n'avons pas d'autres choix!

I stared down at her. Trying to calm myself—

And just how long has he been in there with those doctors?

There's a trick physicians used to do with leeches. In the old days: once the leech attached itself and began to draw blood, the doctor used scissors to sever off its tail. That way, rather than the customary five-to-seven ounces they generally drew—till the leech swelled to capacity and dropped off of its own accord—the leech was fooled into believing it was still hungry. It sucked insatiably, interminably, the blood spurting out its severed end.

The rule was the bigger the leech, the easier it was to fool.

Bleed 'em Blanc had become an expert at performing this trick, or procédé. Exactly how long he and Dr. Bradford worked together over Papee in the tiny operating room at the back of that hospital, I couldn't tell you. I don't have no idea. All I can say is by the time I got up from the bench in the waiting room—without a word to my mother or sisters—and I shoved past the other patients, past the nurse in her starched white headdress, hurrying down the dark corridor to the operating room at the back, I would guess, conservatively, that those doctors had drained *half* Papee's blood. If I didn't get to him first, no doubt they'd've drained him dry.

No doubt—in they combined medical opinions—every one of Papee's symptoms cried out for bleeding: bleeding to slow his rapid pulse, to cool his high temperature; bleeding to drain the contaminant causing the yellow discolouring of his skin and eyes; bleeding to ease his depressed spirits, his clouded-over mind; bleeding to diminish the inflammation of those two vile bruises on his buttocks; bleeding to lessen the blood permeating Papee's bowels.

This is how I found him: alone, unconscious, lying naked and belly-down on the operating table, its two hinged-leaves turned up to make a triangle. Papee lying over them in what I have come to learn physicians call the jackknife position. Papee's bamsee standing up tall in the air, four enamel bowls on the floor at the four corners of the table. Into which Papee's blood dripped—or *didn't* drip, because it was everywhere, the whole of that tiny operating room was swimming in it—from incisions made with the lancet in the veins of his wrists and ankles. Dripping from the welts along the lengths of his arms and legs, resulting from an overtorched glass cup. From numerous raised patches of checkerboard-slashes inflicted with the scarificator. In addition to spurting out the ends of a half-dozen leeches, they tails severed, put to work round the margins of those two blisters on Papee's upturned buttocks. Three more leeches at the margins of his exposed anus.

Papee's trousers discarded in a heap in the corner, his drawers and merino vestshirt—together with the blanket, once sky-blue, now sodden and dripping red. Atop the heap a handful of small glass vials where the leeches had been stored. Prior to the doctors putting them to work.

Son, it was surely the most disagreeable task I've ever been asked to perform. But I was so upset that I couldn't hardly contemplate what my own trembling, blood-dripping fingers were doing. As I picked off those nasty leeches one-by-one, pinched them dead, and pitched them aside. Wherever-the-arse those two doctors were at that moment I couldn't tell you. I didn't have no idea. All I knew for sure was that the French nurse had followed me in—she was standing right there behind me—studying me the whole time. Not speaking a word in no kinda language a-tall.

When I'd finished picking off the leeches from Papee's buttocks I shoved my boot sideways against one of the enamel bowls. Kicking it out the way. Splattering blood up cross the wall as high as the window of spiderweb-encrusted jalousies. I rolled Papee off the tilted-up table—so wet and slippery I was frightened I'd lose him onto the floor—taking him up in my arms. Son, where I got my strength from I couldn't tell you neither. But I managed: I carried my father, naked, dripping, past the nurse and out of that tiny operating room. Down the dark corridor.

He never regained consciousness after that. Whether it was the fever or those doctors that killed him, in the end, I couldn't say. Certainly each contributed they part. But by the time we got Papee home and into his own bed again, he'd stopped bleeding entirely. No pulse left a-tall. No fever neither. We'd taken him away yellow and brought him back brown. His naked body as though beaten with a stick on every square inch—swollen, disfigured, covered over with a dried brown film.

I never saw him again. Not alive. I imagine Mum and my sisters sponge-bathed him once more. I imagine they cleaned & disinfected & dressed each of his thousand-and-one wounds. But I couldn't tell you. All I can say is it did no good for nobody a-tall.

I left Papee with them—I didn't even pause to tell my father an unheard good-bye. I stumbled into the next room and fell face-first on one of my sisters' beds, inadvertently pulling out the mosquito net as I went down. And I wept. I wept for Papee, and Mum, and my three sisters, and I wept for myself. All of us together. And then I slept.

I'd been awake for some time, my back pressed against the wall listening to the silent house, feeling its silence—not a solitary manikin cheeping in the backyard—when Amelia knocked on the door and entered. Still wearing her white frock from yesterday afternoon, stained brown along her left side. I looked straight at her, several seconds, but I could tell by the expression on her face she thought I was still asleep.

Amelia stepped forward. Laying an envelope down gentle on the sheet beside me.

She turned to leave. Then turned round again.

I could see the circles surrounding her eyes—she'd been up crying the whole night, together with my mum and sisters.

But I could also see that she wanted to talk to somebody about something else. Anything else. She was desperate for it. I could see—clearly, unmistakably—that somehow she wanted to move on. Her youthful imagination pressed her forward: already she'd taken the first tiny step. Amelia, Papee's favourite, youngest and most tender of us all.

Seeing me stir, she nodded her chin down at the letter—

Mum sent me to bring it for you. We found it on the shelf in the parlour this morning. But it's a *mystery!* Written on a leaf of writing paper from Georgina's box. One of her envelopes. So whomever left it for you came into the house in order to write it—who knows when?

She took a breath—

Maybe a *thief?* in the middle of the night?

Amelia stood there a few more seconds. Looking at me. Then she shrugged her shoulders, turned, and left the room.

I sat with my back pressing against the wall for several more minutes. My mind blank, listening to the silent house, mosquito netting still bunched up on the bed beneath me. Then I reached and took up the envelope. Seeing my own name—*Willy*—written clearly cross the front. But not yet fully recognising that name as belonging to me. I slipped my filthy, bloodstained fingernail under the folded-in flap, sliding out the letter. And even after reading my name two more times, I remained unconvinced that I was the intended recipient of this letter. That I was the particular container labeled with that particular word.

Then I knew for sure:

Dear Willy—

Capt Maynard, who was to transfer our trunks to the Caroline, the ship upon which we sail tomorrow morning with the tide, has informed us that you and your father are returned from Chaguabarriga, Mr. Tucker under distressed circumstances. Capt Maynard has set off directly for the estate himself. And he has kindly seen to it that our trunks and my aunt were dispatched to the Caroline on another ferry. As your father is ill, and as Mrs. Whitechurch and I have already bid farewell to your mother and sisters, we thought it best not to intrude. And of course we have our own distress and grief to contend with— but Willy, I could hardly leave without attempting to speak to you first! even at the risk of disturbing your family!

So I have sent my aunt on ahead. And I have come straight to your home, which I now find wide open and worrisomely empty. I can only suppose that you and your family have accompanied Mr. Tucker for treatment at the hospital—I'm heartened to think he should have walked there under his own steam, I dare not allow my imagination to drift to darker places—and I can only hope that by the time you read these words Mr. Tucker may be removed from all danger.

My dear Willy, I cannot be sure, given the present circumstances of your father's illness, whether it is best for me to wait here for you to return from the hospital. If, indeed, that is where you are. I cannot even be sure that you would wish to see me at all—especially since our brief meeting would bring only another, perhaps sadder, farewell. I leave that decision up to you. Whichever way you choose I am prepared to accept—for who is to say we are not better off left with our memories? if those memories are not better off left intact? untroubled by further sadness? another farewell and another departure?

You may find me tonight at Le Palais Cramoisi, where I intend to take a room and where I shall wait for you till daybreak, when I must perforce hurry to the harbour and make for my aunt and the Caroline.

In haste, I remain yours—

Marguerite

I sat another minute. Then I reread the letter. I hadn't thought of Marguerite in nearly two days. Now there she was, in a beat, holding in the palm of my hand. I couldn't think what to do. Surely it was late in the morning already—if it *was* still morning? Because I hadn't heard a solitary golden-headed manikin cheeping in the backyard. Then I realised I had to try. I had to at least go to the harbour and see if the *Caroline* had sailed—maybe I could hop on a ferry and be dropped aboard. I could remain with Marguerite till the ship left, even if it meant only to say good-bye.

All-in-a-sudden my mind was working fast. At the risk of outrunning itself.

All-in-a-sudden something *else* occurred—rash & irresponsible & far from thought-through, far from properly thought-through—but it occurred to me nonetheless: I could sail with her.

I could let *fate* make the decision—*if the ship remained in port I'd leave with her; if Marguerite had sailed I'd stay here.* I wouldn't have a hand in it a-tall.

I got up and folded the letter twice and stuffed it inside my pocket. Thinking I didn't want my mum and sisters to see it. Then I thought the reverse, and I took the letter back out and folded it open again. Placing it careful atop the mattress, beside the envelope: the letter would explain to them where I'd disappeared to. After a few days they'd work it out.

I fled my little home feeling like a thief—*as* a thief, in fact—because when I passed through the parlour I grabbed up Georgina's kerchief tied with coins.

I stuffed it into my pocket. Stepping off the front stoop in a single stride and starting down Charlotte Street, towards the harbour—not running exactly, but walking at a swift pace. And

365 ᛥ ROBERT ANTONI

whether or not there were others awake and walking the street at that hour of the morning I couldn't tell you. I felt that even if I did encounter someone, I'd be invisible to them. The same way a thief feels invisible, invincible. Same way a thief walks as though he's trapped inside a dream.

I turned across on Duke Street thinking I'd go first to Le Palais Cramoisi. Then I decided the thing to do was to get to the harbour—the thing to do was to get to the *Caroline*—and I turned round and hurried back to Charlotte Street.

I actually saw the *Caroline* a good while before I reached the harbour—from the hill where Charlotte crosses Queen Street— the only ship of its size in the bay. And although I had no sure way of knowing, I felt in my beating breast that she must be the *Caroline*. She could *only* be the *Caroline*. Still awaiting the tide, two of her aft-sails already raised a blistering white against the sparkling blue. But still at anchor: she hadn't left.

I walked faster, I was practically running. Yet those few remaining minutes seemed to last the longest. I was dripping with sweat, panting by the time I started out onto Kings Wharf, hurrying towards the only ferry tied up. Only vessel moored alongside.

Then I stopped in my tracks: I knew this schooner. I'd sailed on her before—she was Captain Maynard's *Miss Bee*.

But my heart dropped, I had no idea why. I did not know why the sight of Captain Maynard's schooner should suddenly fill me with dread. And yet it did.

Yet I reversed my thoughts just as quick. Now I realised my good fortune at meeting up with this captain I already knew, this schooner I was already familiar with—because certainly Captain Maynard would be most pleased to ferry me out to the *Caroline?* certainly he'd be most obliging?

I continued down the wharf, towards the *Miss Bee*, but the closer I drew the more my pace slackened. The slower my boots moved beneath me.

I walked straight to the side of the dock, positioning myself at the centre of the fingerpier she was moored against. Just beside the gangway. And now I knew that I *was* invisible. I was a thief, dreaming of myself. Because as I stood there on that fingerpier no one said a word to me. They climbed down the slight decline of the wavering gangway—that's how high the tide was—and they walked straight past me.

Not saying a word.

First it was Captain Maynard heself. Carrying a proper canvas hospital stretcher with Esteban lifting behind. And the woman moaning on the stretcher was Mrs. Hemmingway. Then, almost before they'd gotten past, another hospital stretcher appeared with Orinoko in front and Mr. Wood behind. Toting Mr. Hemmingway. They took them both to a wide flatbed-carriage that had backed down onto the wharf, the driver standing beside his rearing horse holding it steady—I'd walked straight past them, I was seeing this horse-and-carriage for the first time—and Mr. and Mrs. Hemmingway were transferred swiftly from they stretchers onto the carriage flatbed.

Not a word spoken in all this. Not a word that I could hear. So far the only sound had been Mrs. Hemmingway's moaning.

Esteban and Captain Maynard returned with they stretcher and ascended the gangway into the *Miss Bee's* cabin again. Now they emerged carrying young Billy Sharpe, Mr. Bundron's nephew. Then Orinoko and Mr. Wood went inside and came out carrying Mr. Bundron.

It went on and on.

Mr. Schofield & Mrs. Spenser & her husband & young son. Taken and transferred to the waiting carriage. Mr. Ford and the young man, Thomas Wilkinson. A long line of them, laid side-by-side cross the wide flatbed. So many I'd lost count. But it was only after watching Captain Maynard climb up onto the flatbed too—and Esteban handed up the stretcher and climbed up behind him, and Orinoko and his stretcher—and I watched the driver climb up heself onto the bench & crack his switch & rein in his still-rearing horse & mutter *ho!*, starting the carriage down the wharf with a jolt. It was only after they'd gone that I saw something else: now I saw clearly that three of those members of our group, removed from the *Miss Bee* and loaded onto the carriage—Mr. Hemmingway, Billy Sharp, and Thomas Wilkinson—those three were not sick a-tall.

They were dead.

I stood on the fingerpier staring at the slightly bobbing *Miss Bee*, at the wavering gangplank, just letting my mind fill with the schooner's whiteness. Letting its whiteness drink me up. Thinking—this is the end, this must be the end. But it was far from over.

Because some minutes later I recognised Mr. Wood, approaching from out the distance. Slow and a bit hazy—as though his feet weren't quite touching the ground—like a spectre out of a dream. Drawing a noisy pushcart behind him. Bouncing it over every blasted rung between the boards of that dock. I was sure he'd departed on the horse-carriage with the others. I was certain I'd seen him climb up behind Orinoko.

Mr. Wood stopped right in front of me. Just at my feet. He lowered the rusty handle of the pushcart and ascended the gangway into the *Miss Bee*'s cabin. Then he reappeared carrying his youngest daughter. Mr. Wood climbed down and laid her on the pushcart, fixing her hands crosswise over her breast.

He brought them out in the order of they ages, youngest-to-oldest, and he laid them side-by-side and fixed they hands over they breasts and returned to the cabin for another of his daughters. Then Mr. Wood emerged carrying his wife.

They'd stayed with us in our own home on Charlotte Street before we left. The entire week. The whole family squeezed into Mary and Amelia's room, the same room I'd slept in last night. The same bed.

I watched Mr. Wood load his wife onto the pushcart bedside his daughters. He turned round to take up the rusty handle, and the only sound I heard out of him the whole time was the gentle *ugh!* as he set the cart slowly into motion. As he set it bouncing over the rungs between the boards.

How I found my way to the end of Kings Wharf I do not know. I cannot remember. But after a time, somehow, I must have wandered as far as the end. I sat down with my legs hanging over the side. I cannot tell you why, but after a time I reached to untie the laces of my ripped-up boots. Letting them slip off my feet and drop down into the water. Only a short distance, with the tide high. But they landed on the surface of the water with a loud *smack* one-after-the-next. Like two clean slaps cross my face. Waking me up.

It was the first time I'd taken my boots off since we'd left Chaguabarriga. I felt the delightful sting of the breeze against my stockingless feet. Against my blisters. My feet suddenly light as air. My boots disappearing straightway under the water, and I was sure they'd sink to the bottom quick. But they didn't. They didn't sink a-tall. One-after-the-other they floated back up, bobbing, and the current carried them off. Slowly out to sea.

I watched a gull squawk and swoop down to inspect them. Then I watched it fold away again.

It was only then that I saw the *Caroline*, all her white sails raised, and I saw that she was headed out to sea too. I watched her go. Till she became nothing more than a blistering speck on the wide horizon. Then I watched the blue swallow her up.

I sat there only a few more minutes, my legs dangling over the edge. Before I picked myself up and started back down the wharf, slow but steady, one burden already lifting, another shifting onto my fifteen-year-old shoulders to take its place. I'd seen and done so much already in my short life. So tender still. I'd carried my father in my arms. And yet I knew already how fortunate I was to have known him, to have loved him so hard, so well, such a short time. As I walked down the empty wharf towards my waiting family, my mum and my sisters, towards home.

Postscript
7 September 1881

Busting a Leave

The moon had long disappeared. That moon cut by a knife into a perfect half. It had travelled its slow course across the sky, disappearing beneath the sea somewhere behind our backs. Then there was only the pitch-oil lamp flickering at my father's feet. The ship beneath us and the air and the sea upon which she floated became a black void. Only the pitch-oil lamp, and the handful of stars still flickering dimly overhead, the two lights tinkling at the end of Kings Wharf: only my father's voice in the dark. Then slowly, vaguely, we got the impression that the ship was moving beneath us—huge, hesitant—slowly shifting round. The tide was turning. But the only indicator of this movement was our position relative to those two tinkling lights, swinging slowly, almost imperceptibly, around behind us too. Till eventually we couldn't see them any longer. Now the *Condor* lay with her stern facing straight out to sea. The tide had turned, but only the stars overhead knew, if we had a way to read them. Because all we could see before us now was the black void.

And as if my father had orchestrated another event to coincide with the telling of his tale, just as he was approaching the end—just as he'd reached the final part about walking to the end of the wharf, sitting himself down and untying his boots— all-in-a-sudden the sun rose up from behind the black wall of the horizon before us. The sea caught fire like a piece of paper held up to a flame—slowly, then all-at-once—igniting & bursting into flames & dying out just as quick. Then the only fire was that flaming ball, so bright it pained our eyes to look at it. And the surface of the sea turned to a flickering of smouldering ash.

We sat in silence, exhausted, filled-up. We didn't move. We *couldn't* have moved—not a muscle—because we didn't exist yet. Neither me nor him. Only the story existed, during those few final moments of silence after my father's voice had come to a halt. The sun wasn't even there before us although it was burning holes into our eyes. Not as yet.

Then my father sighed a soft *ugh!* like he was imitating Mr. Wood, and he leant forward to take up the pitch-oil lamp. He lifted the little glass and blew it out. Setting the lamp down again beside the empty rum bottle, the three empty glasses. He reached for his pasteboard cigar box again. My father briefly stacked the pile of soiled and ragged pieces of paper—his 'artifacts'—and he put them carefully back into the box. Then he took up the small notebook lying there on the deck planking between us, *CHAGUABARRIGA* inscribed cross the cover, and he put it back inside his box too.

My father fitted on the cover. Then, oddly enough, and as though the gesture had no particular meaning, he handed his box to me. He gave it to me to hold—

I got one devil-of-a-weewee to make, R-W. When I tell you!

He walked to the very edge of the deck, and I watched his back as he spread his legs and leant forward slightly, reaching down to open up his fly, the sun shining bright before him. I heard his steady stream splashing down into the water.

I sat reclining against the big coil of weathered rope, watching my father weewee over the stern, as I held his box. And I understood in a flash why he'd given it to me, why he'd wanted me to hold it, if only for a minute: he wanted me to know that it belonged to me too. It was my story now, same as his. But I realised something else, and this other thing I don't even think my father intended. I realised that the story was far from finished.

Far from ended. It was simply resting, sleeping in its pasteboard box. Because all I had to do was lift open the cover to wake it up.

I sat there thinking this, feeling the box in my hands—testing the illusion of its near-weightlessness—listening to my father's stream splashing down into the sea, the morning so quiet it sounded like water splashing into a pan of sizzling grease.

Suddenly we were shaken from out our solitude by Captain Vincent's hoarse voice, booming up to us from down below—

Last ferry ashore! If you don't leave now, we carrying you arse wid us all de way to jolly Englan!

My father returned, buttoning up his fly—

Jesus! Vincent's voice frighten me so much, I almost weeweed myself!

He reached down, taking back his box. Offering a hand to help me onto my feet—

Better hurry, son. Vincent don't make no joke when it come time to bust a leave!

I followed him across the deck.

3 Letters

LETTER FROM WILLIAM SANGER TUCKER

The Morning Star, No. 32, 26 March 1846

Friend Powell—

You may recollect requesting me to send a true statement of Chaguabarriga after I had given it a careful examination. I have not hastily formed my opinion, as it has taken some time to study and learn the property. Now for it. The bay is in the shape of the letter C, tilted onto its back. From side-to-side of the letter, tending inland, is about two miles, and the bay is about half a mile wide. At high tide there is about four fathom of water, shallowing regularly. The beach is of fine hard sand, and near the centre is a stone pathway raised a little, formed on purpose by nature, and with a little expense may be made into a good landing place. The coast abounds with cockles, rock oysters, limpits, periwinkles, and the bay is full of fish. The bay may be compared with Brighton or Weymouth, but the mountain scenery much more pleasing. Turtle, it is said, are plentiful in the season, but only one has been caught so far by harpooning. If nets were set for them I have no doubt a profitable trade may be carried on. The thorn-back or skate is very plentiful.

On landing you find about 100 acres of level land, partly cleared, including our compound and Mr. Carr's gardens, which are cultivated with 50 young cocoanut trees, 400 plantains, various sorts of sweet peas, sweet potatoes, oranges, limes, and much more. The mountains at the back of the estate are about 2000 feet high, and are about 1000 to 1500 acres more, and are not measured. On the declivities are dense forests of all kinds of timber. Some are so high that a bird at the top would be safe from a sportsman. The timber is very valuable for building, paper-milling, and medicinal purposes, and shortly may be exported with great advantage. The game consists of doves, parrots, pheasants, partridges, wild turkey, wild hogs, and red deer. There is a good river running through the gardens that we have embanked, where watercress would thrive. I am convinced that all our peas, beans, &c, would grow abundantly here. As to the climate I cannot speak but from my own feelings. The summer in England is more oppressive than here. The fresh breeze from the sea, morning and evening, is delightful. It is rather oppressive from 11 to 3 o'clock, but not more so than the dog days with you. The mineral productions are abundant. There is lime-stone, brick clay; the beach produces a roman cement-stone, such as found on the Isle of Sheppey. There is copper on the estate, but I have had no time to examine if the lode be worth working. I have seen sulphate of copper almost as pure as purchased in England. The rocks are slightly tinged with green crystals.

My opinion upon the subject of more members coming here is that they must bring good sabres (cutlasses), and good strong arms to wield them amongst the brushwood. Also there must be plenty of axes, billshooks, spades, course canvas trousers, strong shirts, strong high boots, and a straw hat. No engineers, carpenters, blacksmiths, or fancy gardeners are of any use unless they work like countrymen. You may as well send a Bond Street perfumer or a Parisian milliner. A strong country shoemaker, with some leather and all his tackle to repair our torn boots, would be of essential service.

My opinion of our agent, Mr. Carr, is that he is a man of great enthusiasm, but not necessarily a man of business; he is sometimes too cautious, and luffs too near the wind in money matters. If he was to pay off a little more of the Society's money and fill his sails, we would make some headway.

Upon the fever of the country I will offer my opinion. If you have a cramp in the great toe, headache, or any pain, it is sure to be the fever. It more frequently happens that it makes its appearance in this way. There's a good-natured fellow here by the name of John, a black, who has assisted me in repairing the beached schooner. He has been my helpmate. On the Monday after our labours began I said, 'John.' 'Yes suh.' 'Get ready early tomorrow morning for another hard day's work.' 'Yes suh,' he said. In the morning I sung out, 'John,' who replied from underneath a sail, 'Suh, fever, suh.' I was rather taken aback, but left him there and set about strapping to with my son. An hour later the fever abated, as it commonly does, and John rose to join us strong and industrious as ever. I however must acknowledge that it is a dreadful disease in this beautiful country, and it is so contagious that I have caught it nearly as bad myself. It is incurable but in one way, that is by riding it out in your hammock for an hour or two till the fever subsides. Sometimes a few winks of sleep is a palliative for a short time.

I wish you were here, and I am sure you would be of great assistance to Mr. Carr. I have given him a description of you, and he is anxious to see you. Mr. Carr has much anxiety, and attempts so many things all on his own. He takes a cutlass in hand and cuts away like a trooper, and when the work is finished you may wring the wet from his trousers and shirt. It is time some of you were here to bear part of the responsibility; but please remember the spades, &c. Come then and put your shoulder to the wheel. There is lots of hard work, but there is also plenty of good living.*

* Our members will find that the writer, Mr. Tucker, shortly after writing thus far was taken ill and died in Trinidad. On his deathbed this letter, a little packet tied into a small roll with fishing twine, was retrieved from his pocket and sent on to me. Mr. Tucker's widow and son and three daughters intend to remain in Trinidad to carry on the business of dyers. (Ed TP)

5 November 1881

Dear William,

Per your request, please find below the list of your exhibits that I have sold to interested scientific and lay parties (minus the two larger displays you have generously donated to the Museum, and which shall become part of our Permanent Collection). You will also find attached to this letter my cheque, drawn on Coutts Bank of London, to the amount of £15. s18, representing the total moneys collected. I am pleased to inform you that all of your exhibits left behind have found enthusiastic owners—

1. Male & female copper-rumped emeralds (Amazilia tobaci) straight long bills w/nest & egg on allamanda branch in flower. Donated to the Museum.
2. 3 Male ruby-topaz (Chrysolampis mosquitus) w/short slightly decurved bills on heliconia in flower. Donated to the Museum.
3. 2 Male rufus-breasted hermits (Glaucis hirsuta) strongly decurved bills on ixora branch w/blooms. £7. s5
4. Male ruby-topaz (Chrysolampis mosquitus) on heliconia branch w/blooms. £4. s5
5. Female blue-chinned sapphire (Chlorestes notatus) fairly straight bill on red hibiscus in flower. £2. s3
6. Male copper-rumped emerald (Amazilia tobaci) long straight bill on allamanda branch in flower. £2. s5

total : £15. s18

I should like to thank you again on behalf of the Ornithological Society and all of us here at the Museum for your visit to us. Your excitement for your little birds was quite contagious, your lectures and demonstrations most informative. They will not soon be forgotten.

Sincerely,
Dr. Francis M. Evans
Director, Natural History Museum

PS My wife sends her regards.

24 October 1881

Dear Mr. Tucker,

Perhaps you were unaware of the middle-aged woman and her two daughters—both now older than I was when you knew me—sitting towards the rear of the auditorium at the Natural History Museum, whilst you lectured so knowledgeably about your birds. Only that morning I'd chanced to read an announcement in the Guardian that a 'Mr. William Tucker from Trinidad BWI, who is here on a visit to Professor Evans, will be discussing his techniques for preserving and displaying hummingbirds in their natural habitat . . .' and almost before I could finish reading the announcement and catch my breath, I rushed to the Museum to see if this same man could possibly be the 'Willy' I knew some 36 years ago—imagine my surprise! Imagine my daughters' dismay at being dragged off to such a lecture!

But you won Anne and Nicole over as easily as you did me and the rest of your audience. Your illustration of how the short bills of certain sapphire and emerald hummingbirds are perfectly suited for feeding on hibiscus flowers, slightly curved bills for heliconias, and the long straight bills of the copper ones for the tiny tubes of allamanda flowers, &c, &c. I would like to have made myself known to you after your lecture—indeed, I tried my hardest to do só, grasping in my hand a hastily scribbled note of reintroduction—but there were so many others crowded round you and Dr. Evans that I hadn't a chance! So I wrote the Professor next morning asking if he could kindly put us into contact. Professor Evans replied by way of sending the very letter you had written yourself before departing Trinidad, since he now had my postal address. Yet to my great disappointment, by the time your letter reached me and I made inquires at the Museum, you had already sailed again for Port-Spain.

I have since become acquainted with Dr. Evans and his wife, having been invited to visit them at their home. Indeed, Dr. Evans questioned me late into the evening on the Society and my family's experiences with Mr. Etzler in Trinidad, whilst I scribbled out my replies, discovering then that Dr. Evans's father was a close acquaintance of Mr. Whitechurch—as you know of the Professor's connection to the TES and his curiosity on the subject. He and his wife told me everything they'd learnt from you, of your life in Trinidad and your successes in the lighterage and shipping business, of your marriage and your children—also of the recent death of your mother, Mrs. Tucker, and so for a brief moment I found myself dissolved to tears in the Evans's living room.

Dr. Evans then escorted his wife and me to his laboratory in the Museum's basement, where he unveiled for us your various exhibits left behind, several of which you had presented during your lecture. Most spectacularly he showed us the two large scenes that shall become a permanent feature of the Museum's collection. The Professor also explained how you had left in his charge the duty of selling the remaining exhibits to interested parties, the end result being that I now find myself the owner of 'Male copper-rumped emerald on allamanda branch in flower,' which I and the girls watched you demonstrate for your audience, and which has found a place in our home.

Having now this remembrance of the natural beauty of Trinidad constantly in my midst, and having heard you speak so passionately about your birds, I thought it fitting to return your very first attempt at what has become your art. I cannot tell you how often I have admired this tiny creature, which I have kept for 36 years in her little box lined with cotton wool, so curiously labeled 'buttons.' And although you may imagine my sadness at parting with her, I have always felt she truly belonged to that wistful young man I once knew so fondly as 'Willy.' So I return her to him, undoubtedly much changed, yet in some small way preserved in this little bird.

Sincerely,
Marguerite

Final Message

15/11/10

dear mr robot:

i say YES mr robot, say YES YES YES cause i was so happy
when lil buddah & raj reach home last night & tell me how dey
find u in de hilton, where i say u was staying & we did have so
much of sweet jooking in dat hotel 2 sure-as-shiva, & lil buddah
say u had all u bags pack & ready to go back home in amerika, &
so sad & forlorn dat all dis time u have dedicate 2 researching u
book & now u have 2 go home empty-handed, except 4 dem 5-6
photocopies u manage to copy out yesterday pon dis machine
dat i give u permission, plus dat letter from u relative WILLIAM
SANGER TUCKER dat i find 4 u in de STAR, but u say dat aint
enough, u say dat aint noting a-tall, u needs to make PLENTY
PLENTY more copies 4 u research before u could write out dis
book, but now u give up cause u cant fight it no more & u bags
pack, ready to go home empty-handed

so lil buddah & raj invite u 4 drink downstairs in de hotel bar,
dat dey could discuss dis matter wid u men-to-man, & u say ok,
u would take a drink wid dem, & lil buddah say, well u know mr
robot de people gots dey rules, & if de law say no photocopies
pon dis machine in de archives except what miss ramsol make,
cause she in charge, den u gots 2 abide by de rules, & raj chime
in 2 & he say yes, rules is rules & laws is laws, but is not only de
ARCHIVES got dey rules, cause here in t'dad WE got a NEX
law dat say u dont JOOK-WE-LIL-SIS-&-RUN-BACK-HOME-
IN-AMERIKA, not so easy as dat mr robot, not we lil sis, so raj
say mr robot u gots to do what is right & proper according to
de rules, & lil buddah say yes it is mr robot, so let we cease from
beating round de bush & come direc to de point here: lil buddah
say he KNOW u would want to follow de rules mr robot & do
what is right & proper, cause dat mash-face & bust-nose & dem
2 blue-eye is only a lil TASTE of what u would be tasting if u
dont, & lil buddah say, look here mr robot, u want to copy out u

photocopies in de archives? u say is plenty plenty more photocopies u needs to copy out in de archives? well we only offering
u a lil suggestion of how u could do it, as much of photocopies
as u want to copy, as much of copies as u could ever WISH to
copy, & lil buddah say let me tell u someting else mr robot: u tink
dat u could find anyting so sweet as lil sis in amerika? all dem
forceripe hardback womens dey got in amerika, & so stingy 2?
what u going back dere 4? lil buddah say mr robot u could have
dem BOTH, lil sis & photocopies both, as much as u could want,
only ting is u got to do what is right & proper by de rules, u got
to follow de rules

& lil buddah say, & plus mr robot let me tell you someting else:
according to what lil sis say, dis ting between u & she aint no
passing fancy a-tall, cause lil sis say what begin as bullying between 2 of u wind up in hollywood, TRUE hollywood, de real
ting, no trifling fancy neither, cause lil sis say dat is de title of dis
story between u & she: FROM BULLYING 2 HOLLYWOOD,
dat is how dis story bound 2 be call, & mr robot u cant turn u
back pon dat, not hollywood mr robot, cause if is ANYTING
against de law it bound 2 be dat

well raj & lil buddah say u did start to SMILE lil bit now, u was
still sad and forlorn but now u was smiling lil bit 2, now dat
dey plant dis idea in u head, now dat u did feel it inside uself 2,
& mr robot u say ok, u not going back home in amerika, flight
cancel, u staying here in t'dad & u doing what is right according
2 de rules, & u tell raj & lil buddah please to inform miss ramsol
u would be in de archives bright & early tomorrow morning
2 settle everyting up good and proper, & anyway u did always
dream 2 settle down in t'dad, & despite dat a east-indian wife
& half-east-indian popos was never part of dat dream before,
it is now, cause you doing what is right & proper according to
de rules, & raj and lil buddah say dey was smiling now 2, & all
3 of u was smiling happy hugging up 2gether, 2 east-indians &
1 yankee-whiteman, & raj stand-up now 2 he feet & raise-up he

glass & say, well let we toast a toast 2 mr robot, we new yankee brother-in-law!!!

cordial,
miss ramsol
director, t&tna

ps mr robot i would be waiting in de back room wearing my dentalfloss panties & dis machine running charge wid ink & plenty paper waiting 4 u 2

pss MONSOON WEDDING IN U TAIL!!!

Appendix

Page 102, 👁 = www.whatlessboys.com/**silence**

Page 111, ☉ = www.whatlessboys.com/**etzlersplay**

Page 255, ⌸ = www.whatlessboys.com/**etzlersmachines**

Page 300, △ = www.whatlessboys.com/**thoreausreview**

Page 326, 👁 = www.whatlessboys.com/**bruitnoir**

FIN.